JUN 2 6

Y0-CAF-200

BISON FRONTIERS OF IMAGINATION

Jules Verne

THE GOLDEN VOLCANO

Le Volcan d'or

The First English Translation of Verne's Original Manuscript

Translated and edited by Edward Baxter
Preface to the French edition
by Olivier Dumas

University of Nebraska Press
Lincoln

Publication of this book was made
possible by a grant from
The Florence Gould Foundation.

Le Volcan d'or © Société Jules Verne, 1989, pour
une première édition à tirage limité.
© Les Éditions internationales Alain Stanké, 1995.
© L'Archipel, 1995.
Translation and critical materials
© 2008 by Edward Baxter.

Manufactured in the
United States of America

∞

Library of Congress Cataloging-
in-Publication Data

Verne, Jules, 1828–1905.
[Volcan d'or. English]
The golden volcano = Le volcan d'or:
the first English translation of Verne's
original manuscript / Jules Verne; translated
and edited by Edward Baxter;
preface to the French edition
by Olivier Dumas.
p. cm. — (Bison frontiers of imagination)
ISBN 978-0-8032-9633-6 (cloth: alk. paper) —
ISBN 978-0-8032-9635-0 (pbk.: alk. paper)
I. Baxter, Edward. II. Title. III.
Title: Volcan d'or.
PQ2469.V7E5 2008
843'.8—dc22
2007037423

Set in Granjon.

Contents

Preface to the French Edition . . *vii*

Translator's Introduction . . *xv*

PART ONE

1. An Uncle's Legacy . . *3*

2. The Two Cousins . . *13*

3. From Montreal to Vancouver . . *26*

4. Vancouver . . *38*

5. On Board the *Football* . . *48*

6. Skagway . . *58*

7. The Chilkoot Pass . . *68*

8. Lake Lindemann . . *79*

9. From Bennett Lake to Dawson City . . *89*

10. The Klondike . . *104*

11. Dawson City . . *113*

12. From Dawson City to the Alaskan Boundary . . *125*

13. Claim 129 . . *135*

14. Working the Claim . . *146*

15. The Night of August 5–6 . . *155*

PART TWO

1. A Winter in the Klondike . . *169*

2. The Dying Man's Tale . . *181*

3. The Aftermath of a Secret . . *192*

4. Circle City . . *205*

5. A Journey of Discovery . . *216*

6. Fort McPherson . . *226*

7. Golden Mount . . *236*

8. An Engineer's Bold Plan . . *247*

9. The Moose Hunt . . *259*

10. Mortal Dread . . *273*

11. On the Defensive . . *285*

12. Attack and Defense . . *298*

13. The Eruption . . *309*

14. From Dawson City to Montreal . . *320*

Notes . . *331*

Preface to the French Edition

Olivier Dumas

IN 1886, AFTER PUBLISHING about thirty novels in the series Extraordinary Voyages, Jules Verne was at the pinnacle of his renown. During that year, however, he suffered a number of misfortunes: a bullet fired by his nephew left him with a limp that would remain for the rest of his life, and his publisher, Pierre-Jules Hetzel, died. A new life was beginning for the novelist: he had to give up sailing—his great passion— and now that he felt free of the restrictions placed on him by Hetzel, he began to rethink his literary career.

Verne dreamed of breaking out of the "scientific and geographical" framework in which he was "condemned to operate."[1] As he grew older, he wrote gothic novels *(The Sphinx of the Ice, The Yarns of Jean-Marie Cabidoulin)*, novels of passion *(The Castle in the Carpathians)*, and satirical novels *(Topsy Turvy)*, but these works, though appreciated today for their literary value, were not well received at the time. What readers wanted above all from the author of *From the Earth to the Moon* was science fiction featuring extraordinary inventions.

Jules Verne's Posthumous Manuscripts

After the death of Jules Verne on March 24, 1905, his son Michel immediately drew up a list of eleven unpublished volumes. These works consisted of a travel story *(Journey to England and Scotland)*, a futuristic novel *(Paris in the Twentieth Century)*, a collection of short stories, and eight completed novels: *The Lighthouse at the End of the World*, *The Thompson Travel Agency*, *In the Magellanes*, *The Secret of Wilhelm Storitz*, *The Hunt for the Meteor*, *The Danube Pilot*, *The Golden Volcano*, and *Study Trip*. Only the last of these was still in the early stages. Regrettably, under pressure from the publisher Jules Hetzel, Michel Verne began tampering with these with unfortunate results.[2] He completely rewrote his father's works—including *The Golden Volcano*—and introduced new characters, wrote new chapters, and invented new endings. The entire spirit of the original works was misrepresented.

Up until the present time, these posthumous novels were known only in their disfigured form. But now the Société Jules Verne has discovered copies of Jules Verne's manuscripts in the possession of the publisher's descendants. After an initial private, limited edition, now out of print, it now offers to the public at large the original and only authentic version of *Le Volcan d'or*. A hundred years after it was written, this novel has now been restored to its true form.

The Manuscript of *Le Volcan d'or*

In 1896, prospectors were rushing to the banks of streams in the Klondike area of the Yukon Territory after the discovery of an inexhaustible deposit of gold had been reported. Jules Verne's own son tried his hand at prospecting. The author at once described the disastrous gold fever brought on by the metal that he had held in contempt ever since he had worked at the Stock Exchange in 1857—the same gold that provided material for *In the Magellanes* and *The Hunt for the Meteor* and to which he would refer again in 1900 in *Second Fatherland*.[3]

In October 1899, Verne wrote to Jules Hetzel: "I am now deep in the mines of the Klondike. Will I find a precious nugget there? We will see. In any case, I am swinging my pick like a miner!"[4]

A powerful and pessimistic work, *The Golden Volcano* was kept in reserve after its completion. It would be his only posthumous novel to consist of two volumes, an indication of the author's interest in it.

Once it was finished and revised, the work did not need to be corrected or altered. But that was the fate in store for it. The manuscript of *The Golden Volcano* is a finished text, although the final revision of the proofs had not been done. As was his custom, Verne had not decided definitely on the names of his characters. In the course of the story, he sometimes changed the spelling of them, either as a trial run or through absentmindedness, for Verne worked on several novels at the same time. Aware that he made errors of this kind, he put off correcting them, placing a question mark beside an uncertain name, distance, or date to draw his attention to it later. We have corrected mistakes as the author would have done. There remain only a few awkward turns of phrase, repetitions, and missing words; we have respected those and indicated gaps in the text by suspension points in parentheses. A few missing words have also been supplied. All other corrections are indicated by endnotes. Proper names that have been changed maintain their original spelling, but the variants are given in the endnotes. As for geographical names, we have kept their spelling as they were in Jules Verne's time. This new edition has also been revised and corrected.

The Theme of the Work

The Golden Volcano can be summed up in a single phrase: "Death and misery in the Far North." Two themes are developed in the novel: gold fever and travel through a wild and inhospitable land.

Gold fever is described as an illness, using medical terms:

> Ben has definitely not escaped the current epidemic. I hope to God I don't become infected too! What a disease this gold fever is! It isn't a sporadic illness that can be cured with quinine of some sort. No one ever recovers from it, I see.[5]

At the end of the eighteenth century, when getting rich was the goal of the entire middle class, it required a certain audacity to attack the Golden Calf, the capitalists' god. This burden probably compelled Verne to postpone the publication of his novel and explains some of the changes introduced by his son and Jules Hetzel, who were frightened by the writer's contempt for the "vile metal" and afraid that it might have a negative effect on book sales.

While the hatred of gold remained hidden in three posthumous novels (*In the Magellanes*, *The Hunt for the Meteor*, and *The Golden Volcano*), it made its appearance during the author's lifetime in *Second Fatherland*, where there is a brief reference to the discovery of gold nuggets as a scourge that threatens to wipe out the castaway's island colony:

> If people find out about the existence of these gold fields, if it be-
> comes known that New Switzerland is rich in nuggets, hordes
> of gold-seekers will come rushing in, followed by all the evils,
> all the disturbances, all the crimes that the fight to acquire this
> metal brings in its wake![6]

Probably as a result of pressure from the publisher, the "ferment of trouble and ruin" disappears from the story as if by magic; the nuggets cease to exist, and the text reads: "the colony was not invaded by those gold seekers who leave nothing behind them but disorder and misery."[7]

These were the same gold seekers who were described in *In the Magellanes*, swooping down on the colonists' island like a swarm of grasshoppers, leaving nothing but destruction in their wake, and in *The Hunt for the Meteor*, where the golden comet takes on the form of a parody, arousing an outburst of passions and the maddest of speculations.

The Golden Volcano is entirely devoted to this ill-fated quest. In it, Verne describes precisely the methods used in prospecting as well as the living and working conditions of the miners, their setbacks, their moral decline, even their deaths. As if to reinforce his point, he introduces a secondary plot, the story of Jacques Laurier, an unfortunate prospector who believes he has won a fortune but ends his life in the grim Dawson City hospital from which patients "would only leave in a hearse, drawn by a dog team, on the way to the cemetery."[8] This tragic confession seemed to give Verne's son Michel pause for thought. Jacques Laurier was born into a good family. Like Verne—whose name is a synonym for "alder"—

his name was also the name of a tree. Like Verne also, he was French by birth, a native of Nantes. Did Michel Verne understand this allusion? In any case, he changed Laurier to Ledun and deleted the expression "a hearse drawn by a dog team."

The Poetry of the Far North

In this adventure novel, Verne conjured up—as Jack London and James Oliver Curwood would do later—the poetry of the Canadian Far North, the rough, wild country through which the two cousins from Montreal traveled in search of a supposedly gold-bearing claim. Here we have a true western genre: the caravan goes through mountain passes, sails over lakes and rivers, hunts for its food, and is attacked by bears and a gang of bandits. A strange hunting expedition for moose, those mythical and elusive creatures, adds to the novel's ecological and poetic character.

In this rugged universe, with its fearsome cold, women do not face the same dangers—except for two nuns who, true to their vocation, also undertake the long journey to Dawson City to bring comfort and a feminine presence to the wretched victims of the *auri sacra fames*.[9]

Michel Verne's Revisions

Michel Verne rewrote the novel and took it upon himself (possibly out of anticlericalism) to replace the Sisters of Charity by two charming cousins who become prospectors and whose light-hearted banter with the two heroes leads to a double wedding at the end! From being a straightforward and virile adventure novel about a symbolic quest, it sinks to the level of sentimental vaudeville. To add to its picturesque and comical character, Michel Verne has cousin Jane accompanied by a grotesque individual, Patrick Richardson, a market porter, who always addresses his patroness as "Monsieur Jean" since he cannot recognize a woman wearing a miner's trousers! To top it all off, Neluto, the worthy Indian who accompanies the caravan to Golden Mount, the mysterious golden volcano, is ridiculed and made to speak like the caricature of a Norman peasant:

"There! . . . there! . . . Smoke!" he cried.

But he immediately regretted having had the audacity to express himself so positively.

"Or a cloud," he said.

He thought for a second, and added:

"Or a bird!"

The pilot thought some more. Smoke, a cloud, a bird. . . . Had
he really exhausted all the possible hypotheses?

"Or nothing at all!" he concluded.[10]

This stream of interpretations, unworthy of an eagle-eyed Indian, re-
places Jules Verne's concise account:

The fog lifted and Neluto could be heard shouting:

"Look! Look! Smoke!"

At that instant the mountain appeared, the Golden Volcano,
with its crater spewing out sooty vapors.[11]

All these additions, all these changes, far from improving the novel,
make it insipid and mindless.[12] What is even more serious is that Michel
Verne's conclusion, following four supplementary chapters, transforms
defeat into victory. This complete about-face is baffling when one stops
to think that Verne's only reason for describing the search for gold was
to point out the curse attached to the yellow metal: a disastrous quest
from which one returns—if indeed one does return—even poorer than
before.

In his work of transformation, it may be noted that Michel Verne dis-
plays an uncommon talent in changing the novel's final sentences and
succeeds in giving a totally different meaning to his father's words; an
explosion of rancor becomes a superabundance of vitality. For Jules
Verne, Ben Raddle does not admit defeat:

He seemed ready at any moment to burst out in recriminations
against his bad luck.

Then Summy Skim would say cheerfully:

"Yes, poor Ben is always ready to erupt. After all, when you've had a volcano in your life, part of it always stays with you."

In Michel Verne's version, Ben Raddle:

that happy man, is never there, . . . he comes and goes like lightning. . . . Summy Skim . . . does not hesitate to heap the most severe reproaches on Ben Raddle. . . .

But Summy, when his cousin has left for another trip, is the first to make excuses for him.

"You mustn't hold a grudge against my poor Ben," he usually says to Edith, "if he's always about to erupt. After all, when you've had a volcano in your life, part of it always stays with you."

Toward the Final Explosion

Today Jules Verne can finally express himself, cleansed of the slag that disfigured his work, as the cursed gold is doubly purified by water. Reading *The Golden Volcano* in its original version, as the author conceived it, restores the novel's power and beauty, and all its purity.

Verne had always been obsessed by the symbolic aspect of volcanoes—a liberating explosion, an organic outpouring. Often referred to as "fire-spitting" in the Extraordinary Voyages, they vomit fire. Was not an emetic prescribed for Golden Mount in *The Golden Volcano*, to help it disgorge the nuggets from its overburdened stomach? Already, in *Topsy Turvy,* "the volcanoes took advantage of the opportunity . . . to vomit up, like a seasick passenger, the extraneous matter in their stomachs."[13]

From earth to sky, the volcano illuminates all of Verne's writings in a fantastic display of fireworks. In *Five Weeks in a Balloon,* the first novel published by Hetzel, a missionary dies while watching that marvel of nature, a

fiery crater noisily shooting out a thousand dazzling showers of sparks.

"How beautiful it is," he said, "and how infinite is God's power even in its most terrible manifestations."[14]

In the conquest of air, earth, water, and fire, Verne makes full use of his imagination. Volcanoes, as symbols of power, passion, and vitality, give free rein to impulses and express a rejection of constraints. Sometimes the volcano sleeps; let us beware of its reawakening.

Translator's Introduction

Edward Baxter

THERE IS EVERY REASON to believe that if Jules Verne had lived another year he would have made substantial corrections to the manuscript
of *The Golden Volcano*. If he had reread the book carefully, he would
surely have spotted the blanks, the spelling errors (some perhaps caused
by a misreading of his handwriting), and the mistakes in chronology and
geography that are to be found throughout the manuscript.

In this translation, blanks have been filled in and errors in geography
and spelling corrected as far as possible, some by the editor of this edition
and some by the translator.

The most useful source for verifying the spelling of names and iden-
tifying individuals has been *Klondike: The Life and Death of the Last
Great Gold Rush* by the late Pierre Berton (McClelland and Stewart:
Toronto, 1963). "Wallace's Map of the Klondike and Indian River Gold
Fields," dated February 12, 1898, and reprinted in 1962, was also a valu-
able source of information. Other useful works included *The Canadian
Encyclopedia* and *The Oxford Companion to Canadian History*, edited by
Gerald Halowell.

Verne used various units of measurement and currency in this novel:
kilometers, leagues, miles, hectares, francs, sous, piaster, and dollars.
These have all been converted to English units. A kilometer is equal
to about five-eighths of a mile. A league is equal to four kilometers, or
about two and a half miles. A hectare is equal to two and a half acres.

A franc at that time was worth about twenty cents, and a sou was the equivalent of a cent. A piaster was the same as a dollar, and the word is still in common use in colloquial speech in Quebec.

I have been fortunate to have the constant support and advice of my wife, Barbara, who read every chapter as I finished it and gave me the benefit of her keen sense of readable English prose style. She is not responsible, however, for any errors or shortcomings.

The Golden Volcano

PART I

I

An Uncle's Legacy

ON MARCH 16, in the antepenultimate year of this century, the letter carrier whose route included Jacques Cartier Street in Montreal delivered a letter addressed to Mr. Summy Skim, at house number twenty-nine.[1]

The letter read: "Mr. Snubbin, notary public, presents his compliments to Mr. Summy Skim and requests that he call at his office without delay concerning a matter of interest to him."

What did the notary want to see Mr. Skim about? Like everyone in Montreal, Skim knew Mr. Snubbin, a very competent man, a reliable and prudent counselor. A Canadian by birth, he was head of the best law firm in the city—the one headed sixty years earlier by the famous Master Nick, or Nicolas Sagamore, of Huron origin, whose patriotic fervor had led him to play a role in the dreadful Morgaz affair, which created a considerable stir about 1837.*

Skim was somewhat surprised to receive a letter from Mr. Snubbin, with whom he had no dealings at the time. However, he accepted the invitation that had been offered. Half an hour later he was at Bonsecours Market Square, being ushered into the office where Mr. Snubbin was waiting for him.

"A very good day to you, Mr. Skim," said the notary, getting to his feet. "May I present my respects."

*This touching tragedy is the subject of a novel entitled *Family without a Name*, in the series *Extraordinary Voyages*.

"And the same to you," replied Skim, taking a seat near the table.

"You are the first to arrive, Mr. Skim."

"The first, Mr. Snubbin? Have you invited several people to your office, then?"

"Two," replied the notary. "Mr. Ben Raddle, your cousin, should have received a letter, as you did, inviting him to come."

"You should say 'will receive,' instead of 'should have received,' because Ben Raddle is not in Montreal at the moment."

"Will he be back soon?"

"In three or four days."

"I am sorry to hear that."

"What you have to tell us is urgent, then?"

"In a way, yes," replied the notary. "But I will give you the details, and perhaps you will be kind enough, as soon as Mr. Raddle is back, to pass on to him the information I am instructed to give you."

The notary put on his glasses, shuffled a few papers lying on the table, and took a letter out of its envelope. Before reading it, he said, "Mr. Raddle and you, Mr. Skim, are the nephews of Mr. Josias Lacoste . . ."

"That's right. My mother and Ben Raddle's mother were his sisters, but they died seven or eight years ago, and since then we've lost all contact with our uncle. He had left Canada and gone to Europe by that time. Some important issues had kept us apart. We've never heard from him since, and we have no idea what has become of him."

"Well," replied Snubbin, "I have just received word of his death, in a letter dated February 25."

Although all contact between Josias Lacoste and his family had long since ended, this information had a profound effect on Summy Skim. Since he and his cousin had lost both their parents and since each was an only child, they had no immediate family but each other, and their firm friendship made this relationship all the closer. He lowered his head and his eyes filled with tears as he realized that, of the entire family, only he and Ben Raddle were left. They had, of course, made several attempts to find out what had become of their uncle, and they regretted the fact that he had broken off all contact with them. Perhaps they were even hoping they might meet again some time, and now death had shattered that hope.

Besides, Josias Lacoste had always been rather uncommunicative by nature, and of a very adventurous temperament. It was now some twenty years since he had left Canada to make his fortune in the world. He was unmarried and had a small inheritance, which he had hoped to build up through speculation. Had that hope been fulfilled? Was it not more likely, with his well-known penchant for taking enormous risks, that he had been ruined? Would his nephews, his only heirs, receive a few scraps from his inheritance? It is only fair to say that Summy Skim and Ben Raddle had never thought about that, and with his passing, it seemed unlikely that they would think about it now in their grief at the loss of their last relative.

Snubbin left his client to his thoughts and waited to be asked a few questions, which he was prepared to answer. He was well aware of this family's situation and of the fine reputation they enjoyed in Montreal. He knew that, with the death of Josias Lacoste, Summy Skim and Ben Raddle were the last remaining members of the family. And since the governor of the Klondike had notified him of the death of the prospector who owned Claim 129 on the Fortymile River,[2] he had invited the two cousins to come to his office and find out what rights they had inherited from the deceased.

"Mr. Snubbin," asked Skim, "was it on the seventeenth of February that our uncle died?"

"The seventeenth of February, Mr. Skim."

"That's twenty-nine days ago now."

"Twenty-nine, yes. That's how long it took the news to reach me."

"Was our uncle off somewhere in Europe, then, in some distant land?" continued Skim, convinced that Josias Lacoste had never set foot in North America since he left.

"Oh no," replied the notary, holding out a letter bearing Canadian stamps.

"So," said Skim, "he was in Canada and we didn't know about it?"

"Yes, in Canada. But in the most remote part of the Dominion, near the border between our country and the American territory of Alaska. It's a region with which communication is slow and difficult."

"You're referring to the Klondike, I presume, Mr. Snubbin."

"Yes, the Klondike, where your uncle went to live about ten months ago."

"Ten months," repeated Skim, "and it didn't even occur to him as he was crossing the continent on his way to that mining region to come to Montreal and shake hands with his nephews. It would have been our last opportunity to see him!"

Summy Skim was deeply affected by that thought.

"What would you expect?" replied the notary. "Mr. Lacoste was probably in a hurry to get to the Klondike, like so many thousands of others—sick people, I call them, infected with that gold fever that has claimed so many victims and will continue to claim many more! The new placers have been invaded from every corner of the world. After Australia, there was California, after California, the Transvaal, after the Transvaal, the Klondike, and after the Klondike there will be other gold-bearing regions, and so it will go on until Judgment Day—I mean until the last deposit has been exhausted."

Then Snubbin revealed the information contained in the governor's letter. It was, in fact, early in 1897 when Josias Lacoste had set foot in Dawson City, the capital of the Klondike,[3] armed with the obligatory prospecting equipment. Since July of 1896, when gold had been discovered in Gold Bottom Creek, a tributary of Hunker Creek,[4] the Klondike region had been attracting attention. The following year Lacoste came to the gold fields, to which so many miners were already streaming. He wanted to use the little money he had left to buy a claim, never doubting that he would make a fortune. After doing his research, he purchased Claim 129, located on the Fortymile River, a tributary of the Yukon, the great Canadian-Alaskan waterway.

"It seems," Snubbin continued, "that this claim had not yet produced as much profit as Mr. Lacoste expected. However, it did not appear to be exhausted, and perhaps your uncle might have had as much success with it as he hoped. But there are so many dangers threatening the unfortunate immigrants in that far-off region,[5] the terrible winter cold, diseases of epidemic proportions, the privations to which so many unfortunates succumb! So many of them come back poorer than when they left!"

"Could it have been these privations that killed our uncle?" asked Summy Skim.

"No," replied the notary, "the letter does not indicate that he was reduced to that extremity. He succumbed to typhus, which is so terrible in that climate and which claims so many victims. As soon as he was infected with the disease, Mr. Lacoste left his claim and went back to Dawson City, where he died. Since he was known to have come from Montreal, news of his passing was sent to me, so that I could notify the family."

Summy Skim was lost in thought, pondering the situation in which this relative of his might have found himself in the course of what was probably an unprofitable operation. Had he perhaps used up the last of his resources after buying the claim at an exorbitant price as so many imprudent prospectors did? Had he died penniless, still owing money to the workers he had hired? All these thoughts went through Skim's mind.

"Mr. Snubbin," he said, "it's possible that our uncle was heavily in debt when he died. Well—and I guarantee that my cousin Raddle will back me up in this—we'll never let the name of Lacoste default in its obligations. It was our mothers' name, and if there are sacrifices to be made, we won't hesitate to make them. As soon as possible, we must take inventory . . ."

"All right! Let me stop you there, my dear sir," replied the notary. "Knowing you as I do, I'm not surprised to hear you say that. But I don't think there is any reason to anticipate the sacrifices you mention. It is very likely that your uncle died without making his fortune, but we must not forget that he was the owner of a claim on the Fortymile River, and the value of that property may be enough to meet every need. Now this property belongs jointly to you and your cousin Ben Raddle, since you are Mr. Lacoste's next of kin and have a legal claim to his estate."

Snubbin acknowledged, however, that they would have to proceed with some degree of caution. The inheritance could not be transferred until any outstanding debts had been settled. A statement of assets and liabilities would be drawn up, after which the heirs would make a decision concerning the estate.

"I will look after this matter, Mr. Skim," he added, "and obtain the most reliable information available. After all, who knows? A claim is a claim! It may have produced little or nothing so far, but we don't know that yet. One lucky blow with the pick is all it takes to fill your pockets, as the prospectors say."

"I agree, Mr. Snubbin, and if our uncle's claim is of any value, we'll be anxious to get the best price we can for it."

"No doubt, but does your cousin share that view?"

"I should hope so. I don't think it would ever occur to Ben to work the claim himself."

"Who knows, Mr. Skim? Mr. Raddle is an engineer. He might be tempted. What if he were he to learn, for instance, that your uncle's claim is located on a good vein?"

"I assure you, Mr. Snubbin, he will definitely not go out to see it! In any case, he's supposed to be coming back to Montreal in a few days. We'll discuss the matter, and then we'll ask you to proceed, either to sell the claim on the Fortymile River to the highest bidder or, as I fear may possibly be the case, to arrange to honor our uncle's obligations, if it turns out that he went into debt with this operation."

When the conversation was finished, Skim took his leave of the notary, promising to come back in two or three days, and returned to the house on Jacques Cartier Street where he and his cousin lived.

Summy Skim was the son of an English father and a French Canadian mother. This old family traced its ancestry back to the time of the conquest of 1759. They had settled in the Montreal district of Lower Canada, where their principal fortune consisted of an income property that included woods, arable fields, and grassland.

Summy Skim was thirty-two years old, above-average height, with pleasant features, deep blue eyes, a blond beard, and the sturdy build of man accustomed to outdoor life. He was the typical friendly French Canadian, like his mother before him. On his property in that favored part of the Dominion, he led the enviable life of the gentleman farmer, free from cares and ambitions. His fortune, while not large, was sufficient to enable him to satisfy his modest tastes, and he had never wanted or needed to add to it. He was able to indulge his love of hunting in the vast open spaces of the region or in the game-filled forests that covered the greater part of it. He pursued his passion for fishing in the whole network of rivers and streams flowing into the St. Lawrence River, not to mention the many broad lakes to be found in the northern part of the continent.

The house owned by the two cousins, while not luxurious, was comfortable. It was located in one of the quietest neighborhoods of Montreal, away from the industrial and commercial center of the city. There they spent the harsh Canadian winters (although the country is at the same latitude as southern Europe), impatiently awaiting the return of summer. But the fierce winds, unhindered by any mountain range, and the squalls that brought freezing arctic air raged unchecked and with extraordinary violence.

As the capital of the country since 1843, Montreal might have offered Summy Skim an opportunity to participate in public affairs,[6] but he was very independent by nature, seldom mingled with the high society of government officials, and had a deathly fear of politics. Besides, he was quite willing to accept British sovereignty, which was more apparent than real. He had never supported any of the parties that divide the Dominion* and scorned the world of officialdom.[7] He was, in short, a philosopher who liked to take life as it came, with no ambition whatsoever.

In his opinion, any change that might occur in his life could only bring trouble, worries, and a loss of material well-being.

It is not hard to see why this philosopher had never given any thought

---

*Dominion is the name of Canada.

9

to marriage and was not thinking about it now, although he had passed his thirty-second birthday. Perhaps, if he had not lost his mother, he would have provided her with a daughter-in-law just to please her—for mothers, as we know, love to perpetuate themselves in their grandchildren. If he had married, there is no doubt whatever that his wife would have shared his tastes. Somewhere among the many Canadian families that often have more than two dozen children, a suitable heiress would have been found either in town or in the countryside, and the union would have been a happy one. But it was now five years since Madame Skim had died, three years after her husband, and while she had long been thinking about a marriage for her son, the son himself had not given it much thought. In all likelihood, now that his mother was no longer there, the possibility of matrimony would never enter his mind.

As soon as the temperature began to moderate in that harsh climate, and the sun, rising earlier in the morning, announced the imminent return of summer, Summy Skim would get ready to leave the house on Jacques Cartier Street, although he had never persuaded his cousin to return to rural living so early in the year. He would go to their farm at Green Valley, some twenty miles north of Montreal on the north shore of the St. Lawrence River. There he would resume the country life that had been interrupted by the rigors of winter, which covered all the streams with ice and the fields with a thick blanket of snow. He would be back among his farmers, honest folk who had been in the family's service for half a century. How could they not feel a sincere affection and an unfailing devotion to a kind and generous master, who was always eager to do a favor, even at considerable personal sacrifice? There were many demonstrations of joy when he arrived and many expressions of regret when it came time for him to leave.

Year after year, the property at Green Valley brought in about twenty thousand francs, which the cousins shared, because the estate, like the house in Montreal, was owned jointly. A large-scale farming operation was carried on since the soil produced good crops of fodder and grains. The income derived from this supplemented what was provided by the magnificent forests that cover large areas of the Dominion, especially in its eastern region. The farm included a number of well-constructed and well-maintained buildings—stables, barns, cowsheds, a henhouse, storage sheds—and possessed a complete array of modern equipment suitable to the needs of present-day agriculture. As for the master's house, it was a simple but comfortable cottage at the entrance to a vast, lawn-covered, tree-shaded enclosure.

This was the home where Summy Skim and Ben Raddle spent their summers.[8] The former, at least, would not have wanted to exchange it for any wealthy American's palatial mansion. Modest though it was, it was all he needed. He had no plans to enlarge it or embellish it but was content with the beauties provided by nature at its own expense. The days went by, taken up with the pursuit of game, and the nights always brought him a sound slumber.

Needless to say (and this must be emphasized) Summy Skim was quite wealthy with the income from his land, which he exploited methodically and intelligently. But while he had no intention of letting his fortune dwindle, he was not at all concerned about adding to it. Not for anything in the world would he have become involved in the various aspects of business in North America such as commercial and industrial speculation, railroads, banks, mines, shipping companies, and so forth. No! This canny gentleman recoiled in horror from anything that presented even the slightest risk. To get into the habit of calculating the possibilities of gain or loss, to feel that he was at the mercy of events that could be neither foreseen nor prevented, to wake up in the morning thinking, "Am I richer or poorer than I was yesterday?"—that would have seemed horrible to him. Better, he thought, never to have gone to sleep or never to have awakened.

That was the very distinct difference between the two cousins, both of French Canadian origin. That they were the offspring of two sisters and had the same French blood in their veins, there was no doubt. But while Summy Skim's father was English, Ben Raddle's father was an American, and there is certainly a difference between the Englishman and the Yankee, a difference that increases as time goes by. Jonathan and

John Bull may be related,[9] but they are only distant relatives, not even close enough to be legal heirs, and that relationship, it seems, will eventually disappear entirely.

It is worth noting, then, that the two cousins, although they were very close to each other and never imagined that anything could ever separate them, had neither the same tastes nor the same temperament. Raddle was shorter, with brown hair and beard, and two years older than Skim. He did not view life from the same perspective as his cousin. While one was content to live the life of an honest landowner and supervise the harvest, the other was passionately interested in the industrial and scientific activity of his time. He had studied engineering and had already been involved in some of those prodigious projects by which the American seeks to get the upper hand through novelty of conception and boldness of execution. It was also his ambition to become rich, very rich, by taking advantage of those extraordinary but risky opportunities that are so common in North America, especially the extraction of the earth's mineral wealth. His brain was overexcited by the fabulous fortunes of the Goulds, the Astors, the Vanderbilts, the Rockefellers, and so many other billionaires. And so, while Summy Skim hardly ever traveled, except for his frequent trips to Green Valley, Ben Raddle had traveled throughout the United States, crossed the Atlantic, and visited parts of Europe, but had never been able to persuade his cousin to go with him. He had recently come back from a fairly long journey overseas, and since his return to Montreal had been waiting for some opportunity, or rather some large-scale business venture in which he might invest. Summy Skim had reason to fear that his cousin might be lured into one of those risky ventures that he himself regarded with horror.

It would have been a great pity if Summy Skim and Ben Raddle had been forced to go their separate ways, for they loved each other like brothers. While Ben regretted that Summy refused to join him in some industrial venture, Summy regretted that Ben did not confine his ambition to running the Green Valley estate, because it would have guaranteed their independence, and with independence came liberty.

2

The Two Cousins

Back at home, Summy Skim began making the arrangements that the death of Josias Lacoste involved, writing an announcement to be sent to the friends of the family and buying appropriate mourning clothes. He arranged for a religious service at his parish church for the repose of the soul of the deceased, but this would be postponed until Ben Raddle got back from his travels, for he would certainly want to attend.

Once the two cousins had come to an agreement about settling their uncle's personal affairs and claiming the inheritance (which would apparently consist of nothing more than the title to the claim on the Fortymile River), there would have to be a very serious discussion with Mr. Snubbin. The notary simply took the precaution of sending a telegram to the governor of the Klondike, in Dawson City, telling him that Josias Lacoste's heirs would shortly announce the conditions under which they would accept the inheritance, once an inventory had clarified their uncle's financial situation.

Raddle did not return to Montreal until five days later, on the morning of March 21. He had been in New York for a month with a group of engineers who were planning an enormous project, the construction of a bridge across the Hudson River between the metropolis and New Jersey, to match the one joining New York and Brooklyn.

Obviously, the planning of such a project was something that would fire the imagination of an engineer. Raddle had put his whole heart into it and had even offered his services to the Hudson Bridge Company. But it appeared that work on the bridge would not begin soon. A great deal had been written about it in the press, and there were many studies done on paper, but winter, which goes on until mid-April in that part of the United States, was not yet over. Who could tell whether work might start in the summer? Raddle had decided to go home.

Summy Skim found his cousin's absence long and tedious. How he wished he could bring his cousin around to his way of thinking, to get him to share his carefree existence! And even that great Hudson Bridge affair was a continual source of worry to him. If Ben became involved in it, would it not keep him in New York for a long time, perhaps for years? Summy would be left alone in the house they both owned, alone on the farm in Green Valley. But his efforts to keep Ben at home had been futile. The two cousins were so different in character that neither one had much influence over the other.

As soon as the engineer was home, his cousin told him about their uncle's death. He had not informed him in New York by letter or telegram because he was expecting him home any day.

Raddle was sincerely distressed at the news since his uncle Lacoste was the only remaining member of their entire family. He approved the arrangements his cousin had made for the funeral, and the next day they both attended the service, which was held in the parish church.

It was not until that day that Raddle heard the details of his uncle's affairs. He learned that Josias Lacoste had died in Dawson City, leaving behind nothing but Claim 129 on the Fortymile River in the Klondike.

The Klondike! The very sound of the word conjured up visions and could not fail to arouse the instincts of an engineer. The idea of inheriting a gold-bearing deposit definitely did not leave Raddle as indifferent as it did Summy Skim. Perhaps, unlike his cousin, he saw it as a business venture to be pursued rather than liquidated.

He did not want to say anything about it yet, however. It was his habit to study things seriously, and he wanted to give it some thought before announcing his decision. As it turned out, he apparently needed only twenty-four hours to weigh the pros and cons of the situation, for at breakfast the next morning, when Summy found him strangely absorbed in his thoughts, Ben said, "Let's talk a bit about the Klondike."

"If you mean only a little bit, my dear Ben, all right, let's talk about it."

"A little, unless it happens to be a lot."

"Tell me what's on your mind, Ben."

"The notary hasn't sent you the title deed to this Claim 129, has he?"

"No, but he has received it. I didn't think there was any point in looking it over, though."

"That sounds just like you, Summy," replied Raddle. "However, I take this matter a bit more seriously, and in my opinion it deserves serious attention and thorough study."

Skim made no reply to this at first, but after his cousin had gone on further, he said, "My dear Ben, our situation is very simple, it seems to me. Either this inheritance has some value, and we'll sell it for the best price we can get, or it has no value, which is much more likely since we know our uncle had no talent for getting rich. In that case, we won't accept it."

"That would be wise, of course," said Raddle. "But there's no need to act hastily. With these placers, there are so many unknown factors. You think they're poor, you think they're mined out, and one blow of the pick can bring you a fortune."

"Well, my dear Ben, that's exactly what the people familiar with the business should know, the ones working those famous Klondike deposits right now. If the claim on the Fortymile is worth something, we'll try to get rid of it at the best possible price. But as I said, I'm afraid our uncle got himself involved in some worthless venture, and we may have to suffer the consequences. He never made a success of anything in his life, and I can't imagine that he left this world just when he had become a millionaire."

"That's what we have to find out," replied Raddle. "The prospector's trade holds many surprises like that. You're always on the verge of making a lucky strike, and I'm not talking about ordinary luck. I mean finding a gold-bearing lode full of nuggets. After all, there are some gold seekers who have had nothing to complain about."

15

"Yes, one in a hundred, and look at the price they pay in worry, fatigue, and privation."

"Well, I don't intend to be satisfied with theories. I want to see some serious reports before I make up my mind."

Skim could see what his cousin was getting at, and although he was upset, he couldn't appear to be particularly surprised. He fell back on his old familiar theme.

"Don't we have enough, my friend, with the fortune our parents left us? Doesn't our inheritance guarantee our independence and comfort? I'm speaking like this because I can see that you attach more importance to this affair than I do, more than it deserves in my opinion. Do we know what difficulties it has in store for us? Really, aren't we rich enough?"

"You're never rich enough if you can be richer."

"Unless you're too rich, Ben, like some billionaires who have more worries than they have millions and who have more grief keeping their money than they had getting it."

"Oh, come on. Philosophy is all very well, but you mustn't carry it to extremes. Don't try to put words in my mouth. I don't expect to find tons of gold in Uncle Josias's claim, but as I said, it would be just as well to get some information."

"We'll get information, of course, my dear Ben. And when we get it, pray heaven we don't find ourselves in an awkward situation that we'll have to deal with out of respect for our family. Who knows whether the costs of purchasing, setting up, and working Claim 129 out there may not have exceeded our uncle's means? In that case, I assured Mr. Snubbin that . . ."

"You were right to do that, Summy, and I approve what you did," Raddle replied quickly. "We'll have the answer to your question when we know more about the affair. I've done more than listen to stories about these Klondike deposits. I've read everything that's been published about the wealth of that region, even though mining has been going on there for barely two years. After Australia, after California, after South Africa, one might think the last placers on the face of the earth have been exhausted. But lo and behold! Right here in this part of North America, on the border between Alaska and Canada, by some quirk of fate, new ones have been discovered. It seems these northern regions of the continent are highly favored in this respect. Not only are there gold mines in the Klondike, but some have been discovered in Michipicoten, Ontario, as well as in British Columbia, mines like the War Eagle, the Standard, the Sullivan Group, the Alhabarca, the Fern, the Syndicate, the Sans-Poel, the Cariboo,[1] the Deer Trail, the Georgie Reed, and many others whose shares have shot up in value, not to mention the silver, copper, manganese, iron, and coal mines! But as far as the Klondike is concerned, just think, Summy, of the size of that gold-bearing region. Over six hundred miles long and about a hundred wide—and I'm not counting the deposits in Alaska, only those on Canadian territory. Isn't that a huge field for discovery? Perhaps the biggest ever known on the surface of the earth! And who knows? Some day, perhaps, the output of that region will be reckoned, not in millions, but in billions!"

Raddle could have gone on at some length on the same topic, and Skim saw that he was thoroughly familiar with it. But all he said was, "Come on, Ben. You've obviously caught the fever."

"What do you mean, I've caught the fever?"

"Yes, the gold fever, and you can't cure that with quinine, because it isn't an intermittent fever."

"Don't worry, my dear Summy," replied Raddle with a laugh. "My pulse rate is no faster than usual. I wouldn't want you to come in contact with the fever."

"Oh, I've been vaccinated," replied Summy in the same vein. "I have nothing to fear. But I'd be sorry to see you commit yourself . . ."

"My dear fellow, there's no question of committing myself. It's simply a matter of studying an affair and then making a profit from it if there is any to be made. You say our uncle wasn't very lucky with his speculations. I believe that, of course, and it's very likely that this claim on the Fortymile brought him more mud than nuggets. That's possible. But perhaps he didn't have the resources he needed in order to work it.

Perhaps he wasn't operating methodically and on the basis of experience, as would have been done by . . ."

"By an engineer. Isn't that what you mean, Ben?"

"Of course, an engineer."

"You, for instance?"

"Me? Certainly. In any case, that isn't the point at the moment. Before trying to get rid of this claim that we've inherited, you'll have to agree that it would be just as well to send to the Klondike for some information."

"That's reasonable, of course, although I have no illusions about the value of that number 129."

"That's what we'll know after we do our research," replied Raddle. "You may be right, or you may be wrong. What I'm saying is that we go to Mr. Snubbin's office and authorize him to take all the necessary steps. He'll have information sent from Dawson City by mail—or better still, by telegram—and when we know where we stand with regard to the value of the claim, we'll see where we go from there."

The conversation ended there, and all in all, Skim could not object to his cousin's suggestions. It was only natural to get information before making a decision. He had no doubt that Ben Raddle was a serious, intelligent, and practical man. Nevertheless, he was distressed and worried to see how eagerly his cousin looked to the future, how greedily he pounced on the prey that had been so unexpectedly placed in his ambitious path. Would he be able to hold Ben back? Certainly Summy Skim would never desert Ben Raddle. They had a common interest in this affair. He continued to believe it would soon be settled and was now hoping the information from Dawson City would be of such a nature that there would be no need to follow it up. But what an idea, what a bad idea, it was for Uncle Josias to go seeking his fortune in the Klondike, where perhaps he had found nothing but misery and where he had certainly met his death.

That afternoon, Raddle went to the notary's office, where he read the documents sent from Dawson City.

These documents definitely established the location of Claim 129, property of Mr. Josias Lacoste, now deceased. This claim occupied a site on the right bank of the Fortymile River in the Klondike region. This stream runs eastward into the mighty Yukon, which flows all the way through Alaska after draining the western regions of the Dominion. Its water, which is English in its upper reaches, becomes American farther downstream since the vast territory of Alaska had now been sold to the United States by the Russians.

A map showed the exact location of Claim 129. It was located about twenty miles from Fort Cudahy,[2] a village founded by the Hudson's Bay Company.

During this conversation, it became very clear to Snubbin that the engineer took a totally different view of the affair than his coheir did. Raddle studied the deeds in great detail. He could not take his eyes off the rough map spread out in front of him, which included the Klondike and the adjacent part of Alaska. In his imagination, he traveled up the Fortymile, which crosses the one hundred and fortieth meridian,[3] the line agreed on as the boundary between the two countries. There he stopped, near the boundary, at the very spot where stakes marked out the claim of Josias Lacoste. He counted the other claims staked out on both sides of the stream, which had its source in one of the gold-bearing regions of Alaska. Why should they not be as well favored as those on the Klondike River, or its tributary, Bonanza Creek, or on Victoria, or Eldorado, or other streams flowing into Bonanza, so productive at that time and so eagerly sought after by miners? His eyes devoured the marvelous country whose network of streams carried the precious metal down in abundance, a metal which was worth, in Dawson City, $468,000 a long ton.

When Snubbin saw him so absorbed in his thoughts that he did not speak a word, he felt obliged to say something. "Mr. Raddle, may I ask whether it might be your intention to work the claim that belonged to the late Josias Lacoste?"

"Perhaps," was the reply.

"But what about Mr. Skim?"

"Summy doesn't have to make up his mind. As for me, I'll reserve judgment until I've confirmed that this information is accurate, and until I've seen for myself."

"You're thinking of undertaking the long journey to the Klondike, then?" asked Snubbin, shaking his head.

"Why not? No matter what Summy may think, in my opinion this business is worth the trip. Once we're in Dawson City we'll get the facts. Either to sell the claim, or simply to estimate its worth, Mr. Snubbin, you'll agree with me that it's better to have gone to see it."

"Is that really necessary?" asked the notary.

"It's essential," declared Raddle. "And besides, it isn't enough just to want to sell. You have to find a buyer."

"If that is your only concern, you can save yourself a long and tiring journey, Mr. Raddle."

"Why do you say that?"

"Look, here's a telegram that came just an hour ago. I was about to send it to you when you did me the honor of coming to my office."

With that, Snubbin handed Raddle a telegram dated a week earlier, which had been taken from Dawson City to Vancouver and then sent to Montreal by trans-Canada wire.

An American syndicate already owned eight claims in the Klondike, which were being mined by Captain Healy of the North American Trading and Transportation Company (Chicago and Dawson).[4] This syndicate was making a firm offer to purchase Claim 129 on the Fortymile River for five thousand dollars, to be sent to Montreal on receipt of a telegram of acceptance.

Raddle took the telegram and began to read it as intently as he had studied the title deeds.

"Now here, Mr. Raddle," remarked the notary, "is something that will save you the trouble of making the trip."

"I'm not so sure," replied the engineer. "Is the offer high enough? Five thousand dollars for a claim in the Klondike!"

"I can't answer that question for you."

"You see, Mr. Snubbin, if this syndicate is offering five thousand dollars for 129, that means it's worth ten times as much on the market, and perhaps a hundred times as much for anyone who wants to continue mining it."

"Judging by the price, it seems that it was not a great success for your uncle, Mr. Raddle. It remains to be seen whether it might not have been better, instead of embarking on a risky affair of this kind, to save himself all that trouble and put the five thousand dollars in the bank."

"I don't agree with you, Mr. Snubbin."

"So I see, but perhaps Mr. Summy Skim would."

"No. After he's read this telegram, I'll spell out my reasons to him, and he's too intelligent not to understand them. Then, when I've convinced him that we have to make the journey, he'll decide to go with me."

"What?" exclaimed Snubbin. "The happiest, most independent man that any notary ever encountered in the practice of his profession?"

"Yes, he's happy and independent, and I intend to double his happiness and his independence. What have we got to lose, after all, since we can always accept the price offered by this syndicate?"

"Nevertheless, Mr. Raddle, you will have to be very eloquent."

"No, only logical. Give me the telegram, Mr. Snubbin. I'm going to show it to Summy, and we'll come to a decision before the day is out."

"A decision in your favor?"

"In my favor, Mr. Snubbin, and we'll have to put it into effect as soon as possible."

Obviously, it was settled, and whatever the notary may have thought, Ben Raddle had no doubt that he would persuade Summy Skim to make the proposed journey.

After leaving the law office, he went back to the house on Jacques Cartier Street by the shortest route and went straight up to his cousin's room.

"Well," said Skim, "you've just been to see Mr. Snubbin. Is there anything new?"

"Yes, Summy, something new, and some news, too."

"Good news?"

"Excellent."

"Did you read the title deeds?"

"Of course, and they're quite in order. As our uncle's heirs, we're now the owners of the claim on the Fortymile River."

"That'll make a nice addition to our fortune," replied Skim with a laugh.

"Very likely," declared the engineer, "and probably more than you think."

"Ah! What news have you heard to make you talk like that?"

"Just what's in this telegram, which came to Mr. Snubbin's office this morning, with an offer to buy Claim 129."

And Summy Skim learned what was in the offer made by the North American Trading and Transportation Company.

"That's perfect," he said. "What are we waiting for? Let's sell our claim to that obliging company, and the sooner the better."

"Why would we sell something for five thousand dollars, when it's very likely worth a lot more?"

"But my dear Ben . . ."

"Your dear Ben is telling you that's no way to do business and that there's nothing like seeing for yourself."

"You're still thinking that way?"

"More than ever! Think about it, Summy. If someone is making us that offer, it means they know what the claim is worth, that it's worth much, much more. There are other placers in the Klondike, along its streams and in its mountains."

"What do you know about it?"

"I just know, Summy, and if a company that already owns some claims wants to buy 129, it means that it has, not five thousand reasons for offering five thousand dollars, but ten thousand, maybe a hundred thousand."

"Really, Ben, you're playing with figures."

"But figures are life, my dear fellow, and in my opinion, you don't do enough figuring."

"I have no head for mathematics, Ben."

"It isn't a question of mathematics, Summy. Believe me, I'm talking to you very seriously, and after mature consideration. I might have been hesitant at first to leave for Dawson City, but since that telegram arrived, I've decided to deliver my answer in person."

"What! You want to go to the Klondike?"

"It's absolutely essential."

"And without getting any more information?"

"I'll get my information when I'm there."

"So you're going to leave me alone again?"

"No. You're coming with me."

"What, me?"

"Yes, you."

"Never!"

"Oh yes. This matter concerns both of us."

"I'll give you power of attorney."

"No. I'm taking you along."

"But it means traveling five thousand miles."

"Plus another twelve hundred or more."

"And how long will it take?"

"It'll take as long as it takes . . . if it's in our interest to work the claim instead of selling it."

"What do you mean, work it?" exclaimed Skim. "But that would mean a whole year."

"Two, if need be."

"Two years! Two years!"

"Do we need to think about that when every month will add to our fortune?"

"No! No!" exclaimed Skim, curling up and sinking into his armchair like a man who was determined never to leave it.

Ben Raddle made a last effort to convince him. He went over the matter from every angle. He proved by the most urgent reasons that their presence at the claim on the Fortymile was essential and that delay was out of the question.

"As for me, Summy," he concluded, "I've decided to leave for Dawson City, and I can't believe you'll refuse to go with me."

Then Skim began to talk about how much the trip would upset their normal existence. Within two months they were supposed to leave Montreal and move into Green Valley to resume their life of hunting and fishing.

"Fine!" replied Raddle. "There's plenty of game on the open spaces of the Klondike, and plenty of fish in its streams. You'll fish and hunt in a new region, which will have some surprises in store for you."

"But what about our farmers, our honest farmers, who are expecting us?"

"And will they have any reason to regret our absence when we come back rich enough to open up more farms for them and buy the whole district? Besides, Summy, you've been too sedentary up until now. You have to travel a bit in the world."

"Well," said Skim, "there are plenty of other countries I could visit in North America and in Europe if I felt like it. I certainly wouldn't start by rushing off to the heart of that abominable Klondike."

"You'll find it charming, Summy, once you discover for yourself that it's strewn with gold dust and paved with nuggets."

"Ben, Ben, you're frightening me. Yes, you're frightening me. You want to embark on a venture that will bring you nothing but hardship and disillusionment."

"Hardship, perhaps. But disillusionment, never!"

"To begin with, that damned claim is probably not worth as much as a patch of cabbages or potatoes at Green Valley."

"Then why should that company make us an initial offer of several thousand dollars for it?"

"And when I stop to consider, Ben, that it means going out to a country where the temperature drops to fifty below!"

"Excellent! Cold weather keeps you fit."

Finally, after a thousand objections, Summy Skim had to admit defeat. No, he would not let his cousin go to the Klondike alone. He would go with him, even if only to bring him back sooner.

And so, that same day, a telegram announcing the imminent departure of Ben Raddle and Summy Skim was sent to Captain Healy, the manager of the North American Trading and Transportation Company, Dawson City, Klondike.

3

From Montreal to Vancouver

BY TAKING THE CANADIAN PACIFIC RAILWAY, tourists, merchants, immigrants, and prospectors can travel directly, without changing trains and without leaving Canada, from Montreal to Vancouver. On their arrival in this western metropolis, they have a choice of several different means of travel: by land, by river, or by sea, and of various means of transportation: by boat, on horseback, by wagon, or even on foot for most of the way.

Once their departure date had been fixed, Summy Skim could simply leave it up to his cousin to make all the arrangements for the journey, such as buying supplies and choosing the route. That would probably have suited the ambitious and intelligent engineer, the sole promoter of the enterprise, on whom all the responsibility fell—and who accepted it.

In the first place, Raddle quite rightly pointed out that the departure could not be delayed more than two weeks. It was important for Josias Lacoste's heirs to be in the Klondike before the beginning of summer, a summer, be it noted, that provides warmth only four months of the year in that far northern region located almost at the Arctic Circle.

Indeed, when he consulted the book on Canadian mining law, which governed the Yukon Territory, he came across Article 9, which reads:

"Any claim on which no digging is carried out for a period of seventy-two hours during the summertime (to be defined by the commissioner) shall revert to the public domain, unless special permission has been granted by the commissioner."

Summer, even when it comes early, begins in the second half of May. At that time, then, if work on Claim 129 was interrupted for more than three days, Josias Lacoste's property would revert to the Dominion government and in all probability the American syndicate would be quick to buy it up, probably at a lower price than they had offered to the two heirs.

"Now you understand, Summy," said Raddle, "that we really can't let anyone get ahead of us and that it's urgent for us to be on our way."

"I understand whatever you want me to understand, my friend," was the reply.

"Which is, after all, perfectly reasonable," added the engineer.

"I have no doubt of that, Ben, and I don't mind leaving Montreal as soon as possible if it means that we can also come back as soon as possible."

"We won't stay in the Klondike any longer than necessary, Summy."

"All right, then, Ben. When do we leave?"

"On the second of April, two weeks from now."

Summy Skim stood with his arms crossed and his head bent forward. He wanted desperately to shout "What? So soon?" But he said nothing, because it would have made no difference. Since he had agreed to go, he had sworn to himself that he would not utter a word of recrimination during the trip, no matter what might happen.

It was a wise move on Raddle's part to set April 2 as the latest possible departure date. With his eye on his itinerary, he launched into a series of comments, bristling with statistics that he manipulated with undeniable competence.

"For the time being, Summy," he said, "we don't have to choose between two routes to the Klondike, because there's only one. Some day, perhaps, it will be possible to get to the Klondike via Edmonton, Fort St. John, and the Peace River, which passes through the Cassiar district in the northeast corner of British Columbia."[1]

"I've heard there's plenty of game in that country," remarked Skim, whose love of hunting was getting the better of him. "Why don't we take that route, by the way?"

"Because after we left Vancouver we'd have to go five hundred miles by water and then nearly nine hundred by land," replied Raddle.[2]

"What route do you plan to follow, Ben?"

"We'll decide that after we get to Vancouver, where we'll be in a position to compare the advantages of different routes. Anyway, here are some exact figures that will show you the length of our itinerary: the distance from Montreal to Vancouver is 2,922 miles, and from Vancouver to Dawson City, one 1,555."

Skim did the mathematics. "Five and two make seven, five and two make seven again, five and nine make fourteen, and carry one; one and three make four, so the total is 4,477 miles."

"Exactly right, Summy!"

"Well then, Ben, if we bring back three pounds of gold for every mile we travel . . ."

"At the current rate of $212 a pound, that would come to $2,847,372."

"Perfect!" said Skim. "That would be a nice return on our investment."

"And why not?" replied Raddle.[3] "According to the geographer John Muir, Alaska will produce more gold than California, which yielded eighty-one million in 1861 alone.

"Why shouldn't the Klondike contribute its fair share to our planet's five-billion-dollar fortune in gold?"

"You've got an answer for everything, Ben."

"And the future will prove me right."

Of that, Summy Skim had no doubt.

"Besides," he added, "there's no going back on what we've agreed on."

"Right you are," replied Raddle. "It's just as if we'd already left."

"I'd rather it was just as if we were already home again, Ben."

"But you have to leave first, Summy," quipped Raddle, "before you can come back."

"Your logic is perfect, Ben. And now let's think about getting ready for our trip. You don't go out to that incredible country with one spare shirt and two pairs of socks."

"Don't worry about a thing, Summy. I'll look after everything. All you have to do is get on the train in Montreal and get off in Vancouver. As for our preparations, we won't be like some immigrant setting out aimlessly for a distant land, lugging a heavy load of equipment. Our equipment is there already. We'll find it on Uncle Josias's claim. It's what he used for working number 129 on the Fortymile. All we have to do is get ourselves there."

"But even that is something," replied Skim, "and we deserve every precaution—especially against the cold! Brrr! I feel chilled to the bone already."

"Come on, Summy. When we get to Dawson City, it will already be summer."

"If only we can get home before winter."

"Don't worry," replied Raddle. "Even in the winter you'll have everything you need. Good clothes, good food. You'll come home fatter than when you left."

"Ah, no. I don't ask for that much," said Skim, who had wisely decided to give in. "I warn you, if I'm going to put on as much as ten pounds, I'm staying home."

"Make light of it if you like, Summy, but trust me."

"Yes, of course, I have no choice but to trust you. On the second of April we'll start out like pilgrims on the road to Eldorado."

"Yes, the second of April. That'll give me time to make all our preparations."

"Well, Ben, since I have two free weeks, I'd like to spend that time in the country."

"All right, but the weather isn't very pleasant yet at Green Valley."

Summy Skim might have replied that the weather would be at least as pleasant as it would be in the Klondike. Besides, even though winter was still not over, it would be a great pleasure for him to spend a few days among his farmers, to see his fields again, even though they would be white with snow, the beautiful forests covered with hoarfrost, the nearby streams sheathed in ice, and the St. Lawrence solidly packed with ice jams. And then, the cold weather gives the hunter an opportunity to shoot a few fine furred or feathered trophies, not to mention the bears, cougars, and other wild beasts that prowl about the neighborhood. It would be Summy Skim's way of saying good-bye to all the inhabitants of the region. He was setting out on a journey that might be very long. Who could say when he would be back again?

"You should come with me, Ben," he said.

"Do you think so? And who would look after the preparations for our trip?"

The next day, Summy Skim took the train to Green Valley, found a well-equipped coach waiting for him at the station, and was at the farm that afternoon.

Needless to say, the farmers were somewhat surprised at his arrival, but pleased as well. As usual, he was deeply moved by the warm welcome he received. But when the farmers heard that their master would not be with them all summer, they could not hide their disappointment at the news.

"Yes, my friends," said Skim, "Ben Raddle and I are leaving for the Klondike. It's the devil's own country, and he holds it in his power. It's so far away that it takes four months to get there, and just as long to get back."

"And all that just to pick up some nuggets," said one of the peasants, with a shrug.

"Even supposing you do find any," added a philosophical old fellow, shaking his head discouragingly.

"You also have to be careful not to fall," said Skim, "because sometimes you can't get up again. But what can you do, my friends? It's like a fever, or perhaps an epidemic, that sweeps the world from time to time and carries off a great many victims."

"But why are you going out there, sir?" asked one of the farm women.

Skim replied that he and his cousin had just inherited a claim, following the death of their uncle, Josias Lacoste, and explained why Ben Raddle considered their presence in the Klondike indispensable.

"Yes," the old man went on, "we've heard about what goes on in the far outposts of the Dominion, especially about the hardships that take the lives of so many poor people. After all, Mr. Skim, it's out of the question for you to stay in that place. After you've sold your pile of mud, you'll come back."

"You can count on that, my friends. But, assuming that everything goes smoothly, five or six months will go by before we return, and the warm weather will be over. That means a whole summer wasted!"

"Yes, a wasted summer and an even sadder winter," said an old woman, crossing herself and adding, "May God protect you, sir."

After a week at Green Valley, Skim thought it was time to go back to his cousin. He had a few personal things to get ready. When he said good-bye to the good people on the farm, it was an emotional leave-taking for all concerned. In only a few weeks, he thought to himself, the April sun would be rising over the horizon at Green Valley, the first green sprouts of spring would be pushing up through all the snow, and if it were not for that damned journey, he would come back as he did every year and settle into the cottage until the first cold spells of winter. He was even hoping a letter from Ben might arrive at Green Valley, telling him there was no need to go ahead with their plan. But the letter had not come. Nothing had changed. They would leave on the appointed day. And so Summy Skim was driven back to the station, and on the morning of March 31 he was back in Montreal with his formidable cousin.

"Nothing new?" he asked, standing in front of him like a question mark.

"Nothing, Summy, except that everything is ready for our trip."

"So you've bought . . ."

"Everything," replied Raddle, "except for food, which we'll find in Vancouver. I only got clothes. As far as guns are concerned, you have yours and I have mine. They're excellent firearms, and we know how to use them. Two good rifles and a complete hunting outfit. But since we won't be able to replenish our wardrobes out there and since there are no department stores yet in the capital of the Klondike, here are the various articles of clothing that each of us will take, just to be on the safe side: four flannel shirts, two sets of two-piece woolen underwear, a heavy knitted sweater, a corduroy suit, two pairs of heavy pants, two pairs of canvas outer pants, a blue denim suit, a fur-lined leather coat with a hood, a sailor's raincoat with a waterproof hat, a rubber coat, six pairs of fitted socks and six pairs of socks one size larger, a pair of fur mitts, leather gloves, a pair of hobnailed hunting boots, two pairs of knee-length moccasins, a pair of snowshoes, a dozen handkerchiefs, towels . . ."

"Hey!" exclaimed Skim, raising his hands heavenward, "that's enough for ten years."

"No, only two years."

"Only, Ben? That 'only' is very frightening. Look, all we have to do is go to Dawson City, sell Claim 129, and come back to Montreal."

"Of course, Summy, if anyone will pay us what the claim is worth."

"And if not?"

"Then we'll think about it, Summy."

Since it was impossible to get any other answer, Skim did not insist. In the two days prior to their departure he wandered like a lost soul between the house on Jacques Cartier Street and Snubbin's office.

To make a long story short, on the morning of April 2 the two cousins were at the Montreal railway station, where their luggage was waiting for them. There was not a lot of it, and it would not really be a burden to them en route until they added more to it in Vancouver.

The travelers could have bought steamship tickets to Skagway from the Canadian Pacific Railway before leaving Montreal, but Ben Raddle had not yet decided what route to take to Dawson City. He could either travel up the Yukon River from its mouth to the capital of the Klondike, or go from Skagway across the mountains, plains, and lakes of British Columbia.

Finally the two cousins were on their way, one dragging the other along, one resigned to his fate, the other full of confidence. They would travel in style, too, in a very comfortable first-class car. The least they could ask for was to have all their creature comforts during the six days of the 2900-mile journey from Montreal to Vancouver.

During the first part of the trip the train traveled through the varied regions of eastern and central Canada. They would have to pass the Great Lakes before entering the sparsely populated, and sometimes uninhabited, part of the country, especially as they approached British Columbia. It was the first time either of them had visited that part of North America.

The weather was fine, the air bracing, the sky overcast with a light haze. The mercury hovered around zero degrees centigrade, with a dry, biting wind when it rose and brief snow flurries when it dropped.

White plains stretched as far as the eye could see. In a few weeks they would be green again, and their numerous streams would be free of ice. Flocks of birds went flapping their way westward ahead of the train. On either side of the track, footprints of wild animals could be seen on the snow, leading back to the forests on the horizon. Those tracks would have been easy to follow and might have led to a lucky shot! Summy Skim's impatience and regret can well be imagined, imprisoned as he was aboard the train, unable to give free rein to his hunting instincts.

But hunting was out of the question for the time being. If there were hunters on the train heading for Vancouver, they were only nugget hunters, and the dogs that accompanied them were not there to retrieve partridges or hares, or to chase down deer or bears. No! Their masters had bought them in Montreal with only one plan in mind: to use them for hauling sleds across the frozen surface of lakes and streams in that part of British Columbia between Skagway and the Klondike.

Among the travelers who had boarded the train in Montreal or at the various stations along the Canadian Pacific Railway were immigrants, both country folk and city people.

Yes, the gold fever was only beginning. But news kept coming in, announcing the discovery of gold on Eldorado Creek, Bonanza Creek, Hunker Creek, Bear Creek, Gold Bottom Creek, all the tributaries of the

150-mile-long Klondike River. There was talk of claims where a prospector could pan as much as three hundred dollars' worth of gold. The flood of immigrants continued to grow. They were rushing headlong into the Klondike just as they had rushed into Australia, California, and the Transvaal, and the transportation companies were being swamped. Besides, the people traveling on the train were not representatives of companies or syndicates founded with the support of big American or European banks, equipped with the best material, well supplied with food and clothing, and with no fear for the future, since they continually received fresh supplies of clothing and food through a special service. No! They were only poor people, trapped by all the hardships of life, driven from their homeland by misery. They could gamble everything since they had nothing to lose, and their brains were addled by the hope of making a rich strike. Besides, while they were not in a position to work on their own, they could hire themselves out to the owners of claims that often shut down for lack of workers. Wages were probably extremely high, as much as fifteen dollars a day. But that was because the cost of living was exorbitant in the Klondike and the most essential items cost twenty times as much as they did elsewhere. There was really no way of getting rich except by a stroke of luck.

But the transcontinental train was speeding on, full steam ahead. Summy Skim and Ben Raddle had no reason to complain about lack of comfort on their long journey. They had a drawing room at their disposal during the day and a bedroom at night, a smoking room where they could smoke to their hearts' content just as they could in the best restaurants in Montreal, a dining car where the quality of the food and service left nothing to be desired, and a bathing car where they could take a bath en route. But Skim still longed for his cottage at Green Valley.

In four hours the train reached Ottawa, the country's capital,[4] which overlooks the surrounding countryside from the top of a hill. It is a splendid city and lumbering center, which claims, with more or less justification, to be the center of the world. Farther on, near Carlton Place,[5] one might have caught sight of Toronto, its rival and one-time Dominion capital. (It seems as if a number of Canadian cities took turns at being the capital.)

Now running due west, the train reached Sudbury, an area made rich by nickel mining. Here, where the track forks, they took the northern line along Lake Superior, to Port Arthur, near Fort William. At Heron Bay, Schreiber, and all the other stations on the huge lake, the train stopped long enough for the two cousins to note their importance as lake ports. Then they went on past Bonheur, Ignace, Eagle River, Rat Portage, through a region holding a fortune in mineral deposits, and arrived at the large city of Winnipeg.

The few hours they stopped there seemed all too short to Skim, who wanted to retain a few memories of the trip. He would gladly have spent a day or two visiting that city of forty thousand souls and the fine neighboring farms of western Canada. But railway timetables are inflexible, and the passengers boarded the train again. Most of them were not traveling for the sake of traveling but in order to get to their destination by the shortest and fastest route. The train that served the many little towns in that region, such as Portage la Prairie, Brandon, Elkhorn, and Broadview, was indifferent to the fact that the land was intensively cultivated or that it contained vast hunting grounds that were home to thousands of buffalo.[6] Summy Skim would rather have spent six months there than six weeks in the Klondike.

"Oh well," Raddle kept telling him, "if there are no buffalo near Dawson City, you'll make up for it with moose."

The train passed Regina, stopped for a few hours in Calgary, then headed for the Crowsnest Pass through the Rocky Mountains, crossing the border into the coal-rich province of British Columbia, where other animals were seen.

From Calgary another route branched off, and some of the immigrants had chosen that route to reach the Klondike. It was the one Summy Skim would have preferred since it was a route for hunters. It cuts across the Cassiar district, famous as a hunting area; passes through Edmonton and Fort St. John; crosses the Peace, Dease, Francis, and Pelly rivers; and connects northeastern British Columbia with the Yukon. But it is long and difficult, and the traveler must replenish his supplies frequently over a distance of more than 1200 miles. True, the region is very rich in gold, which can be panned in almost all its streams, but it lacks resources and will not be viable until the Canadian government sets up relay posts every forty or fifty miles.

On their way through the Rockies, the travelers caught a glimpse of Mount Stephen and Cathedral Peak as the railway turned on its upward way. Especially magnificent were the immense Selkirk Mountains, with their eternal caps of snow and glaciers as far as the eye could see. In the midst of this solitude reigned the "silence of all life," disturbed only by the puffing of the locomotive.

Before leaving Montreal, Skim had bought the *Short*, a guidebook published by the Canadian Pacific Railway. While he could not visit all the famous spots mentioned in the book, at least he read the descriptions. He also relied on the guidebook's editor in choosing hotels at the various stations where the train stopped. Some, like Skyte House at Field and Glacier House with its magnificent view over the Selkirks, were truly luxurious and exceptionally comfortable, and their excellent cuisine provided a welcome change from the dining car's regular fare.

As the train traveled west, new regions opened up before it. These were not the rich, fertile lands where man's labor is rewarded by fine harvests from soil that has not yet been exhausted. No! These were the Kootenay region and the gold fields of the Cariboo, where gold was found and is still being found in abundance, as a whole network of streams wash down flecks of the precious metal. One might well wonder why the prospectors did not spend more time and effort in an area that was easier to reach instead of embarking on the long and tiring journey to the Klondike with its exorbitant costs.

As the train carried him farther from Montreal and Green Valley, Summy Skim said to himself over and over again, "Really, Uncle Josias ought to have tried his luck in the Cariboo. We'd be there by now. We'd know already what his claim is worth. We'd have cashed it in within twenty-four hours, and been back home within a week."

That was true enough, but it was undoubtedly written in the great book of destiny that Summy Skim would venture into the terrifying Klondike region and wade about in the mud of the Fortymile River.

The train continued on its way toward the Pacific coast of British Columbia, veering to the southwest. The last part of the journey of 2900 miles passed without incident, and after six days the two cousins stepped down from the Canadian Pacific Railway car and set foot in Vancouver.

4

Vancouver

THE CITY OF VANCOUVER is not located on the large island of the same name that lies off the coast of British Columbia but on a point of land protruding from the mainland. It is a major city, but the provincial capital is Victoria, a city of some sixteen thousand inhabitants on the southeast shore of the island. New Westminster, with its six thousand inhabitants, is also on the island.[1]

Vancouver lies at the inner end of a harbor opening onto the winding Juan de Fuca Strait, which continues to the northwest.[2] Behind the harbor, the spire of a chapel rises among the thick branches of pines and cedars tall enough to conceal the high towers of a cathedral.

From the southern tip of Vancouver Island (which has borne the names of its first two occupants, the Spaniard Quadra in 1786 and the Englishman Vancouver in 1789),[3] the channel turns north between the island and the mainland, where it becomes known as Georgia Strait to the east of the island, and Johnstone and Queen Charlotte straits farther north. The port of Vancouver is therefore easily accessible to ships from the Pacific, whether they come along the Canadian coast or up the coast of the United States.

Did the founders of Vancouver overestimate what the future held in store? It is impossible to answer that question, although the discovery of gold in the Klondike has given rise to lively and exuberant activity. One thing is certain: it could accommodate a population of a hundred thousand, and traffic would move easily through its checkerboard of streets intersecting at right angles. It has churches, banks, and hotels; is lit by gas and electricity; and draws its water supply from springs located north of Burrard Inlet. There are bridges across the False Bay estuary, and on the northwest peninsula there is a park covering 950 acres.

After leaving the station, Skim and Raddle, following the advice of their guidebook, went to the Westminster Hotel, where they planned to stay until they could leave for the Klondike.

With so many people in town, however, the problem was to find a room in that hotel. Travelers were flooding in as trains and steamships disgorged up to 1200 passengers every twenty-four hours. It is easy to imagine how much profit the city derived from this, especially the citizens who were in the business of lodging and feeding visitors, and charging them exorbitant prices. The visitors would very likely spend as little time there as possible, eager to get to the area where gold attracted them like iron to a magnet. But they still had to find a way to leave, and space was limited on the many northbound steamers that stopped at various ports in Mexico and the United States.

Some took the Pacific route to St. Michael, at the mouth of the Yukon River on the west coast of Alaska.[4] From there they traveled upstream as far as Dawson City, the capital of the Klondike. Most, however, headed for Victoria or Vancouver, and from there followed the coast up to Dyea or Skagway. Ben Raddle had already decided which route to follow, but in the meantime he and Summy Skim had to make do with a room in the Vancouver Hotel. At least they had no complaints about the food or the service there.

As soon as they had checked in, Skim's first question was, "And how long will we be staying in Vancouver, my dear Ben?"

"About four days," was the reply. "That's when the *Football* is due to arrive."[5]

"The *Football*? And just what is the *Football*?"

"It's a Canadian Pacific steamer that will take us to Skagway. I'm going to book passage on it for us today."

"So Ben, you've picked the route that will take us to the Klondike?"

"The choice was obvious, Summy, once I had decided not to go up to the mouth of the Yukon. That's a journey of more than 2800 miles. We'll take the most frequently followed route, up the coast of British Columbia in the lee of the islands. We'll get to Skagway without wearing ourselves out. At this time of year there are still ice floes on the Yukon River, and it isn't unusual for ships to get caught in the ice and sink. Or they could be delayed until July. The *Football*, on the other hand, will take no more than a week to get to Skagway, or even to Dyea. Mind you, after we disembark we'll have to cross the rugged slopes of the Chilkoot Pass or the White Pass.[6] But after that we'll travel partly by land and partly across lakes until we reach the Yukon River, which will take us to Dawson City. My guess is we'll get to our destination by the beginning of June, which is a good time to arrive. Now we just have to wait patiently for the *Football*."

"And where is it coming from, this ship with the athletic name?"

"Right from Skagway. It does a regular run between there and Vancouver. It's due here on the fourteenth of this month, at the latest."

"Well, Ben, if that's your decision, I wish we were already on the *Football*."

"You approve of my plan, then?"

"Absolutely, and since we're destined to go to the Klondike, I'm counting on you to get us there the best way possible."

The two cousins would have some time on their hands during their stay in Vancouver. For one thing, they already had all their gear. For another thing, they did not have to buy equipment to work the claim, since Uncle Josias's equipment would be at their disposal. On board the *Football* they would still find the comfort they had enjoyed on the Pacific Transcontinental. But at Skagway Raddle would have to make special arrangements to acquire some means of transportation to Dawson City. They would need a collapsible boat for crossing lakes and a team of dogs to haul their sleds across ice-covered plains. He would also see whether it might be better to deal with a local carrier who would agree to take

them to Dawson City and provide enough food for several weeks in case
it might be difficult to obtain any on the way. Obviously, that was bound
to be very expensive, but surely one or two good nuggets would be more
than enough to make up for that expense.

There would also be the matter of dealing with Canadian customs
officials, who were rather difficult, not to say irritating.

There was so much lively activity in the city, such a crowd of travelers, that Skim was not bored for a moment. Nothing could have been
more fascinating than the trains arriving from eastern Canada and the
United States. Nothing could have been more interesting than the thousands of passengers disembarking from the steamers that brought them
to Vancouver. There were so many people wandering about the streets,
waiting to leave for Skagway or St. Michael, that most them were reduced to huddling in corners of the port or under the timbers of the
electrically lighted docks.

The police were kept busy with surveillance and maintaining order,
what with that swarming crowd of adventurers of all types without
hearth or home, attracted by fantastic posters promoting the Klondike.
At every step of the way police officers, wearing drab uniforms the color
of dead leaves, stood ready to intervene in the many quarrels that threatened to end in bloodshed, for a miner is quick with his knife.

In the midst of this seething mass of immigrants from all social classes,
and especially perhaps, from the underworld, the constables carried out
their difficult and dangerous duties with all the zeal and courage required
by their important office. Perhaps, too, they were thinking it would be
more profitable and less dangerous to pan for gold in the tributaries of
the Yukon. How could they forget that five Canadian constables, at the
very beginning of the Klondike gold rush, had gone home two hundred
thousand dollars richer? It required great moral courage on their part
not to become intoxicated as so many others had done.

Sometimes looking through his guidebook, Summy Skim had been
rather impressed to read that the temperature in winter fell to minus
fifty degrees centigrade. Surely he thought, that was a bit of an exaggera-

tion, even though Dawson City is close to the Arctic Circle. But what really set him thinking was to see in a store in Vancouver that sold optical instruments several thermometers that were graduated down to ninety degrees below freezing.

"Clearly," he said to himself, "that's an exaggeration! The Klondikers are proud of their cold weather and like to show it off."

He went into the store and asked to see a few thermometers so that he could choose the one he wanted.

The proprietor took several different models from his window and handed them to him. They were not graduated in the Fahrenheit scale, which is still in use in the United Kingdom, but in centigrade, which is more commonly used in Canada because of the influence of French customs.[7]

"Are these thermometers accurate?" he asked.

"Yes indeed, sir," was the reply. "I'm sure you will be satisfied . . ."

"Not on the day when they register seventy or eighty degrees below zero," said Skim gravely.

"But the main thing," he was told, "is that they show the temperature as it really is."

"As you say, sir. And does the mercury sometimes fall to sixty degrees below zero?"

"Very often, sir, and even lower."

"Come now," said Skim, "it's hard to believe that the temperature can fall so low, even in the Klondike."

"And why not?" There was a note of pride in the proprietor's voice. "Would you care to have an instrument that registers that far down on the scale?"

"No thanks, no thanks," replied Skim. "I'll settle for this one, which only goes down to sixty below."

And after all, he might have said to himself, what is the use of buying this? When your eyes are chapped under eyelids reddened by the bitter north wind, when your breath falls around you in snowflakes, when your half-frozen blood nearly clogs your veins, when you can't touch a metal object without losing the skin off your fingers, when you are freezing in front of a blazing fireplace as if the fire itself had lost all its heat, it makes no difference whether the temperature is sixty degrees below zero or eighty, and you don't need a thermometer to tell you.

The days went by, however, and Ben Raddle, having completed his preparations, could not conceal his impatience as he waited for the *Football* to arrive. Had the ship been delayed at sea? They knew it had left Skagway on April 10. It should have been within sight of Vancouver by now, since it was only a six-day trip.

It was true that the stopover would be very short, just long enough to take on the several hundred passengers who had booked their passage in advance. There would be no cargo to load or unload, since this ship carried immigrants and their luggage, but no merchandise. It would only have to clean out its boilers, fill its bunkers with coal, and take on a supply of fresh water. That would take twenty-four hours, or thirty-six at the most, and there was no cause for concern about the slowness of the trip along the coast, in the lee of islands for most of the way.

Dawson City's food supply was replenished by cargo ships that brought flour, liquids, preserved meat, and dried vegetables to Skagway, but no passengers. After the *Football*, other passenger ships were expected, which would take on thousands of Klondike-bound immigrants. Since Vancouver's hotels and inns could not accommodate them all, whole families were sleeping in the open. Their present hardships were a foretaste of what was in store for them in the future, without shelter in such harsh weather.

For most of these poor people, life would be no more comfortable on board the ships taking them to Skagway or during the interminable, frightful journey from Skagway to Dawson City. The ship's bow and stern cabins could barely hold the passengers who were willing to pay the price. Some families were crowded into the steerage for the voyage of six or seven days, during which they would have to attend to their own needs. There were even some who allowed themselves to be shut up in the hold like animals, and even that was better than being on the open deck exposed to the severe weather conditions, the icy squalls and snow-storms so frequent in the region near the Arctic Circle.

It was not only immigrants from the distant lands of the Old and New Worlds who came swarming into Vancouver at that time. There were also hundreds of miners who had no intention of spending the cold winter season in the iceboxes of Dawson City, when it was impossible to work their claims. All activity comes to a halt when the ground is covered with ten or twelve feet of snow. In temperatures of forty or fifty degrees below zero it becomes as hard as granite and breaks the pickaxes.

And so, those prospectors who could afford it, who had enjoyed a certain measure of good fortune, preferred to return to the larger towns and cities of British Columbia. They had gold to spend, and they spent it with a carefree abandon that staggers the imagination. They were convinced that fortune would not forsake them . . . that the next season would be a good one . . . the new strikes discovered along the tributaries of the Yukon and the Klondike would fill their hands with piles of nuggets. The end of April or the beginning of May it would be time to go back to the placers and begin again. These men had the best hotel rooms for the six or seven months of winter, just as they would have the best cabins on the voyage to Skagway, where they would continue their northward journey.

Summy Skim soon realized that this class of miners included the most violent, the most uncouth, and the most quarrelsome types, the ones who indulged in every excess in the gambling houses and casinos, where, money in hand, they talked as if they owned the place.

And here is how Summy Skim came to make the acquaintance of one of these disreputable prospectors. Unfortunately, the contact that began on that occasion would not end there, as we shall see.

On the morning of April 15, Skim and Raddle were walking along the dock when they heard the sound of a steam whistle.

"Is that the *Football* at last?" asked the more impatient of the two cousins.

"I don't think so," said the other. "That sound is coming from the south, but the *Football* will be coming from the north."

It was indeed a steamship on its way to the port of Vancouver. Since it was coming up Juan de Fuca Strait, it could not be coming from Skagway.

However, Raddle and Skim walked out to the end of the dock and joined the crowds that the arrival of a ship always attracts. Several hundred passengers were about to disembark and wait to book passage on one of the northbound steamships.

The ship was the *Smyth*, a vessel of 2500 tons, which had stopped at every port on the North American coast from the Mexican port of Acapulco onward. After leaving its passengers in Vancouver it would return to its home port since it was assigned specifically to the coastal service. Its passengers would swell the throng of people who had to decide in Vancouver whether to make their way to the Klondike via Skagway or via St. Michael. The *Football* could certainly not carry everyone, and most of the immigrants heading for Dawson City would be obliged to wait for other vessels to arrive.

Of course, Skim and Raddle would have preferred that the steam whistle, whose screeches grew louder as the ship entered the harbor, had been announcing the arrival of the *Football*, but even though it was the *Smyth*, they watched out of curiosity as the passengers disembarked.

When the steamer reached the landing stage, one of the passengers was seen struggling furiously to be among the first to reach the gangplank. No doubt he was in a hurry to book his passage on the *Football*. He was a large man, rough and energetic, with a bushy black beard, the bronzed complexion of a southerner, a forbidding look in his eyes, an unpleasant face, and a disagreeable manner. There was another passenger with him who seemed to be of the same nationality and who appeared to be equally impatient and unsociable.

There must have been others in just as much of a hurry to disembark as this arrogant and noisy passenger. But it would have been difficult to get ahead of him as he elbowed his way to the landing stage, paying no

45

heed to the orders of the officers and the captain, pushing his neighbors aside and insulting them in a harsh voice that added to the fierceness of the insults spoken in a mixture of English and Spanish.

"Well," exclaimed Skim, "that's what you might call a pleasant traveling companion. If he's going to book passage on the *Football* . . ."

"The voyage will only last a few days," replied Raddle, "and we can manage to keep our distance from him during that time."

At that very moment, an onlooker standing near the two cousins shouted out, "Right! There's that damned Hunter. Well, there'll be a ruckus in the bars tonight if he doesn't get out of Vancouver today."

Skim gathered that Hunter was well known, and not favorably. He must have been one of those adventurers who had spent the summer in the Klondike and then gone home to wait for a suitable time to start work again.

One of those violent types of mixed American and Spanish blood, Hunter was indeed coming back from his native state of Texas. This confused world of gold seekers was exactly the kind of milieu that suited his unscrupulous instincts, his disgusting habits, his brutal passions, and his taste for an unorthodox existence where everything is left to chance. If he arrived in Vancouver on that day with his friend, it was precisely to wait for the *Football*. But when he learned that the boat would not arrive for thirty-six or forty-eight hours, he went to the Vancouver Hotel where Skim and Raddle had been staying for the past six days.[8]

They certainly had no reason to rejoice on finding themselves in the company of such a man, and they would be careful to avoid him both in the hotel and during the voyage from Vancouver to Skagway.

When Skim inquired who this Hunter was, he was told, "Oh, everyone in Vancouver knows him, and in Dawson City, too."

"Does he own a claim?"

"Yes, and he works it himself."

"And where is his claim located?"

"On the Fortymile River."

"What number is it?"

46

"127."

"Right!" said Skim. "And ours is 129. That horrible Texan is our neighbor!"

The next day, the *Football* signaled its arrival as it left Queen Charlotte Strait,[9] and after a twenty-four-hour layover, it put to sea again on the morning of April 17.

5

On Board the *Football*

THE *FOOTBALL* WAS A STEAMBOAT of 1200 tons, and if the number of passengers did not exceed the tonnage, it was because the marine inspector had not authorized it to carry any more than that. The waterline, shown by a crossed zero painted on the hull, was already below its normal level. In twenty-four hours the cranes on the dock had put aboard a load of heavy equipment, plus about a hundred head of cattle, horses, and mules; some fifty reindeer; and several hundred dogs for pulling sleds across the icy wastes.[1]

These dogs, it should be noted, were Saint Bernards and huskies. They were usually bought at markets in Canadian cities where the price was low even after adding the cost of transportation, which was about ten dollars by rail from Montreal to Vancouver and the same again from Vancouver to Skagway.

The *Football's* passengers were of every nationality: English, Canadian, French, Norwegian, Swedish, German, Australian, North and South American, some alone and some with their families. Those in the cabins could be separated into first and second class, but there was obviously no way to prevent overcrowding on deck. The number of spaces in each cabin had already been increased from two to four. The steerage looked like a long dormitory, with a row of trestles set up on one side and hammocks slung between them. On deck, it was very difficult to move about. Masses of poor people were crowded along the deckhouses and railings, for a place in a cabin cost thirty-five dollars. True, the passengers could still make do as long as they could find shelter from the cold gusts, and since they were in the lee of the islands, there was no risk of heavy seas between Vancouver and Skagway.

Ben Raddle had managed to reserve two places in one of the stern cabins. The third place was occupied by a Norwegian named Boyen, who owned a claim on Bonanza Creek, a tributary of the Klondike. He was a calm and mild-mannered man, daring and cautious at the same time, of the Scandinavian race that has produced the Audrecs and the Nansens. He was from Christiania and was returning to Dawson City after spending the winter in his hometown.[2] He was in short not a troublesome traveling companion, only rather uncommunicative, and Summy Skim could only exchange a few pleasantries with him.

Fortunately for the cousins, they did not have to share a cabin with the Texan. Hunter and his friend had reserved a cabin for four, even though there were only two of them. Several passengers who had not been able to find any available space on board vainly pleaded with the two uncouth individuals to let them have the two vacant places. Their efforts were wasted, and their pleas were met with a blunt refusal.

Obviously, to Hunter and his friend (whose name was Malone), money was not a problem. They realized a substantial income from working their claim, but they were big spenders, extravagant gamblers and debauchees, denizens of the bars that tended to increase in number in the shady quarters of Dawson City. Since there was a card room on board the *Football*, they would very likely spend long hours there. Besides, most of the passengers had no desire to associate with them, and they made no attempt to associate with anyone.

By six o'clock the next morning the *Football* had left the port of Vancouver and was steering a course up the channel toward the northern tip of the island. From there it would have only a short distance to travel along the North American coast, sheltered most of the way by the Queen Charlotte Islands and Prince of Wales Island.

The stern passengers would hardly ever leave the poop deck, which was reserved for them. The main deck was cluttered with sheds containing the animals—oxen, horses, mules, and reindeer—which could not be allowed to run loose. That was not the case with the pack of dogs, which ran around howling among groups of second-class passengers, young men already scarred by hardship and exhausted women surrounded by sickly children. Their object in coming was not to pan for gold on their own but to find work with the syndicates and compete for wages.

"At last," said Skim, "this is what you wanted, Ben, and this time we're on the way to Eldorado. After all, since we had to make this journey, what I've seen so far and what I'll see later on is certainly very curious. I'll have an opportunity to study this world of gold seekers. They don't seem to be the most commendable of types."

"It could hardly be otherwise, my dear Summy," replied Raddle. "We have to take things as they are."

"Always provided, Ben, that we don't become part of it, which we aren't and never will be! You're a gentleman, and so am I. We've inherited a claim, which, I'd like to think, is full of nuggets, but we aren't going to keep even the tiniest piece of it."

"All right," said Raddle, with an imperceptible of shrug of the shoulders that Skim did not find reassuring.

"We're going to the Klondike to sell Uncle Josias's claim," he went on, "although it would have been easy to close the sale without making the trip. Good Lord! When I think that I might have acquired the instincts, the passions, and the desires of that mob of scoundrels!"

"Be careful, Summy, or you'll have me quoting Virgil to you: *auri sacra fames.*"[3]

"You're right, Ben. Yes, I have a deathly horror of that atrocious thirst for gold, that mad desire for wealth that makes people endure so many hardships. That isn't work, it's just gambling! It's a race for the jackpot, for the big nugget. When I think that I could have been in Montreal, getting ready to spend an idyllic summer at Green Valley instead of sailing off to some incredible region on board this steamship . . ."

"You promised me you wouldn't complain, Summy."

"That's all, Ben, that's the last time. Now I'm only thinking about . . ."

"About getting to Dawson City?" asked Raddle, with a touch of irony in his voice.

"About coming back, Ben, about coming back," was the frank reply.

As long as the *Football* was sailing in Queen Charlotte Strait without reaching its top speed, the passengers suffered no discomfort. The rolling was barely perceptible. But when it had passed the northern tip of Vancouver Island, it was exposed to the long swell from the open sea.

The distance from there to the Queen Charlotte Islands, some 140 miles, was the longest stretch the ship would have to travel under those conditions.[4] It would meet the open sea again as it crossed Dixon Entrance—between the Queen Charlottes and Prince of Wales Island— but only for about fifty miles. From there on, it would be sheltered all the way to Skagway.

It was a cold, cloudy day, with a bitter wind coming out of the west. A strong swell was pounding the British Columbia coast. A driving rain was coming down, mixed with snow. The suffering of the immigrants who could not find shelter either on the poop deck or in the steerage can well be imagined. Most of them were plagued with seasickness, for by now the ship was rolling and pitching, and it was impossible to go from the bow to the stern without holding on to the rigging. The animals, too, were in great distress, and above the whistling of the wind could be heard lowing, whinnying, and braying in a terrifying concert that is hard to imagine. It was impossible to enclose or leash the dogs, which were running and rolling along the deckhouses. Some of them had become fierce and were rushing at the passengers, leaping at their throats and trying to bite them. The boatswain was forced to shoot some of them with his revolver. This created a serious disturbance, which the captain and his officers had difficulty putting down.

Needless to say, Summy Skim, as a determined observer, braved the inclement weather and did not go to his cabin until bedtime.

Neither of the cousins suffered from seasickness and neither did their traveling companion, the stolid Norwegian Boyen. Nothing that happened on board ship seemed to have any effect on him.

The same was true of the Texans, Hunter and his friend Malone. From the very first day, they managed to round up a group of gamblers and ensconced themselves around the card table. Their angry shouts and taunts, in all their savage ferocity, could be heard day and night.

Among the passengers who arrived on the last train from Montreal to Vancouver were two who had attracted Summy Skim's attention.

They were nuns, and they had arrived in Vancouver the day before the ship was to sail. Passage aboard the *Football* had been reserved for them in advance. They were native French Canadians, aged twenty-eight and thirty-two, and belonged to the Congregation of Sisters of Mercy. The order was sending them to the hospital at Dawson City, where the sister superior had asked for additional staff.

Skim was overcome with emotion at the sight of those two nuns who had been given an order by their convent in Montreal and had set out at once, without protest and without hesitation. What a dangerous journey they were undertaking! What a dreadful world of fortune hunters, wretches of every description and every background, they would be exposed to! What suffering they would have to endure during their long journey, and what privations were in store for them in the Klondike, from which they might never return! But they were upheld by the spirit of charity and intoxicated by the spirit of devotion. Their mission was to aid the unfortunate, and they would not fail in their duty.

Aboard the steamship that was carrying them to their distant destination, they were already busily offering relief to the poor folk without distinction, giving aid to the women and children, even depriving themselves in order to provide for others' comfort.

It was not until the fourth day that the *Football* came under the lee of the Queen Charlotte Islands.[5] Sailing conditions were now less difficult since the swell was not coming in from the open sea. On the land side there was a succession of fjords similar to those found in Norway, which must have brought many memories of his homeland to Skim and Raddle's cabin mate. Around these fjords rose tall cliffs, tree covered for the most part, among which appeared little fishing villages or hamlets, but most often there was a small, isolated dwelling, home to aboriginal people who lived by hunting and fishing. As the *Football* went by, they came out to sell their products, which found ready buyers.

Away off beyond the cliffs, mountains reared their snow-capped peaks through the mist, while on the Queen Charlotte Islands nothing could be seen but long plains and thick forests covered with hoarfrost. Here and there the occasional small cluster of huts could be seen at the edge of a narrow inlet, where fishing boats waited for a favorable wind.

After passing the northern tip of the Queen Charlotte Islands, the *Football* was again exposed to the open sea as it crossed Dixon Entrance, bounded on the north by Prince of Wales Island. The crossing took twenty-four hours, but since the wind had shifted around to the northeast and was now coming off the mainland, the pitching and rolling were less violent. Once it reached Prince of Wales Island, the ship would always be protected by a chain of islands and by the Sitka peninsula until it entered port at Skagway. They were now sailing on a river, as it were, rather than on the sea.

The name "Prince of Wales" applies to a whole complicated archipelago whose most northerly points are lost in a jumble of tiny islands. The capital of the main island is Shakan on the west coast, where ships can take refuge from the storms of the open sea.

Farther on lies Baranof Island, where the Russians built the fort of New Arkhangel, and whose principal town, Sitka, is also the capital of the whole territory of Alaska. When Alaska was sold by the Muscovite Empire to the United States, Sitka was not given back to Canada or to British Columbia, but remained in American hands.

The first Canadian port that the *Football* passed was Port Simpson, on the coast of British Columbia at the end of Dixon Entrance, but it did not stop there nor at the port of Jackson on the southernmost island of the Prince of Wales group.

While the forty-ninth parallel forms the boundary between Canada and the United States a little south of Vancouver, the longitude separating Alaska from Canada will have to be clearly drawn across the gold-bearing territories of the north. Who can tell whether, in some more or less distant future, there may not be grounds for dispute between the flag of Great Britain and the fifty-one-star flag of the United States of America?[6]

On the morning of April 24 the *Football* docked at the port of Wrangell, at the mouth of the Stikine River. At that time, the town consisted of only about forty houses, a few active sawmills, a hotel, a casino, and some gambling houses that kept very busy during the season.

At Wrangell they parted company with the miners who wanted to go to the Klondike via Telegraph Creek rather than by crossing the lakes on the other side of Skagway. They would have some 170 miles to cover under the most difficult conditions, although the cost would be lower. About fifty immigrants left the ship, determined to face danger and exhaustion crossing the endless plains of northern British Columbia

After they left Wrangell the channels became narrower and more winding. The vessel slipped through a veritable labyrinth of little islands. A Dutchman might have thought he was in the middle of the maze of Zeeland, but he would soon have returned to harsh reality on feeling the bitter arctic wind whistling around him, seeing the whole archipelago buried under a thick layer of snow, and hearing the roar of avalanches thundering down into the fjords from the height of the coastal cliffs. A Russian would have found the situation quite normal because he would have been at the same latitude as St. Petersburg.

It was just off Mary's Island, near Fort Simpson, that the *Football* left behind the last American customs office. At Wrangell, the ship was once again in Canadian waters,[7] and although a number of passengers had disembarked to continue their journey by land, they had been warned that the route was not yet negotiable by sled.

The steamboat, meanwhile, pressed on toward Skagway through increasingly narrow channels, following the coast of the rugged mainland. After passing the mouth of the Taku River, it stopped for several hours at Juneau, which was still only a village on the way to becoming a town.

To the name of Joe Juneau, who founded it about 1882, must be added that of Richard Harris. Two years earlier, they had discovered the gold deposits of Silver Bow Basin, which yielded twelve million dollars in nuggets a few months later.

That period saw the first influx of miners attracted by reports of this discovery and of the work going on in the gold fields to the north of Telegraph Creek, before the Klondike gold rush began. Since that day, the Treadwille Mine, with 240 pestles at work, has crushed up to 1500 tons of quartz every twenty-four hours, yielding over five hundred thousand dollars' worth of gold. A hundred years of mining would still not exhaust its supply.

When Ben Raddle told him about the good luck miners were having in that region, Summy Skim replied, "It's too bad our uncle's claim wasn't on the Taku River instead of on the Fortymile."

"Why is that?"

"Because then we wouldn't have to go all the way to Skagway."

If it had only been a matter of getting to Skagway, of course, there would have been nothing to complain about. The *Football* would be there the next day. But their real difficulties and extreme hardships would begin then, when they would have to go through the Chilkoot Pass and make their way across the lakes to the left bank of the Yukon River.

And yet there they all were, those passengers, eager to be off the *Football* and to venture out into the region drained by the great Alaskan waterway. If they were thinking only about the future, it was not of its exertions, trials, dangers, and disappointments, but of the mirage that it held out before them.

Leaving Juneau behind, the steamer made its way up the Lynn Canal to Skagway, which is the end of the line for ships of a certain tonnage, although flat-bottomed boats can continue for another five miles to the village of Dyea. Off to the northwest was the shining Muir Glacier, 240 feet thick, whose thundering avalanches kept falling into the Pacific. A few boats manned by natives provided an escort for the *Football*, which took some of them in tow.

During the last night on board, the card room was the scene of a tremendous game, during which some of the passengers who had been regular patrons during the voyage would lose everything, down to their last dollar. Not surprisingly, the two Texans, Hunter and Malone, were among the most avid of the players and especially the most violent. The others, whatever their nationality, were no better. They belonged to the same class of scoundrels as are usually to be found in the bars of Vancouver, Wrangell, Skagway, and Dawson City.

Up until now, it seemed, fortune had smiled on the two Texans. Since they had embarked on the *Football* in the port of Acapulco, their good luck at cards had brought them several thousands of piasters, or dollars. They were hoping, no doubt, that luck would stay with them during their last evening on board.

Such was not the case, however, and the noise emanating from the card room made it obvious that deplorable scenes were being enacted there. Shouts and coarse insults rang out. It seemed as if the captain of the *Football* might be forced to intervene to restore order, but he, being a cautious man who knew exactly where he stood with everyone, would do that only as a last resort. On their arrival in Skagway he could notify the police, who would then arrest the troublemakers if necessary.

It was nine o'clock when Skim and Raddle decided to return to their cabin. On their way down they passed the card room, just astern of the deckhouse.

Suddenly, the door opened with a crash, and about a dozen passengers spilled out onto the deck.

Among them was Hunter, in a towering rage, wrestling with one of the gamblers and spewing out a torrent of insults. A discussion about a hand of cards had led to this dreadful scene, which threatened to set the whole band of maniacs at each other's throats.

It appeared, moreover, that Hunter did not have the majority on his side. People were hurling threats at him, to which he replied with the most terrible stream of abuse. It seemed as if it might end with revolver shots mingling with the furious clamor.

Just at that moment, Hunter broke loose from the group surrounding him and sprang forward.

The two nuns, who were returning to the deckhouse, happened to be in his way, and the elder of the two was knocked down onto the deck.

Skim was outraged. He rushed at Hunter while Raddle helped the nun to her feet.

"You villain!" shouted Skim. "You ought to be . . ."

Hunter turned around and was putting his hand to his belt to draw his knife from its sheath when he thought better of it and said, "Ah, it's you, the Canadian. We'll meet again out there, and you'll get what's coming to you then."

As he was returning to his cabin with his friend Malone, the nun came up to Skim.

"Thank you, sir," she said. "But that man didn't know what he was doing. You must forgive him—as I forgive him."

6

Skagway

SKAGWAY, LIKE EVERY SETTLEMENT hidden away in a region where there were no roads or means of transportation, began as a campground where the first prospectors stopped to rest. Soon this jumble of huts gave way to a cluster of more carefully built cabins, to be replaced in turn by small houses erected on lots that became more and more expensive. And who knows? Perhaps some day when there is no gold left, these towns created to meet the needs of the time will be abandoned and the region will be deserted once more.

There is really no comparison between these territories and those of Australia, California, and the Transvaal, where villages became towns and sometimes large cities even after the panning for gold came to an end. The surrounding region was habitable, the soil was fertile, commerce and industry could take on real importance, and the land, after giving up its metallic treasure, could still reward human labor.

But here, in this part of the Dominion on the Alaskan boundary and close to the Arctic Circle, in this freezing climate with its eight-month winter, in this region without resources and already half-exhausted by the fur traders, what prospects are there and what will there be to do once the last nuggets have been taken out?

In Skagway, Dyea, and Dawson City, which were established quickly, there is now brisk business activity with travelers coming and going. But it is quite possible that they may gradually decline when the Klondike mines are empty, even though there are now financial institutions to establish better communications between them, and plans are afoot to build a railway between Wrangell and Dawson City.

At the time, Skagway was bursting at the seams with immigrants, some of whom had come by Ocean Pacific steamships, others by Canadian railways and American railroads, but all heading for the Klondike.[1]

Some of the travelers went as far as Dyea, a village at the head of the Lynn Canal. But since the canal was too shallow for ships to go beyond Skagway, they and their equipment were taken on flat-bottomed boats built to navigate the five miles between the two villages, thus shortening the difficult land route.

It was at Skagway that the really hard part of the journey began, after the relatively easy voyage by coastal steamer.[2]

First of all, there was the insufferable harassment by American customs.

Beyond Skagway, which is on Canadian soil, there is a twenty-mile strip of American territory.[3] The Americans, in order to prevent travelers from trading while they cross this strip, require them to be escorted to the border. The high cost of this escort is rigorously charged and collected.

Skagway already had several hotels, and the two cousins had chosen one. They booked a room for two, at a price considerably higher than they had paid in Vancouver, and would make every effort to leave as soon as possible.

Needless to say, the hotel was swarming with travelers waiting to go on to the Klondike. People of every nationality rubbed shoulders in the dining room. The food was acceptable at best, but why should all these immigrants complain, when they would be exposed to so many hardships for several months?

During their stay in Skagway, Skim and Raddle would not have occasion to encounter the two Texans, whom they had carefully avoided on the *Football*. Hunter and Malone had left for the Klondike as soon as they arrived. They were going back to where they had come from six months earlier, and their transportation had been arranged in advance. All they had to do was set out with their guides with no equipment to burden them down since it was already at their claim on the Fortymile River.

"My goodness," said Skim, "we're lucky not to have those louts for traveling companions. I feel sorry for the people who will be going along with them . . . unless, of course, they're all alike, which is very probable in this lovely world of gold seekers."

"True enough," replied Raddle, "but those louts are lucky not to have to wait around in Skagway, whereas we'll be here for several days."

"Oh, we'll get there, Ben, we'll get there, and when we do, we can look forward to finding those two villains on Claim 127, right next door to 129. A pleasant prospect. So we'll waste no time selling our claim for the best price we can get and then head home again."

If Summy Skim had no further need to worry about the two Texans, such was not the case with the two nuns who had got off the *Football*. The cousins were moved to pity as they thought of the danger and fatigue to which those saintly women would be exposed. And what support, what assistance, would they ever be able to find, if they needed it, among that mob of immigrants whose envy, greed, and lust for gold drowned out any sentiment of justice or honor? Yet they had left without hesitation and started out on the long road to the Klondike, a road already strewn with hundreds of dead bodies. They did not shrink back in the face of dangers that the most resolute of men might be pardoned for fearing.

The next day, Skim and Raddle happened to meet the Sisters of Mercy as they were making arrangements to join a caravan that would be ready to leave in a few days. The caravan was made up mostly of wretched, uneducated, and uncouth people, hardly suitable company for the nuns during a long journey of more than four hundred miles through the lake region from Skagway to Dawson City.

The cousins went up to them as soon as they saw them, hoping to be of some service. The nuns had spent the night in a small church house in Skagway.

Summy Skim asked very respectfully whether they planned to rest a bit after their tiring sea voyage.

"We can't," replied Sister Martha, the elder of the two.

"Are you going to the Klondike?" asked Skim.

"Yes, sir" replied Sister Martha. "There are many sick people in Dawson City. The sister superior at the hospital is expecting us, and unfortunately we still have a long way to go."

"Where are you from?" asked Raddle.

"From Quebec," replied Sister Madeleine, the younger one.

"You'll be going back there, I suppose, when your services are no longer required."

"That we don't know, sir," replied Sister Martha. "We left because our superior asked us to, and we'll go back whenever God wills."

There was so much resignation in her voice, or rather so much faith in divine goodness, that the cousins were deeply moved. Then they spoke about far-off Dawson City, about the long distances to be covered every day across the lake region and the Yukon Territory, about the difficulties of transportation and the arduous travel by sled across the hard snow of the plains and the frozen surface of the lakes.

When the nuns reached their destination, all their obstacles and troubles would be over. If there were deadly epidemics there, if the sisters had to work day and night treating dangerous illnesses, that was their job, and they would enjoy the satisfaction of having done their duty. Their lives belonged to the unfortunate, the afflicted, to all those who were suffering. They had to find a way of getting to those people in the Dawson City hospital, for which the sister superior was requesting more nuns from her order. And that was why Sister Martha and Sister Madeleine were trying to find transportation within the limits of their modest means.

"Are you Canadians, sisters?" asked Skim.

"Yes, French Canadians," replied Sister Madeleine, "but we have no family left, or rather we only have the extended family of the unfortunate."

"We're familiar with the Sisters of Mercy," said Raddle. "We know about the work they've done and are still doing all over the world."

"So," added Skim, "as fellow Canadians, we're at your disposal, and we'd be happy to be of service to you."

"Thank you, gentlemen," replied Sister Madeleine, "but I hope we'll be able to join this caravan, which is getting ready to leave for the Klondike."

"Are you going to Dawson City, gentlemen?" asked Sister Martha.

"As a matter of fact, we are," said Skim. "Why would anyone come to Skagway if they weren't going on to Dawson City?"

"Do you intend to spend the whole season there?" asked Sister Madeleine.

"Oh, no!" exclaimed Skim. "Just long enough to settle our business there, which may take a few days. But since we're on our way to the Klondike, sisters, if you can't make arrangements with that caravan, we're at your service."

"Thank you, gentlemen," replied Sister Martha. "Whatever happens, we'll meet again in Dawson City. Our superior will be happy to meet some fellow Canadians."

As soon as he got to Skagway, Ben Raddle had set about arranging transportation to the capital of the Klondike. Acting on the advice he had been given in Montreal, he had inquired about a certain Bill Steel,[4] who had been recommended to him and with whom he planned to get in touch.

Bill Steel happened to be in Skagway at that very time. He was a Canadian and had been a runner on the prairies. For a number of years he had been highly regarded by his superior officers for his service as a scout for the Canadian forces and had taken part in their long battles with the Indians. He was considered a man of great courage, nerve, and energy.

The scout was now in the business of transporting immigrants being drawn (or drawn back) to the Klondike by the return of warm weather. Not only was he a guide, but he also had employees working for him and owned all the essential equipment for such a difficult trip. He had men to row the boats across the lakes and dogs to pull the sleds over the ice-covered plains that stretched out beyond the Chilkoot Pass. He also provided food for the caravans he organized.

It was precisely because he intended to make use of Bill Steel's services that Ben Raddle had left Montreal without burdening himself down with heavy luggage. He knew the scout would provide everything they would need to get to the Klondike, and he had no doubt they would settle on a reasonable price for the return journey.

When Raddle went to Steel's house the day after arriving in Skagway, he was informed that the scout was not home.[5] He had gone to lead a caravan through the White Pass to the tip of Bennett Lake, but as it was now some ten days since he had left, he was expected back soon. If he had not been delayed on the way or if his services had not been required by other travelers as he left the pass, he could be in Skagway the very next day.

That is exactly how it turned out, and on the following day Raddle went back to Steel's house to make contact with him.

The scout was a wiry man of about fifty, of average height, with short, coarse hair, a beard that was turning grey at the sides and a steady, piercing look in his eyes. Complete honesty was written all over his friendly face. While serving with the Canadian army as a scout, he had acquired those rare qualities of wariness, vigilance, and prudence. He was thoughtful, methodical, and resourceful and would not have been easily tricked. He was also a philosopher in his own way and looked on the bright side of life—for it always has a bright side. He enjoyed his work, and it had never been his ambition to follow the example of the men he led into the gold country. He knew only too well that most of them succumbed to hardship or came back from their strenuous campaigns more wretched than when they left.

Ben Raddle explained to the scout his plan to leave for Dawson City on the earliest possible date. He had contacted Steel, he said, because he had been told in Montreal that he could not find a better guide in Skagway.

"Well sir," was the reply, "you're asking me to take you to Dawson City. Guiding travelers is what I do for a living, and I've got all the staff and equipment we need for the trip."

"I know that, Scout," said Raddle, "and I also know that you're dependable."

"You're only planning to stay in Dawson City for a few weeks?" asked Bill Steel.

"Very likely."

"You won't be working a claim there, then?"

"No. The claim my cousin and I own is one we inherited. We've had an offer to buy it, but we wanted to get some idea of its value before we sell."

"That's wise, Mr. Raddle, because in dealings of this sort there's no end to the tricks that are used to cheat people. You have to be careful."

"That's why we decided to make the trip to the Klondike."

"And when you've sold your claim, you'll go back to Montreal?"

"That's our plan, and after you've taken us out there, we'll ask you to bring us back."

"We can come to an agreement on that," replied Steel, "and since I don't make a practice of overcharging, here are my terms, Mr. Raddle."

It would be a journey of thirty to thirty-five days, for which the scout would provide horses or mules, dog teams, sleds, boats, and tents. Skim and Raddle were not burdened down with all the equipment that prospectors have to acquire in order to work their claims. In addition, Bill Steel would undertake to provide supplies for his caravan. They could rely on him for that, for he knew better than anyone the needs and essential requirements of such a long journey through territory barren of resources, especially in the winter.

The price of the journey from Skagway to Dawson City was fixed at $260, everything included, and the same amount for the trip back.

Raddle knew who he was dealing with, and it would have been inappropriate to bargain about terms with as conscientious and honest a man as the scout.

Besides, the price of transportation at that time, just to go through the passes as far as the lake region, was fairly high because of the difficulties of the two routes: four or five cents per pound of luggage for one, six or seven cents for the other. In view of that, Bill Steel's terms were quite acceptable.

"It's a deal," said Raddle, "and don't forget, we want to leave as soon as possible."

"Forty-eight hours is all I need," replied the scout.

"Do we have to go to Dyea by boat?" asked Raddle.

"There's no need to, because you're not carrying a lot of equipment with you. It seems to me it would be better to stay in Skagway until it's time to leave and avoid that extra trip of five or six miles."

Now they had to decide which route the caravan would take through the mountainous area before the lake region, where the greatest difficulties are encountered.

To Raddle's question, Steel replied, "There are two routes, or rather two tracks, the White Pass and the Chilkoot Pass. Once a caravan has gone through one of those passes it only has to go down to the tip of Bennett Lake or Lake Lindemann."

"And which one do you plan to take, Scout?"

"The Chilkoot Pass. It will bring me directly to the tip of Lake Lindemann after an overnight stop at Sheep Camp to replenish our supplies. My equipment will be waiting for me at Lake Lindemann. That way I don't have to bring it back over the mountains to Skagway."

"As I said before," said Raddle, "we're relying on your experience. Whatever you do will be done well. As far as we're concerned, we're ready to leave whenever you give the word."

"In two days, as I told you," replied Steel. "I need that much time to make my final preparations, Mr. Raddle. If we leave early in the morning, it'll be possible to cover the ten miles between Skagway and the top of the Chilkoot Pass."

"How high is that?"

"About three thousand feet, but the pass is narrow and winding. What makes traveling more difficult is the fact that it's crowded right now with a swarm of miners, vehicles, and teams, to say nothing of the snow that sometimes blocks the way."

"But you still prefer it to the other pass," remarked Raddle.

"Yes, because by the north face of the Chilkoot I can go straight down to Lake Lindemann."

Once everything was settled with Bill Steel, Raddle only had to tell Summy Skim to be ready to leave Skagway in forty-eight hours. He gave him the message that same day. It was a stroke of good luck, he said, to have dealt with the scout, and he had the utmost confidence in him. Steel was taking care of everything necessary for an extremely arduous journey under difficult conditions. And the price they had agreed on was not exorbitant considering that it would take at least five weeks to cover the distance from Skagway to Dawson City.

Summy Skim could only approve of what his cousin had done.

"I see," he said, "that things will go along as well as possible, my dear Ben. But I've had an idea, which I hope you'll agree is a good one and won't create a burden for us."

"What's your idea, Summy?"

"It's about those two nuns who got off the boat in Skagway at the same time as we did. I saw them again, and I really felt sorry for them. They couldn't arrange anything with that caravan, which wasn't suitable for them anyway, and they don't know how they're going to get to the Klondike. Well, why don't we invite them to come along with us, with the scout to guide us?"

"That's a very good idea," said Raddle, without a moment's hesitation.

"Of course there'll be a few additional costs for transportation and food."

"We'll take care of that, Summy. That goes without saying. But have you got any reason to think the sisters will agree to . . ."

"Come on, Ben. Canadian women and Canadian men traveling together—isn't that an ideal arrangement?"

"All right. Go and see Sister Martha and Sister Madeleine, Summy, and tell them to be ready."

"They're good souls, Ben. They'll be ready to leave in an hour."

It was certainly a lucky turn of events for the two nuns to be able to travel under the protection of their fellow Canadians. They would not be exposed to those overcrowded caravans made up of disreputable people from all corners of the world. They would be given every consideration and every assistance, if need be, on that long journey.

That same day, then, Skim and Raddle went to see the two sisters, who were trying in vain to arrange transportation to the Klondike.

Sisters Martha and Madeleine were deeply moved and accepted the offer that was made to them. As they were trying to express their gratitude, Summy Skim interrupted, "It's not you who should thank us, sisters, but those poor sick people who are expecting you out there and who are in such dire need of your care."

7

The Chilkoot Pass

BILL STEEL HAD MADE THE RIGHT decision in choosing the Chilkoot Pass over the White Pass. The latter, it is true, can be reached via Skagway, whereas the other begins farther on, at Dyea, which immigrants and their heavy equipment can easily reach in flat-bottomed boats suitable for traveling to the end of the Lynn Canal.

Here is what travelers must do once they reach the highest point of a pass. If they have taken the White Pass, they still have about twenty miles of very heavy going in order to get to Bennett Lake. If they have taken the Chilkoot Pass, a mere ten miles will bring them to Lake Lindemann,[1] which is only about fourteen miles long. From its northern tip, it is only two miles along the Caribou River to the southern tip of Bennett Lake.

Of course, the Chilkoot Pass is harder to climb than the White Pass since there is an almost vertical slope of a thousand feet to be scaled. But this is a problem only for the immigrants who have heavy baggage to drag along with them, and as we have seen, this was not case with the two Canadians and their guide, the scout. Beyond the Chilkoot they would find a fairly well-maintained road leading to Lake Lindemann. If they had brought mining equipment with them, Bill Steel would probably have advised them to go by the White Pass. Through the Chilkoot, however, the first part of the trip across the mountain barrier might be tiring but would not present any great difficulties.

As for the immigrants heading for the lake region, there were as many in the White Pass as in the Chilkoot. There were thousands of them risking their lives in an effort to get to the Klondike by the beginning of the working season.

On the morning of May 2, Steel gave the signal for departure. Sisters Martha and Madeleine, Summy Skim and Ben Raddle, the scout, and his six men left Skagway and started on the road to the Chilkoot Pass. Two mule-drawn sleds would suffice for the journey as far as the south end of Lake Lindemann, where Steel had set up his main camp. This would take at least three or four days even under the most favorable conditions.

The two nuns were sitting on the sled assigned to them, well wrapped in blankets and furs for protection against an extremely strong north wind. They had probably never imagined they would be traveling in such a fashion and continued to express their thanks, but Skim would not hear of it. He and Raddle were happy to be of use by helping them to accomplish their mission and had insisted on paying the additional costs that would be owing to Steel, who in turn, made no secret of his delight that the nuns had accepted their compatriots' offer. Was he not after all a Canadian by birth, just as they were?

Besides, the scout had explained to Sisters Martha and Madeleine how eagerly their arrival in Dawson City was anticipated. The sister superior was completely overwhelmed by all the demands made on her, and several nuns had become ill while caring for the patients hospitalized by a variety of epidemics.

Typhoid fever in particular was ravaging the capital of the Klondike at that time. The victims numbered in the hundreds. These unfortunate immigrants, who had left so many of their companions behind on the way from Skagway to Dawson City, had now fallen prey themselves to persistent epidemics.

"A charming country indeed!" said Summy Skim to himself. "But we'll only be passing through, and here are these two saintly women, going off unhesitatingly to face such great dangers . . . and they may never get back."

It had not seemed necessary to bring food for the trip through the Chilkoot Pass, with its steep slopes. Although there were no hotels, the scout knew of some rudimentary lodges, or inns, that offered food and lodging for the night. The price of a board that served as a bed was half a dollar, and a meal (consisting invariably of bacon and sourdough) cost a dollar. But Bill Steel's caravan would not be reduced to such straits while crossing the lake region.

The weather was cold, holding steady at ten degrees below zero centigrade, with a freezing north wind. At least, once they were on the track, the sleds would slide easily over the hard snow, but the steep climb would be hard on the dog teams. Large numbers of mules, dogs, horses, oxen and reindeer perished along the way, and the Chilkoot Pass, like the White Pass, was often cluttered with their dead bodies.

On leaving Skagway, the scout had headed along the east bank of the Lynn Canal toward Dyea. His sleds, which were less heavily loaded than many others climbing toward the mountain, could easily have outstripped them, but the congestion was already severe. The way was blocked by laggards, vehicles of every kind sliding back across the path or overturned, and animals that refused to move despite blows and shouts. There were violent efforts by some to get through and equally violent efforts by others to stop them. Equipment had to be unloaded and reloaded on the wagons bought in Skagway, and arguments and brawls led to insults and blows, occasionally punctuated by revolver shots. Sometimes, too, dog teams got tangled together, and it was a lengthy process for the drivers to unsnarl them, with the half-savage animals howling around them. And all the while, storms raged through the narrow defiles of the Chilkoot and White passes, with swirling eddies that could cover the ground to a depth of several feet in a matter of minutes.

Boats on the Lynn Canal usually take half an hour to travel between Skagway and Dyea. By land, despite the obstacles to progress, the distance can be covered in a few hours, and the scout's caravan arrived in Dyea before noon.

Dyea was still merely a collection of tents and a few houses and cabins scattered around the end of the canal. It was the unloading point for the equipment that a miner has to transport across the mountain.

There might have been, at a rough estimate, at least 1500 travelers squeezing into that embryonic town at the entrance to the Chilkoot Pass at that time.

Bill Steel had wisely decided not to stay longer than necessary in Dyea, wanting to take advantage of the cold, dry weather that favored travel by sled. The best plan would be to have something to eat and then to start out on the pass, so as to spend the next night in the encampment of Sheep Camp.

The scout and his party set out again at noon with the nuns back on their sled and Ben Raddle and Summy Skim on foot. It would have been hard for them not to admire the wild grandeur of the scenes that came into view at every turn in the pass: clumps of frost-covered pines and birches rising to the top of the slope and streams that the cold had not been able to freeze over bounding tumultuously down into bottomless abysses.

Sheep Camp was only about ten miles from Dyea, a journey of a few hours. To be sure, the pass consisted of a series of very steep grades. The dog teams, which were not going faster than a walk, made frequent stops, and it was not easy for the drivers to get them moving again.

As they went along, Raddle and Skim kept up a conversation with the scout. "I expect," he said, in answer to a question, "to reach Sheep Camp around five or six o'clock and spend the night there."

"Will we find an inn where the two ladies can get some rest?" asked Skim.

"Yes," replied Steel. "Sheep Camp is a stopping place for immigrants."

"But isn't it likely to be overcrowded?" asked Raddle.

"No doubt it will be," was the reply, "and anyway, the inns are not very inviting. Perhaps it would be better to pitch our tents and spend the night in them."

"Gentlemen," said Sister Martha, who had heard this conversation from her sled, "we don't want to create problems for you."

"Problems, sister?" replied Skim. "How could you create problems for us? We have two tents, haven't we? One will be for you and we'll take the other."

"And with our two little stoves, which will keep burning until morning," added Steel, "there'll be no need to worry about the cold, even though it's very intense right now."

"Thank you, gentlemen," said Sister Madeleine, "but whenever it suits you to travel by night, you mustn't let us stand in your way."

"Have no fear, sister," exclaimed Skim with a laugh. "You may be sure we won't spare you any difficulty or exertion."

When the caravan reached Sheep Camp, around six o'clock, the mule teams were exhausted. They were soon unhitched, and the scout's men gave them something to eat.

Bill Steel had been right when he said that the inns in the village had little in the way of comfort. They were barely up to the standard of the shelters where poor folk find a night's lodging.² In any case, there was no room there. The scout had the two tents pitched in the shelter of some trees a short distance away from Sheep Camp so as not to be disturbed by the frightful noise of the crowd.

As soon as the tents were set up, the blankets and furs were brought in from the sleds and the stoves were lit. Although they had to make do with cold meat, at least there was plenty of hot tea and coffee. At last, left to themselves, Sisters Martha and Madeleine bundled up in their blankets side by side, not forgetting to pray for their helpful and generous compatriots.

In the second tent, the evening went on longer in a cloud of pipe smoke. It was just as well that they fired up the stoves to a red heat, for the temperature that night dropped to minus seventeen degrees centigrade.

It is not hard to imagine the suffering that must have been endured by the immigrants who had not been able to find shelter in Sheep Camp. There were perhaps several hundred of them including women and children, many of whom were already exhausted at the beginning of a journey whose end they would never see.

Bright and early the next morning, Bill Steel had the tents taken down and folded. It was better to leave at daybreak and get ahead of the crowd in the Chilkoot Pass.

The weather was still dry and cold, and even if the thermometer had fallen still lower, that would have been much preferable to the heavy squalls, swirling snow, and violent blizzards that are so feared in the high latitudes of North America.

Sisters Martha and Madeleine had been the first to emerge from their tent and load their modest luggage onto the sled. After an early meal, or rather, a few cups of hot coffee or tea, they all took their places on the sleds, and the mules, under the drivers' whips, started off again.

Their pace was no more rapid than it had been the day before. The grade grew steeper as the pass approached the summit of the mountain. The scout had wisely chosen to use a mule team instead of the dogs, which were reserved for taking the sleds down the other side of the mountain to the lakes. The sturdy mules were quite capable of hauling the sleds over the uneven and rocky ground with its deep ruts. It would be more difficult to negotiate if a rise in temperature caused it to turn soft.

As on the previous day, Raddle and his cousin found it better to cover part of the journey on foot, and occasionally the nuns, numbed by the cold, decided to follow their example.

There was always the same noisy, milling crowd, always the same obstacles that make the Chilkoot trail so arduous, always the forced and sometimes lengthy halts, when a pileup of sleds and teams blocked the way. Several times, the scout and his men had to use their fists to make their way through.

Sad to say, it was not only the bodies of animals that were to be seen scattered here and there at the bottom of the slope. It was not unusual to see, lying abandoned under the trees at the bottom of a precipice, some poor immigrant who had perished from cold and exhaustion and who would not even have a grave. Frequently, too, there were families, men and children, lying on the frozen ground, unable to go any farther, and no one was making any effort to pick them up. Sisters Martha and

Madeleine, assisted by their friends, tried to help these poor unfortunates and to revive them with a little of the brandy that was kept in reserve on their sled. But what more could they do? Either these hapless people had no way of crossing the Chilkoot except on foot, or else the animals pulling them had been scattered along the way to die of exhaustion and hunger. And this was not surprising, since the animals were horses, mules, and reindeer, which had to be fed regularly. Between Skagway and the lake region, the price of feed became exorbitant—four hundred dollars for a ton of hay, three hundred dollars a ton for oats. Fortunately, the scout's teams were well provided for in this respect, and there was no fear of their running short before they got to the north slope of the mountain.

In fact, of all the working animals, the dogs seemed to be best supplied with food. At least they could satisfy their hunger by eating the carcasses of horses and mules lying here and there along the pass. They fought over them, howling, to the very last scrap.

The slow, backbreaking climb continued. Every fifteen minutes, they had to stop two or three times because it was impossible to make their way through the crowd. At some spots where there was a sharp turn, the pass was so narrow that equipment could not get through. This was the case mainly with the immigrants' prefabricated boats, the larger parts of which were wider than the path. The result was that the sled had to be unloaded and the parts hauled through one at a time by horses or mules. This led in turn to a considerable loss of time as the following sleds were crowded together.

There were also places where the grade was so steep—sometimes more than forty-five degrees—that the animals refused to go up, even though they were shod with special shoes for travel on ice. The studs on their shoes left deep marks on the blood-stained snow.

About five o'clock in the afternoon the scout halted the caravan. His weary animals could not have taken another step, even though their load was light compared to many others. To the right of the pass a sort of ravine opened up, with many evergreens growing in it. Under their branches the tents would find shelter that might enable them to withstand the gusts forecast by the rise in temperature.

Bill Steel was familiar with the place, for he had spent a night there more than once, and camp was set up as usual.

"Are you afraid there may be a high wind?" asked Ben Raddle.

"Yes, it will be a bad night," replied the scout. "We can't take too many precautions against the snowstorms. They sweep through here as if they were going through a funnel."

"But we'll be protected a bit here," Summy Skim pointed out, "because of the position of the ravine."

"That's why I picked this spot," replied Steel.

It was a wise move on his part. A terrible storm began about seven o'clock in the evening and raged until five in the morning. Through the swirling snow they could not see each other five paces away. It was very hard to keep the stoves burning because the force of the wind drove the smoke back inside, and it was not easy to find more firewood in the midst of the fierce gusts. Nevertheless, the tents held up, but Skim and Raddle had to sit up part of the night, fearing that the nuns' tent might be blown away at any minute.

That was exactly what happened to most of the tents that had been pitched along the slope outside the ravine. When daylight returned, the extent of the disaster could be seen. Most of the teams had broken loose from their tethers and run off in all directions. Sleds were overturned and some had slid over the precipices that lined the path and fallen into the raging streams at the bottom. There was equipment that could no longer be used. There were families in tears, pleading, begging for help, which no one was in a position to give them.

"Those poor people, those poor people!" murmured the nuns. "What will become of them?"

But the scout was in a hurry to leave and push on to the summit of the Chilkoot. He gave the signal to start, and the caravan resumed its slow upward journey.

By daybreak the storm had subsided. With the sudden change in temperature typical of those northern regions, the wind had swung around to the northeast and the thermometer had dropped to twelve degrees below zero.

The ground, now covered with a thick layer of snow, became extremely hard. This would make the sleds slide along more easily, as long as the grade was not too steep, and Bill Steel was able to set his friends' minds at rest on that point.

The appearance of the region had now changed. For a distance of eight or ten miles there were no trees at all. Beyond the slopes stretched dazzling white plains that hurt the eyes. It would have been worse if the snow had been on the point of melting. Since this often causes ophthalmia, travelers who have sunglasses put them on, while those who have none have to smear charcoal on their eyebrows and eyelids.

That was what Raddle and Skim did, on Bill Steel's advice. As for the sisters, they pulled down their broad-brimmed hats and had nothing to fear from the effects of the dazzling snow. In any case, since they were now back on their sled, they did not need to use their eyes and sat huddled under the blankets.

More accustomed to giving help than to receiving it, the two nuns were touched by the attentions of their compatriots. But Summy Skim always replied that it was not for their sake, but for the sake of the sick people in Dawson City, that he wanted them to arrive safe and sound in the capital of the Klondike.

"Besides," he kept saying, "Ben or I will probably end up in the hospital, and we'll be sure of being well cared for. It's pure selfishness on our part." On the evening of May 4 the caravan stopped at the summit of the Chilkoot Pass, and the scout made camp. The next day, they would make whatever preparation was needed for going down the north face of the mountain.

The altitude of the plateau at that point was about 3500 feet as compared to the 2900 feet of the White Pass.[3]

It is easy to imagine how congested that spot must have been, without any protection and exposed to the full force of the weather. There were more than two thousand immigrants there at the time, making caches for storing part of their gear. In fact, the descent presented extreme difficulties, and it was necessary to proceed with small loads in order to avoid disaster. And after they had gone down to the foot of the mountain, all those people, whom the vision of gold claims in the Klondike had endowed with supernatural energy and tenacity, went back up to the top, picked up a second load of equipment, brought it down, and went up again, fifteen or twenty times if need be, for days on end. That was where the dog teams rendered yeoman service in hauling the sleds (or the ox hides that replaced them because they slid more easily over the hard snow of the slopes). But then the north wind beat with all its force on that side of the Chilkoot, causing dreadful suffering among those who had to fight against it. But all the poor wretches saw the plains of the Klondike open before them. They said to themselves that these territories would bring them fortune, but in fact they would bring only disappointment.[4]

Bill Steel and his caravan did not have to prolong their stay at the summit or cache any equipment, since they had nothing but their own personal luggage. After they reached the foot of the mountain, they would not have to go back up the pass. Once they had set foot on the plain they would only have a few miles to go in order to reach the tip of Lake Lindemann.

The next day, May 5,[5] the scout would take down his tents and, instead of hitching the mules to the sleds, replaced them with the dog teams that one of his men was keeping in reserve on the plateau.

The usual arrangements were made. But this last night was an extremely bad one. The temperature had risen suddenly, and the storm returned with renewed violence. This time, the tents were not sheltered by a ravine as they had been the night before. Neither Summy Skim nor Ben Raddle nor the nuns could take shelter in them. Several times, the storm pulled the tents off their pegs, and in the end they had to be folded up to prevent them from being carried away in the swirling snowstorms. There was nothing for it but to wrap themselves in their blankets and wait philosophically until daylight returned.

"Really," thought Summy Skim, "it would take all the philosophy of all the philosophers, ancient and modern, to endure such an abominable journey, especially when there was no compelling reason for going."

During the rare lulls in the storm, in pitch darkness and without any fire (which it would have been impossible to keep going), they heard cries of pain and terror, and horrible curses. To the groans of the injured rolled along the ground by the storm were added the barking, whinnying, and bellowing of the terrified animals across the plateau.

Dawn came at last, and Bill Steel gave the word to move on. The dogs were hitched to the sleds, which as a precautionary measure carried no passengers this time. Following the scout's advice and example, the two cousins had put on three pairs of socks plus a kind of moccasin that made walking easier. They would have quickened their pace if they had not wanted to stay with the two nuns, who could not have kept up with them. That was especially necessary since it was hard to keep from falling on the icy slopes.

However, thanks to the precautions they took and to the scout's experience, they made their way down without accident, though not without fatigue, and the two sleds reached the plain at the end of the Chilkoot Pass. The weather had taken a turn for the better, the wind had come round to the east and was less violent, and the temperature was rising, but not enough to bring on a thaw that would have made walking more difficult.

At the end of the pass, a large number of immigrants had gathered together in an encampment, waiting for their equipment to catch up with them. It was a huge area, less congested than on the higher plateau. There were trees all around, and tents could be set up in complete safety.

There the caravan came to spend the night. The next day it would start out again along a fairly well-maintained road and would reach the south tip of Lake Lindemann, ten miles away, by noon.

8

Lake Lindemann

THE AFTERNOON OF THAT DAY was spent resting.[1] There were also preparations to be made for sailing across the lakes, and the scout promptly busied himself with that. Summy Skim and Ben Raddle could only congratulate themselves that the man they had chosen to work with was so cautious and got along so well with them and their traveling companions.

Bill Steel's equipment was stored at the tip of Lake Lindemann in an encampment already occupied by about a thousand travelers. His main installation was located at the back of a hill and consisted of a small house divided into several separate rooms, with sheds nearby where the sleds and other vehicles were stored. There were stables at the back for the draft animals and kennels for the sled dogs so essential for the descent.

The Chilkoot was already becoming more heavily traveled than the White Pass, even though the latter leads directly to Bennett Lake, by-passing Lake Lindemann altogether. Conditions for transporting men and mining equipment were better on Lake Lindemann, whether it was frozen over or clear of ice, than across the long plains and through the heavily wooded area between the end of the White Pass and the south shore of Bennett Lake. As a result, the encampment the scout had picked was growing larger all the time. By offering this kind of transportation from Skagway to Dawson City, he was doing a thriving business, one that was certainly less risky than panning for gold in the Klondike.

But Bill Steel was not the only one plying this profitable trade. There were others doing the same thing, both at Lake Lindemann and at Bennett Lake. In fact, there were not enough of these Canadian and American entrepreneurs, because immigrants were flooding in by the thousands at this time of year, eager to be in Dawson City by the beginning of the mining season, which usually started during the first half of May.

Many of the immigrants, of course, for reasons of economy had no dealings either with the scout or with his colleagues. But that meant they were obliged to bring their equipment from Skagway, loading their sleds down with prefabricated wooden or sheet-metal boats, and we have seen the difficulties involved in crossing the Chilkoot Pass with those heavy loads. Travel through the White Pass was no less arduous, and on both routes a good part of the equipment was in danger of being lost.

Some, however, either to avoid overloading or to save money, adopted a different expedient. Instead of bringing their boats right up to the edge of the lake, they found it more advantageous to have them built on the spot or to build them themselves. In this wooded region there was no shortage of building materials. There was, however, the risk of delay because of the time required to fell trees, cut them up into ribs and planks, and fit them solidly together, (since they would all too frequently come into violent contact with blocks of ice or with rocks). There were already a few construction sites in the vicinity, with sawmills functioning and construction actively under way.

When Steel's caravan arrived, he was met by his foreman, who lived in the little house with a few men, Canadians like himself. Usually they found employment piloting boats from lake to lake, as far as the Yukon River. They were skilled and dependable men, thoroughly familiar with the demands of this kind of water travel, which is difficult even after the ice has gone out.

Since the air was bitterly cold, Skim, Raddle, and the nuns were very glad to take lodging in the scout's house, where the best rooms were put at their disposal. The difference in temperature between the inside and the outside was more than twenty degrees centigrade. They would not be staying more than twenty-four hours, however, since the boats were ready to be loaded, and they would take on supplies at Bennett Lake, where conditions would be more favorable.

Sisters Martha and Madeleine retired at once to their little stove-heated room. As he showed them the way, Summy Skim assured them that the hardest part of the journey from Skagway to Dawson City was over.

When he came back to the common room, the scout, who had overheard that remark, felt obliged to comment on it.

"Yes," he said, "the most exhausting part is over, but not the longest part. We still have hundreds of miles to go before we get to the Klondike."

"I know that, Bill my hearty," replied Skim, "but I have an idea the second part of our journey won't be so dangerous or strenuous."

"That's where you're wrong, Mr. Skim," answered the scout.

"But all we have to do is let ourselves drift down with the current of the lakes and rivers."

"Very likely, but winter is far from over. When the breakup comes, our boat will be surrounded by drifting blocks of ice, and we'll have several hard portages to make."

"There certainly is a lot to be done before a tourist can travel through this part of the Dominion in comfort," said Skim. "And I think it may never happen."

"Why not?" interrupted Ben Raddle. "It's just a matter of putting through a railway. Work on the line from Skagway to Bennett Lake is going to start shortly, isn't it? And then it will go on to Fort Selkirk. A five-hour trip to the lake, with three trains a day, ten dollars for a ticket, six dollars a ton for freight. Hawkins, the engineer, is going to hire two thousand men for this project, and pay them thirty cents an hour."

"All right, all right," exclaimed Skim. "I know your information is always exact, my dear Ben. But there's something that you're forgetting, and so are the engineers. Before the railway is finished, the Klondike will be stripped clean of its gold. No more gold deposits, no more prospectors, no more business . . . the country will be abandoned."

"Oh, come on," countered Raddle. "Is that your opinion too, Bill Steel?" The scout simply shook his head and said nothing.

In reply to another question from Raddle, he spread out a rough map of the whole Yukon basin from the lake region to the Alaskan boundary beyond the Klondike.

"First of all," he said, "here is Lake Lindemann, which lies at the foot of the Chilkoot Pass. We'll have to travel the full length of it."

"How far is that?" asked Summy Skim.

"Only five miles," replied the scout. "It doesn't take long when the surface is frozen smooth or when it's completely clear of ice."

"And then?" asked Raddle.

"Then we'll have to portage for about a mile to get our boat and our gear to the site at Bennett Lake. There again, how long the portage will take depends on the temperature, and you've seen already how much it can change from one day to the next."

"So we have," confirmed Ben Raddle. "Differences of fifteen or twenty degrees, depending on whether the wind is coming from the north or the south."

"The best thing," said Steel, "would be a dry cold that hardens the snow on the ground because then we can slide the boat along like a sled. One good team of dogs would be enough for that."

"So now we've arrived at Bennett Lake," said Skim.

"Yes," said the scout. "It's about thirty miles in length, from north to south. But we'll have to allow at least three days for that trip, because we'll need to make rest stops. Besides, the ice isn't out yet."

Summy Skim looked at the map. "Is there another portage after that?" he asked.

"No, there's the Caribou River, two or three miles in length. It connects Bennett Lake with Tagish Lake, eighteen or twenty miles long, and leads to Marsh Lake, which is about the same length. After you leave that lake you have to follow a winding river for about thirty miles until you come to the Whitehorse Rapids, about two and a half miles in length. They're very difficult to negotiate, and sometimes very dangerous. Then you come to the point where the river joins the Takhini, which brings you to the head of Lake Laberge. That's where we may be held up the longest when we have to make our way through the Whitehorse Rapids. I once had to stop there for a whole week, upstream from Lake Laberge."

"And what about that lake?" asked Raddle. "Is it navigable?"

"All thirty-two miles of it," replied Steel. "But it would not be pleasant to get caught in the breakup, because only a miracle could keep a boat from being crushed by the blocks of ice drifting down toward the Lewes River. It's better to drag the boat over the ice, as long as the cold weather lasts."

"That takes a lot longer," Skim pointed out.

"It's a lot safer," replied the scout, "and I'm speaking from experience because I've been caught in the breakup more than once, and I thought no one would come out alive."

"When we get to Lake Laberge we'll see what has to be done," said Ben Raddle.

"Oh, I don't think we'll have any trouble," replied Steel. "It doesn't look as if we'll have an early summer this year."

"How do you know that?" asked Skim.

"By the fact that there aren't any game birds like partridges or grouse."

"And that's really too bad," said Skim, "because I'd have had a chance to take a few shots."

"All in good time," said the scout. "First of all, let's think about getting out of this lake region. After that, when our boat is going down the Lewes and Yukon rivers, if any game appears, Mr. Skim, you can shoot as much of it as you like."

"I'll certainly do that, Bill, even if only to replenish our supplies."

"Scout," asked Raddle, "with the exception of a few portages, will our boat take us all the way to Dawson City?"

"Directly, Mr. Raddle. All things considered, the water route is the easiest way to go."

"And by way of the Lewes and the Yukon," asked Raddle, "how far is Lake Laberge from the Klondike?"

"About 375 miles, counting all the detours."

"I see we're not there yet," said Skim.

"Definitely not. And when we get to the Lewes and the north end of the lake, we still won't be halfway, as you can see on this map."

"But I'm inclined to believe," remarked Raddle, "that we won't encounter any more difficulties as great as there were in the Chilkoot Pass."

"And we can say for sure," declared Steel, "that in five or six weeks, when the ice is out of the rivers, it'll be an easy trip. But at the beginning of May, it's too early in the season, and it'll take a lot longer."

"Can you give us an estimate, even under favorable conditions?" asked Skim.

"No, not even within two weeks," was the reply. "I've seen people go from Skagway to Dawson City in three weeks, and I've seen others take as long as two months. As I said before, it depends on when you start out."

"I really hope we'll be in the Klondike by the first week in June," said Raddle.

"I hope so too," said Steel, "but I don't want to guarantee it."

"Well," replied Skim, "with a long trip ahead of us, let's save our strength. Since we have a chance to spend a good night here at Lake Lindemann, let's get some sleep."

It was indeed one of the best nights the two cousins had spent since leaving Vancouver. The little house was well sheltered and weather-proof, and the well-stoked stoves kept it warm.

The next day, May 8, Sisters Martha and Madeleine were the first to appear in the common room, where they set about making coffee. Skim and Raddle would find two hot cups waiting on the table. That would be their only meal before the scout and his friends set out for the trip over Lake Lindemann.

The departure time was set for nine o'clock. Bill Steel estimated it would take half a day to get to the end of the lake, and then on to the site at Bennett Lake, where they would spend the night in somewhat similar conditions.

In any case, it was best to let him handle everything connected with the trip. He had experience and, having seen him at work, the two cousins intended to let him do as he thought best.

While the temperature inside the house was more than seven degrees above zero, the outside thermometer showed fifteen below. This difference necessitated certain indispensable precautions, and so Summy Skim, while drinking his coffee with the nuns, urged them to keep themselves very warmly covered up on the boat, which the dog team would pull over the surface of the lake.

"We have plenty of blankets," he said, "and the cold is as pitiless for Sisters of Mercy as for any other travelers. Whether the rules of your order permit it or not, please wrap yourselves in furs from head to foot."

"That is not forbidden," replied Sister Madeleine with a smile.

"Very well," replied Skim, "but what is forbidden is to expose yourself to the cold needlessly. When we're in Dawson City, sisters, we expect you to take all the necessary precautions in this abominable climate where the temperature sometimes drops to fifty degrees below freezing."

"That's winter for you," interjected Raddle.

"Yes, that's winter," agreed Skim. "Thank heaven it isn't summer! And now Sister Martha, and you, Sister Madeleine, wrap yourselves up and we'll be off."

At nine o'clock the signal to start was given. The men who had been with the scout since they left Skagway would stay with him as far as the Klondike. Their services would be very useful for handling the boat, now transformed into a sled, until it could sail over the lakes and down the Lewes and Yukon rivers.

The dogs were of a breed remarkably well acclimatized to that region. Because they had no hair on their feet, they were better able to run on the snow with no risk of getting stuck in it. But while they were acclimatized, it should not be assumed that they were any the less wild. Indeed, they seemed to be just as wild as wolves and foxes. It was not exactly by stroking them and offering them treats that their handlers managed to control them.

Among Bill Steel's crew was a pilot who would be in charge of the boat when it was in the water.

He was an Indian from the Klondike, named Neluto, very experienced in his trade and familiar with all the various kinds of difficulties encountered on lakes, rapids, and rivers. He had worked for Steel as a pilot for nine years, and his skill could be depended on.

Neluto was about forty years old, strong, clever with his hands, and a tireless walker. Skim noticed that he was different from the other Indians of that territory.

The natives of northern British Columbia, as well as those of Alaska, are generally unattractive and ungainly, with narrow shoulders and slender bodies, members of a vanishing race. They are not Eskimos, although they have the same very dark complexion as those northern tribes, but they resemble them most in having long, oily, flowing hair, which they allow to grow down to their shoulders.

There is no doubt that Neluto earned good wages by his trade, which kept him in constant touch with strangers (although these were obviously not of the finest caliber, what with the influx of immigrants from all parts of the world into the Klondike). Besides, before taking a job with the scout's crew, he had worked for the Hudson's Bay Company as a guide for fur trappers throughout that vast territory. He was thoroughly familiar with the country, having traveled the length and breadth of it and even part of the areas downriver from Dawson City and north to the Arctic Circle.

Neluto was not very talkative, but he knew enough English to understand and make himself understood. Apart from things related to his own work, he said very little. As the saying is, the words had to be dragged out of his mouth. Raddle and Skim would not learn much from him about working a claim in the gold fields.

He was used to the climate in the Klondike, however, and could provide much valuable information on that subject. Ben Raddle began by asking him his opinion of the weather and if he thought the ice on the lakes would soon go out.

Since he made no reply (probably because it was a stranger who was asking), Bill Steel intervened and repeated the question.

Neluto then announced that, in his opinion, the worst of the cold weather would be over within two weeks and that there was no way of knowing before then when the snow would melt or when the ice would go out.

The logical conclusion to be drawn from this was that the boat would not find open water at the beginning of the journey unless there was a sudden change in the weather, as often happens in the north.

In any case, they would not be sailing through Lake Lindemann, but dragging their boat over it. The nuns could still take their place in the boat, which would slide along on one side of its hull, with the men walking behind.

The dog team required some encouragement with voice and whip before they seemed ready to start out, but at last they were on their way. The lake was alive with the comings and goings of hundreds of immigrants on vehicles of every description.

Since the ice was fairly smooth, Raddle and Skim were wearing their moccasins. If they had not been obliged to stay with the boat they could have crossed the lake in half an hour, but it was better for the caravan to stay together under the scout's direction.

The weather was calm. The sharp wind of the previous day had died down and was shifting around to the south. It was still cold, however—a dozen degrees below zero. On the whole, this was fortunate because it created favorable conditions for walking, which becomes so difficult during a snowstorm.

Still, progress was slow, and besides the nuns preferred to walk part of the way. In some places the ice was so uneven and the boat was jolted about so much that it was difficult to stay in it and it was in danger of turning over.

In short, the five-mile passage of Lake Lindemann was not finished until eleven o'clock. The distance from there to Bennett Lake, only about a mile, took nearly an hour. It was noon when the scout and his caravan came to a halt at the campsite at the southern tip of the lake.

9

From Bennett Lake to Dawson City

BENNETT LAKE, one of the largest in the region, is twenty-five miles long from south to north.

If steamboats (there is some talk of establishing this service) were to carry immigrants as far as the Whitehorse Rapids and if, after a portage around those rapids, other steamboats were to deposit them at the northern end of Lake Laberge, what a lot of exertion, privation, and suffering those travelers would avoid on their way to the Lewes River, which becomes the Yukon at Fort Selkirk. This could not happen, of course, until after the spring breakup when the lakes and rivers would be clear of the masses of ice that sometimes continue to float downstream until nearly the end of May. Then there would still remain the long journey to Dawson City, estimated at 300 to 325 miles at least.

In any case, there was no steamboat service at that time on the lakes or on the Lewes. Like the railway that was supposed to start at Skagway, it was still in the planning stage, and the immigrants had to face a very difficult journey.

Obviously, when the last gold deposit in the Klondike has been stripped clean, the swarm of miners will leave the country, never to return. But half a century may go by before the pick has dug out the last nugget.

The Bennett Lake settlement was as badly overcrowded as the one at Sheep Camp on the Chilkoot Pass or the one at Lake Lindemann. It was filled with thousands of immigrants waiting for an opportunity to move on. There were tents everywhere, which would soon be replaced by cabins and houses if the rush to the Klondike were to go on for a few more years.

This embryonic settlement, later to grow into a village and then a town, already had a number of inns, which would become hotels. To judge by the exorbitant prices they charged for food and lodging despite the total lack of comfort, they were hotels already. There was also a police station, and on the heavily wooded shores of the lake there were sawmills and construction sites where boats were being built.

It should be mentioned that policemen are not assigned to this settlement alone. The Dominion government posts them here and there over the whole territory. The job they do among all those fortune seekers at large throughout the region is sometimes dangerous, and there are barely enough of them to maintain law and order on the Klondike's roads.

Neluto, the Indian, had predicted the weather accurately. It underwent a sudden change in the afternoon. With the wind now blowing from the south, the thermometer rose to zero centigrade. There were unmistakable signs that the cold season was coming to an end, that a thaw would soon cause the ice to break up, opening the lakes and streams to navigation.

Furthermore, during the first week in May, Bennett Lake was no longer completely frozen over. Between the ice fields there were winding, open channels where a boat could get through and still make good time, even though its route was no longer a straight line. The twenty-five miles between the north and south ends of the lake would probably be doubled, but there would be no need to use sleds. In fact, the boats would save time whether they were propelled by oars or by sails. In any case, the journey would be less tiring.

The temperature rose still more in the afternoon, and the thaw quickened. A few blocks of ice were beginning to drift north, and unless there was a sudden return of cold weather during the night, the scout would have no difficulty in reaching the north end of the lake.

Summy Skim, Ben Raddle, and the Sisters of Mercy were able to find shelter overnight in one of the little houses at the settlement. Although their lodging was not quite as comfortable as it had been the previous night at the scout's house, at least they did not have to put up with the overcrowding that prevailed in the tenting area.

The thermometer did not fall during the night, and at daybreak on May 9 Bill Steel declared that conditions were reasonably favorable for navigation. The south wind showed no sign of freshening, and the clouds were motionless high in the sky. If the breeze continued, Steel's party would be able to sail with the wind behind them.

At sunup the scout was already getting the boat ready and loading the luggage and supplies with the help of Neluto and the four Canadians who made up his regular crew when he carried travelers from Skagway to Dawson City.

"Well, what do you think about the weather?" Summy Skim asked him when the two cousins joined him at the shore. "Have we seen the last of the winter cold in the Klondike?"

"I wouldn't like to say for sure," was the reply, "but it certainly looks as if the lakes and rivers will soon be free of ice. Anyway, by following the open channels, even if we have to take longer, our boat . . ."

"Won't have to leave its natural element," Skim finished for him. "That will be best."

"And what does Neluto think?" asked Raddle.

"He agrees with me," replied the scout.

"But don't we have to worry about drifting blocks of ice?"

"Our pilot knows what he's doing. He'll find a way to avoid them," replied Steel. "Besides, the boat is solid. It's proved that already by sailing through the breakup, and if there's any danger, we can easily take refuge on the shore."

"It would be very exhausting if we had to disembark," Skim pointed out. "Let's hope we can spare the ladies that ordeal."

"We'll do all we can, Mr. Skim," replied the scout. "After all, if would be better if we didn't have to drag the boat for twenty-five miles or so. That would take at least a week."

91

He called out to Neluto, who had just come down to the shore, "When do you think the ice will go out?"

"It's two days now since the first blocks of ice started drifting. That means the upper part of the lake must be clear."

"And the wind?"

"The wind is fair. It sprang up a couple of hours before dawn."

"But will it hold steady?"

Neluto turned and scanned the horizon, where the Chilkoot rose about two and a half miles away. The clouds were barely moving, and a light mist was drifting across the face of the mountain.

Stretching out his hand in that direction, the pilot replied, "I think the breeze will keep up until evening."

"But what about tomorrow?" asked Raddle.

"Tomorrow, we'll see," was Neluto's brief reply.

"All aboard," ordered Steel, and the nuns promptly joined him.

The scout's vessel was a sort of open boat or barge thirty-five feet long. The after deck was covered with a tarpaulin under which two or three people could find shelter for the night or during the day if there was a snow squall or heavy rain and wind. Its flat bottom enabled it to navigate in a minimal depth of water, and with its six-foot beam, it could carry a fairly large sail, cut like the foresail of a fishing smack, which could be hoisted to the top of a small, fifteen-foot mast. In foul weather the mast could easily be taken down and laid across the benches, and the oarsmen would take over.

Given the arrangement of the sail and the shape of the hull, this craft could not sail very close to the wind, but with a stern wind it made good time. Because of the twists and turns of the channels between the ice fields, it happened all too often that the pilot found himself heading directly into the wind. It that case, he furled the sail, took down the mast, and brought out the oars. Manned by four sturdy Canadians, they drove the boat along at a brisker speed.

Bennett is not a large lake, not to be compared with the vast inland seas of North America, where storms of unimaginable violence spring up. The northern regions of Canada and Alaska, like Hudson Bay, have no mountains to protect them from the Arctic winds and are sometimes overwhelmed by storms that churn the lakes into enormous waves. Clearly, an unseaworthy craft could not hold out and would soon be lost unless it had enough time to reach port.

By eight o'clock the gear was on board and everything was ready. The scout had some supplies of food in reserve: canned meat, biscuits, tea, coffee, a cask of brandy, coal for the stove set up on the foredeck. They also expected to do some fishing since those waters were teeming with fish and to bag some of the partridge and grouse found along the shores of the lake.

Since the scout had completed the formalities at the customs, which are very strict and never fail to create a few problems for travelers, he was now free to leave. The sail went up and the boat pulled away from the shore.

Neluto, the pilot, was at the tiller, just behind the tarpaulin, and the nuns had taken their places in front of it. Skim and Raddle were leaning against the rail, near Bill Steel. His four men, standing near the bow, used their gaffs to push away the floating blocks of ice. The boat was following a fairly wide crack in the ice, oriented in such a way that they could sail for a little more than a mile with a stern wind. But then they had to come about and head west with the wind on their quarter. All in all, they did not make very good time.

The pilot's main concern was to avoid the masses of ice floating downstream, which would have damaged the boat on contact. This was not always easy, since there were a great many boats in the channels. Several hundred of them, taking advantage of the breakup and the favorable wind, had left the Bennett Lake settlement at dawn. In the midst of that flotilla it was sometimes difficult to avoid a collision. When that happened, angry cries, insults, and threats were heard on all sides, not to mention the gunfire exchanged between boats.

Raddle and Skim's curiosity was aroused by the view on the right bank, to which they were heading. There were clumps of yellowish spruces growing on the shore, and farther back loomed the dense forest, covered with snow still undisturbed by the wind. There were also mechanical sawmills in operation, sending up clouds of steam above the level of the bark roofs and emitting metallic, grating sounds.

There were cabins scattered here and there along the banks, sometimes a village of huts occupied by Indians who lived by fishing. Their canoes were pulled up onto the sand, waiting until the lake was open for navigation.

In the background, on the far distant horizon, rose a few barren peaks which offered little or no protection against the icy north winds.

The wind, which was beginning to die down, had not dissipated the mists that had been building up in the south since morning. The sun had not broken through, and there was reason to fear that the fog might settle over the surface of the water. To sail under those conditions, with ice drifting all around, was practically impossible. The best thing to do would be to put in to shore and wait there until the weather changed.

During the afternoon they met a police boat traveling through the channels. All too often it had to intervene to settle a brawl.

The scout knew the man in charge of that boat, and they had a brief conversation.

"We're still getting immigrants coming from Skagway on the way to the Klondike."

"So we are," replied Steel, "and more of them than we need."

"And more than we'll see on their way back."

"That's for sure! How many have come across Bennett Lake, do you think?"

"About fifteen thousand."

"And they aren't all here yet?"

"Far from it."

"Do you know if the ice has gone out farther downstream?"

"So they say."

"We can get to the Yukon River by boat, then?"

"Yes, unless we get another cold spell."

"Is there any hope that we won't?"

"Yes. We can always hope."

"Thanks."

"Have a good trip."

The weather was calm, however, and although Bill Steel had no serious problems to deal with on Bennett Lake, his progress was slow. After putting in to shore for two nights, they finally reached the end of the lake on the afternoon of May 10.

The little Caribou River (which is really no more than a channel) flows out of the lake at this point and into Tagish Lake, no more than two miles away.

They stopped there for the night, planning to leave again the next day. There was no need to set up camp, since the boat would provide shelter for the scout and his passengers.

Summy Skim decided to take advantage of the last hours of daylight to go hunting in the nearby fields for partridges and green-feathered grouse. He brought back several brace of them as well as a number of ducks. The lake region was teeming with them, enough to keep the party supplied for the whole journey. Skim was a good hunter, and Steel, who went along with him, proved to be no less skillful. They made a wood fire on the shore and cooked the game over a crackling flame. It was pronounced excellent.

Tagish Lake, nearly twenty miles long, is connected to Marsh Lake by a short opening, which had filled up with drifting ice during the night. Rather than wait until it was open again, the scout hired a team of mules and hauled the boat for about a mile. That way he was able to resume his journey the same day through the channels on Marsh Lake.

At this point, twelve days after leaving Skagway, Bill Steel and his companions had covered only a hundred miles.

It would take them at least forty-eight hours to cover the length of Marsh Lake, even though it was only eighteen or twenty miles long. The wind had shifted to the north. It was not strong, but it was a contrary wind, making it impossible to use the sail, and with the oars they could not expect to make rapid progress.

Since the lake was only two miles wide, both the eastern and western shores were in view all the way along. The high hills surrounding the lake, white with frost and snow, presented a picturesque appearance. There were fewer boats now than there had been on Bennett Lake since some of them had encountered difficulties and stayed behind.

On the afternoon of May 13 they made a halt at the end of Marsh Lake. After looking at the map Ben Raddle asked the scout, "We only have one more lake to cross, don't we? Isn't this the last one in the region?"

"Yes, Mr. Raddle," replied Steel. "Lake Laberge. But that's the hardest part of our journey."

"But surely, Scout, we won't have to drag our boat between the two lakes along the Lewes River, and then farther on north, will we?"

"On the river, no, but on the land, yes," replied Steel, "if it's impossible to get past the Whitehorse Rapids without portaging. It's always a dangerous run, and more than one boat has gone down with all hands."

These rapids constitute the gravest danger for river traffic between Skagway and Dawson City. They cover two miles of the fifty-three between Marsh Lake and Lake Laberge, and over that short distance the river falls no less than thirty-two feet. To make matters worse, the passage is obstructed by rocks that inevitably smash any craft driven against them by the current.

"Can't you follow along close to shore?" asked Skim.

"It's not practical," replied the scout. "But a tramway is being built to transport fully loaded boats to a point below the rapids."

"So if the tramway is being built, that means it isn't finished yet," remarked Skim.

"Not yet, but there are hundreds of men working on it."

"And you'll see, Bill my hearty, that it still won't be finished when we come back."

"Unless you stay in the Klondike longer than you expect," replied Steel. "You know when you're going, but you never know when you're coming back."

"You hear that, Ben?" said Skim to his cousin.

There was no reply.

On the following afternoon, May 15, the boat reached the Whitehorse Rapids on its way downstream. It was not the only one to venture into that dangerous stretch of water. Other boats were following it, and many of those that started out above the rapids would not make it through.

It is understandable that the pilots who work on the Whitehorse Rapids charge a high price for going through those two miles. Their fee of thirty dollars gives them a good income, and they would not consider exchanging their lucrative trade for that of a prospector.

It is often necessary before launching out into the current to unload part of a boat's cargo, which is picked up later. With a lighter load, boats can be guided more safely between the rocks.

Since the scout's boat was not weighted down with heavy equipment, he did not consider this precaution essential, and Neluto was of the same opinion. After all, they were both perfectly familiar with the rapids.

"Don't be frightened," the scout advised the nuns.

"We have confidence in you," replied Sister Martha.

At that point, the current was moving at the rate of about twelve miles an hour, and it should not have taken long to go through the two miles of rapids. But the many detours needed to avoid the basalt rocks scattered helter-skelter between the banks of the river, and the floating blocks of ice, like moving shoals that could shatter the sturdiest boat, made the trip much longer. Several times the boat, listing sharply, had to do an about-turn to avoid colliding with a block of ice or another boat. Neluto's skill got them out of more than one tight spot.

"Look out! Look out!" cried the scout, when the boat was three-quarters of the way through.

It was important to keep a firm grip on the benches in order not to be thrown overboard. The last fall in the rapids is the most fearsome, and the scene of many disasters. But Neluto had a good eye, a steady hand, and an unshakable nerve. The scout knew he could depend on him.

In spite of his efforts, a few waves broke over the boat as it pitched

97

downward, but the men soon bailed it out and conditions improved once the rapids were past.

The two cousins experienced a bit of a fright when the boat seemed to head straight down into the abyss. As for the nuns, they closed their eyes and crossed themselves with trembling hands.

"And now," exclaimed Summy Skim, "is the worst over, Bill?"

"There's no doubt about it," added Raddle.

"In fact, gentlemen," declared the scout, "we just have to sail through Lake Laberge and follow the Lewes River down for about four hundred miles. There are only one or two rather difficult stretches, but they can't be compared to the Whitehorse Rapids."

"So, sisters," said Skim with a laugh, "no more than four hundred miles. We might as well say we've arrived, and you'll have nothing more to fear."

"Oh, but we'll be afraid for you, gentlemen," replied Sister Madeleine, "because when you come back you'll have to go up the rapids, and that may be even more dangerous."

"You're right, sister," answered Skim. "It would definitely be better for us not to come back at all."

"Unless the tramway is in operation," Raddle pointed out.

"As you say, Ben. All we have to do is wait a year or two."

What would have been an even greater advantage and made the journey even easier would have been the railway then under consideration, running from Skagway to the Whitehorse Rapids and from the Whitehorse Rapids to Dawson City. With that completed, there would be no more lake travel, no more portages anywhere along the way. The journey from the Chilkoot to the Klondike would be a matter of days instead of weeks. But when would these projects get under way, and who knows whether they would ever be undertaken?

On the evening of May 16 the scout's caravan reached the southern tip of Lake Laberge, a hundred and ninety miles from Skagway.

After talking it over with Neluto, Bill Steel decided to make a twenty-four-hour stop at that settlement. There was a powerful north wind, and the pilot was not eager to attempt a crossing of the lake under those conditions for fear of being caught in a violent storm. Besides, even with the crew manning the oars, the boat would barely be able to get away from the shore because the strong winds had brought the ice to a stop and driven it back against the southern shore of the lake. There was even the possibility of another freeze-up since the temperature was falling and the thermometer now registered two degrees below zero.

This settlement, built along the same lines and to meet the same needs as the ones at Lake Lindemann and Bennett Lake, already had about a hundred houses and cabins. One of the houses called itself a hotel—with exorbitant prices, needless to say, and lacking even minimal comfort. Nevertheless, Skim, Raddle, and the nuns were able to find rooms there.

That evening the two cousins and Bill Steel met in the lower hall of the hotel to discuss the probable length of their journey.

"After we get through Lake Laberge," said the scout, "we can't make more than ten or twelve miles a day going down the Lewes, and since we're still four hundred miles from Dawson City, I don't expect to get there before the first week in June."

"We won't be sailing at night, then?" asked Ben Raddle.

"That wouldn't be wise," replied Steel, "because the Lewes is full of floating ice, and Neluto wouldn't want to take a chance on it."

"In that case," remarked Skim, "we'll tie up on one bank or the other, will we?"

"Yes, Mr. Skim, and if there's any game around, you'll have time for some good hunting."

"I'll be sure to get off a few shots, Scout."

"And I'm sure you won't miss."

"But if we don't get to the Klondike until the first week in June," Raddle pointed out, "won't we be too late to work the claim?"

"No, Mr. Raddle," replied the scout. "Just think of the thousands of immigrants who are still behind us and who won't get there until long after we do. Placer mining can't start until the middle of June, when the ground is completely thawed."

"It doesn't matter to us anyway," added Skim. "We aren't going there to pan for gold on Claim 129 but to sell it for the best price we can get. Even if that takes us until July, we'll still have time to be back in Montreal before winter."

Lake Laberge, about thirty miles long, is made up of two parts connected at the point where the Lewes River flows northward. Starting out on the morning of May 18, the boat took forty-eight hours to travel through the first part of the lake.

It was about five o'clock on the afternoon of May 20 when the scout and his companions, after enduring a good many heavy winds, reached the Lewes River, which angles off to the northwest on its way to Fort Selkirk.[1] The following morning the boat set out through the floating ice, keeping as much as possible to the center of the river, where the current kept the passage clear.

At five in the afternoon the scout gave the order to pull up against the right bank, where he planned to spend the night. Summy Skim was the first one ashore. A little later, shots rang out and a couple of ducks and grouse replaced the usual canned meat on the supper menu.

The other boats going down the Lewes also made overnight stops, just as Bill Steel's did, and numerous campfires lit up the river banks.

From that day on the thaw seemed to have come to stay. The south wind kept the thermometer at five or six degrees above zero, and there was no longer any danger of the river freezing over. The immigrants did not have to worry about dragging their boats or making portages. The ice on all the lakes—Lindemann, Bennett, Tagish, Marsh, and Laberge—had now broken up, and the current was carrying it rapidly downstream.

During the nights under canvas there was no danger of being attacked by wild beasts. There was no sign of bears in the vicinity of the Lewes River, and Summy Skim—to his great regret, perhaps—did not have the opportunity to shoot one of those formidable plantigrades.[2] On the other hand, they had to defend themselves against the innumerable mosquitoes swarming around the river banks, and even by keeping fires

going all night the travelers could barely escape their painful and annoy-
ing bites.

On the afternoon of May 23, the scout and his companions were about
thirty miles down the Lewes, where it was joined by its tributary the
Hootalinqua.[3] The next day they came to the Big Salmon River, another
tributary. They could see there how the blue water of the river changed
color when mixed with the water of the tributaries. The following day
the boat passed the mouth of the Walsh River, which had been by then
abandoned by the miners, although it had produced gold worth ten cents
to the pan. It was now reported to have been stripped clean to its last
nugget. Then there was the Cassiar, a sandbank that emerges when the
water is low. A few prospectors gleaned six thousand dollars' worth of
gold from it in one month, and a few grains of the precious dust are still
being found.

The journey continued, in fair weather and foul, but the cold was not
severe enough to cause any undue suffering. The boat continued on its
way, sometimes under sail, sometimes propelled by the oars. Sometimes,
in very winding passages, the men had to haul it along by a rope. They
had to take care, however, when they approached the high cliffs lining
the shore at places, which occasionally sent enormous avalanches crash-
ing down.

By May 30 they had gone down most of the Lewes (which would
shortly become the Yukon) under reasonably favorable conditions. The
caravan was now about a hundred and fifty miles from Lake Laberge,
and still had to go through the Five Finger Rapids. This would entail
some difficulty. The river is obstructed at that point by five islands,
which create large whirlpools and sudden rapids, requiring the utmost
caution on the part of the pilot. On Neluto's advice, it seemed prudent to
go ashore because the high water level made the current almost torrential. But after the boat had negotiated those rapids, and the Rink Rapids
a short distance downstream, the passengers all went back on board and
would encounter no further serious obstacles until they arrived at Fort
Selkirk, some fifty miles away.

On May 31 the scout made camp at the Turenne encampment, located on a cliff blanketed with the first spring anemones, crocuses, and sweet-smelling juniper. A great many immigrants had already pitched their tents there. Since the boat was in need of a few repairs, it remained there for twenty-four hours, giving Summy Skim an opportunity to indulge in his favorite activity. There was an abundance of game, especially thrushes, and he could have hunted all night since at that latitude and that time of year there is only partial darkness between sunset and sunrise.

During the next two days the boat made rapid headway downstream, thanks to a current flowing at seven or eight miles an hour. On the morning of June 2, after passing the labyrinth of the Myersall Islands, it swung over to the left bank and tied up at the foot of Fort Selkirk.

This fort was built in 1848 for use by Hudson's Bay Company agents but was destroyed by Indians in 1852. What used to be a fort is now nothing more than a well-supplied general store. It is surrounded by Indian huts and immigrants' tents and covers an open space beside the great waterway that from that point on is usually known as the Yukon. It is then swollen by the water of the Pelly River, its principal tributary flowing in from the right.

The scout had to take on fresh supplies at Fort Selkirk, and he found everything he needed there, at exorbitant prices to be sure, since even in the smallest inn a very simple meal cost three dollars.

On the morning of June 3, after a layover of twenty-four hours, the boat moved back into the current of the Yukon. The weather was very uncertain, with rain and occasional sunny spells, but there was no longer any danger of severe cold as the temperature approached ten degrees above zero.

The scout did not stop on the way past the mouth of the Stewart River, which was beginning to attract a number of gold seekers and would soon be lined with claims all the way back to its source a hundred and eighty miles to the east. At Ogilvie, on the right bank of the Yukon, the boat tied up for half a day.

Downstream the river was already much wider, and boats could sail without hindrance among the many blocks of ice drifting northward.

On June 6, the scout and his companions passed the Indian River and the Sixtymile River, which flow into the Yukon from opposite sides thirty miles from Dawson City, and Baker Creek, which flows in from the right, and finally set foot in the capital of the Klondike that afternoon.

10

The Klondike

THE PART OF NORTH AMERICA known as Alaska is a vast region washed by the waters of two oceans, the Arctic and the Pacific, and covering nearly six hundred thousand square miles. The Russian Empire sold it to the Americans as much out of sympathy for the Union, they say, as out of hostility to Great Britain. In any case, it was almost inevitable that the region should become American, rather than adding to the area of the Dominion of Canada and British Columbia. And besides, will not the future justify the famous Monroe Doctrine: All of America for the Americans?[1]

Apart from its gold fields, is there any great profit to be derived from the half-Canadian, half-Alaskan Yukon River watershed, part of which lies north of the Arctic Circle and whose soil is not suitable for any agricultural use? Probably not.

It must not be forgotten, however, that this region, including Baranof, Admiralty, and Prince of Wales islands, which belong to Alaska, as well as the Aleutian archipelago, has a coastline of more than eight thousand miles. It has ports that offer shelter to ships in these stormy waters from Sitka, the capital of Alaska, to St. Michael, near the mouth of the Yukon, one of the largest rivers in the New World.

Alaska was discovered by the Russians in 1730 and explored in 1741,[2] when its total population did not exceed thirty-three thousand inhabitants, mostly of Indian origin. It is now being invaded by hordes of immigrants and prospectors, attracted to the Klondike over the past few years by the discovery of gold.

The one hundred and forty-first meridian, running from Mount St. Elias (which rises to a height of 19,212 feet) to the Arctic Ocean, has been chosen as the boundary between Alaska and the Dominion of Canada, although the southern part of the boundary, which twists and turns so as to include the inshore islands, may not have been established so precisely.

A glance at the map of Alaska will show that most of its land is flat. Its orographic system is found only in the south, with a chain known as the Cascade Range that extends through British Columbia and California.

Most striking of all is the course of the Yukon River, whose waters flow through Canadian territory on the way north to Fort Cudahy. With its tributaries and subtributaries, an immense network of rivers and streams including the Pelly, Big Salmon, Hootalinqua, Stewart, Sixtymile, Fortymile, Indian, and Klondike rivers, this magnificent watercourse curves around to Fort Yukon and then flows southwest,[3] emptying the last of its water into the Bering Sea near St. Michael.

In short, the Yukon is the river of gold par excellence. Together with its tributaries, it flows through the richest gold deposits in Alaska and the Dominion of Canada. How many nuggets would rise to the surface of those streams, if only they could float!

The Yukon is greater than the Father of Waters, the Mississippi itself. Its discharge is no less than thirty thousand cubic yards a second, its course extends over a distance of 1,430 miles, and it drains an area of approximately four hundred thousand square miles.*

While the land through which it flows is not suitable for agriculture, the forested area is very large. It consists mostly of dense stands of yellow cedar, enough to supply all the rest of the world if the forests were exhausted. The wildlife includes black bears, moose, caribou, mountain sheep, white long-haired mountain goats, and feathered game by

*Twice the area of France.

the tens of thousands: grouse, snipes, thrushes, ptarmigans, and ducks in numbers sufficient to feed the native population at the time of the country's discovery.

The waters surrounding this immense coastline are no less rich in sea mammals and fish of every kind. One fish in particular should be mentioned because of the use to which it can be put. It contains so much oil that it can be lighted and used as a candle, hence the name "candle fish" by which it is known to Americans.

But the greatest wealth of this region lies in its deposits of gold. They may possibly yield more than Australia, California, and the mines of South Africa.

It was in 1864 that the first deposits were discovered in the Klondike.

At that time, the Rev. McDonald found gold that could be collected by the spoonful in a little river near Fort Yukon.[4]

In 1882 a group of former miners from California, including the Boswell brothers, braved the Chilkoot Pass and worked the first placer mines.

In 1885 some gold seekers in the Lewes-Yukon River area discovered the Fortymile gold field on the boundary between Alaska and the Dominion of Canada, a little downstream from what would become the site of Dawson City. In 1887, the same year when the Canadian government began proceedings for defining the boundary, they took out more than $120,000 worth of gold.

In 1892 the North American Trading and Transportation Company of Chicago founded the village of Fort Cudahy near the confluence of the Fortymile and Yukon rivers. Two years later, Fort Constantine was built to protect it. Thirteen constables, four noncommissioned officers, and three officers, who were working there, collected no less than three hundred thousand dollars' worth of gold on the claims at Sixtymile, a little above Dawson City.

The rush was on, and prospectors began streaming in from every direction. In 1895 at least a thousand Canadians, mostly French, crossed the Chilkoot and spread out over the area along the river.

But it was in 1896 that the startling news spread: the discovery of gold on Eldorado Creek, a tributary of Bonanza Creek, which is a tributary of the Klondike, which in turn flows into the Yukon. Gold seekers came swarming into the region. In Dawson City, lots that had sold for five dollars were soon worth thirty thousand, and the federal government in Ottawa recognized it as the Yukon capital in June of 1898.

The region specifically known as the Klondike is only a district of the Dominion. As part of British Columbia, it belongs to the vast English territory of Canada.[5] The one hundred and forty-first degree of longitude, which marks the boundary between Alaska (now American) and the British possessions, forms the western limit of the district.

Its northern limit is the Klondike River, ninety miles long, which flows into the Yukon from the east at Dawson City and divides it into two unequal parts.

The Yukon crosses the boundary some fifty miles to the west,[6] a little to the northwest of the capital, after being joined on its right bank by the Stewart River, the Indian River, Baker Creek, and the famous Bonanza Creek with its tributary Eldorado Creek.

To the east, the Klondike borders on the part of the Dominion where the first ranges of the Rocky Mountains appear, on territory through which the Mackenzie River flows northward.

The center of the district rises in high hills, the tallest of which, the Dome, was discovered in 1897. These are the only elevations in this generally flat region, where the network of rivers and streams attached to the Yukon basin has its source. Its size can be estimated by the sheer number of its direct tributaries: the Klondike, fed by creeks with names such as Too Much Gold, Hunker (rising in the bowels of the Dome), Bear, Quigley, Bonanza, Bryant, Swedish, Montana, Baker, Westfield, Geneenee, Montecristo, Ensley, the Sixtymile River, the Indian River, gold-bearing waterways on which hundreds of claims are already being worked.[7]

But the gold country par excellence is still the area along Bonanza Creek, which flows out of the domes at Cormack's, and its many tributaries: Eldorado Creek, the Queen, the Boulder, the American, the Pure Gold, Cripple Creek, the Tail, etc.

It is not hard to understand why prospectors rushed in such great numbers into a territory whose numerous creeks and small streams are completely ice free for the three or four months of summer, and onto the many deposits that were relatively easy to work. It should be pointed out that their number is increasing every year, despite the exertions, hardships, and disappointments of the journey between Skagway and the capital of the Klondike.

A few years ago, at the confluence of the Klondike and the Yukon, there was nothing but a marsh, which was often submerged during the flood season. The only buildings were a few Indian huts, log cabins built in the Russian style, where native families lived a miserable existence.

Dawson City, which now has eighteen thousand inhabitants, was founded on that very spot. The town's founder, a Canadian named Ladue,[8] began by dividing it into lots for which he charged no more than five dollars and which are now selling for anywhere between ten thousand and forty thousand dollars.

If the Klondike's first deposits are not destined to be mined out in the near future, if other placers are discovered in the basin of the mighty river, if the claims eventually number in the thousands, are there not grounds for believing that Dawson City will become a metropolis like Vancouver, British Columbia, or Sacramento, California?

From its very beginnings, the new town was in danger of being overwhelmed by floods, as had happened to the swamp that it replaced. It lies on the right bank of the Yukon and is divided into two parts by the Klondike. When the ice breaks up in the spring, the rising water level threatens to cause severe damage.

Solid dikes had to be built as protection against these floods, which occur only during a short time each year. Indeed, the water level in the Klondike River drops so low in the summer that pedestrians can cross dry-shod from one part of the town to the other.

As we can see, the new town had a difficult beginning, but that did not prevent its population from increasing rapidly.

As we know also, Ben Raddle had a thorough knowledge of the district's history. For several years he had kept up-to-date on all the discoveries. He was aware of the constant increase in the yield of the placer mines and of the lucky strikes that had been made. Of course, he had only come to the Klondike to take possession of the claim on the Fortymile River, to assess its value, and to sell it at the best price he could get. But Summy Skim had a feeling that as they got closer to Dawson City his cousin was taking a greater interest than he would have liked in the miners' work, and he was still afraid Ben might be tempted to try his hand at it. He would oppose that of course; he would not let his cousin engage in such an enterprise; he would not allow him to settle down in this country of gold and misery!

At that time, there were no fewer than eight thousand claims in the region, numbered from the mouth of each tributary or subtributary of the Yukon back to its source. The parcels varied in area from 250 to 500 square feet, as stipulated by an amendment to the law of 1896.

It should be pointed out that the infatuation of the prospectors, and the preference of the syndicates, always led them to the deposits on Bonanza Creek and its tributaries and to the low mountains on its left bank. Was it not in that highly favored area that Georgie MacCormack sold several claims of twenty-four by fourteen feet, which yielded nuggets worth eight thousand dollars in less than three months?

The deposits on Eldorado Creek were so rich that, according to the government surveyor Ogilvie,[9] the average value of each pan was between five and seven dollars. If, as everything seems to indicate, the vein is thirty feet wide, five hundred feet long, and five feet deep, it is reasonable to assume that it will produce up to four million dollars.

From then on, companies and syndicates tried to buy these claims, and bid sky-high prices for them. It is hard to predict how high the bidding will go for placers where the pans yield anywhere from three hundred to eight hundred dollars' worth of pure gold valued at fifteen or sixteen dollars an ounce on the Dawson City market.

It was truly unfortunate—at least, that is what Ben Raddle must have been telling himself, although Summy Skim gave it very little thought—that Uncle Josias's legacy had not been one of the claims on Bonanza Creek, instead of in the Fortymile region across the Yukon River. Whether they had decided to work it or to sell it, they would have made a substantial profit. The heirs might even have received offers high enough to persuade Raddle not to undertake the journey to the Klondike. Skim would have been vacationing on his farm at Green Valley instead of tramping around the streets of Dawson City through mud that possibly contained bits of the precious metal.

There was still, of course, the offer made by the syndicate for the claim on Fortymile, unless it had expired in the absence of a reply.

After all, Ben Raddle's reason for coming was to see, and see he would. Although Claim 129 had never yielded nuggets worth six hundred dollars—the value of the biggest one ever found in the Klondike—it was apparently not exhausted, since there had been offers to buy it. The American and British syndicates did not enter into such negotiations with their eyes closed. In any case, if the worst came to the worst, the two cousins would certainly make enough to pay for their trip.

As Raddle knew, there was already talk of new discoveries on Hunker Creek, which flows into the Klondike fifteen miles above Dawson City. It runs for seventeen miles between 1500-foot mountains containing gold deposits richer than those of Eldorado Creek. There were also rumors about a tributary of Gold Bottom Creek in which, according to Ogilvie's report, there was a vein of gold-bearing quartz that yielded up to a thousand dollars a ton.

The newspapers were also calling attention to Bear Creek, which flows into the Klondike only ten miles from Dawson City. It was divided into about sixty lots over a distance of seven miles, which were said to have yielded handsome profits during the last working season. Rumor had it that these claims were better than the ones on Bonanza Creek because their more regular features made them easier to work.

Perhaps Ben Raddle was saying to himself that they might head in that direction if nothing could be done with Claim 129.

Summy Skim, on the other hand, sometimes said to himself, "That's just perfect! Bonanza, Eldorado, Bear, Hunker, Gold Bottom—they're all very well, but we're on Fortymile, and I have no intention of hearing Fortymile spoken about as if it didn't exist!"

It did exist, however, and Bill Steel's map showed it flowing into the Yukon below Dawson City.

It would indeed have been a deplorable bit of bad luck if the Fortymile River had not contributed its share to the gold output of the Klondike, which, according to the MacDonald report, had produced at least twenty million dollars during the working season between May and September of 1898.

This was a region whose reputation could not be overrated and which had touched off, for good reason, a growing influx of miners from all over the world, despite the strain of the journey. How could Ben Raddle, or even Summy Skim, have had doubts about its wealth? Had it not produced $1,500,000 worth of nuggets in 1896 and $2,500,000 in 1897? And would the output for 1898 not reach $6,000,000? No matter how many immigrants there were, would they not still have a share in the $50,000,000 that Ogilvie estimated as the value of the Klondike's wealth? The millionaires would be in a very tiny minority, but torrents of gold would issue from the bowels of the earth.

It should be noted, too, that the Klondike is not the only area in that region that is crisscrossed with gold-bearing veins. Others were known to exist elsewhere, not only on the territory of the Dominion but also on the other side of the Yukon in the immense territory of Alaska, parts of which have still not been fully explored. And even on the right bank of the great river, in Canadian territory, at the southern edge of the Klondike, is there not talk of the Indian River, whose deposits rival those of the Klondike itself? Are there not miners already working three hundred claims as far upstream as the junction of Sulphur Creek and Dominion Creek, which join to form the Indian River? Are there are not already more than 2,500 of them washing sixty to eighty dollars' worth from every panful?

It is not only the tributaries on the Yukon's right bank that carry gold flakes and nuggets along in their course. Prospectors are now rushing to the ones on the left bank. Claims are being filed on the Sixtymile River, the Geneenee, the Westfield, and the Swedish, which contain at least 680 lots. Last but not least there is the Fortymile River—for it does exist, no matter what Summy Skim may think—and Uncle Josias's claim really is number 129, just as the telegram had informed Mr. Snubbin, the Montreal notary.

Furthermore, even in the part of the Klondike between the Indian River and the Ensley, another tributary of the Yukon, there is an unexplored area where miners will soon discover new wealth.

A glance at the map of the Dominion will show gold-bearing regions apart from the Klondike already marked there. There are, for example, those adjoining the Chilkoot range, drained by the Pelly River before it joins the Yukon, and those at the Cassiar Mountains, to the north of Telegraph Creek, and south of the mining camp at Centreville.

It can be seen also that these gold-bearing regions are even more numerous in Alaska, and there is no doubt that the Americans, the new owners of that territory, will not let them sit idle. To the south of the great river are those at Circle City, Rampart City, and the Tanana Mountains and to the north is the one at Fort Yukon. Finally, north of the Arctic Circle lies a vast area drained by the Nootok and Colville rivers, where Point Hope protrudes into the Arctic Ocean.

When Ben Raddle dangled the prospect of these future treasures before his cousin's eyes, Skim only smiled and answered, "The Yukon definitely flows through a region favored by the gods. Just think! We own a little bit of it, and my only concern is to get rid of Uncle Josias's legacy at last."

I I

Dawson City

"A COLLECTION OF CABINS, huts, and tents, a sort of camp set up on a swamp, always threatened by the floodwaters of the Yukon and Klondike rivers, with crooked, muddy streets and potholes at every step of the way, not a city by any means, but something like a huge kennel fit only for the thousands of dogs that can be heard barking day and night—that's what you thought Dawson City was, Mr. Skim. But the town has changed visibly thanks to the fires that have opened up the terrain. It has its Catholic and Protestant churches, its banks and hotels, it's going to have its Mascott Theatre, and it will soon have its grand opera house, with seating for 2,200 Dawsonians, et cetera (and you can't imagine what that *et cetera* implies)."

This was Dr. Pilcox speaking, a rotund English Canadian about forty years of age, vigorous, active, resourceful, and in robust health. His constitution was proof against all diseases and seemed to enjoy incredible immunity. It was a year now since he had moved to this town, which was an ideal place to practice his profession since it seemed to be a favorite rendezvous for epidemics, not to mention the endemic gold fever, against which, by the way, he was as effectively vaccinated as Summy Skim himself.

In addition to being a physician, Dr. Pilcox was a surgeon, pharmacist, and dentist. Since he was known to be both skilful and conscientious, patients flocked to his comfortable home on Front Street, one of the main streets of Dawson City.

It should be mentioned also that Dr. Pilcox had been appointed chief of medicine at the clinic whose sister superior was awaiting the arrival of the two Sisters of Mercy.

Bill Steel had known Dr. Pilcox for a long time, going back to his days as a scout in the Canadian Army and had always recommended him to the immigrant families that he brought from Skagway to the Klondike. It was only natural then that he should have thought of putting Ben Raddle and Summy Skim in touch with someone so zealous, so public spirited, and so highly regarded in the community. Where could they have found anyone better informed about what was going on in the country than this doctor, with his intimate knowledge of so many fortunes and misfortunes? If anyone could provide good advice, as well as a sound medical opinion and effective medicine, it was certainly that excellent man. Moreover, in the midst of the frightful overexcitement that prevailed in town whenever there was news of a discovery, he had always kept his head and never had any inclination to go prospecting himself.

Dr. Pilcox was proud of his town, and he made no secret of that when Summy Skim paid his first visit to him.

"Yes," he said, "it well deserves the title of capital of the Klondike, which the Dominion government has conferred on it."

"But it seems to me, doctor," observed Skim, "that it's hardly built yet."

"It may not be completely built yet, but it soon will be because its population is growing every day,"

"And how many people live here now?" asked Skim.

"More than twenty thousand, sir."

"But perhaps they're only passing through."

"Excuse me, but they've settled here with their families and have no more intention of leaving than I have."

"But still," continued Skim, who took a delight in needling the good doctor, "I don't see any of the usual characteristics of a capital in Dawson City."

"What!" exclaimed Dr. Pilcox, puffing himself up until he looked more rotund than ever. "This is the home of Maj. James Walsh, the commissioner of the Yukon Territory and a whole hierarchy of civil servants such as you won't find in the cities of British Columbia or the Dominion of Canada."[1]

"Who are these people, doctor?"

"Mr. Justice McGuire of the Supreme Court; gold commissioner Thomas Fawcett, esquire; crown lands commissioner Wade, esquire; the consul of the United States of America, and the French consul."[2]

"Yes," replied Skim, "those are high-ranking administrators, but what about the business sector?"

"We already have two banks," replied the doctor, "the Canadian Bank of Commerce, with its head office in Toronto, managed by Mr. H. T. Wills, and the Bank of British North America."

"And churches?"

"Dawson City has three, Mr. Skim. There is a Catholic church, served by Father Judge, a Jesuit,[3] and Father Desmarais, an Oblate, as well as a Reformed church and an English Protestant church."

"That's fine, doctor, as far as the salvation of people's souls is concerned. But what about public safety?"

"What do you think of this, Mr. Skim? We have Captain Stearns, a French Canadian,[4] as commander in chief of the mounted police, and Captain Harper as head of the postal service. Between them, they have about sixty men under their command."

"What I say, doctor, is that this police squad may not be sufficient, because the population of Dawson City is growing every day."

"Well, then, the squad will be increased too, to meet the need. The Dominion government will do whatever is necessary to ensure that the inhabitants of the capital of the Klondike are safe."

The way the good doctor pronounced the words "capital of the Klondike" was something to hear!

"But after all," Skim continued, "it certainly looks as if Dawson City is doomed to disappear once the gold deposits in the district have been exhausted."

"Exhausted!" exclaimed Dr. Pilcox. "The gold deposits in the Klondike! But they're inexhaustible, Mr. Skim. New placers are being discovered every day along the creeks. New claims are being worked every day. I don't know of another town in the world whose longevity is more certain than the capital of the Klondike."

Skim had no desire to continue a discussion that was, on the whole, quite pointless. What did it matter to him whether Dawson City lasted two years or two thousand? He was only going to be there for two weeks.

No matter how inexhaustible the doctor declared the gold fields to be, however, they would eventually be mined out, and it seemed hardly likely that the town would survive when it had no further reason to exist, located as it was near the Arctic Circle and with its abominable living conditions. But since the doctor promised it a vitality greater than that of any other town in the Dominion—Quebec City, Ottawa, or Montreal—there was no point in contradicting him. The important thing for Ben Raddle and Summy Skim was that Dawson City had a hotel.

In fact, it had at least three, the Yukon Hotel, the Klondike Hotel, and the Northern Hotel. The two cousins managed to book a room in the Northern.

No matter how small the influx of miners into Dawson City, the hotel owners could not fail to make a fortune. A room cost seven dollars a day, meals were three dollars, and the service charge was a dollar a day. It cost a dollar to have one's beard trimmed and a haircut was a dollar and a half.

"Fortunately," remarked Skim, "we're not in the habit of getting shaved. And as for our hair, we'll wait until we get back to Montreal to have it cut."

On the basis of the aforementioned figures, it will come as no surprise to learn that everything in the capital of the Klondike was exorbitantly priced. Anyone who did not get rich quick through some stroke of luck was sure to go bankrupt in short order. The high prices on the market price list of Dawson City speak for themselves: sugar sold for thirty or forty cents a pound; salt pork, twenty-five cents; canned meat, forty cents a can; a glass of milk, fifty cents; corn and oat flour, twenty-five cents; rice, beans and apples, twenty-five cents; dried potatoes, sixty cents; onions, seventy-five cents; butter, a dollar; eggs, two dollars and forty cents a dozen; honey, seventy cents; coffee and tea, from a dollar to two dollars and forty cents; salt, twenty cents; pepper, a dollar; tobacco, two dollars and fifty cents; oranges, five for sixty cents; lemons, five dollars a dozen; beef, a dollar thirty; mutton, a dollar; moose meat, a dollar; fish, fifty cents. An ordinary bath cost two dollars and fifty cents, and a Russian bath was thirty-two dollars. Summy Skim would settle for the ordinary baths.

At that time Dawson City extended for a mile and a quarter along the right bank of the Yukon River. The distance from that bank to the nearest hills was about three-quarters of a mile. The town covered an area of 220 acres and was divided into two parts by the Klondike River, which flows into the Yukon River at that point. Its seven avenues and five streets crossed each other at right angles. The one closest to the river was named Front Street. The streets had wooden sidewalks and were traveled by sleds during the long winter months. For the rest of the year, large carriages and heavy wheeled wagons drove noisily through them, surrounded by packs of dogs.

The many vegetable gardens around Dawson City grew turnips, cabbages, kohlrabi, lettuce, and parsnips, but they could not produce enough to meet the needs of the inhabitants, and vegetables had to be imported from Canada, British Columbia, and the United States. Canned meat, fresh meat, and game were brought in by refrigerator ships, which steamed up the Yukon River after the ice went out, from St. Michael to Dawson City, a distance of over 1,100 miles.[5] From the first week in June the Yukon steamers made their appearance downstream, and the docks rang with the screaming of their whistles.

On the day they arrived in Dawson City, the two nuns had of course been taken to the hospital run by the Catholic church. They were warmly welcomed by the sister superior, who was profuse in her thanks to Skim, Raddle, and the scout for the help and care they had given to Sisters Martha and Madeleine.

Dr. Pilcox's welcome to the nuns was equally touching, and indeed their presence was really essential since the staff of the clinic could no longer cope with so much work.

Following a severe winter, the wards were overcrowded, and it is impossible to imagine the condition to which exhaustion, cold, and privation had reduced those poor people who had come from so far away. In Dawson City at that time there were epidemics of scurvy, diarrhea, meningitis, and typhoid fever. The death toll rose with every passing day, and a constant stream of hearses pulled by dog teams went along the streets, taking many unfortunate victims to the cemetery where a simple grave dug out of the bowels of the gold-bearing earth awaited them.

And yet, despite this lamentable spectacle, the Dawsonians, or at least the miners passing through the town, were constantly indulging in excesses. They frequented the casinos and gambling houses whether they were making their first trip to the gold fields or going back there to recoup the money they had squandered in the course of a few months. One would not have suspected, watching the crowds packing the restaurants and bars, that an epidemic was decimating the town or that alongside the few hundred pleasure seekers, gamblers, and scoundrels with strong constitutions, there were so many homeless wretches, entire families of men, women, and children, stranded at the entrance to the town and too ill to go any farther.

All these people so keen on violent pleasures and continuous thrills could be found in establishments like the Folies-Bergères, the Monte-Carlo, the Dominion, and the Eldorado. It could not be said that they were there from evening until morning, because at that time of year near the solstice there was neither morning nor evening. Games of poker, monte, and roulette were in full swing. It was not guineas or dollars that were being wagered but nuggets and gold dust against a background of shouts, challenges, attacks, and sometimes revolver shots. The police were unable to suppress these dreadful goings-on in which individuals like Hunter and Malone played a leading role.

Then, too, the restaurants were open all night, and supper was served at any hour. Chickens were offered at twenty dollars apiece, pineapples at ten dollars, eggs (guaranteed fresh) at fifteen dollars a dozen. People drank wine at twenty dollars a bottle and whisky at equally exorbitant prices and smoked cigars that cost seventy cents.[6] Three or four times a week, prospectors came in from the neighboring claims to the gambling houses, where they wagered everything they had panned out of the muck of Bonanza Creek and its tributaries.

It was a sad and distressing sight, revealing the most deplorable vices of human nature, and the little that Summy Skim saw of it from the time of his arrival in Dawson City only increased his disgust for this world of scoundrels.

But he probably would not have an opportunity to study it in greater depth. He still expected their stay in the Klondike to be of short duration, and besides, Ben Raddle was not a man to waste time.

"Our business here is our top priority," he said, "and since a company has offered to buy Claim 129 on the Fortymile River, let's go and have a look at it first."

"Whenever you like," replied Skim.

"Is the Fortymile River far from Dawson City?" Raddle asked Bill Steel.

"I've never been there," replied the scout, "but according to the map it flows into the Yukon at Fort Cudahy, northwest of Dawson City."[7]

"Judging from its number, then," remarked Skim, "I don't think Uncle Josias's claim is very far away."

"It can't be more than about seventy-five miles," replied the scout, "because that's how far it is to the Alaska-Canada border, and number 129 is on Canadian soil."

"We'll leave tomorrow," announced Raddle.

"Of course," replied his cousin, "but before we check out the value of 129, wouldn't it be a good idea to find out whether the group that offered to buy it is still interested?"

"Right. And we can have an answer to that in an hour."

"As a matter of fact," added Steel, "I'll show you where Captain Healy of the North American Trading and Transportation Company has his office. It's on Front Street."

Having reached that decision, the two cousins left the Northern Hotel in the afternoon, and the scout took them to the building occupied by the Chicago company.

There was a big crowd in the neighborhood. A Yukon steamer had just disembarked a large number of immigrants. While they were waiting to make their way to the various tributaries of the river, some to work their own claims, others to earn high wages by the strength of their arms, they swarmed through the town. Front Street was more crowded than any other street because the main agencies had their offices there. At the same time, a canine crowd mingled with the human crowd. Every step involved an encounter with these undomesticated animals and their ear-splitting howls.

"This Dawson City is a city of dogs," Summy Skim kept repeating. "The mayor must be a Great Dane."

Through a gauntlet of bumps, shoves, name-calling, and insults, Raddle and Skim made their way along Front Street to the company's office, where Steel left them at the door, promising to meet them later at the Northern Hotel.

They were welcomed by the assistant manager, Mr. William Broll, to whom they explained the purpose of their visit.

"Ah yes," he said. "You must be Mr. Raddle and Mr. Skim from Montreal, then? I'm pleased to see you."

"The pleasure is ours," said Skim.

"You are the heirs of Josias Lacoste, the owner of Claim 129 on the Fortymile River?"

"Exactly," confirmed Raddle.

"And now that we have come on this endless journey, can we assume that the claim has not disappeared?" asked Summy Skim.

"You may be sure, gentlemen," was the reply, "that it is exactly at the spot the surveyor has assigned to it, on the boundary between the two countries, which is still not precisely settled."[8]

What could that unexpected sentence mean? What effect could the boundary between Alaska and the Dominion of Canada have on Claim 129? Was Josias Lacoste not its rightful owner during his lifetime, and had it not been legally bequeathed to his natural heirs, no matter what controversy might arise concerning the boundary?

"We were informed in Montreal, Mr. Broll," Raddle went on, "that the company of which Mr. Healy is the manager was offering to buy Claim 129 on the Fortymile River."

"Quite so, Mr. Raddle."

"So we have come, my coheir and I, to find out what the claim is worth. We would like to know whether the offer is still in effect."

"Yes and no," replied Broll.

"Yes and no!" exclaimed Skim.

"Please explain to us, sir," said Raddle, "what you mean by yes and no."

"It's very simple, gentlemen," replied the assistant manager. "It's yes, if the location of the claim is settled in one way, and no if it's settled in another."

That decidedly needed to be explained, but without waiting for an explanation, Skim exclaimed, "No matter which way it's settled, was Mr. Josias Lacoste the owner of the claim, and are we not the owners in his place, since his estate has been passed down to us?"

In support of this declaration, Ben Raddle drew from his briefcase the title deeds confirming their right to take possession of Claim 129 on the Fortymile River.

"Gentlemen," continued the assistant manager, "I have no doubt at all that those title deeds are quite in order, but as I said, that is not the point. Our firm sent you an offer concerning the purchase of Mr. Josias Lacoste's claim, and when you ask me whether that offer is still in effect, I can only answer by . . ."

"By not answering," retorted Skim, who was getting a little irritated, especially when he noticed Broll's somewhat derisive attitude, which was not to his liking.

"Mr. Broll," went on Raddle, "your telegram offering to buy Mr.

Lacoste's claim reached Montreal on March 22. Today is June 7. More than two months have gone by, and I'd like to know what has happened in that time to make it impossible for you to give us a definite answer."

"You're talking about the claim as if its location wasn't definitely established," added Skim. "I'd like to think that it's still where it's always been."

"Certainly, gentlemen," replied Mr. Broll, "but it occupies a spot on the Fortymile River, right at the boundary between the Dominion of Canada, which is British, and Alaska, which is American."

"It's on the Canadian side," said Raddle sharply.

"Yes, if the boundary between the two countries is really settled," declared the assistant manager. "No, if it isn't. Since ours is a Canadian company and can only work deposits that are Canadian in origin, I haven't been able to give you an affirmative answer."[9]

"Does that mean," asked Raddle, "that there's still a controversy as to the border between American and British territory?"

"Exactly, gentlemen," replied Mr. Broll.

"I thought the one hundred and forty first meridian had been chosen as the dividing line," said Raddle.

"Yes, it was, gentlemen, and rightly so. Ever since 1867, when Russia sold Alaska to the United States of America, it has always been agreed that that line would constitute the boundary."

"Well," said Summy Skim, "I think lines of longitude don't move around even in the New World, and the one hundred and forty-first hasn't moved, either to the east or to the west."

"No, but apparently it isn't where it's supposed to be," replied Broll, "because serious arguments have arisen on that subject over the past two months, and it's possible that the meridian may have to be shifted a bit to the west."

"Several miles?" asked Skim.

"No," said Broll, "only a few hundred yards."

"And there's a dispute about so little!" exclaimed Skim.

"So there should be, sir," said the assistant director. "What is American must be American, and what is Canadian must remain Canadian."

"And which of the two countries is protesting?" asked Raddle.

"The United States," replied Broll. "It claims a strip of territory to which Canada also lays claim."

"And what have those discussions got to do with us?" Skim wanted to know.

"If the United States wins out, some of the claims on the Fortymile River will become American territory."

"And 129 will be one of them?"

"Exactly. And in that case the company would withdraw its offer."

Here at last was a definite answer.

"But at least," asked Raddle, "has work begun with a view to correcting the boundary?"

"It has, gentlemen, and the survey is being carried out with the utmost precision."

What was at issue was only a fairly narrow strip of territory along the one hundred and forty-first degree of longitude, and if both countries continued to press their claims, that meant that the disputed territory had gold in it. Who could tell whether there might not be a rich vein running through that strip from Mount St. Elias in the south to the Arctic Ocean in the north, which the Republic could profit from just as well as Canada could?

"To come to the point, then, Mr. Broll," asked Raddle, "if Claim 129 stays on the east side of the boundary, the company's offer is still in effect?"

"Exactly."

"And if, on the other hand, it ends up on the west side, the deal is off?"

"Exactly."

"Well then," declared Skim, "we'll go somewhere else. If our claim is absorbed into American territory, we'll get dollars for it instead of banknotes."

With that, the meeting ended and the two cousins went back to the Northern Hotel.

There they met the scout and explained the situation to him.

"In any case, gentlemen," he advised them, "it would be just as well for you to go to the Fortymile River as soon as you can."

"That's what we intend to do," said Raddle. "We're leaving tomorrow."

"It seems," added Skim with a laugh, "that work on correcting the boundary has begun. I'm curious to see whether it's nearly finished. A meridian must be a heavy thing to move around."

"Yes, you'll see that," replied Bill Steel, "but you'll also see that Claim 127, next to yours, is owned by an individual that you'll have to beware of."

"Yes," said Skim. "Hunter, the Texan."

"He and his friend Malone," the scout went on, "are working 127, which is their property. But since they aren't trying to sell it, it makes no difference to them whether it's located in Alaska or in Canada."

"I hope," added Raddle, "we won't have anything to do with those uncouth individuals."

"It will be much better if you don't," said the scout.

"And what about you, Bill? What are you going to do?" asked Skim

"I'm going back to Skagway to bring another caravan to Dawson City."

"How long will you be away?"

"About two months."

"We're counting on you to take us back."

"You can depend on it, gentlemen. But you'd better not waste any time if you want to leave the Klondike before winter."

12

From Dawson City to the Alaskan Boundary

INDEED, BEN RADDLE AND SUMMY SKIM had not a day to lose before settling their business. The Arctic cold arrives early in those high latitudes. It was already the second week of June, and before the end of August the lakes and creeks are frozen over and the air is filled with wind-driven snow. Two and a half months—that is as long as summer lasts in the Klondike, and for the two cousins part of that time would be taken up going from Dawson City to Skagway through the lake region, or, if they should decide to change their itinerary, down the Yukon to its estuary near St. Michael.

The day after they arrived, Raddle and Skim had prepared for the possibility that their stay at Claim 129 might be an extended one and that they might not be able to buy what they needed at Fort Reliance.

There was no need to buy or carry in equipment, since Josias Lacoste's equipment was already there, or to hire personnel since they had no intention of working the claim on the Fortymile River.

It did seem wise, however, to hire a guide who knew the country well. Since the scout had met another of his pilots in Dawson City, he offered to make Neluto available to Raddle until he got back. The Indian was willing, they had already seen him at work, and they knew what he was capable of, although he had not become any more talkative. A better choice for their trip would have been hard to find, and the two cousins could only thank Bill Steel for his kindness.

All that remained to do now was to lay in a supply of food regardless of the price, which was of course very high. But they had little trouble in purchasing a supply of fresh and salted meat, pork, bacon, flour, dried vegetables, tea, coffee, gin, and whisky sufficient for a stay of two weeks.

Raddle chose a cart as their vehicle rather a sled. Sleds are normally pulled by dogs even when the ice and snow are gone, and those animals were very expensive at the time, costing as much as $1,500 or $2,000 apiece.

Before leaving Dawson City, the scout had managed to obtain a cart that could carry three people and had room for their supplies as well. It was a two-wheeled vehicle with a leather top that could be raised or lowered and was solidly built to withstand bumps and shocks. They paid $270 for it and $175 for the sturdy horse that would be harnessed to it. There was no need to be concerned about its food, because at that time of year there were pastures to be found all along the roads. Under those conditions, a team of horses would find their own food more easily than a team of dogs would.

Neluto told them what utensils they would have to take with them, and Raddle could be sure of having everything he needed for the trip.

Meanwhile, Skim entertained himself by wandering calmly through the streets of Dawson City, looking at the shops, taking note of the prices of foodstuffs and manufactured articles. All in all, it was fortunate that he and his cousin had bought their supplies from merchants in Montreal.

"Do you know, Ben," he said, "what a pair of shoes costs in the capital of the Klondike?"

"No, I don't, Summy."

"Anywhere from ten to eighteen dollars. And a pair of stockings?"

"I don't know that either."

"Two dollars. And woolen socks?"

"Let's say four dollars."

"No, five. And suspenders?"

"We can do without those, Summy."

"A good idea. They cost three dollars and a half."

"We'll get along without them."

"And women's garters?"

"I couldn't care less, Summy."

"Eight dollars, and $180 for a dress made by a good seamstress. In this incredible country, it really pays to be a bachelor."

"We'll be bachelors, then," replied Raddle, "unless you've decided to marry some rich heiress."

"There's no shortage of those, Ben, nor of scheming women who own rich claims on Bonanza or Eldorado. But after all, I left Montreal a bachelor and I'll go back a bachelor. Ah! Montreal! Montreal! It's so far away, Ben!"

"What can you expect, Summy?" replied Raddle, with a trace of sarcasm in his voice. "The distance from Montreal to Dawson City is exactly the same as the distance from Dawson City to Montreal."

"I rather suspected as much," answered Skim, "but that doesn't make it any shorter."

Needless to say, Summy Skim made a point of visiting the hospital. The nuns always welcomed him with gratitude, and he, for his part, felt great admiration as he watched them going about their charitable work.

As for Dr. Pilcox, he enjoyed talking to Skim, giving him encouragement and advice and extolling the beauties of the admirable Klondike.

"You'll love it! You'll love it!" he kept saying. "If only you had a chance to see it during the winter."

"I certainly hope I won't have that good fortune, doctor."

"You never know. You never know."

That was an answer that Skim did not and could not take seriously.

At five o'clock on the morning of June 9 the cart was harnessed and waiting at the door of the Northern Hotel. Their supplies and their light camping equipment had been loaded, and Neluto, who would be driving, was already in his seat.

"Let's not forget anything," said Raddle, as they were about to leave.

"And especially, let's not forget that we have to be back in Montreal in two months."

The distance from Dawson City to the Alaskan boundary, as it was established at that time, was ninety-one miles. Since Claim 129 on the Fortymile River was right on the border, it would take at least three days to get there, at the rate of thirty miles every twenty-four hours.

Here is how Neluto planned to break up the journey so as not to over-work the horse. Each day's travel would be divided into two stages, the first from six in the morning until eleven, followed by a two-hour stop-over, and the second from one o'clock until six, when they would make camp for the night. That was the most they could expect to do through this rough country, following the course of the creek.[1]

If Ben Raddle and his cousin were unable to find a room in some inn along the way between Dawson City and Fort Reliance or between Fort Reliance and the border, they could simply pitch their tent in the shelter of some trees and camp there for the night.

Traveling conditions were favorable for the first two legs of the jour-ney. The weather was fine, the temperature about ten degrees above zero, and a light breeze was blowing from the east. The clouds, high in the sky, gave no sign of rain. The country was hilly with many streams emptying into the Yukon or its tributaries from the west, some of them flowing north into the Fortymile River and others flowing south into the Sixtymile. The hills on either side of the streams were not more than a thousand feet high. Anemones and crocuses in all their springtime glory grew in profusion on the nearby plains and on the slopes of the ravines. Spruce trees, poplars, birches, and pines grew in dense thickets.

Since Summy Skim had been told he would find no shortage of game on the way and that there were even bears in that part of the Klondike, he and Ben had made a point of bringing along their hunting rifles, but they had no opportunity to use them against the plantigrades.

Moreover, the territory was far from deserted. They saw hundreds of miners working their two-hundred-square-foot mountain claims. Some claims, such as the ones on Bonanza Creek, were very productive, yield-ing as much as two hundred dollars per man per day.

In the afternoon the cart reached Fort Reliance, a bustling little village at that time, located on the right bank of the Yukon River where it turns to the northwest.

Like many other forts (Forts Selkirk, Norman, Simpson, Providence, Resolution, Good Hope, McPherson, Chipewyan, Vermillion, and Wrangell in Canadian territory, and Forts Yukon, Hamlin, Kenay, Morton, and Get There in Alaska), Fort Reliance had been built by the Hudson's Bay Company in order to carry on the fur trade and defend itself against Indian tribes. Most of them, including Fort Selkirk and Fort Yukon, were no longer being used for their original purpose. They had become supply depots since the discovery of gold in the Klondike. Raddle had been wise to buy his supplies in Dawson City since the price of foodstuffs and manufactured goods was much higher in Fort Reliance.

In Fort Reliance the two cousins met Maj. James Walsh, the commissioner of the Yukon Territory, who was making a tour of inspection, and mentioned to him the names of some officials in Montreal. In that region, swarming with foreigners, those references were more helpful than they might have been elsewhere. Major Walsh gave them an extremely cordial welcome, for which they thanked him.

He was a man of about fifty, an excellent administrator, and had been stationed in that district for the past two years. The Dominion government had sent him there at the time when thousands of immigrants were flooding into the gold fields in a stream that showed no sign of abating soon.

It was not an easy assignment. Problems of all kinds arose every day concerning the granting of rights to individuals or companies, the assignment of claims, the collection of license fees, and the maintenance of law and order in this region where the Indian tribes reacted to the influx of newcomers with protests and sometimes active resistance.

In addition to these problems caused by the discovery of new placers, there was the controversy about the one hundred and forty-first meridian, which had to resurveyed. It was precisely this matter that had brought Major Walsh to the western part of the Klondike.

According to him, this boundary adjustment was always creating difficulties, even though the solution, being a mathematical one, could not have been more exact. The one hundred and forty-first meridian could only be where it was supposed to be.

"But who brought this question up, Major Walsh?" asked Raddle.

"The Americans," replied the commissioner. "They claim that the survey done when Alaska still belonged to Russia was not sufficiently accurate. According to them, the boundary represented by the one hundred and forty-first degree of longitude should be moved to the east, thereby giving the United States possession of most of the claims on the tributaries flowing into the Yukon from the west."

"Including," added Skim, "number 129, which we have inherited from our uncle, Josias Lacoste."

"Precisely, gentlemen."

"And that is why," said Raddle, "the company that had made us an offer to purchase now refuses to honor that offer as long as the issue remains unsettled."

"I know that, gentlemen," replied the commissioner, "and I can understand your concern."

"But," Skim went on, "do you have any reason to think, Major Walsh, that the work of adjusting the boundary will soon be finished?"

"All I can tell you," answered the major, "is that the ad hoc commission appointed for the task has been working on it for several weeks, and we certainly hope the frontier between the two countries will be definitely settled before winter."

"In your view, major," asked Raddle, "is there any reason to suppose that an error was made and that it will have to be corrected?"

"No, gentlemen, not according to my information. It seems to me like a nasty quarrel that some American companies are trying to pick with Canada."

"In that case," added Skim, "it may be worth our while to extend our stay in the Klondike longer than we had planned."

"Well, gentlemen," said Major Walsh, "I'll do everything in my power to speed up the work of the commission. But I have to admit it's sometimes hampered by ill will on the part of the owners of some claims near the border. Especially number 127."

"That's near ours!" exclaimed Skim.

"Right."

"A Texan named Hunter . . ."

"Precisely. You've heard of him, then?"

"Not only that, commissioner, we actually heard that uncouth individual when he got off the boat in Vancouver."

"I see that you know him, then. He's a violent, brutal man. And his crony Malone, who comes from the same background, is no better, they say."

"This Hunter," asked Raddle, "is he one of the people pushing hardest for a change in the boundary, Major Walsh?"

"He certainly is, Mr. Raddle. In order not to be subject to Canadian authority, he wants his claim to be on American soil. That's why he's stirring up the owners of claims lying between the left bank of the Yukon and the present boundary line. If it's moved to the bank of the river, that entire strip of land would belong to the Union, and a Texan would then be in his own country. But, as I said before, I doubt that the Americans will win their case, and Hunter will have nothing to show for his efforts. However, I'd advise you to have nothing to do with these scoundrels. They're men of the worst sort, and my police have already had run-ins with them."

"Have no fear on that score, commissioner," replied Skim. "We didn't come to the Klondike to wash the muck out of Claim 129 but to sell it. Once we've done that, we'll head back through the Chilkoot and take the train from Vancouver to Montreal."

"Well, gentlemen," was the reply, "there's nothing for me to do now but wish you *bon voyage* on your way to the Fortymile River. If I can be of service to you, you can count on me."

"Thank you, major," said Raddle.

"And if you can speed up the question of the one hundred and forty-first by telegram . . ." added Skim.

"Unfortunately, that doesn't depend on me," said Walsh.

Since the major had to go back to Dawson City, and the two cousins were on their way west, it was time to say good-bye.

The next day, the cart set out again. After crossing the Yukon by ferry, Neluto followed along the left bank almost all the way.

The sky was not as clear as on the previous day, and the northwest wind brought on several violent squalls, but the two cousins were protected by the leather top and did not suffer unduly from the weather.

Since Neluto, quite understandably, wanted to conserve his horse's strength, he could not urge it to move along very quickly. The ground was becoming very rough. The ruts, without the ice that had filled them for the past several months, made for a bumpy ride that was perhaps harder on the vehicle than on the horse.

The region was heavily wooded, with pines, birches, poplars, and aspens. The miners would have enough wood for a long time to come, both for their own personal use and for working the claims. Furthermore, the ground in this part of the district contains coal as well as gold. Four miles downstream from Fort Cudahy, on the Coalcreek, eight miles farther down, on the Cliffecreek, and again five and a half miles farther on, on the Flatcreek, deposits of excellent coal have been discovered, which leave a residue of not more than 5 percent. Coal had already been discovered in the basin of the Five Fingers, and it would serve as an excellent substitute for wood, which the steamships, even medium-powered ones, burn at the rate of one ton per hour. Perhaps, the district will take on a new lease on life if it attracts miners to work in its coal mines after it has given up all its veins of gold.

That evening, at the end of a very tiring second leg of their journey, Neluto and his friends reached Fort Cudahy, on the left bank of the Yukon, where they planned to spend the night in some inn if they found one that suited them better than their tent.

Fort Cudahy was founded in 1892 by the North American Trading and Transportation Company of Chicago, which was trying to take over the business of selling provisions in the Yukon gold fields from the Alaska

Commercial Company. The settlement was built right at the mouth of the Fortymile River, with Fort Constantine to protect it.

It was noticed at the time that the placers in that region were very productive, such as those on the Morse and the Davis, small tributaries of the Fortymile River on American territory,[2] and Miller Creek, a tributary of the Sixtymile. A few of them could be compared in productivity to those on the lower reaches of Bonanza Creek.

It was now six o'clock, and the two cousins set off in search of a place to spend the night. A sort of inn was pointed out to them (but not recommended) by the head of the mounted police detachment, who lived in the village most of the time. His sphere of activity extended over the area between the Alaskan boundary and the left bank of the Yukon.

Ben Raddle and Summy Skim, eager to get a few hours of rest in any kind of a bed, were not about to haggle over the facilities or the price and spent a reasonably comfortable night.

Beyond Fort Cudahy, the Yukon continues to flow northwest until it crosses the one hundred and forty-first meridian as it appeared on maps at that time. The Fortymile River flows in a northeasterly direction, following a winding course through a region of alternating woods and hills. It is about forty-five miles in length, of which twenty are in British territory and twenty-five in American. It crosses the meridian that was disputed at that time as does the Yukon itself. The Sixtymile River and other creeks cross the boundary before flowing into the river from the west.

By leaving early in the morning, Neluto hoped to reach the site of Josias Lacoste's claim during the evening. The horse did not seem to be overly tired after two days of walking and had been given plenty of good, nourishing fodder. If one last effort was needed, it would be forthcoming, and besides, the sturdy animal would rest while the cousins were at Claim 129.

When Ben Raddle and Summy Skim left the inn at three o'clock in the morning, the sun was already well up in the sky. With the arrival of the solstice in about ten days, it would hardly disappear at all over the northern horizon.

The cart followed the right bank of the Fortymile River,[3] which was very crooked and sometimes surrounded by hills separated by deep gorges. The country was far from being deserted. All around, mountain claims and river claims were being worked. At every turn in the stream there were stakes at the entrance to ravines, indicating the limits of the claims and displaying their numbers in large figures. The equipment was not complicated: a few machines operated by hand or water from a diverted creek. Most of the prospectors, either by themselves or with their hired workers, were drawing muck out of shafts dug in the claim and working with a plate or a pan. All that activity would have gone on in silence if it had not been for the noisy demonstrations and the shouts of joy uttered by the miners when they pulled out a valuable nugget.

The first halt lasted from ten o'clock until noon since the horse had been somewhat overtaxed and needed that much time to rest. He was turned loose to graze in a nearby field. After a lunch of canned meat and biscuits, followed by cups of coffee, Raddle and Skim had time to sit and smoke their pipes.

Neluto set out again a little after noon and maintained such a vigorous pace that the cart reached Claim 129 by seven o'clock in the evening.

Its new owners had left Montreal on April 2. On June 11, less than two and a half months later, they had reached their destination.

13

Claim 129

AT THAT POINT WHERE they were standing, the Fortymile River curved gently toward the east. For a distance of about 450 yards along the curve, there was a series of claims, one after the other, marked off by stakes according to the terms of the mining law for the district, which reads as follows:

"Any person over the age of eighteen years, who holds a special hunting, fishing, and mining permit, valid for one year on payment of ten dollars, has the right to occupy a placer claim 250 feet in length along the course of the stream, and not more than 1000 feet in width from one bank to the other, as measured by a horizontal line three feet above the surface of the water."

Claim 129, the property of Josias Lacoste, had been established in accordance with that law. It was the farthest upstream of all the Fortymile River claims in the Klondike region. It was adjacent to the Alaska-Canada boundary and was marked off by two stakes, one of which bore its number and the other the date on which it was registered.

Since it was a river placer claim, it occupied only one bank of the stream, in this case the right bank. The western edge of number 129, as we have seen, was the Alaskan boundary, and if the members of the commission decided to move that boundary eastward, the claim would no longer be in Canadian territory. It was important, therefore, that the process of adjustment should be completed, fixing the location of the one hundred and forty-first meridian once and for all. It was not only Josias Lacoste's claim, but all claims lying adjacent to the boundary between Alaska and the Klondike, that would be affected.

Beyond Claim 129, to the north in the space between moderately high hills, lay a green expanse with stands of birches and aspens on either side. The water of the Fortymile River, which was fairly high at that time, flows quite rapidly through a valley framed by hills on both sides. A great many prospectors' houses, cabins, and huts could be seen, and there were several hundred prospectors at work over a distance of about two miles.

Across the border, in American territory, there were similar buildings. But since the valley broadened out farther upstream, there were in addition to the river claims many mountain claims, which could be longer than 250 feet, but not more than 1000.

As Ben Raddle and Summy Skim were well aware, number 129 was adjacent to number 127, separated from it only by the meridian which both countries were asking to have adjusted. Number 127 was owned by Hunter, the Texan, who had been working it for a year and had just begun his second season. Now that they knew him, the two cousins had no doubt that he had had disagreements with his neighbor, Josias Lacoste. Claim 129, needless to say, had been properly established when Lacoste took possession of it in accordance with the rules then in effect. The discovery had been reported, accepted by the authorities, and registered within the required deadline at the office of the Dominion mines commissioner on payment of an annual fee of fifteen dollars. In addition, a deposit of 10 percent of the gold taken from the claim would be collected and would be forfeited in case of fraud in the output of the placer. And Lacoste had never run afoul of the law stipulating that any claim left idle for seventy-two hours during the summer would revert to the public domain. Mining had stopped only after his death, until his heirs could take possession of their inheritance.

The work begun by Lacoste had gone on for eighteen months and had not been very profitable on the whole. The costs of setting up, hiring workers, transportation, etc., were rather high. Then, too, a sudden flood on the Fortymile River had caused considerable damage and interfered with the work. In short, the owner of Claim 129 had barely covered his expenses when death overtook him.

But in such uncertain ventures, where is the prospector who ever loses hope, who does not continue to believe that he is on the verge of striking a rich vein, of finding a few very valuable nuggets, of panning anywhere from two hundred to eight hundred dollars at a time?

All things considered, Josias Lacoste might have succeeded even with the limited equipment at his disposal. He did not use rockers and confined himself digging shafts fifteen to twenty feet deep into a gold-bearing layer, which might average five or six feet in thickness.

Lacoste's foreman provided complete information about the working of the claim. After the work had stopped and the workers were laid off, he had stayed on to guard it until work should resume, either for the heirs or for another purchaser. The foreman's name was Lorique. He was a French Canadian about forty years of age and very knowledgeable about the prospector's trade. He had worked for several years in the gold fields of California and British Columbia before moving to the Yukon. There was no one in a better position than he to provide Raddle with exact data about the present condition of 129, about the profits already made and still to be made, and about its true value.

First of all, Lorique undertook to find the best possible lodgings for Raddle and Skim, who would likely be spending several days at the Fortymile River. Rather than camping in a tent, they settled for a very modest but clean room in the little house that Josias Lacoste had had built for himself and his foreman. It stood at the entrance to the ravine, within a stand of birches and aspens, and provided adequate shelter for that time of year when the worst weather was over. During the winter, however—that is to say, seven or eight months out of twelve—it was closed, the workers were laid off, and Lacoste and Lorique went back to Dawson City until work could begin again.

At the moment, however, while prospectors and their crews were working day and night on other claims, number 129 had been abandoned since the death of its owner four months earlier. As for food, the foreman would have no difficulty in meeting the needs of his guests. There were companies in that area, as there were everywhere in the Klondike, that sold provisions. Organized in Dawson City, where their supplies were brought up the great river by the Yukon steamers, they served the placers one after the other, making handsome profits in the process, given the prices of food items and the number of workers in the district.

The day after their arrival at the Fortymile River, Lorique took Raddle and Skim to visit the location of the claim. They stopped to look at the shafts, now free of the winter's ice, and at the precious muck lying at the bottom.

Lorique told the how the work had begun after their uncle had completed the formalities, paid his fees, and taken possession of Claim 129.

"Mr. Lacoste," he said, "had about fifty employees. At first he didn't put them to work digging shafts on the riverbank, but just proceeded to skim the surface, all that was required by law, with three months' residence a year at the placer. It wasn't until near the end of the first season that they dug down to a metal-bearing layer."

"And how many shafts did you dig at that time?" asked Raddle.

"Fourteen," replied the foreman. "Each one had an opening of nine square feet, as you can see. They're still in working order, and all you have to do is dip into them to start the operation going again."

"But before you dug those shafts," asked Skim, "what profit did you make by surface skimming? Did you get enough to cover your expenses?"

"Definitely not, sir," replied Lorique, "and the same is true of almost all the deposits if all you do is wash the gravel and gold-bearing pebbles."

"You only work with a plate and a pan, then," observed Raddle.

"That's correct, gentlemen, and a pan didn't often produce three dollars' worth."

"But on Bonanza," exclaimed Skim, "a pan sometimes yields four or five hundred, they say."

138

"You can be sure that's the exception," declared the foreman. "Anyone would be satisfied with an average of twenty dollars. On Claim 129 the average was never more than a little over a dollar, and since a worker's wages might be as high as a dollar and a half an hour . . ."

"Isn't that pitiful!" said Skim.

Raddle had another question. "Why did you wait so long before digging the shafts?"

"Because we had to wait for the water, which was slowly filling them, to freeze. That formed a sort of armor plating that supported the walls and made it possible to dig more holes without causing a cave-in."

"That means, then," said Raddle, "that you had to wait until winter was over before you could use the shafts."

"And that's what we did, Mr. Raddle," said the foreman.

"How deep are they?"

"From ten to fifteen feet;[1] in other words, down to the layer where gold-bearing deposits are usually found."

"And how thick was that layer, as a rule?"

"About six feet."

"And how many panfuls would there be in a cubic foot of the material you took out of the shaft?"

"About ten, and a good worker can wash a hundred a day."

"So your shafts haven't been used yet?" asked Raddle.

"Everything was ready to put them into operation when Mr. Lacoste died, and work had to stop."

While Ben Raddle was interested in this information, it was obvious that his cousin was taking a certain interest in it as well. It was important to know the value of Claim 129 as accurately as possible, and that could only be based on its yield during the first season. He put that question to the foreman.

"We took out about six thousand dollars' worth of gold," was the reply, "and nearly all of it went for expenses. But I'm sure the vein on the Fortymile River is a good one. On the neighboring claims, when the shafts were in operation, the yield was high."

"Well, Lorique," said Raddle, "as you probably know, a company in Chicago has made us an offer to purchase."

"I know that, sir. Its agents came and looked at the placer three months ago."

"Can you tell me, then," Raddle went on, "what Claim 129 might be worth, in your opinion?"

"Based on the results obtained on other claims on the Fortymile River, I'd estimate it at not less than forty thousand dollars."

"And how much was it bought for?"

"Mr. Lacoste paid ten thousand for it."

"Forty thousand dollars," said Summy Skim.

"That's a handsome sum indeed. We'd have no reason to regret coming out here if we got that price. But the company won't honor its offer until the question of the boundary is finalized."

"What does it matter," asked the foreman, "whether 129 is in Canada or Alaska? Its value is the same either way."

"That's absolutely right," declared Ben Raddle, "but it's also true that the offer has been withdrawn, although that hardly explains . . ."

Skim turned to the foreman. "Lorique," he asked, "do you have any reason to think the boundary issue will be settled soon?"

"All I can tell you, gentlemen," said Lorique, "is that the commission has begun its work.[2] As to when it'll finish, I don't think any of the commissioners could say. They're being assisted, by the way, by one of the most highly regarded surveyors in the Klondike, Mr. Ogilvie. He's a very experienced man and has done a precise survey of the district."

"And what do you think the outcome will be?" asked Raddle.

"I think it'll go against the Americans," replied the foreman, "and if the boundary isn't where it should be, then it'll have to be moved to the west."

"In that case," concluded Summy Skim, "129 will still definitely be part of the Dominion."

"That's right," agreed Lorique.

Ben Raddle went on to ask the foreman about the relationship between Josias Lacoste and the owner of 127, the claim next to his.

"You mean the Texan and his friend, Hunter and Malone?"

"Exactly."

"Well, gentlemen, it was a very unpleasant relationship I can tell you. They're two scoundrels, those Americans. They tried to pick a fight with us about everything, and they're quick on the draw with a knife. For the last little while, we always carried a revolver to work. The police had to intervene several times to bring them to their senses."

"That's exactly what the police chief told us when we met him in Fort Cudahy," said Raddle.

"I think he'll have to get involved a few more times," added Lorique. "You know, gentlemen, we'll never have any peace until the day those two rogues are expelled."

"And how will that happen?" asked Summy Skim.

"There's nothing easier. Believe me, gentlemen, it'll happen if the boundary is shifted to the west. Number 127 will then be in Canadian territory, and Hunter will have to abide by all the regulations of the Canadian government."

"I suppose," remarked Skim, "he's one of the people who claim that the one hundred and forty-first meridian should be shifted to the east."

"Naturally," replied the foreman, "and he's stirred up all the Americans along the frontier, both on the Fortymile and the Sixtymile. They've threatened more than once to invade our territory and take over our claims. It's Hunter and Malone who are behind all this. The authorities in Ottawa have sent protests to Washington, but it seems the American government is in no hurry to look at them."

"They're probably waiting until the boundary question is settled," said Raddle.

"That's very likely the case, Mr. Raddle, and until you've sold number 129, you'll have to be on your guard. When Hunter finds out that the new owners have arrived at the Fortymile, who knows what underhanded trick he may try?"

"We've been warned, Lorique," said Skim, "and we know how to give those rogues what's coming to them."

After going up to the northern edge of the placer, the two cousins and the foreman walked through it and went back down to the right bank of the river. There they stopped near the stake that marked the division between the two claims. While number 129 was deserted, work on 127 was in full swing. Hunter's men were working at the shafts that had been dug upstream, and the muck, after it was washed, was carried away by rivulets and disappeared in the current of the Fortymile River. There were also a few boats heading downstream, having paid the duty owing at the border, where the customs service maintained a strict surveillance.

Raddle and Skim tried unsuccessfully to spot Hunter and Malone among the workers on Claim 127. They were not to be seen, and Lorique thought they must have left after spending a few days at the placer and headed west to a part of Alaska where new gold fields had been reported.

After their visit to the claim, the two cousins and the foreman went back to the house, where lunch was waiting for them. They did not have to concern themselves about Neluto. The cart was all the Indian needed, and the horse could be sure it would be well looked after.

After lunch, Skim asked Raddle what his plans were, and whether he intended to stay any longer at their claim.

"You're familiar with it now," he added. "You know what condition it's in and what it's worth. I don't suppose you can learn any more about it by staying here."

"I don't agree with you there," was the reply. "I have to have a long talk with the foreman and go over Uncle Josias's accounts. I don't think another forty-eight hours would be too long to stay on our placer."

"All right, forty-eight hours. But while you're checking the accounts, I assume I have permission to do some hunting in the vicinity."

"Yes, as long as you don't get lost or run into some kind of danger."

"Don't worry, Ben. I'll take good old Neluto along. He knows the country."

"Do what you like, but as I said, I think it's essential to spend a few days here."

Skim smiled. "Well, well," he said. "So the forty-eight hours you were talking about have already turned into a few days."

"Well, of course," replied Raddle. "If only I had been able to see the men at work and watch them wash a few panfuls."

"Easy now, Ben," exclaimed Skim. "We didn't come to Claim 129 as prospectors, but only to estimate how much it's worth."

"Of course, Summy, of course. Don't forget, though, that we can't complete the sale of our claim right now. The commission of adjustment has to finish its work, and the surveyor has to make his report. In the meantime, I don't see why Lorique shouldn't get the work going again."

"So now," said Skim, "we're condemned to sit around here until that damned meridian is put in its proper place."

"Where else would we spend the time, Summy?"

"In Dawson City, Ben."

"Would we be any better off there?"

Summy Skim did not answer. He felt sure the engineer was getting the upper hand over him, that his cousin was itching to set his hand to the plough (or rather to the muck). Once he acquired a taste for it, might he not be tempted to continue Uncle Josias's work?

"Oh no," he said to himself. "I'll find a way to stop him, whether he likes it or not."

He picked up his rifle, called Neluto, and the two of them headed north, up the ravine.

Summy Skim had guessed right. Now that he had the opportunity, Raddle had decided to study the workings of a placer, and especially a placer that had come into his possession. Certainly, when he left Montreal, the engineer's only thought was to sell Claim 129 after getting an appraisal of its value. But now unforeseen circumstances were forcing him to stay longer at the Fortymile, perhaps for several weeks. How could he resist the temptation to use the shafts that were already prepared and see what they might produce? Then, too, had Uncle Josias done everything necessary to get the best results, or had he just followed the old system of panning, which was obviously too rudimentary? But Raddle was an engineer. Would he not find a quicker and more productive method? And if there were tens of thousands, or tens of millions, of dollars waiting to be extracted from under the ground that belonged to him, did it make sense to hand it over to that company for a ridiculously low price?

Those ideas were swirling around in Ben Raddle's mind. It did not bother him that he had to wait because of the boundary issue and because the North American Trading and Transportation Company had withdrawn its offer. He would find a way to make Summy wait patiently, too. He even said to himself that his cousin might eventually acquire a taste for it.

When he had immersed himself in Uncle Josias's accounts and when the foreman had given him all the documents that might provide any information, he asked him, "If you had to recruit a crew now, Lorique, would it still be possible?"

"I'm sure it would, Mr. Raddle. There are thousands of immigrants in the district looking for work and not finding it. They come here to the claims on the Fortymile every day. In fact, considering their numbers, I think they might not be able to demand very high wages."

"You'd only need about fifty miners?"

"About fifty. Mr. Lacoste never hired more than that."

"And how long would it take you to get such a crew together?"

"Twenty-four hours," replied the foreman. He paused a moment and added, "Were you thinking of prospecting yourself, Mr. Raddle?"

"Perhaps, until we sell number 129 for a fair price."

"That would definitely give you a better idea of its value and put you in a stronger position to negotiate with the companies that might offer to buy it from you."

"Besides," said Raddle, "what is there to do here until the boundary issue is settled one way or another?"

"That's true," said the foreman. "After all, number 129 is worth whatever it's worth, whether it's American or Canadian. I've always believed that the claims on the tributaries to the west of the Yukon River are just as good as the ones on the right bank. You know, Mr. Raddle, you can make a fortune just as quickly on the Sixtymile or the Fortymile as on Bonanza or Eldorado."

"I'll remember that, Lorique," replied Raddle, well satisfied with the answers he had received since they were exactly what he had hoped to hear.

Realizing, perhaps, that one last possibility might still occur to the engineer, Lorique added, "Yes, Mr. Raddle, whatever the adjustment commission may decide, Claim 129 will still be what it is now. You have nothing to worry about, I assure you. Your claim is Canadian, as Canadian as it can be, and Canadian it will remain."

"I hope so," replied Raddle. "I'll consult my cousin Skim and suggest to him that we resume the work our uncle began."

When Ben Raddle said he would "consult" his cousin, he meant that he would inform him of his plans without giving him too much opportunity to discuss them. And so, when Summy Skim came back from hunting with Neluto, carrying a string of partridges and snipes, his cousin simply said to him, "I've been thinking about this, Summy, and since we're stuck here for a few months, the best thing to do is to start working on number 129 again."

"You mean we should become prospectors!" exclaimed Skim.

"Yes, until we can sell our claim."

14

Working the Claim

As it turned out, Summy Skim's longstanding fears were not unfounded. While waiting for an opportunity to sell number 129, Ben Raddle was going to reactivate it, and who could tell whether he would ever agree to dispose of it? Indeed, if the operation proved to be only slightly profitable, would there be any cause for regret?

Skim, in his wisdom, kept saying to himself, "This was bound to happen, and I feel like cursing Uncle Josias! It's all his fault that we've become miners, or gold panners, or prospectors, or whatever name you want to attach to those gold seekers that I, for one, prefer to call trouble seekers. Yes, I should've put my foot down right at the start of this adventure. If I'd refused to leave Montreal and come with Ben to this frightful country, he probably wouldn't have come either, and we wouldn't find ourselves involved in this deplorable business. And even if there were millions in the muck of number 129, isn't it unbearable to say to yourself that you're going to be a mucker by trade? Well, once the hand gets caught in the machinery, the whole body follows, and next winter will be here before we can start back to Montreal. A winter in the Klondike at fifty below, where you need nice thermometers that register the temperature as far below zero as other ones do above zero! What a prospect! Ah, Uncle Josias, Uncle Josias, what a lot of grief you've caused your nephews!"

This was Summy Skim's line of reasoning. But he was a philosophical type after all and could take things as they came. As for regretting that he had not opposed this trip to the Klondike, that was all well and good, but deep down he knew very well he would not have been able to stop Ben from leaving, even by refusing to go with him, and that in the end he would have gone along, too.

The season for the Yukon gold fields was only beginning with this first week of June. It was not more than two weeks since the ground had thawed and the ice had gone out of the creeks, making it possible for work to begin. The earth, hardened by the extreme cold, still offered some resistance to the pick, but at least a start could be made. It was fairly easy now to reach the vein through the shafts without having to worry that their walls, now frozen by the winter, might collapse. They would only have to be joined together by tunnels in order for the work to be carried out as usual.

It was obvious, too, that in the absence of more sophisticated equipment—machines that he could have used to good advantage—Raddle would be reduced to using a dish or a plate, what the miners call a "pan." Still, these rudimentary devices would be adequate for washing out the muck in the nearby section of the Fortymile River. It is the quartz claims, not the river claims, that have to be worked mechanically; and machines equipped with a pestle for crushing quartz, like the ones used in other mining areas of Canada and British Columbia, were already being set up on the Klondike gold fields.

Raddle could not have found a more valuable assistant than the foreman Lorique. He was very experienced, very knowledgeable about this kind of work, and could be left to work on his own since he had been in charge of similar work in British Columbia. He was also quite capable of adopting any improvements that the engineer might suggest.

It should be noted that if Claim 129 remained unoccupied for too long, the authorities would issue a complaint. Greedy for the taxes they levied on the placers' output, they would revoke the licenses of the ones where work stopped even for a relatively short period.

The first item on the foreman's agenda was to hire a crew. This was more difficult than he had expected. Many gold deposits had been reported in the vicinity of the Domes, and miners had rushed there in great numbers, for manpower promised to command a high price. Of course, caravans were constantly arriving in Dawson City since it was easier to cross the lakes and sail down the Yukon during the warm season. But workers were in demand everywhere at a time when machines were not generally in use.

Lorique did manage to hire about thirty immigrants, however, instead of the fifty that Josias Lacoste had employed, but only by offering them very high wages, over a dollar an hour.

That was the going rate at the time in the Bonanza region. Many workers earned fifteen or sixteen dollars a day. How many would become rich if only they did not spend their money as freely as they earned it!

Not surprisingly, wages continued to rise. On the Skookum and other gold deposits, a worker could pan as much as a hundred dollars an hour. In fact, however, they were paid only a hundredth part of that.

The equipment on Claim 129 was, as we have seen, very rudimentary, consisting only of what the prospectors used when gold was first discovered—a plate and a dish. No doubt Josias Lacoste intended to upgrade this primitive equipment, and now his nephew tried to do what he had left undone.

Thanks to the foreman, and by paying a high price, two rockers were added to 129's equipment.

A rocker is simply a box, three feet long by two feet wide, a kind of coffin mounted on a see-saw. Inside it is a screen, fitted with a piece of woolen cloth, which holds the gold dust and allows the water and sand to escape. A quantity of mercury is deposited at the lower end of this apparatus, which can be agitated regularly by using the see-saw. The mercury forms an amalgam with the gold dust if it is too fine to be picked up by hand.

Raddle would have preferred to set up a sluice rather than a rocker, and since he had not been able to buy one, he considered building one. A sluice is a wooden trough with transverse grooves every six inches. When a stream of liquid muck is poured into it, the earth and gravel are carried off, while the heavier gold is held back by the grooves.

These two procedures are both fairly effective and bring good results, but they need a pump to raise water to the upper end of the sluice or rocker. That is the most costly part of the apparatus. On mountain claims it is sometimes possible to use natural waterfalls, but on river claims, mechanical means must be used, involving a rather large expenditure.

Work on Claim 129 started up again under improved conditions. Summy Skim, with his philosophical nature, never wearied of observing the ardor and passion with which Raddle attacked this work.

"Ben has definitely not escaped the current epidemic," he said to himself. "I hope to God I don't become infected too! What a disease this gold fever is! It isn't a sporadic illness that can be cured with quinine of some sort. No one recovers from it, I see, even after making a fortune, and having enough gold is not sufficient. No! You have to have too much, and perhaps too much is still not enough."

In any case, the owners of Claim 129, Uncle Josias's heirs, were not at the point of having too much yet—far from it. While the deposit may have been rich, as the foreman said, it was certainly not generous in giving up its riches. They had problems reaching the pay streak running through the ground from east to west along the course of the Fortymile River. Raddle was forced to conclude that the shafts were not deep enough, and that further drilling would be necessary. This was heavy work because by now the temperature was no longer low enough to harden the walls of the shafts as would have been the case in sub-zero weather.

But had it really been wise to embark on this costly undertaking? Should they not leave the work for the companies or individuals who might buy the claim? Should Ben Raddle not stick to the pan and the rocker? Was it wise to gamble on expenditures that were not likely to increase the value of the claim?

Indeed, each pan produced barely a quarter of a dollar. With the wages they were paying their employees, profit was minimal. Were the foreman's predictions based on solid evidence? That was the question.

The weather was generally fine during the month of June. There were several thunderstorms, some of them very violent, but they soon passed over, and work resumed all along the Fortymile River.

It was now July, and there were barely two months of summer left. The sun set at half past ten and reappeared over the horizon before one o'clock. And even between sunset and sunrise there was a kind of twilight in which the circumpolar constellations were barely visible.[1] With a second team to relieve the first, the prospectors could have kept on working as was being done in the placers on the other side of the Alaskan boundary, where the Americans were working at an incredible pace.

Given Ben Raddle's temperament, it is not surprising that he wanted to be directly involved in the work. He did not consider it beneath him, even while he was supervising his employees, to pick up a pan and join them in washing the muck of Claim 129. He was also in charge of operating the rockers, and Lorique worked with him as if it had been his own claim.

"What about it, Summy?" he kept saying to his cousin. "Aren't you going to give it a try?"

The answer was always the same. "No, I don't think I'm cut out for that."

"It isn't hard, though. You shake the pan, you wash out the gravel, and the bits of gold are left at the bottom."

"No, Ben, not even if you paid me two dollars an hour."

"I'm sure you'd be good at it."

One day Ben Raddle handed him a pan and said, "Try it, just to humor me."

"All right, Ben. Just to please you."

Skim dutifully took the pan, filled it with a bit of the earth that had just been taken out of one of the shafts, stirred it up into a liquid mixture, and poured it off little by little. If it had contained a few bits of gold, they would have stayed at the bottom of the pan.

There was not the slightest trace of the metal that Summy was always cursing.

"You see," he said, "not even enough to buy me a pipeful of tobacco."

Raddle had no intention of giving up. "Perhaps," he suggested, "you'll have better luck some other time."

"Anyway," replied Skim, "hunting works better for me. I can make up for it with game."

He called Neluto, picked up his gun, and was gone for the whole afternoon.

He seldom came home empty-handed, not only because of his skill as a hunter, but also because there was an abundance of furred and feathered game in the neighboring plains and gorges. Moose and caribou were frequently seen in the woods, heading north to where the Yukon River curves around to the west. The swamps on either side of the Fortymile River were teeming with snipe, snow ptarmigan, and ducks. Skim made the best of his prolonged stay, although he yearned for the game-filled countryside of Green Valley.

It is worth noting that panning on Claim 129 brought better results during the first half of July. The foreman had finally struck the real pay streak, which became richer as it approached the Alaskan boundary. Pans and rockers were producing a wealth of gold dust. Although no nuggets of any great value had been found, the output for those two weeks was at least $3,400, enough to justify Lorique's assertions and fuel Ben Raddle's ambition.

On Claim 127, as the prospectors worked their way eastward, the quality also continued to improve. No doubt it was the same vein, running along the right bank of the Fortymile River,[2] that went through the American claim upstream and the Canadian one farther down.

This meant that Hunter and Malone's crew and Raddle and Skim's crew were heading toward each other. The day was not far off when they would meet on the disputed border between the two countries.

The Texans' employees—about thirty men—were all Americans. It would have been difficult to assemble a more disreputable band of suspicious-looking scoundrels and savages, men who would stop at nothing. They were violent, brutal, and quarrelsome, fitting companions for the Texans whose reputations in the Klondike region were so unsavory. Almost all of them had worked on 127 the previous season since Hunter and Malone had bought their claim at the time of the first discoveries after the sale of Alaska by the Russians.[3]

There was a certain difference between the Americans and Canadians working on the gold fields. The Canadians were generally more easygoing, calmer, and more disciplined, and the syndicates tended to prefer them. A small number of them worked for American companies, which usually sought out their fellow Americans, despite their unruliness, their rebelliousness, their tendency to get carried away in almost daily scuffles, when they were overexcited by strong drink (especially cocktails, which wreak havoc in the gold fields). Hardly a day went by without the police having to intervene on one claim or another. Knives were drawn and revolvers fired. Sometimes a man would be killed, and the wounded would have to be taken to the clinic in Dawson City, already overcrowded with a constant stream of patients suffering from epidemic diseases.

No doubt it would have seemed more logical to take the Americans to Sitka since it is the capital of Alaska. But Sitka is very far from the Klondike. They would have had to go back over the long and difficult route through the lake region and over the Chilkoot Pass, and that was out of the question. And so, both to get the treatment they needed and to enjoy the many pleasures that everyone was so eager for, they all poured into Dawson City.

During the third week of July mining continued to be very profitable, although neither Raddle nor Lorique nor their men ever found one of those nuggets that had made the fortune of Bonanza and Eldorado. But by now profits were considerably higher than expenses, and it was quite possible that they might finish the season twenty thousand dollars to the good. That would justify maintaining a high price for 129, whenever purchasers might appear on the scene.

In any case, Summy Skim had no serious reason to complain, and in fact he would not have complained if only he and Raddle had been able to leave the Klondike before the cold weather set in. But—and this is what irritated him beyond measure—that did not depend solely on their wishes. They could not leave the region until they had sold Claim 129, and that could not be done until the boundary question was settled. Days and weeks went by, and the members of the commission did not seem to be getting any closer to a conclusion on which they could all agree.

Skim remarked one day, logically enough, "I don't see, Ben, why we should have to stay here until the position of that damned hundred and forty-first meridian is settled."

"Because," replied Raddle, "we won't be able to negotiate with the North American Trading and Transportation Company, or any other company, until the adjustment is completed."

"All right, Ben, but that can be done by mail, or through an agent, in Mr. Snubbin's office in Montreal just as well as in the Front Street offices in Dawson City."

"But not under as favorable conditions."

"Why not, since we know now what our claim is worth?"

"In a month or six weeks, we'll have an ever better idea," said the engineer, "and then they won't be offering us forty thousand dollars for 129, but eighty or a hundred thousand."[4]

"And what will we do with all that money?" asked Skim.

"We'll make good use of it, never fear," declared Raddle. "Don't you see that the vein gets richer as it moves west?"

"Right! And if it keeps on going it will eventually meet the vein on 127," Skim pointed out, "and when our men come into contact with that horrible Hunter's crew, I don't know what will happen."

Indeed, there was reason to fear that a fight might break out between the two crews, who were getting closer and closer every day to the boundary between the two placers. Insults had been exchanged and threats of violence were heard. Lorique had already had a run-in with the American foreman, a brutal and uncouth kind of strongman; and who could tell whether those insults might not escalate to acts of violence when Hunter and Malone came back to supervise the work? The position of the stake marking the division between the two claims would be disputed. More than once, stones had been thrown from one claim to the other (but not without first making sure that they did not contain any bits of gold).

Under the circumstances, Lorique definitely did everything in his power, with Raddle's help, to keep his men in line. The American fore-man, on the other hand, was always egging his crew on. He obviously never missed an opportunity to pick a quarrel with Lorique. Besides, he was less fortunate in his work, since Claim 127 was not as rich as 129. It appeared, in fact, that the vein Lorique was prospecting tended to swing toward the north, away from the left bank of the Fortymile, instead of extending through the bordering claim.

In short, the two crews were now no more than twenty-five yards apart, and within two or three weeks they would meet on the boundary.

Summy Skim's predictions and fears of a conflict were not far off the mark.

On July 27, as it happened, an incident occurred that aggravated the situation, an incident that could lead to unfortunate complications.

Hunter and Malone had just returned to 127.

15

The Night of August 5–6

THE DOMINION OF CANADA is not the only territory, of course, where gold-bearing regions are to be found. There are some across the immense expanse of North America lying between the Atlantic and the Pacific, and many deposits will probably soon be discovered. The area between the Kootenay in southern British Columbia and the Arctic Ocean is said to be rich in deposits of gold and other metals. Nature has given generously of her mineral treasures to this region but has deprived it of agricultural wealth.

The placers in Alaska are located mainly in the vast curve described by the Yukon River as it flows north from the Klondike to Fort Yukon on the Arctic Circle and then back down to its estuary near St. Michael.

One of these regions is located near Circle City, a village on the left bank of the great river, 230 miles downstream from Dawson City. Birch Creek, which rises nearby, flows into the river at Fort Yukon.

At the end of the previous season it had been rumored that the gold deposits of Circle City were as rich as those on Bonanza Creek. That was enough to send miners rushing there in droves.

After arriving at Dawson City, Hunter and Malone got work going again on 127, then took one of the Yukon steamboats to Circle City. They visited the area around Birch Creek and presumably did not see fit to spend the whole season there, since they had just come back to 127.

It was obvious that the Texans' journey had been fruitless since they

had returned to the Fortymile River and were now making preparations to stay there for the rest of the season. If they had found a rich harvest of nuggets and gold dust in the Birch Creek deposits, they would
have hurried on to Dawson City, where the gaming houses and casinos
offered them so many opportunities to squander their earnings. That
was the general custom, and they had no reason not to follow it. They
would have done the same if 127 had shown a profit after work started
there again.

That was what Lorique told Ben Raddle and Summy Skim when he
informed them that the two Texans had arrived.

"With Hunter here," he added, "there's no way we'll have peace on
the border claims, especially the ones on the Fortymile."

"All right," replied Skim, "we'll be on our guard."

"That would be wise, gentlemen," said the foreman, "and I'll advise
our men to stay well away from those hooligans."

"Will the police be informed that the two Texans are back?" asked
Raddle.

"They must know by now," replied Lorique, "and we'll also send a
message to Fort Cudahy to ward off any attack."

"That's all very well," declared Skim, "but I still believe, with your
permission, that there isn't too much to fear from that individual. If he
should feel like resorting to his usual violence against us, he'll find me
ready for him."

"That's all very well, too," said Raddle, "but I have no intention of letting you have anything to do with that man."

"He and I have an old account to settle, Ben, and I insist on paying . . ."

"You have nothing to pay," objected Raddle, who wanted at all costs
to keep his cousin from getting involved in any dangerous affair. "You
stuck up for the two nuns in Vancouver, which was only natural. You
put Hunter in his place, and I would have done the same. But here,
when the crew of one claim is threatened by the crew of another, that's a
matter for the police."

"And what if the police aren't there?" countered Summy, who was not
about to yield a point.

"If they aren't there, Mr. Skim," said the foreman, "we'll defend ourselves. We won't be pushed around by those Texans."

"But after all," concluded Raddle, "we didn't come here to get rid of the thugs infesting the Fortymile, but to . . ."

"To sell our claim," interrupted Skim, who always kept coming back to his own agenda and was now starting to get a little excited. "Tell me, Lorique, isn't there some way of finding out what the boundary commission is doing, whether they're getting on with the job of adjusting the boundary, and when it will be finished?"

"I'll try to find out, Mr. Skim," replied the foreman.

"And where are those devils of commissioners right now?"

"According to the latest word from Dawson City, they've gone south."

"Then I'll go and get them moving," exclaimed Skim.

"Take my advice, Summy, and do nothing of the sort," replied Raddle, trying to calm his cousin. "Just be patient."

"Besides, it would be quite a long trip," Lorique pointed out, "because Mr. Ogilvie and the commissioners have gone down to the foot of Mount St. Elias, and unless you go back through Dyea you would have to make your way through a long stretch of wilderness."

"Damn this country!" Skim shouted.

"Come on, Summy," said Raddle, clapping him on the shoulder. "You need to calm down. Why don't you go hunting? Take Neluto with you. There's nothing he'd like better. Bring us back some choice game for this evening. Meanwhile, we'll go shake our rockers. Let's hope it will bring good results."

"Well," added the foreman, "why shouldn't we find what Colonel Harvey found at Cripple Creek in October 1897?"[1]

"And just what did your colonel find?" asked Summy Skim in a somewhat scornful tone of voice.

"He found on his claim, only seven feet down, a lump of gold worth one hundred thousand dollars."

"Bah!" said Skim, "a measly hundred thousand dollars."

"Go get your gun, Summy," said Raddle. "Spend the rest of the day hunting. And watch out for the bears!"

Since Skim realized he had nothing better to do, he and Neluto went back up the ravine. Fifteen minutes later their first shots rang out.

As for Ben Raddle, he went back to work, after first ordering his men not to react to any provocations that might come their way from Claim 127.

Nothing happened that day to set off a conflict between the crews of the two claims.

In the absence of Summy Skim, who might not have been able to hold himself back, Raddle had an opportunity to observe Hunter and Malone. The little house where the Texans lived was identical to Lorique's cottage at the bottom of the opposite slope. For the time being, until it was finalized, the boundary line followed the thalweg of the ravine, running north and south. From his room, Raddle could watch Hunter and Malone as they were visiting Claim 127, where their men were working under the direction of an American foreman.

They walked obliquely across the claim, going down the path between the shafts. A rocker and a sluice were in operation at the time, and the clicking of the see-saws together with the roar of the water rushing down toward the stream made a deafening noise.

Raddle showed no desire to pay any attention to what was happening on 127. He made no attempt to conceal himself but stood leaning on the sill of the open window on the ground floor of the cottage.

Hunter and Malone walked up to the claim marker and stopped, talking in an animated tone. They apparently showed little consideration for their men, for a number of them were very harshly reprimanded, sometimes by the foreman himself.

After looking toward the stream and studying the claims on the right bank, indicated by even numbers,[2] they took a few steps toward the ravine. They were obviously in the foulest of moods, no doubt because the output of 127 had been very mediocre since the beginning of the season, barely covering expenses. And how much more irritated they would be, knowing that the Lacoste claim had shown fairly substantial profits over the previous few weeks.

Hunter and Malone kept walking up toward the ravine and stopped when they were abreast of Lorique's cottage. From there they could see Raddle leaning on the window sill, apparently paying no attention to them. But Raddle clearly saw that they were pointing at him and that their violent gestures and angry voices were an attempt to provoke him.

Wisely, he paid no attention, and after the Texans had left, he went back to operating the rocker with Lorique.

"You saw them, Mr. Raddle," said the foreman.

"Yes, Lorique, but their provocations aren't going to get a rise out of me."

"Mr. Skim doesn't seem to be so patient."

"He'll really have to calm down," declared Raddle. "We mustn't even let on that we know those people."

The next few days went by without incident. Skim—at his cousin's urging—went off hunting every morning with the Indian and did not return until late in the afternoon. There were no encounters with Hunter. It was becoming more and more difficult, however, to prevent the American and Canadian workers from coming into contact with each other. Their work on the vein brought them closer every day to the stake marking the line between the two claims. The time was certainly not far off when, to use the foreman's expression, they would confront each other "pick to pick." The slightest difference of opinion could give rise to a dispute, the dispute to a quarrel, and the quarrel to a fight, which could soon degenerate into a battle. When these men were thrown against one another, who could stop them? Would Hunter and Malone not try to stir up trouble on the claims of all their fellow Americans against the Canadian claims adjacent to the boundary? With scoundrels like them, anything could happen. The police from Fort Cudahy and Dawson City would be powerless to restore order.

For forty-eight hours the Texans were nowhere to be seen. Perhaps they had gone to look over the placers on the Alaskan part of the Fortymile River, with a view to making a move.

While they were away a few altercations broke out between the workers. There was even one incident involving Lorique and the foreman of 127. The miners may even have been on the point of joining in to help their bosses, but matters went no further than that.

Since the weather seemed very unsettled, with a strong north wind, Skim had not gone hunting, but Raddle had managed to keep him from becoming involved, which he probably could not have done if Hunter and Malone had been there.

For three more days it was impossible for Skim to indulge in his favorite pastime. The rain came down, sometimes in torrents, and they had to take shelter in the cottage. It became very difficult to pan gravel in those conditions. The shafts filled to the brim, and the overflow spilled onto the surface of the claim, transforming it into a thick muck in which they sank up to their knees.

As a result, work had to be stopped on both sides and could not be resumed until the afternoon of August 3. After a rainy morning, the southeast wind brought a clear sky. But there was a danger that it might also bring thunderstorms, which are often very severe at that time of year and sometimes have disastrous consequences.

The Texans had come back to 127 the previous day and did not leave their foreman's house until the next day.

Summy Skim had taken advantage of the fine weather to go hunting again. A few grizzly bears had been reported farther down the Fortymile River, and there was nothing he wanted more than to encounter one of those fearsome plantigrades. It would not be the first time for him, however, since he had already bagged a few of them in the forests of Green Valley.[3]

"I'd still rather see him fighting with a bear," said Raddle to himself, "than with Hunter."

On August 4 Lorique made a lucky strike with his pick. While digging a hole on the edge of the claim, almost at the end of the vein, he discovered a nugget that could not have been worth less than four hundred dollars.

The foreman could not contain himself for joy, and shouted at the top of his voice, "Come here! Look at this!"

His workers came running, with Raddle close behind.

The nugget, the size of a walnut, was set, so to speak, in a piece of quartz.

The people on 127 quickly realized what the shouting was all about. There was an outburst of jealous anger, justified perhaps, because for some time now the men had not been able to find a vein and their work was becoming more and more onerous.

Then a voice was heard—Hunter's voice—repeating, "So those are only for the prairie dogs from the Far West!"

That was his uncouth way of referring to the Canadians.

Ben Raddle heard the insult. He turned white, the blood rushed to his head, and he was about to leap forward when Lorique grabbed him by the arm and held him back. Shrugging his shoulders scornfully, he turned his back.

"Hey, Mr. Montreal," said Hunter, "that's you I'm talking about."

"You're an insolent fellow," replied Raddle. "I don't want to have anything to do with your kind."

"You will, though," retorted the Texan. "I don't know what's stopping me from . . ."

He was about to cross the line marked by the stake and attack Raddle, but Malone stopped him. The workers on the placers were ready to charge at each other, and it would have been impossible to come between them.

Skim returned in the evening, delighted to have shot a bear (at some personal risk) and described his hunting exploit in detail. Raddle did not want to tell him about the day's incident, and after supper they both went back to their room, where Skim slept the refreshing sleep of a hunter.

Was there any reason to fear that the affair might have consequences? Would Hunter and Malone, more worked up than ever, try to pick a fight with Raddle? They would probably egg on the crew of 127 against the crew of 129 since their picks would meet the following day on the boundary between the two claims.

On that very day, much to his cousin's annoyance, Summy Skim did not go hunting. The weather was overcast. Heavy clouds were rising in the southeast. There would be a thunderstorm before the day was out, and it was better not to be caught far from home.

The entire morning was taken up with panning the muck taken from the shafts already in operation, while a team under Lorique's direction dug another one on the border line, almost at the foot of the stake, with its little wooden sign marked "127" on one side and "129" on the other.

Hunter's workers were along the border at that time, but no complications arose during the morning. The Americans made a few offensive remarks, to which the Canadians retorted sharply. But matters did not go beyond words and gestures, and the foremen did not have to intervene.

Unfortunately, things did not go so well when work was resumed in the afternoon. By an unusual stroke of bad luck, Hunter and Malone were walking back and forth on their placer, and Summy Skim was doing the same on his when Ben Raddle joined him. He was wondering whether the Texans were going to repeat their threats of the day before.

"Well, well," said Skim to his cousin, "so those two thugs are back. I didn't see them before. Did you, Ben?"

"Yes, I saw them yesterday," said Raddle evasively. "But do as I do and ignore them."

"But Ben, I don't like the way they're looking at us."

"Summy, you're not to pay any attention to them."

The Texans had come a little closer, but although they cast insulting glances at the two cousins, they did not utter any of their usual invectives.

Skim wisely decided to pay no attention to them, except to answer them if the occasion arose.

Meanwhile, the two crews of workers continued working at the line between the claims, digging into the earth, collecting the muck and carrying it to the rockers and sluices. They were no more than six feet apart, and their picks, intentionally or not, were in danger of hitting each other at any moment. Sometimes a few stones rolled across the dividing line.

So far, no one had paid any heed to this, but about five o'clock one of Lorique's men pried a stone out of the ground with his pick, and it landed at the feet of the American foreman.

It was a piece of quartz weighing four or five pounds, and appeared to be a kind that contains bits of gold. There might possibly have been a valuable nugget in it.

When Lorique asked for it back—quite legitimately—his claim met with a blunt refusal.

Until now there had only been an exchange of words, but Lorique, intending to get back what belonged to him, went past the stake.

Three or four Americans jumped on him to stop him, and several Canadians rushed to help him.

A fight broke out amid the commotion and shouting that set the neighboring claims buzzing as well. It threatened to develop into a full-scale battle between Americans and Canadians.

Meanwhile, Lorique had managed to get away from the men who were holding him and ran to the spot where the stone had stopped rolling.

Just at that moment, he found himself face to face with Hunter, who gave him a powerful shove, knocking him to the ground.

On witnessing this violent scene, Summy Skim rushed to the assistance of the foreman, who was being held down by the Texan.

Raddle quickly followed him and stopped Malone, who was coming to help his friend.

It was now a complete donnybrook. Picks and mattocks were being used as weapons—dangerous weapons in those powerful hands—and there would soon have been bloodshed, injuries, perhaps even deaths if the militia, on patrol in that part of the Fortymile River, had not appeared on the scene.

Thanks to those fifty men and their competent commander, the trouble was brought under control in a matter of minutes.

Ben Raddle, Summy Skim, and the two Texans were now facing each other. Hunter was speechless with anger, and Raddle was the first to speak.

"What gives you the right," he said, "to stop us from recovering our own property?"

"Your property?" bellowed Hunter in an insultingly familiar way. "Your property was on my land, and it belongs to me."

"You villain!" shouted Skim, hurrying to the scene and almost running into Hunter.

"Ah!" said the Texan. "It's the champion of ladies in distress."

"Ladies whom you were bullying, you hooligan. If they'd been men, you'd have been the biggest coward in the world."

"Coward, you say?"

Hunter was about to jump on Skim when Malone stopped him.

Summy was beside himself.

"Yes," he said, "and too cowardly to back up his insults with action."

"All right, you'll see," shouted Hunter. "I'll meet you tomorrow."

"Tomorrow morning," retorted Skim.

"Tomorrow," said Hunter.

Then the miners went back to their placers. Lorique was unable to take the piece of quartz back with him, because one of the Americans, rather than give it up, threw it into the waters of the Fortymile River.

Raddle and Skim returned home, and Ben did his best to persuade Summy not to pursue the matter any further.

"Summy," he kept saying, "you simply can't fight with that ruffian."

"Yes I will, Ben."

"No, Summy, no!"

"I'll do it, I tell you, and if I put a bullet in his head, that will the best hunting I've ever done, hunting a stinking beast."

Raddle realized that, no matter what he said, he would not be able to prevent the duel from taking place.

But a totally unexpected disaster was about to prevent this affair from reaching its conclusion, at least for the time being.

The weather had been getting more and more overcast throughout the day. By five o'clock the air, charged with electricity, was riddled with lightning flashes, and thunder rumbled in the southeast. Although the sun was still above the horizon, the gathering clouds made the darkness deeper.

During the afternoon, disquieting signs had been noticed on various claims along the Fortymile River. Dull tremors were running through the ground, accompanied by prolonged rumblings. Foam appeared on the river in places, and jets of sulfuric gas escaped from the shafts. There were definitely subterranean forces at work.

About half past ten, as Skim, Raddle, and the foreman were about to go to bed, they felt a series of violent shocks.

"An earthquake!" shouted Lorique.

Hardly had he spoken those words when the building suddenly overturned as if its base had abruptly given way.

With great difficulty the two cousins and the foreman managed to extricate themselves from the wreckage. Fortunately, they were not hurt.

But outside, what a sight met their eyes by the light of the fiery sky! The entire claim had disappeared under a torrential flood. Part of the stream had overflowed and was cutting a new channel for itself through the gold-bearing area.

Cries of despair and pain were heard on all sides. The miners, taken by surprise in their cabins on both sides of the river, were trying to escape the flood, which was gaining on them. It was so violent that the underground convulsions must have been terrible. Nearby trees, torn up by the roots or broken off, were being swept along on the Fortymile River and its new channel with the speed of ice going out in the spring.

"Run! Run!" cried Lorique, who had now been joined by Neluto, "or we'll be carried away by the flood."

Indeed, the water was already rising to the spot where the cottage, destroyed by the earthquake, was lying. They could still feel the ground rising and falling under their feet as if it were caught in the swell of the ocean.

Just then the trunk of a birch tree, snapped off above the roots, was driven by the current into the wreckage. Unfortunately, it struck Ben

Raddle and knocked him over. He would have been lost in the raging flood if Skim and Lorique had not managed to grab him.

Raddle could not walk. The violence of the shock had broken his right leg below the knee.

Most of the claims within a mile on both sides of the border were destroyed, either upset by the earthquake or engulfed by the flood.

PART II

I

A Winter in the Klondike

AN EARTHQUAKE, albeit a very localized one, had just struck the central part of the Fortymile River where it runs through the Klondike between the Alaskan boundary and the Yukon River. The shock had been felt for more than a mile upstream from the boundary.

The Klondike, although not subject to frequent seismic activity, carries in its belly quartz-bearing aggregates and volcanic rocks, showing that subterranean forces were at work at the time it was formed. These forces, which are only dormant, sometimes awaken with extraordinary violence. In the entire region of the Rocky Mountains, whose first ranges rise near the Arctic Circle, there are several volcanoes that may not be completely extinct.

Although the possibility of earthquakes or volcanic eruptions is not a serious threat in the region, the same is not true of the floods that occur when melting snow causes a sudden rise in the water level of the streams.

While the Yukon River has not been a threat, its tributary, the Klondike, which separates Dawson City from its suburb, has often overflowed its banks and washed out the bridge connecting the two parts of the town.

The area around the Fortymile River had suffered a double disaster. The complete upheaval of its surface led to the destruction of claims over a distance of a few miles on both sides of the border. The flood had caused the stream to carve a new bed for itself through the ravine to the south of Claims 127 and 129.[1] It seemed likely, in fact, that any further work in the area would be impossible.

It would have been difficult at first to estimate the extent of the catastrophe. At night the area was plunged into pitch darkness, even though the sun had dropped below the horizon for only two and a half hours. It would not be known until the next day whether cottages, cabins, and shacks of the miners had been destroyed, leaving most of them homeless, or how high the toll of dead and injured would be—how many had been crushed under the wreckage or drowned in the new stream bed. Nor would it become known, until the extent of the disaster had been assessed, that all the immigrants working on the placers would be forced to abandon the region since work could no longer be carried on there.

The apparent cause of this absolutely irreparable catastrophe was the diversion of part of the water from the Fortymile River onto the adjacent gold deposits on both its banks. The river bed must have been raised under the pressure of subterranean forces and would have been completely emptied of water if the bottom had risen to the level of the river banks. There was reason to believe, therefore, that this was not just a temporary flood. Under these conditions, how could digging start again on land covered by five or six feet of running water that could not be diverted? The new stream would continue to flow southward until it joined another creek.

Struck by this sudden catastrophe, the unfortunate people spent the night in terror and anguish. They had had to climb to high ground in order to escape the rising water. They were without shelter, and the thunderstorm lasted until five o'clock in the morning. The stands of birch and poplar, where families had taken refuge, were repeatedly struck by lightning. At the same time, a torrential rain, mixed with hail, fell without letup. If Lorique had not pointed out a cave in the right-hand slope as they were climbing up the ravine, they would have had no shelter. He and Skim carried Raddle into the cave.

It is not hard to imagine what must have been going through their minds. Was it only to fall victim to this disaster that the two cousins had undertaken the arduous journey to the Klondike? All their efforts seemed to have been for naught. They would have nothing left of their uncle's inheritance, not even the fruits of six weeks' work. Of the nuggets and gold dust collected since work began under the engineer's direction, nothing remained. After Lorique's cottage collapsed, the flood had overtaken it. Not a single article had been saved from it and now its wreckage was drifting away in the current.

When the storm was over, Summy Skim and the foreman left the cave briefly—for they did not want to leave Ben Raddle alone for long—and were able to assess the extent of the catastrophe. Both 127 and 129 had disappeared under water. As to the fate of Hunter and Malone, that was the least of Skim's worries. In any case, as far as they were concerned, the boundary issue seemed to have been resolved. It made no difference to the two claims whether the one hundred and forty-first meridian was moved to the east or to the west. It was of no importance whether the territory was Alaskan or Canadian. A new stream was flowing over it, that was all.

Until an investigation was carried out it would not be known whether the earthquake had claimed many victims. There was no doubt that some families had been taken by surprise in their cabins and shacks, either by the earthquake or by the flood. Sad to say, most of them had probably perished before they had time to escape. It was only by a miracle that Raddle, Skim, and Lorique had survived, and even at that, the engineer did not get off unscathed.

The only thing Skim could do now was go back to Dawson City and find some way of getting Raddle there as soon as possible.

Needless to say, the Hunter-Skim affair was now a dead issue. The rendezvous for a duel on the following day was automatically canceled. Other concerns were claiming the attention of the two adversaries, and they might never come face to face again.

When the sun cast its light on the scene of the disaster, neither of the Texans was anywhere to be seen. There was not a sign of the house they had occupied at the entrance to the ravine, through which the new branch of the Fortymile River now flowed. As for Claim 127, the flood had engulfed it, as it had engulfed 129, and all the claims that came after them on the right bank of the river. Of the equipment installed on them—rockers, sluices, and pumps—not a vestige remained. The previous day's storm had swollen the stream, making the current flow even faster. The gap opened on the right bank did not lower the water level, although it had probably prevented the river from overflowing on the left bank as well, which would have greatly increased the overall damage.

And what about the Texans? Had they been able to escape unharmed, or were they among the victims? No one knew what had happened to them or to their workmen. It never occurred to Summy Skim to worry about that in the least. His only concern was to get Ben Raddle to Dawson City, where he would be cared for, and to wait until he recovered. Then, if there was still time, they would be on their way to Skagway, from there to Vancouver, and then back to Montreal. He and Raddle had no incentive to prolong their stay in the Klondike. Claim 129 would find no buyers now that it was lying under seven or eight feet of water.[2] It would be best to get away as soon as possible from this abominable country where, as Skim put it with some justification, "people of sound mind and body should never have set foot."

His most doleful thoughts arose from the quite understandable fear that Ben's recovery might take several weeks.

It was now near the middle of August. Before the end of the month, winter, which comes so early in those high latitudes, would have arrived, making it impossible to travel through the lake region and the Chilkoot Pass. Soon the Yukon River itself would not be navigable, and the last steamboats would have headed downstream toward the river's mouth.

The prospect of spending seven or eight months buried in the snow of the Klondike, with the temperature dropping to fifty or sixty degrees below zero, was anything but pleasant. There was not a day to lose. They had to get back to Dawson City, put Ben under the care of Dr. Pilcox and Sisters Martha and Madeleine, and order him to get well forthwith.

The first thing to be done was to arrange some means of transportation. By good luck, Neluto found his cart intact because he had left it on an escarpment out of reach of the water. The horse, which had been grazing at large and was overcome with terror, came back down the slope of the ravine and was reunited with its master.

"All right, let's go, let's go now!" Skim kept saying.

"Yes," agreed Raddle. "I'm really sorry to have got you involved in this miserable business."

"This isn't about me, it's about you," replied Skim. "We'll wrap your leg up as best we can and put a good bed of dry grass in the cart for you to lie on. I'll get in with Neluto, and Lorique will join us in Dawson City when he can. We'll travel as fast—no, I mean as slowly as necessary to avoid jostling you around. Once you're in the hospital you'll have nothing more to worry about. Dr. Pilcox will get you on your feet again, and God willing, we may be able to leave before the cold weather sets in."

"My dear Summy," said Raddle, "it may take several months for my leg to heal, and I know how keen you must be on getting back to Montreal. Why don't you go back alone?"

"I'd never do that," said his cousin. "I'd rather break a leg myself, and then Dr. Pilcox would have two to set instead of one."

That same day, along the roads crowded with people looking for work on other placers, the cart set out for Fort Cudahy, carrying Ben Raddle. It followed the right bank of the Fortymile River below the point where the diversion was flowing south. All along the way there was activity on claims that had not been affected by the flood. There were a few, however, where work could not be carried on, even though they had not been engulfed by the water. Shaken by the earthquake, which had reached as far as three or four miles from the Alaskan border, they were a sorry sight. Equipment was broken, shafts filled in, stakes knocked down, and cabins destroyed. Still, the devastation was not total, and work could be resumed without any great interruption.

The cart was not traveling quickly, since the bumps on those bad roads caused the injured man excruciating pain. Food was expensive, but not

hard to find since companies in the Klondike had recently brought provisions to the gold fields.

Two days later the vehicle stopped at Fort Cudahy.

Summy Skim did everything he could to care for the injured man, but
he could not set his broken leg. Raddle was in great pain, but bore his
suffering without complaining.

Unfortunately, there was no doctor at Fort Cudahy nor at Fort
Reliance, where the cart arrived forty-eight hours later.

Summy Skim had good reason to worry since he was afraid the passage of time and the lack of medicine might make his cousin's condition
worse. He could tell that Ben was holding himself in so as not to alarm
them unnecessarily, but he could not suppress the occasional cry of pain.
It was only too clear that he was racked by violent attacks of fever. And
so they had to start out again, traveling up the right bank of the Yukon,
which leads directly to the capital of the Klondike.[3] Only there, in the
Dawson City hospital, could Raddle be given the care he needed. After
two more days, he was finally admitted on the afternoon of August 16.

Needless to say, Sisters Martha and Madeleine were deeply distressed
to see their compatriot in that condition. He hardly recognized them, for
his burning fever made him delirious. Skim gave the nuns and the sister
superior a brief account of what had happened. The patient was placed
in a small private room, and word was quickly sent to Dr. Pilcox.

"You see, sisters," said Skim to the two nuns, "I was right in saying, when I brought you to Dawson City, that we'd have a personal
interest."

"Mr. Skim," replied Sister Martha, "your cousin will be treated like
the dearest of our patients, and he will be healed—when God wills."

"Well, sister, I pray God that it will be as soon as possible, and before
winter prevents us from leaving."

Dr. Pilcox was immediately summoned to the hospital and was there
an hour after Raddle was admitted.

News of the earthquake in the Fortymile River area had reached
Dawson City several days earlier. It was known that the dead and in-

jured numbered about thirty, but Dr. Pilcox could not have suspected that the engineer would be among them.

"What!" he exclaimed, in his usual garrulous way. "It's you, Mr. Raddle, and with a broken leg!"

"Yes, doctor," replied Skim. "Poor Ben is suffering terribly."

"Yes, I know," said the doctor, "but this is nothing serious. We'll fix his leg up for him. What he needs is not a physician, but a surgeon, or maybe a bonesetter. Don't worry. We'll get that leg set, right by the book!"

The doctor examined Raddle, who was lying on his bed, fully conscious and in great pain. The examination revealed only a simple fracture below the knee. The doctor set it very skillfully, and the leg was placed in a device to keep it completely immobile.

"My dear patient," said the doctor, "you'll be fitter after this than you were before. You'll have the legs of a deer or a moose—one leg at least."

"But when?" asked Skim.

"In a month or six weeks. You know, of course, Mr. Skim, bones can't be welded together like two pieces of red-hot iron. No, it takes time, as in any . . ."

"Time, time," muttered Skim.

"What can you expect?" said the doctor. "Nature is at work here, and as you know, nature is never in a hurry. That's why she invented patience."

"And resignation," added Sister Madeleine.

Resignation would be the best policy for Summy Skim. It was obvious to him that winter would set in before Ben Raddle was back on his feet. Just imagine a land where winter starts before the end of September! And what a winter it is, with its snow and ice that make the region impassible! And how could Ben, unless his leg was completely healed, undertake an exhausting journey in the freezing Klondike weather, go through the Chilkoot Pass to Skagway and board a steamboat bound for Vancouver? As for the Yukon steamers, the last of them would leave for St. Michael in about two weeks, with the river freezing up behind it.

On August 20, the scout, who had been guiding several parties during the season, arrived in Dawson City.

Bill Steel's first concern was to find out whether Raddle and Skim had settled the business of Claim 129, whether they had sold the property and were getting ready to go back to Montreal.

Since the best way to find out was to ask the two nuns, off he went to the hospital.

What was his surprise to learn that Ben Raddle was undergoing treatment and would be in hospital for another six weeks. He went to see Summy Skim.

"Yes, Bill," said Skim, "this is the situation we're in. Not only have we not sold 129, but 129 no longer exists. And not only does 129 no longer exist, but it's impossible to get out of this atrocious Klondike and into a country that's fit to live in."

The scout now heard for the first time about the catastrophe that had struck the Fortymile region and how Ben Raddle had been seriously injured.

"And that's the worst of it," declared Skim. "After all, we would have mourned the passing of one two nine, and I didn't care all that much about one two nine, and what was Uncle Josias thinking about when he bought one two nine and then died and bequeathed one two nine to us?"

How he emphasized that number, "one two nine," which he had come to detest so passionately!

"Ah, Bill," he exclaimed, "I'd really have blessed that earthquake if poor Ben had not been one of its victims. It would have taken a troublesome legacy off our hands. No more claim, no more work, and my cousin would have had to give up the idea of becoming a prospector, or even making a deal with some company."

"So then," said the scout, "you're going to spend the whole winter in Dawson City?"

"You might as well say at the North Pole," retorted Skim.

"And here I was coming with my men to take you back."

"You won't be taking us back, Bill. You'll go back alone."

"With Neluto, at least?"

"No, the good old Indian has promised to stay with us."

"All right," said the scout, "but I can't leave any later than the first of September if I want to make it back to Skagway."

"Then you'll leave, Bill old chap," said Skim, with a note of resignation, almost despair, in his voice.

And so it turned out that on September 1 the scout said good-bye to his friends and left, promising to come back and get them in the spring.

Skim was exceedingly frustrated. "Yes," he said, "in eight months."

Meanwhile, Raddle's treatment continued as usual. There had been no complications, and Dr. Pilcox declared that he could not have been more satisfied. His patient's leg would be stronger than ever, he said, and would be the equal of two ordinary legs.

The two nuns were taking good care of Raddle, who was patiently putting up with his situation. While his cousin went hunting with the faithful Neluto whenever the weather permitted, he kept himself up to date on the Dawson City markets and new discoveries in the gold fields. With newspapers like the *Yukon Sun*, the *Midnight Sun*, and the *Klondyke Nugget*,[4] he could not fail to be well informed. Just because Claim 129 no longer existed, did that mean there was now nothing to do in the region? Might there not be some other claim to buy and exploit? With his engineer's instinct, he had acquired a taste for working on the Fortymile River. But he was careful not to mention that to Summy Skim, who would not have been able to keep his indignation—quite justified, after all—in check.

And so, while the fever caused by his injury had left Raddle, the gold fever—that endemic fever that was claiming so many victims—was still with him, and he did not seem to be close to a cure. What was important to him was not so much the possession of the precious metal as the desire to be prospecting rich placers.

How could his imagination not be fired by the daily press reports of mountain claims on Bonanza, Eldorado and Little Skookum creeks, where they were panning $100 an hour per worker? A hole twenty-four feet long by fourteen feet wide yielded $8000. A London firm had just bought two claims on Bear Creek and Dominion Creek for $350,000. Claim 26 on Eldorado was for sale for $400,000, and the workers there were taking in as much as $12,000 per man per day. Mr. Ogilvie had offered his expert opinion that there would be $30,000,000 to be taken out of the ground at the Dome on the divide between the Klondike and Indian rivers.

And yet, in spite of this mirage, the warning given by the curé of Dawson City to M. Arnis Semiré, a French traveler who had made the most careful study of the gold fields, must not be forgotten.

"If you also contract gold fever during your stay here," he said, "you must make sure you have a bed in my hospital. You'll wear yourself out, especially if you find even a tiny bit of gold—and there's gold everywhere in this country. You'll certainly contract scurvy. For fifty dollars a year, I'm selling subscriptions that entitle you to a bed and free medical care. Everyone is buying them from me. Here's your ticket."

Ben Raddle had been surrounded by attention at the hospital. But would his irresistible passion not draw him out of Dawson City and into the new regions where deposits were being discovered? Might he not share the misery of the many people who were dying before they could get back? Yes, the newspapers kept reporting that the Klondike had produced $1,500,000 in 1896 and $2,500,000 in 1897. They predicted at least $6,000,000 for 1898.[5]

Meanwhile, Summy Skim had asked the authorities whether the two Texans, Hunter and Malone, had been seen since the Fortymile disaster.

It was certain that neither of them had returned to Dawson City, where their usual boisterous behavior would have made their presence known. They would have been seen in the casinos, the gambling dens, and all those pleasure spots where they were the first in line. This was the time of year when those who stayed in the capital of the Klondike, instead of going back to their own country after making their fortune, waited for the next season to begin. And there, for seven or eight months, they squandered most of their profits in extravagant spending of all kinds and in enormous gambling losses. That was what Hunter had done before and what he would have done again if he had been there. But there was no news. No one knew what had happened to him and his friend. Perhaps they had died in the earthquake at the Fortymile, swept away in the raging water of the new stream. However, since none of the Americans working on Claim 127 had been seen again and since it was impossible to believe that they had all died in the disaster, there was reason to think Hunter and Malone had left with their crew for Circle City and Birch Creek, where they had begun their season.

By the middle of October Ben Raddle was able to get out of bed. Dr. Pilcox was tremendously proud of the recovery he had made. His treatment had helped, of course, but Sisters Martha and Madeleine had also done their share. Those dedicated nuns had continued to work unstintingly, caring for the other patients in the crowded hospital, most of whom would only leave in a hearse drawn by a dog team on the way to the cemetery. But although Raddle was back on his feet, he still had to take certain precautions and could not risk the journey from Dawson City to Skagway. It was too late, anyway. The first snow of winter was falling thick and fast, the streams were beginning to freeze over, and navigation on the Yukon River and the lakes was no longer possible. Summy Skim knew only too well that he was doomed to stay in the Klondike for the entire winter of seven or eight months. The average temperature was now fifteen degrees below zero, and it would fall to fifty or sixty below.

The two cousins had booked a room in a hotel on Front Street and were taking their meals at the French Royal Restaurant, where the prices were exorbitant, but they did not go so far as to treat themselves to chickens at thirty dollars a pair.

Sometimes Skim would say, shaking his head, "The worst of it is we weren't able to leave Dawson City before winter set in."

To which Raddle would reply, "The worst of it is we didn't sell our claim before the disaster occurred, unless—and this may be even worse—it's that we can't go on working it."

And with that, not wanting to engage in a thoroughly pointless conversation, Skim would pick up his rifle, call Neluto, and go off hunting on the outskirts of town.

It may be noted also that Lorique had come back to Dawson City a few days after Raddle, and the two of them had long conversations. It is not hard to guess what the foreman and the engineer talked about since they were in complete agreement about the only item on the agenda.

Another month went by. The level of the mercury in the thermometer showed wide variations, dropping to minus thirty or forty degrees, then rising to minus fifteen, depending on the direction of the wind. After the blizzards came the cold.[6]

Whenever the weather permitted, Summy Skim went hunting with Neluto and had the good fortune to shoot several bears driven from the mountains toward the town by the cold weather.[7]

On November 17 he and Neluto were a few miles to the north of Dawson City. The hunting had been good, and they were getting ready to go home when the Indian stopped and pointed to a tree about fifty paces from a stream.

"A man . . . there." he said.

"A man?" asked Skim.

Sure enough, there was a man lying on the snow under a birch tree. He was not moving. He might have been dead, perhaps frozen to death since the temperature was very low.

They ran toward him. He was a man of about forty with a long beard. His eyes were closed, and his face showed signs of great suffering. He was still breathing but so weakly that he might have been drawing his last breath.

Skim opened the fur jacket the man was wearing and found in a pocket a leather wallet containing a number of letters. They were addressed to M. Jacques Laurier and had a Paris postmark.[8]

"A Frenchman!" exclaimed Skim.

A moment later the man was in the cart, heading at top speed toward the capital of the Klondike.

2

The Dying Man's Tale

SUMMY SKIM'S CART stopped at the door of the hospital that afternoon. The man it was carrying was brought into one of the wards containing about thirty beds and placed in the adjoining office, which Ben Raddle had occupied during his convalescence.

In this small room, the sick man would not be disturbed by the proximity of the other patients. Summy Skim had gone to see the sister superior.

"He's a Frenchman," he told her, "almost a fellow countryman. What you did for Ben, I'm asking you now to do for him, and I hope Dr. Pilcox will cure him just as he healed my cousin."

Sisters Martha and Madeleine had echoed his request, and soon Dr. Pilcox was at Jacques Laurier's bedside.[1]

Ben Raddle, informed of the situation by Neluto, hurried to the hospital and was present at the doctor's first visit.

The Frenchman had not regained consciousness and his eyes were still closed. Dr. Pilcox found his pulse very weak and his breathing barely perceptible. He found no wounds on the man's body, which was terribly emaciated by deprivation, fatigue, and misery. The unfortunate fellow had probably dropped from exhaustion under the tree where Skim came across him. It was likely, too, that he was suffering from congestion, due to the cold, after a night in the open with no one to help him.

"This man is half frozen," said the doctor.

He was wrapped in blankets, given hot drinks, and massaged to restore circulation. Everything that could be done was done, but all efforts to bring him out of his weakened state and revive his spirits were in vain.

It was not a corpse that Skim had brought back, but would the poor man recover? Dr. Pilcox refused to offer an opinion on that question.

Jacques Laurier—that was the name on the letters found in his wallet. The most recent one, dated five months earlier, had been mailed from Nantes. A mother was writing to her son in Dawson City, Klondike, and waiting for a reply, which perhaps he had not yet sent.

Skim and Raddle read the letters, which provided a few details about their recipient. If he did not survive, they would surely have to write to his poor mother and tell her that she would never see him again.

What could be established from this collection of four letters was that Jacques Laurier had left Europe two years earlier, but he had not gone directly to the Klondike to work as a prospector. Some of the addresses indicated that he must have tried his luck first on the gold fields of Ontario and British Columbia. Then, attracted no doubt by the amazing news published in the Dawson City newspapers, he had joined the throng of miners. He apparently did not own a claim, since there was no deed of ownership in his wallet, but along with the letters there was one document in particular that attracted Raddle's attention.

It was a rough map, drawn in pencil, whose irregularly traced lines marked out a stream flowing west with several tributaries running into it. At least, that is what the natural orientation of the map would lead one to believe. However, it did not seem possible that the stream could be the Yukon River or its tributary the Klondike. A number written on one corner of the map indicated a higher latitude, above the Arctic Circle. If this was a map of some Canadian region, it straddled the sixty-eighth parallel. But because the number for the longitude was missing, it was impossible to tell in what part of North America it was situated.

Was Jacques Laurier heading for this region or on his way back when Summy Skim came across him near Dawson City? If the unfortunate

Frenchman died without regaining consciousness, that question would never be answered.

It was fairly certain, too, that he belonged to a family with some social standing. His mother's letters, written in a delicate hand, certainly bore witness to that. He was not an ordinary laborer, but what vicissitudes, what misfortunes, had brought him to this state of destitution and misery that would probably end on a hospital bed?

Several days passed, and despite Dr. Pilcox's medications and the care and attention of the nuns, Jacques Laurier could barely answer Raddle's questions. It was even doubtful whether he was in full possession of his faculties. Who could tell whether his sanity had been able to resist the stresses of the adventurous existence that claims so many victims in the world of the gold seekers?

When asked about that, Dr. Pilcox replied, "I'm afraid our patient's mind has been violently disturbed. Whenever he opens his eyes a little, I notice a blank look that frightens me."

"But what about his physical condition?" asked Skim. "Is it improving?"

"Not so far," declared the doctor. "It seems to me to be as serious as his mental state."

"But you'll save this poor Frenchman," the two nuns kept repeating.

"We'll do everything we can," replied the doctor, "but I haven't much hope."

If the usually confident Dr. Pilcox used that kind of language, it meant that he did not believe Laurier would recover.

But Ben Raddle refused to give up hope. In time, he said, there would be a remission. Even if Laurier did not recover his health, he would at least get his faculties back, he would talk, he would answer questions. They would find out where he was going and where he was coming from. They would write to his mother. If his death was inevitable, he would have made known his last wishes and would die with the consolation of saying to himself that they would be faithfully carried out. He would know that friends, almost fellow countrymen, had been at his bedside.

Well, perhaps there was some reason to suppose Dr. Pilcox had shown too little faith in the effectiveness of his treatment. Two days later there appeared to be signs of the remission that Raddle was waiting for so impatiently. Laurier seemed to be gradually recovering from his state of complete exhaustion. His eyes stayed open longer, and his gaze was steadier. Yes! His questioning eyes definitely revealed his astonishment at seeing the room and the people grouped around him—the doctor, Ben Raddle, Summy Skim, and the two nuns. "Where am I?" the eyes seemed to say. "Who are you?" But everyone could tell that they would soon close again, that they showed only a dim glimmer of light, one of life's final reactions as its end drew near. They all knew the unfortunate man was at death's door.

The doctor shook his head like a man who could not be mistaken. Intelligence was returning, but it was on the verge of disappearing forever.

Sister Martha leaned over the bed, and Laurier murmured a few words in a barely audible voice broken by sighs.

"You're here, in a room at the hospital," he was told.

"Where?" asked the patient, trying to sit up.

Supporting him with his arm, Ben Raddle answered, "In Dawson City. We found you lying unconscious six days ago as we were coming along, and we brought you here."

Laurier's eyelids closed for a few minutes. The effort seemed to have exhausted him. The doctor administered a few drops of a stimulant, which brought the color back to his pale cheeks and words to his lips.

"Who are you?" he asked.

"We're French Canadians," replied Skim, "friends of France. You can trust us. We'll take care of you until you're well."

A kind of smile spread over the patient's face as he uttered a feeble "thank you" over and over and fell back on his pillow. On the doctor's advice, there were no more questions. It was better to let him rest. They would keep watch at his bedside and be there to answer as soon as he regained enough strength to speak. But perhaps he felt that his end was near, for the tears welled up in his eyes.

For the next two days Laurier's condition neither improved nor deteriorated. He was still as weak as ever, and there seemed to be some danger that he would not respond to treatment. But at long intervals and with great effort he managed to speak again and answer questions, which he appeared to be inviting. They could tell that he had many things to say and was eager to say them.

Ben Raddle did not leave him but stayed nearby, ready to hear what he might say. And that was how he came to learn the story of Jacques Laurier, both from what the Frenchman told him and from what he said in his moments of delirium. On some points, though, he seemed reluctant to give a full explanation as if he had a secret that he would not reveal as long as he believed he had some chance of surviving.

And here, without going into too much detail, is the story of his life.

Jacques Laurier was forty-two years old and in robust health. He must have suffered terribly to have been reduced to the state he was now in.

He was a Breton, born in Nantes, where his mother still lived on the small widow's pension left to her by her husband, an infantry officer who had never risen above the rank of captain.

Laurier had wanted to be a sailor, but just when he might have taken his entrance examination for the naval school, a serious illness cut short that career. Having then passed the age of eligibility, he had to sign on as an apprentice aboard a merchant ship. After voyages to Melbourne and San Francisco, he was promoted to master mariner. It was in that capacity that he entered the navy as a sublieutenant, hoping to reach the rank of lieutenant.

He served for three years, but he was always behind his comrades who had come out of the *Borda*.[2] He realized that he would always be left behind, barring some rare circumstance in which a sailor might distinguish himself. He resigned and looked for a position on one of the merchant ships whose home port was Nantes.

It was difficult to find a command, and he had to be satisfied with a posting as second mate on a sailing ship heading for the South Seas.

Four years went by. He was now twenty-nine years old. His father had just died, leaving Madame Laurier in a rather precarious situation. He tried in vain to move up from second mate to captain in the merchant marine but could not afford to buy a share in the ship he wanted to command, as was the usual custom. As long as he was only a second mate, what a bleak future was in store for him! And how could he ever reach the state of modest affluence that he dreamed of for his mother? Yes, especially for her.

His voyages as a master mariner had taken him to Australia and California, where the gold fields attracted so many immigrants. As is always the case, a very few became rich, while the vast majority found nothing but ruin and misery. And yet, dazzled by the example of so many others, Jacques Laurier resolved to make his fortune by following the perilous path of the gold seekers.

At that particular time, the whole world's attention had just been drawn to the mines in Canada, even before its metallic wealth had been so amazingly increased by the discoveries in the Klondike. In other less remote and more easily accessible regions, such as Ontario and British Columbia, Canada possessed gold-bearing areas that could be more easily exploited with no interruption by the terrible winters of the Yukon Territory. One of these mines, perhaps the largest, known as "Le Roi," was purchased in 1890 for the ridiculous sum of three cents per share. In two years it paid dividends of nine hundred thousand dollars and still distributes monthly profits of one hundred thousand dollars.

This was the company for which Laurier went to work. But anyone who has only his intellectual or physical labor to offer seldom gets rich under those conditions. One must own a share of the business and be there when the profits are divided up. To become a shareholder one must buy shares, and the one thing that this courageous but perhaps too imprudent Frenchman lacked was money. He dreamed of making a quick fortune by some lucky quirk of fate, but how could that happen as long as he was an employee or even a day laborer at Le Roi?

There was talk at the time of new discoveries in the Yukon River basin. The name "Klondike" was as dazzling as the names "California,"

"Australia," and "Transvaal" had been previously. The crowd of miners betook themselves to the Klondike, and Laurier followed the crowd.

While working in the mines of Ontario, he had met a Canadian of English descent named Harry Brown. They were both driven by the same ambition, consumed by the same urge to succeed. Harry Brown was a strong influence on Laurier. He persuaded him to leave his job and head out into the unknown, an unknown that usually holds more disappointments than advantages. With the meager savings they were able to accumulate, they made their way to Dawson City.

This time they were determined to work for themselves. But, understandably, on the placers of Bonanza and Eldorado creeks and the Sixtymile and Fortymile rivers, even if claims had not been commanding exorbitant prices, they would not have found one for sale. Bids of thousands and thousands of dollars were already being offered. They would have to go farther, to the northern reaches of Alaska or the Dominion, well beyond the great river, where a few hardy prospectors were reporting the presence of gold fields. They would have to go where no one had ever gone before. They would have to find some new deposit, which could be claimed by the first one to occupy it. And—who knows?—they might be rewarded by a quick and profitable operation.

That is certainly what Laurier and Brown said to themselves. With no equipment and no crew, they spent the last of their money to buy enough supplies for eighteen months and left Dawson City. They lived by hunting and ventured to the north of the Yukon, through the region lying beyond the Arctic Circle.

Summer had begun with the first weeks of June, six months before that day in the winter of 1897–98 when Laurier was found dying on the outskirts of Dawson City. How far had the expedition of those two adventurers led them? Had they traveled to the edge of the continent, to the shores of the Arctic Ocean? Had the discovery of some rich deposit repaid them for all that effort and fatigue? Apparently not, considering the state of exhaustion and deprivation in which one of them had been found. And he was alone. Was there no news of his partner? Had

Harry Brown perished in those distant regions since he had not come back with Laurier? Yes, but if he had met his death while coming to Dawson City, that meant that he and his friend had been attacked on the way by Indians and robbed of a precious nugget they had found—where?[3] Jacques Laurier was not saying.

Ben Raddle was able to get no more information from him. And even that whole sad story had come to him only in bits and snatches when the patient became lucid for a short time. As Dr. Pilcox had predicted, he was getting weaker every day.

As to the results of the expedition, whether it had proved profitable or fruitless, and as to the region Laurier and Brown had reached and from which they were returning with the nugget the Indians stole, the engineer was still not clear. Perhaps he would never learn any more about it, for the secret seemed likely to be carried to a grave in the Dawson City cemetery, where the poor Frenchman would soon be lying.

And yet, there was a document in existence, an incomplete one to be sure, but one that the end of Laurier's story would no doubt have completed. It was the sketch found in Laurier's wallet, certainly a map of the region where he and his partner had spent the previous season. But where was that region? Where was the creek that followed its winding course from east to west? Was it a tributary of the Yukon or the Porcupine? Did it flow through part of the Hudson's Bay Company's territory around Fort McPherson, near the spot where the mighty Mackenzie River empties into the Arctic Ocean? When Raddle held before Laurier's eyes the map he himself had probably drawn, his face lit up for a moment. He recognized it and seemed to be saying, "Yes, that's where it is! That's exactly where it is!" Neither Raddle nor the foreman could doubt that he had made a major discovery there. And they had the impression that even if the patient had had the strength to speak, he would not have wanted to tell them everything he knew about it.

Yes, deep within that soul now ready to leave its exhausted body, there may still have been some hope of returning to life. Perhaps the poor fellow was saying to himself that he would not lose the prize so dearly won, that he would see his mother again and bring her some comfort in her old age. Perhaps he was dreaming of setting out on another expedition when winter was over and he was well again.

Several days passed. The cold weather was now at its most severe. Several times the temperature dropped to minus fifty degrees centigrade. It was impossible to go outdoors during these dry cold spells. When they were not at the hospital, the two cousins spent their time in their hotel room. Sometimes they bundled themselves up in furs from head to foot and went to some casino or gambling house—but not to play. There were not many people there anyway, since most of the miners had gone to Dyea, Skagway, or Vancouver before the severe cold set in, while the roads were still passable. Faro and monte were being played with an unbelievable fury.

Perhaps Hunter and Malone had moved to one of those towns for the winter. It was certain, at least, that no one had seen them in Dawson City since the Fortymile disaster. On the other hand, they were apparently not among the earthquake's victims identified by the Canadian and American police.

During this time of frequent snowstorms, it was obviously impossible for Summy Skim and Neluto to go hunting, to their great regret, for the bears came prowling right to the outskirts of Dawson City.

The diseases that developed as a result of this excessively cold weather continued to decimate the town's population. The hospital did not have enough room to admit more patients, and those whom death dispatched to the cemetery were promptly replaced. There would soon be a place available in the room occupied by Jacques Laurier.

He had certainly not lacked care. He was the object of very special attention. The nuns worked tirelessly on his behalf, and Dr. Pilcox used every possible means to restore strength to that poor, exhausted body. Ben Raddle and Summy Skim treated him like a fellow countryman. But now he could not take any nourishment, and his life was visibly slipping away day by day, even hour by hour.

During the morning of November 27 Jacques Laurier suffered a violent attack. It looked as if he would not recover from it. He was struggling, and weak though he was, precautions had to be taken to keep him in his bed. He kept muttering over and over, "There . . . there . . . the volcano . . . the eruption . . . gold . . . golden lava!"

Then, like a cry of despair, he shouted, "Mother . . . Mother . . . it's for you . . . only for you!"

After a long period of anguish, his agitation died down, and the unfortunate man fell into a state of prostration. His only sign of life was his faint breathing, but he did not appear to be dying. According to the doctor, he could certainly not survive a second attack like the first. It would end with his last breath.

During the afternoon, when Raddle came to sit by the patient's bedside, he found him calmer and apparently fully conscious again. There had been a kind of remission as sometimes happens when death is near.

Laurier opened his eyes and was staring fixedly at Ben Raddle, the man to whom he had spoken most about his adventurous existence, the man who had often said to him, "Consider us your friends, friends who will not abandon you. We'll do everything we can do for you—and for your mother."

Laurier reached out and took Raddle's hand. "Listen carefully," he said. "I'm going to die. My life is slipping away. I can feel it."

"No, my friend, no," replied the engineer. "You'll get your strength back."

"I'm going to die," the patient repeated. "Come closer, Mr. Raddle. Listen and remember what I'm going to tell you."

In a gradually weakening but clear voice, the voice of a man whose mind has not been damaged and who is in full possession of his wits, he confided this story to Ben Raddle.

"This map you found on me, the one you showed me, show it to me once more."

Raddle did as he was asked.

"This is a map of the region where I've been," Laurier went on. "The richest deposits in the entire world are located there. You won't even have to dig to get the gold out. The earth itself will throw it out from its entrails. Yes! There . . . I discovered a mountain, an extinct volcano containing an immense quantity of gold. Yes! A golden volcano, Golden Mount."

"A golden volcano?" asked Raddle in a somewhat incredulous tone of voice.

"You must believe me," cried Laurier violently, trying to sit up in bed. "You must believe me, if not for yourself, then for my mother . . . an inheritance that you'll share with her. I climbed that mountain. I went down into the crater. It's filled with gold-bearing quartz and nuggets. You just have to pick them up."

After this effort, the patient fell back into a state of prostration from which he recovered in a few minutes. His eyes turned first toward the engineer.

"Good," he murmured. "You're here . . . still here . . . near me . . . you believe me . . . and you'll go there . . . to Golden Mount."

His voice fell lower and lower as Raddle, whom he was pulling by the hand, leaned over his bed.

"It's there," he said, "at the point marked X on the map . . . in the region . . . near this creek, Rubber Creek, which flows out of the left branch of the Mackenzie, straight into the northern part of the Klondike . . . a volcano that will spew out nuggets the next time it erupts, and the cinders will be gold dust . . . there . . . there."

Half sitting up in Raddle's arms, Laurier stretched a trembling hand toward the north.

Then these last words issued from his lips: "For my mother! For my mother!"

He was shaken by a final convulsion and fell back lifeless on his bed.

3

The Aftermath of a Secret

THE UNFORTUNATE FRENCHMAN'S FUNERAL was held the following day. Ben Raddle and Summy Skim followed him to the cemetery, where so many victims of the migration to the Klondike gold fields were already buried. A wooden cross bearing the name "Jacques Laurier" was erected over the grave after one of the priests from the church in Dawson City had offered the final prayers.

On his return, Raddle fulfilled the promise he had made to the dying man. He wrote to Europe, to France, to Brittany, to Nantes, to the poor mother who would never see her son again.

Naturally, Raddle was completely obsessed by the secret of Golden Mount. It never occurred to him for a moment that Laurier's revelation did not have a solid basis. He had no doubt that the Frenchman and his partner had discovered a mountain on the bank of Rubber Creek, a tributary of the Mackenzie, in the Canadian north. They had recognized it for what it was, an enormous pocket of gold that would sooner or later disgorge its contents. If there was an eruption, millions of nuggets would be thrown out. If not, if the volcano was definitely extinct, they could simply be gathered up in the crater of Golden Mount.

It seemed, too, that there were rich placers in the region drained by the Mackenzie and its tributaries. While the Indians who traveled through the territory near the Arctic Ocean had not said anything about the mountain shown on Jacques Laurier's map, they reported that there was gold in the streams. Companies were considering extending their explorations to the part of the Dominion between the Arctic Ocean and the Arctic Circle. Prospectors were already thinking about moving there for their next expedition, and the first to arrive would have the best chance. And who knows? They might come face to face with that mountain known only to Ben Raddle, who had learned its secret from Jacques Laurier.

It is understandable, then, that the engineer wanted to keep abreast of all the news that was going around, and that Lorique, the foreman, was equally interested. He could not get over the loss of the Fortymile claim, and they had many conversations about it. Raddle was still reluctant, however, to reveal the secret of the golden volcano to the foreman, and in fact it was only after careful consideration that he would tell his cousin about it. There was no urgency in any case. Of the Klondike's eight-month winter, only three months had elapsed.

At this juncture, the commission announced the results of its deliberations concerning changes to the boundary. After a very careful study of the matter, it concluded that neither the English nor the American claim was valid. No mistake had been made in drawing the one hundred and forty-first meridian west of Greenwich. The border between Alaska and Canada had been accurately drawn and would be moved neither to the west, to the advantage of the Canadians, nor to the east, to their disadvantage. The claims lying on the border would not undergo any change of nationality whatsoever.

"That's a big help," said Skim on the day he heard the news. "It makes no difference whether 129 is in American or British territory, since it no longer exists."

"It still exists under the stream that branches off from the Fortymile River," said the foreman, still unwilling to give up hope.

"All right, Lorique, go ahead and work it then, under five or six feet of water. Unless a second earthquake puts everything back the way it was."

"Anyway," added Skim, shrugging his shoulders, "if Pluto and Neptune are going to collaborate in the Klondike again, I hope they finish that dreadful place off once and for all, upset it and flood it so thoroughly that no one will be able to collect a single nugget!"

"Oh, Mr. Skim!" said the foreman.

"You're wrong to talk like that, Summy," said Raddle.

"No, I'm right. The world will get along just as well without the Klondike's millions."

"Well," said Raddle, being careful not to say more than he intended, "there are other gold fields in Canada besides the ones in the Klondike."

"And furthermore," retorted Skim a bit testily, "I include all the others in my catastrophe, both in Alaska and in Canada . . . and, frankly, in the whole world."

"But Mr. Skim," said the foreman, "gold is gold."

"No, Lorique, it's nothing. It only deceives poor people by muddling their brains, and its victims number in the thousands."

The conversation might have gone on a long time on the same topic without any of the participants gaining any ground, but Summy Skim brought it to a conclusion.

"After all," he said, "I'm only looking out for our own interests. One twenty-nine has disappeared, and I think that's reason enough for us to be on our way back to Montreal."

Skim never imagined that this plan might be thwarted just when the time came to put it into effect.

The day was still far off when the two cousins could undertake the return journey either by the lake route to Vancouver or down the Yukon to its estuary. The year had just ended. Summy Skim would never forget that Christmas week. The temperature, though it did not fall below minus twenty degrees, was still dreadful. A much lower temperature, with brisk, dry north winds, might have been better.

During that last week the streets of Dawson City were almost deserted. No light could have shone through the swirling snow, which piled up more than six feet deep, making the streets inaccessible to vehicles and teams. If the cold returned with its usual intensity, picks and mattocks would not be able to cut a path through the accumulated drifts. It would be necessary to use explosives. In some neighborhoods along the Yukon and Klondike rivers several houses were snowed in up to the second floor and could only be entered through the windows. Fortunately, the buildings on Front Street were not blocked in that way, and the two cousins could have left their hotel if it had not been absolutely impossible to move along the streets. After taking only a few steps outdoors, they would have been buried up to the neck in snow. These storms known as blizzards are very frequent in all parts of North America,[1] but none are as violent as those that occur in Alaska and northern Canada.

At that time of year the daylight lasted only a few hours. The sun barely made an appearance between morning and afternoon over the hills that rise to the east and west of the city. Even when the snow squalls subsided, its rays did not reach the center of Dawson City. The wind-driven flakes came so hard and thick that electric lighting could not have penetrated them. The city was plunged into pitch darkness for twenty hours out of twenty-four.

Since communication was now impossible, Summy Skim and Ben Raddle were confined to their rooms. The foreman and Neluto, who were staying in a modest inn in one of the lower quarters, were unable to visit them as they were in the habit of doing. As for the hospital, where Dr. Pilcox had had to take up residence in order to continue the daily routine, the two cousins did not visit it now. Skim made one attempt to go out, braving the gusts, and was nearly buried in the snow. With considerable effort, the people from the Northern Hotel managed to pull him out safe and sound. They carried him back to his room and massaged him. When he came to, he exclaimed, "We might as well have spent the winter at ninety degrees north latitude. At least we would have had the glory of setting foot at the North Pole."

Needless to say, no services were functioning in the Klondike. Letters did not arrive, newspapers were not delivered, and telegrams probably froze as they traveled along the telegraph wires. There was also a very serious fear that people might run out of food. If it had not been for the reserves built up in hotels and private houses in anticipation of such a dreadful eventuality, Dawson City would have faced starvation. The casinos and gambling houses, of course, were idle. Never before had the city been in such an alarming situation, and the authorities were helpless to do anything. The governor's residence was inaccessible, and all administrative functions, in both the Canadian and American territories, had ceased. Every day the epidemics claimed more victims, but they could not be carried to their final resting place, and now it was not even cold enough to prevent decomposition.[2] If a plague had broken out, no one in Dawson City would have been left alive.

The first day of 1899 was certainly a dreadful one. During the previous night and throughout the day, so much snow fell that it threatened to envelop houses in Dawson City up to the second floor. On the right bank of the Klondike River some buildings were completely covered except for their roofs. One might have thought the entire city was about to disappear under those white layers of snow as Pompeii and Herculaneum had disappeared under the ashes of Vesuvius. And if the storm was followed by a drop in temperature to minus forty or fifty degrees, the masses of snow would harden, and the city (whose entire population would have perished) would not reappear until the snow began to melt under the first rays of the sun in April or May.

On January 2 there was a sudden change in the weather. The wind shifted direction, the thermometer quickly rose to zero centigrade, and there was no further danger that the snow banks might turn to ice. They melted in the space of a few hours.[3] As the saying is, it had to be seen to be believed. But the flood that followed caused heavy damage. The streets became raging torrents and the debris-laden water rushed to join the Yukon and Klondike rivers, flowing noisily over the icy surface. Avalanches came rushing down from the top of the hills around Dawson City. The flood covered the whole district. The Fortymile River was greatly swollen and covered the downstream claims. It was another disaster, and if Ben Raddle had cherished any hope of regaining possession of 129, he definitely had to abandon that hope now.

As soon as the streets were passable, the foreman and Neluto put in an appearance at the Northern Hotel as eager to have news of the two cousins as the latter were to have news of them.

Then Skim and Raddle made their way to the hospital, where Sisters Martha and Madeleine greeted them warmly. Dr. Pilcox had lost none of his usual good humor.

"Well," Skim asked him, "are you still proud of your adopted country?"

"Come now, Mr. Skim," replied the doctor. "This Klondike is an amazing place, amazing! It may have nearly disappeared under the snow, but it has recovered and is none the worse for it. I don't believe so much snow has ever fallen within living memory. There's something to put down in your travel journal, Mr. Skim."

"You can be sure I will, doctor."

"If the severe cold had come back before the thaw, we'd all be mummified by now. There's a news item for the European and North American papers!"

"Is that how you look at it, doctor?"

"Yes, Mr. Skim, and that's how you have to look at it. It's a question of philosophy."

"Yes," said Skim, "philosophy at fifty degrees below zero."

The city soon resumed its usual appearance and routine, but during the next few days many victims of the epidemic, whose burial had had to be postponed, were taken to the Dawson City cemetery.

In January, however, the cold weather is far from over in the Klondike. During the latter half of the month it was extremely cold, but it was still possible to get around by taking certain precautions. The temperature dropped to fifty below, but that did not deter Skim from going on the occasional hunting trip with Neluto.

Raddle, the doctor, and the nuns had all failed to dissuade him from going out into the countryside near the city. He was not tempted by the excitement of gambling or the entertainment offered in the casinos, and the time hung heavy on his hands. One day, when he was being pushed too hard, he replied in all seriousness, "Well, I promise you I'll stop hunting, but only when . . ."

"When?" Dr. Pilcox wanted to know.

"When it's so cold the gunpowder won't ignite."

All that month, conditions were better, in the sense that the blizzards were less frequent and not so violent. Instead, the people in the Klondike had to suffer spells of bitter cold. When the air was calm, this could still be endured, but when a strong north wind blew down from the north from across the polar region, cutting people's faces and making their breath fall like snow, it was wise to stay in one's room.

Ben Raddle and Lorique met frequently in the hotel, and scarcely a day went by when one of them did not pay a visit to the other. When Summy Skim came back from hunting with Neluto, he usually found them together. As was to be expected, their conversation centered on the disaster that had occurred at the claim on the Fortymile River. But to hope that it could ever again be worked would have been to court disappointment.

Skim wondered somewhat uneasily whether his cousin and the foreman might not be discussing another venture, and that was a cause of great concern to him.

"What can they be talking about?" he kept saying to himself. "Hasn't Ben had enough—too much in fact—of this abominable country? What can he want? To try his luck on some new deposit? To let himself be led around by Lorique? To go prospecting next summer? Oh no! Even if I have to use force, I'll find a way to make him leave as we agreed as soon as the scout comes back to take us to Skagway. If May finds me still in this horrible city, it will be because good old Pilcox has amputated both my legs, and even then I'd make the trip as a legless cripple."

Although Skim was still unaware of the secrets Jacques Laurier had told Ben Raddle, the foreman knew everything. As a matter of fact, since the disaster at the Fortymile, he had been constantly urging the engineer to undertake a new expedition. Since he had put so much effort into coming to the Klondike, why should he not try to buy another claim? Claims on Bonanza and Eldorado were still showing splendid results. By going farther upstream, they would find new deposits just as good as 129. Over toward the Domes lay a vast, still untapped gold field. Its placers would belong to whoever got there first. The foreman offered to hire a crew. In addition to the river claims, there were also mountain claims, which were often even more productive.

As can be easily imagined, the engineer lent a willing ear to this proposal, and that was how he had come to tell Lorique the secret of Golden Mount.

The effect of this revelation on the foreman was predictable. He did not doubt for a moment either the accuracy or the magnitude of the discovery. It was a claim, but more than a claim. It was a mountain containing millions of nuggets, a volcano that willingly gave up its treasures to anyone who took the trouble to pick them up. It was an opportunity not to be missed. The profits to be made from such an operation must not be left to others. Gold seekers were beginning to flock to the northern regions of the Klondike. Following Jacques Laurier's example, Americans and Canadians would go up toward the Mackenzie and its tributaries. They would find the mountain. In a few weeks they would collect more nuggets than all the tributaries of the Yukon had produced in two years. No! There was no time to lose. Within three months the northern routes would be passable, and what a harvest was in store for the daring ones—or rather the well-informed ones—who would be the first to travel along them.

Ben Raddle and the foreman spent hours studying the map traced out by the Frenchman. They had transferred it onto the overall map of the Klondike. From its latitude and longitude, they had calculated that the distance from Dawson City to the Golden Volcano was not more than 280 miles, or about 125 leagues.

"Mr. Raddle," said Lorique, "with a good wagon and a good team it's possible to get to the mouth of the Mackenzie in about ten days, starting the second week in May."

While the foreman was urging the engineer to undertake this expedition, Summy Skim kept repeating to himself, but without saying anything, "What are those two cooking up now?"

Although he was not privy to the secret, he suspected that those frequent conversations must have something to do with a new expedition, and he was determined to oppose that in every way he could. If Raddle had not been injured during the earthquake, they would both have been back in Montreal three months ago. The decision to leave had been made, and since it could not be carried out in September of the previous year, at least it would be done in May of the current year.

The beginning of March brought severe cold spells. For two days the thermometer registered minus sixty degrees centigrade. Skim pointed this out to his cousin on the instrument he had bought in Vancouver, adding that if the cold weather kept up the temperature would certainly drop below its range.

Raddle made no reply at first. Finally he said, "It's bitter cold, but because there's no wind, it's not as unbearable as I expected."

"Yes, Ben, yes, it's really very healthy. I like to believe that it's killing myriads of microbes."

"I might add," said Raddle, "that it doesn't seem likely to last, according to the observations of the local people. There's even some hope, Lorique tells me, that the winter will not be very long this year and that work can start again by the beginning of May."

"Work!" declared Skim. "That's no concern of ours. We'll take advantage of an early spring to be on our way. The scout will be here by that time."

"However," remarked the engineer, who probably thought the time had come to reveal all, "it might to a good idea to pay a visit to 129 before we go."

"Right now, Ben, 129 looks like the old sunken hull of a ship at the bottom of the sea. There's no reason to worry about it any more."

"But there are millions there, millions that we've lost."

"I don't know if there are millions, Ben, but there's no denying the fact that they're lost, completely lost. I see no reason to go to the Fortymile River again. It'll just bring back unpleasant memories."

"Oh, I'm completely cured of that, Summy."

"Perhaps not as thoroughly as you want me to think, Ben. I think the fever—the famous fever, you know, the gold fever—may attack you again if you aren't careful."

Ben Raddle looked at his cousin, looked away, and then like a man who has made up his mind, he said, "Listen to me, Summy, and don't lose your temper as soon as I start."

"But I will lose my temper," shouted Skim, "and nothing can stop me, if you make any reference to a project or a delay."

"Listen, I said. I've got a secret to tell you."

"A secret? From whom?"

"From the Frenchman you found half-dead and brought back to Dawson City."

"Jacques Laurier told you a secret, Ben?"

"Yes, Summy."

"And you've kept it from me?"

"Yes, because it gave me an idea for a project worth considering."

"First, let's hear the secret and then we'll talk about the project," said Skim, who felt that he would have a fight on his hands about the latter.

Then Ben Raddle told him of the existence of a mountain called Golden Mount, whose exact location near the spot where the Mackenzie empties into the Arctic Ocean had been revealed by Jacques Laurier. Skim took a look at the sketch then at the map onto which the engineer had transferred the location of the mountain. Its distance from Dawson City was also marked, bearing north-northeast, approximately on the one hundred and thirty-sixth meridian. Then he learned that the mountain was a volcano, a volcano whose crater contained masses of gold-bearing quartz, and which held in its belly thousands and thousands of nuggets.

"And you believe in this *Thousand and One Nights* volcano?" asked Skim sarcastically.

"*A Thousand and One Nights,* Summy, not to say thousand and one millions," replied Raddle, who seemed to have decided to cut off discussion on that subject.

"All right," continued Skim. "So there's a volcano. But what difference does it make to us?"

"What difference does it make to us?" retorted Raddle excitedly. "What? We hear a secret like that and we don't make use of it? We leave it up to other people to profit from their efforts?"

Trying to control himself, Skim simply replied, "So then, Ben, you intend to take advantage of Jacques Laurier's secret?"

"Is there any reason to hesitate, Summy?"

"But we found him on the way as he was coming back from his expedition, and he died from exhaustion and privation."

"Because winter caught him by surprise."

"But, in order to mine that mountain, we'd have to travel north about 250 miles."

"That's right, about 250 miles."

"But we're supposed to leave for Montreal at the beginning of May."

"Well, we'll just postpone our departure for a few months, that's all."

"But by then it'll be too late to leave."

"If it's too late, we'll spend another winter in Dawson City."

"That I will never do!" exclaimed Skim in such a determined tone of voice that Raddle thought he had better end their interesting conversation right there.

He intended to bring the subject up later though. And so he did, in spite of everything his cousin could say. He had plenty of arguments, and he found an equally determined ally in the foreman. They would make the journey with no difficulty after the spring thaw. In the space of two months, they could reach Golden Mount, make themselves several millions richer, and return to Dawson City. There would still be time enough for them to leave for Montreal, and at least the trip to the Klondike would not have been a total loss.

Then Raddle added one last reason. If Laurier had given him this information, it was not only for him, Ben Raddle. The Frenchman had left behind in Europe a mother to whom he was devoted, a poor, unfortunate woman for whom he had wanted to amass a fortune. If her son's last wishes were carried out, her security would be assured in her old age.

Skim had let Raddle go on talking without interrupting him, wondering which of them was crazy, Ben, because he was saying such preposterous things, or he himself, for listening to them. When the story was finished, his cousin asked him what he thought.

"What I think, Ben," said Skim, no longer able to contain himself, "is that you're making me sorry I ever rescued that poor Frenchman instead of letting him take his secret with him to the grave."

Needless to say, there were many other discussions between the two cousins, often involving the foreman. He was equally fanatical about carrying out the plan to travel up to Golden Mount. Summy Skim tried in vain to defend himself, to resist with his best arguments, recalling the promises that had been made and even maintaining that there was no serious basis for Laurier's revelations. No! It would be one more disappointment after so many others to say nothing of the dangers involved in heading out into the unknown. After the disaster at the Fortymile River, after the destruction of 129, the only option left was to get out of the Klondike as soon as weather permitted, and since spring seemed likely to come early, that would give them a chance to get out of this terrible country a little sooner.

But Ben Raddle held his ground. Summy Skim realized he had made up his mind to see the venture through to the end, and that nothing would deter him. Should he decide, then, to let his cousin embark on this second expedition alone? Should he go back to Montreal without him? But then how much worry and mental anguish would he suffer?

Naturally, Dr. Pilcox had been kept informed of these frequent and interminable conversations. While he knew nothing about a golden volcano, he knew at least that Jacques Laurier, just before he died, had revealed to Raddle the secret of a great discovery—a prodigiously rich deposit in the Canadian north.

Skim told him one day that he would definitely find a way to prevent his cousin from venturing into the hyperborean regions.

"No," said the doctor, "you can't stop him."

"In any case, I won't go with him."

"Yes you will, my dear Skim. You came here against your will from Montreal to Dawson City, and you'll go against your will to the farthest point in the Klondike, and even to the North Pole, if Ben Raddle wants you to."

And perhaps the good Dr. Pilcox was right.

4

Circle City

It is a well-known fact that the wealth of northern Canada and Alaska is not confined to the gold fields of the Klondike. They would soon be subjected to an extremely intense exploitation, and the prices of mining concessions in the area surrounding Bonanza Creek and its tributaries were already becoming unaffordable. American and English companies were competing for them with their dollars and their pounds sterling. Although they were not all sold yet by any means, it would soon be impossible, except for powerful companies, to buy new river or mountain claims even in the Domes region or in the area drained by the tributaries of the upper Yukon. Prospectors, singly or in groups, would be forced to extend their exploration northward by going down the Mackenzie and Porcupine rivers, and they would certainly not shrink from any exertion or any danger. Human greed knows no obstacles.

Rumors of all kinds, moreover, were constantly fueling the miners' ambitions. In these far-off regions, less well-known than Australia, California, or the Transvaal when mining operations began there, the field was wide open, both for ambition and for disappointment. Reports kept coming in, brought by unknown persons from unknown sources and circulated mainly by the Indian tribes that pass through the vast northern solitudes near the Arctic coast. Unable to make use of the gold deposits themselves, the natives tried to attract immigrants to the north in order to obtain employment as guides or workers. If they were to be believed, the greatest number of gold-bearing creeks were to be found in the part of North America beyond the Arctic Circle. These Indians sometimes brought back samples of nuggets they had picked up near Dawson City, claiming to have found them in the area north of the sixty-sixth parallel.[1] Naturally, it must have been a great temptation for the miners, whose hopes had too often been disappointed to accept these finds as genuine. Equally great, even irresistible, was the temptation to venture out to those hitherto unexploited placers.

It should be mentioned also that reports of a gold-bearing volcano had already been gaining ground in the Klondike, almost from the time when the surveyor Ogilvie and his companions discovered the first gold deposits in the vicinity of Dawson City. It was possible, then, that this rumor had led Jacques Laurier to pinpoint its exact location and then to mine it himself. It was possible too that he was not the only one who knew of the secret, although there were good reasons for believing that he was. In the time since he had left the Mackenzie estuary, might other adventurers not have discovered the location of Golden Mount?

In any case, it seemed certain now that, apart from Ben Raddle and his friends, no one else had plans to set out along Jacques Laurier's trail. But the legend of the Golden Volcano still had its believers, and since some miners were inclined to seek their fortunes in the northern regions of the Dominion, the supposition that Golden Mount had been discovered might soon become a reality.

The engineer was understandably worried that someone might reach the Arctic coast ahead of him, and he was impatient to get under way, no matter what Summy Skim might do to dissuade him.

Some immigrants, of course, had already gone in search of new claims along the Yukon downstream from Dawson City since numbers 127 and 129 and several others on the Fortymile River were now destroyed. Some, especially Americans, had even set out in the direction of Circle City. Among them, as it happened, were the two Texans, Hunter and Malone.

At the beginning of the season, as has been mentioned already, the Texans had been working in the gold deposits at Circle City, Alaska, along the banks of Birch Creek, which flows into the Yukon from the left. Since the results of these operations were only mediocre, they had returned to Claim 127, which they had owned for a year. Then came the catastrophe on the Fortymile River, the earthquake that caused the flood, the flood that engulfed the claims under the raging torrents of a new stream and brought about the complete destruction of the gold deposits along the Canada-Alaska border.

Neither Hunter nor Malone nor any of their men had fallen victim to the disaster, and while their property had been wiped out, at least they had come through it unscathed. But because they had decided to return immediately to Circle City once they had recognized that the damage was irreparable, it was believed that they had perished in the cataclysm.

It is easy to imagine that, under the circumstances, Hunter gave no more thought to his proposed encounter with Summy Skim than Skim himself did. It seemed that nothing would come of the affair.

When the Texans got back to the gold deposits at Circle City, there were still two months of summer left.[2] It would not end until early in September. With their crew, they resumed work where they had left off. Their purchase of that placer had not brought them good luck. The profits barely covered their expenses, and if Hunter had not made some money at the gambling table, his men would undoubtedly have been in financial difficulty during the coming winter, with eight months to spend in the Klondike.

One particular turn of events—which will surprise no one, considering the kind of men these were—would soon free them from any concern in that regard.

Wherever these violent types had come in contact with their fellow men, whether Americans or others, arguments and quarrels had broken out. With their insolent assumption that they could impose their will on anyone, ignore the rights of others, and act as if they were in an occupied country, they continually attracted trouble. We have seen how things turned out at the claims on the Fortymile River. Before their arrival, the men at Claim 127 had already been trying to pick a quarrel with those at 129, and Hunter and Malone's presence had only made matters worse.

It was the same at the claim on Birch Creek. They did not attack foreigners, but their compatriots suffered from their dishonesty and violence.

Eventually, the governor of Alaska had to act, and he acted against them. The police got involved and then the justice system. Following a clash between the police and Hunter's men, everyone was placed under arrest, bosses and workers alike. They were sentenced to ten months in prison and locked up in the Circle City jail.

Under these circumstances, the Texans and their companions could stop worrying about finding lodgings for the winter, and the question of food would not cause them any concern either. The authorities even decided it would be pointless to transport them to Sitka, the capital of Alaska. They would serve their sentences in Circle City.

And so Hunter and Malone had to forego the many pleasures available during the winter in Vancouver, Skagway, and Dawson City. The casinos of those three cities would not be honored by the presence of the two Texans.

During their incarceration, they had plenty of time to think about the future. What would they do with their crew? What would the men themselves do when they were out of jail? There was no hope of ever resuming work at the claim on the Fortymile River, and the results of their operation at Circle City were unsatisfactory. Their resources would soon be exhausted unless they met with a stroke of luck. Unscrupulous and with no sense of moral values, they could not afford to be too fussy. Their men would do whatever they were told and follow wherever they were led, even to the remotest regions of Alaska or the Dominion rather than return to their own country, which they had probably left with some charges pending against them.

Yes, Hunter and Malone could count on the loyalty of the band of scoundrels they had recruited several years earlier. This time, to be sure, bad luck had taken a hand. They had not found the Alaskan police any more patient than their Canadian counterparts. They had lost, and with their conviction the country was rid of them for a while. But their sentences would come to an end with the return of summer, and what would they do once they were released? Would some occasion arise that they would try to take advantage of?

Such an occasion did present itself in the following way.

Among the prisoners with whom the Texans shared prison life, Hunter had noticed an Indian named Krasak, who in turn seemed to be keeping a close eye on Hunter. There is a very natural sympathy between rogues who respect each other. These two men were ideally suited to understand one another, and a certain closeness soon developed between them.

Krasak was about forty years of age, stocky and powerful, with cruel eyes and a fierce face. In short, he was just the sort of character who could not fail to appeal to Hunter and Malone.

The Indian had been convicted of theft, and his sentence still had several years to run. A native of Alaska, he was thoroughly familiar with the region, having roamed through it since his youth. He would certainly have made an excellent guide, and his intelligence could have been relied on but for the fact that his whole person inspired a well-deserved mistrust. The miners for whom he had worked had always complained about him, and it was following a major robbery—at the Birch Creek mines as it happened—that he was imprisoned in the Circle City jail.

For the first month Hunter and the Indian kept their distance but observed each other closely. Feeling that Krasak wanted to tell him something in confidence, Hunter waited.[3] He was not mistaken in thinking that this Indian, who had spent so much time in the northern part of Alaska and the Dominion, might prove useful to him and provide him with information about the area.

One day, in fact, the Indian told him about his wanderings through that almost unknown part of North America while serving as a guide for some Hudson's Bay Company agents exactly in the region between Fort Yukon on the Porcupine, Fort McPherson, and the Arctic Ocean.

Hunter must have been especially interested in knowing whether there were any gold deposits to be found north of the Arctic Circle. He was aware of the stories told by the Indians, and Krasak might give him precise information.

As it happened, the Indian had devised a plan that could not be carried out without the Texans' help. Hunter and his men would be released in a few months; whereas he still had several years to serve. He wanted the Texan, once he was out of jail, to have some incentive for helping him to escape. Alone, it would have been difficult to break out, but with outside help there was some chance of success.

As a result, Krasak revealed only enough to excite Hunter's greed. His English was quite understandable because of the contacts he had had while working for the Hudson's Bay Company.

"Yes," he said one day, "there's lots of gold in the north, near the ocean. Before long there will be thousands of miners on the Arctic coast."

"Well then," said Hunter, "there's only one thing to do—get there ahead of them."

"Of course," replied Krasak, "but you still have to know where the deposits are located."

"And you know where there are some?"

"I know quite a few, but the terrain is difficult. You could wander around there for months and walk right past claims without seeing them. Ah! If only I was out of here."

Hunter looked him in the face.

"If you were, what would you do?" he asked.

"I'd go to the place I was going to when I was picked up."

"For a measly nugget that probably caught your eye as you were going across a claim and that you pocketed."

"Nuggets belong to everybody," declared the Indian.

"Of course they do," replied Hunter, who wanted to encourage his man, "but not after they've been discovered."

"Yes they do," declared Krasak, who obviously had strong opinions of his own about personal property. "But that got me locked up in here. Ah! If only I was free!" he repeated, stretching his hand to the north.

"But where were you going, then, when the police nabbed you?"

"There, where you can fill a wheelbarrow with gold."

But for all Hunter's questions, Krasak would say no more.

Hunter knew about the legend of Golden Mount, but like the great majority of miners, he did not believe it. Perhaps he thought that was what the Indian was referring to, which meant in his opinion that the man was dreaming. However, Krasak never said a word about that mountain in the splendors of the Klondike, whose fame was as great as was the unlikelihood of its existence. Was his silence due to ignorance or to caution? Did he possess the secret of the discovery that Jacques Laurier thought was his alone? No one could say. Both Hunter and Malone (who was kept informed) seemed to have no doubt that Krasak knew about a number of gold deposits near the Arctic Ocean. The same thought occurred to them both—that they had to find out everything the Indian knew in order to undertake an expedition as soon as they and their men were out of jail.

There followed endless conversations during their long hours of inactivity, but while the Indian remained as positive as ever about the existence of the placers, he maintained an absolute silence about their exact location near the Arctic Ocean.

The last weeks of April brought an end to a winter that was as severe at Circle City as it had been in the Klondike, with its dreadful blizzards and spells of extreme cold. The prisoners had suffered greatly. Hunter and his men were waiting very impatiently for the time when they would be released and were determined to undertake an expedition to the far north of the continent.

But while they were not facing a long prison term and would be released in a few weeks, such was not the case for Krasak. He would spend several more years in the Circle City jail unless he managed to escape, and for that he needed Hunter's help. In return for that help, he promised to work for him and lead him to the deposits he knew about in the northern part of the Klondike.

The only way of escaping was by digging a tunnel under one of the walls of the courtyard adjoining the prison. It was impossible to make this opening from inside without tools and without attracting the attention of the guards, but from the outside at night and by taking certain precautions, it might be done.

A bargain was struck. On May 13 Hunter and his crew finished their sentences and took their leave of Krasak.

All the Indian had to do now was keep on the lookout. Since he was not locked in a cell, it was easy for him to leave the common dormitory and sneak across the courtyard without being seen.

That was just what he did the following night. Lying near the wall, he waited.

It was an exercise in patience, for there was not a sound to be heard between sundown and sunup.

Hunter and Malone had not been able to make their move yet. Perhaps the police were surprised at not seeing them leave Circle City immediately and wanted to keep them under surveillance. They had to take a few precautions, therefore, in order to help the Indian escape. They did not lack tools, since they still had the picks left over from their last expedition. These they found at the inn where they had been staying and where they took up residence again after getting out of jail.

Moreover, there was already some activity in the little settlement. Prospectors from the Alaskan deposits on the lower Yukon were streaming in now that the second half of May had arrived. The prospects were good thanks to an early summer.

At ten o'clock the following evening, Krasak was able to return to his post beside the wall. Night was falling and a fairly strong breeze was blowing from the north.

About eleven o'clock, putting his ear to the ground, the Indian thought he heard a noise at the base of the wall.

He was not mistaken. Hunter and Malone had set to work. Using a pick, they were digging a tunnel under the wall so that it would not be necessary to move any stones.

From his side, Krasak dug away the earth with his hands as soon as he could tell what spot they had chosen. The Texans must have heard him working, just as he heard them.

There was no alarm. The guards were not attracted to the courtyard nor were any other prisoners, although they were free to go there during the night. The cold, brisk wind kept them inside the hall, and Krasak had managed to leave without being noticed.

Finally, a little before midnight, the passageway was finished. It was wide enough for a man of ordinary size to get through it.

"Come on," said a voice. It was Hunter speaking.

"There's nobody outside?" asked Krasak.

"Nobody."

A few moments later he was through the opening, free at last.

On that side a vast plain, still dotted with the last patches of snow, stretched beyond the bend in the Yukon, where Circle City lies on the left bank.

The spring breakup had already taken place, and blocks of ice were floating downriver. It would have been dangerous for a boat to venture out into it, and besides, Hunter would probably not have been able to get one without arousing suspicion.

But the Indian was not one to let a little thing like that stand in his way. He could easily jump onto an ice pan drifting near the shore and, if need be, leap from one to another until he reached the other side. Once he was there, the whole countryside would be open before him, an uninhabited countryside that he knew well, and he would be far away before the guards realized he had escaped. But it was important for the fugitive to be out of reach before sunup. He had not an hour to lose.

"It's all agreed, then?" asked Hunter.

"Agreed."

"Where will we meet?"

"Where we said, ten miles from Fort Yukon, on the bank of the Porcupine."

That was the place they had agreed on. In two or three days Hunter and his companions would leave Circle City and head downstream toward Fort Yukon, about sixty miles to the northwest.[4] From there they would turn to the northeast and go back up the Porcupine to the spot where the Indian would be waiting for them. And he, once he had crossed the great river, would head straight north toward its tributary.

But since Krasak could not start out penniless, Hunter gave him twenty dollars. And since he could not venture into that region without being able to defend himself against robbers or wild beasts, Hunter gave him also a rifle, a revolver, and a well-filled cartridge pouch.

As they were going their separate ways, Hunter asked again, "Everything is settled, then?"

"Everything."

"And you'll take us . . ." said Malone.

"Straight to the placers. And who knows?" he added. "Perhaps to Golden Mount."

That was the first time he had mentioned the Golden Volcano. Did he believe it really existed? Did he perhaps know where it was?

They shook hands. Then Krasak leaped onto an ice pan that had come out of an eddy and was immediately caught up in the current. Although it was dark, Hunter and Malone could see him move from one ice pan to another and finally jump ashore on the other side of the river.

They went back to their inn, and the next day began to prepare for their new expedition.

Needless to say, the Indian's escape was discovered in the morning, but the police tried in vain to pick up his trail. They never suspected, and never could have suspected, that the Texans had facilitated his escape.

Three days later, Hunter and his men, about thirty in all, with a much reduced load of equipment, boarded a barge, a sort of heavy boat built to resist the shocks of floating ice. It would take them downriver to Fort Yukon, about sixty miles away, roughly the distance between Fort Selkirk and Dawson City. The journey took forty-eight hours.

On the twenty-second, after taking on fresh supplies at Fort Yukon and with their sled loaded with supplies and drawn by a sturdy dog team, the caravan headed northeast, up the left bank of the Porcupine. If the Indian was punctual at the rendezvous, they would meet him that evening.

"Let's hope he's there," said Malone.

"He'll be there," Hunter replied. "No one ever keeps a promise better than the good people of that race."

The Indian was right where he was supposed to be, and under his guidance the group continued along the left bank of that large tributary of the Yukon.

5

A Journey of Discovery

AND SO IT WAS WRITTEN in the indestructible book of destiny that Summy Skim, after accompanying Ben Raddle to the Klondike, should now accompany him to the most northerly regions of North America. He had put forward every possible argument against this new expedition and lodged every possible complaint. Nothing had succeeded in changing the engineer's plans. Unless he waited for Raddle in Dawson City (and Skim would not have had the patience for that) or headed back to Montreal (and he could not have made up his mind to do that), he would eventually follow his cousin to the conquest of Golden Mount.

"If you give in once," he kept saying to himself, "you leave yourself open to giving in a second time, and who knows whether you may not have to do it a third time? I have only myself to blame. Ah! Green Valley! Green Valley! You're so far away! And how much farther away you'll be in a few weeks!"

Thanks to the early season, the scout had returned to Dawson City during the first few days of May after coming over the Chilkoot Pass and sailing across the lakes and down the Lewes River under favorable conditions. As they had arranged, Bill Steel had come to take the two cousins back to Skagway, where they would board a steamboat to return to Vancouver.

Bill Steel was not greatly surprised to hear about Ben Raddle's plans. He knew only too well that whoever sets foot on the soil of the

Klondike runs the risk of taking root there. Although the engineer had not quite reached that point, neither did he seem ready to pack his bags for Montreal.

"That means . . ." said the scout to Summy Skim.

"Yes, Bill old boy, that's the way it is."

And that was the only answer the scout was to get.

Skim took some comfort, however, on hearing that Steel had agreed to go with them on their new expedition.

Ben Raddle had wisely decided to reveal to the scout, in whom he had every confidence, the object of this expedition. What he had kept secret from the others, even from Doctor Pilcox, namely, Jacques Laurier's secret, he had no hesitation in confiding to Bill Steel.

At first Steel refused to believe in the existence of Golden Mount. Although he knew about the legend, he would not admit that it had the slightest credibility. But after Raddle had given him all the information he had received from Jacques Laurier and shown him the map giving the precise location of the Golden Volcano, the scout began to pay attention, and the engineer's views on the subject were so firm that he finally came to share them.

"Well," said Raddle, "since there are boundless riches there, why shouldn't you have your share?"

"You're inviting me to go with you to Golden Mount?" asked Bill.

"Not just to go with us, Scout, but to be our guide. You've already been through those northern regions. You have the equipment, teams, and wagons we need for this expedition. If it doesn't work out, I'll pay you well for your services. If it succeeds, why shouldn't you dip a few handfuls out of that volcanic treasure chest, too?"

Philosophical though he was, the good scout felt himself weakening. Such an opportunity had never come his way before, assuming of course that the Frenchman's story could be taken seriously.

What frightened him, however, was the length of the journey. After calculating that the best route would be the one going through Fort McPherson, which he had already visited, he announced that the distance would not be less than 350 miles.[1]

"Fine," replied the engineer. "That's about the distance from Skagway to Dawson City, and you've never had any trouble doing it."

"True enough, Mr. Raddle, and I might add that the traveling is easier between Dawson City and Fort McPherson. But after that, to get to the mouth of the Mackenzie . . ."

"It's no more than 150 miles," said Raddle.

"Making a total distance of at least five hundred," added Steel.

"Which we can cover in five or six weeks, and we'd be back in Dawson City before winter."

Yes, it was all possible provided they did not encounter one of those unfortunate circumstances that occur so often in the far north.

Ben Raddle's arguments had been supported by those of the foreman Lorique and Neluto, who was delighted to see his boss, Bill Steel, once again. And it must be admitted that Summy Skim took the same position and argued very persuasively. Now that the journey had been decided on, the scout's participation became crucial and increased the chances of its success.

As for Neluto, the expedition suited him perfectly. What wonderful hunting there would be for him and Skim in this almost untouched region.

"Good hunting for whom?" remarked Skim.

"Why, for us," replied Neluto, somewhat surprised by this reaction.

"Unless we're the quarry. There's a good possibility the country may not be safe. There may be all kinds of criminals there."

In fact, during the summer, parties of Indians up to no good roam around the northern regions. The Hudson's Bay Company agents have often had to defend themselves against their attacks.

Preparations were quickly made. The scout and his men were ready to leave for the north instead of for the south with their equipment, wagons, portable boat, tents, and mule teams, much preferable to dog teams since there would be fodder for them on the grassy plains. As for food, in addition to what they would get by hunting and fishing, it was easy to obtain enough canned meat and vegetables, tea, coffee, flour, sugar, and brandy for several months. Dawson City had just had its supplies replenished by the companies that served the Klondike gold fields now that communications had been reopened between that city, Skagway, and Vancouver. There would be no shortage of ammunition either, and should there be any need to use their rifles, they would be fully loaded.

The caravan under the scout's direction would consist of the two cousins, Lorique, Neluto with his horse and wagon, six Canadians who had worked on Claim 129, and nine Canadians working for Bill Steel, making a total of twenty,[2] enough to do the work at Golden Mount. According to Jacques Laurier's information, the work would be simply a matter of picking up the nuggets in the volcano's crater.

Preparations for the expedition (whose objective was known only to Ben Raddle, Summy Skim, the scout, and Lorique) went ahead so quickly that the departure date was set for May 6.

Of course Raddle wanted to get one last report on the condition of the claims on the Fortymile River before leaving Dawson City on this new expedition. He sent the foreman and Neluto back to the source of the new northward-flowing stream.

Nothing had changed. Claim 129, like 127 and others along the border, was completely inundated. The new stream followed a regular course in the bed created by the earthquake. The task of deflecting it would have been so enormous and costly that there was no point in undertaking it, and no one even considered it. Lorique returned convinced that any hope of ever working those deposits had to be abandoned.

Preparations were completed by the afternoon of May 5. On that last evening, the evening for good-byes, Summy Skim and Ben Raddle went to the hospital to take their leave of the sister superior and the two nuns. Sisters Martha and Madeleine were very apprehensive at the thought of their compatriots venturing out through the northern regions where Jacques Laurier and Harry Brown had endured the many privations that had cost them their lives.

Raddle reassured the sisters as best he could, and Skim tried to appear as confident as his cousin. In any case, the little caravan would be back in Dawson City before the end of summer, hale and hearty. If they were exhausted it would apparently be from the weight of the nuggets!

"Speaking for myself," said Dr. Pilcox, "I'm delighted to see you leaving for the north. If you had gone south, it would have meant you were returning to Montreal, and we'd never see you again in the Klondike. Now, at least, we'll see you when you come back."

"Please God it may be so," murmured Sister Madeleine.

"May he guide you there and back," added Sister Martha.

"Amen!" said the superior.

At five o'clock the next morning, the caravan left Dawson City through the upper part of town on the right bank of the Klondike River and headed northeast.

The weather was ideal, with a clear sky, a light breeze, and a temperature of only about twelve degrees above zero. Most of the snow had melted, leaving only a few dazzling white patches on the grass.

It need hardly be mentioned that the itinerary had been worked out in detail. Ben Raddle, Lorique, and the scout had carefully marked on the large-scale map of the area the details indicated by Jacques Laurier's sketch. It must be remembered, too, that the scout had already made the trip from Dawson City to Fort McPherson, and the accuracy of his memory could be depended on for the 350 miles between those two points.

All in all, it was a fairly flat region with several streams running through it. The first of them were tributaries or subtributaries of the Yukon or Klondike rivers, but beyond the Arctic Circle the streams were tributaries or subtributaries of the Peel River, which skirts the base of the Rocky Mountains before flowing into the Mackenzie.

For the first part of the journey from Dawson City to Fort McPherson, then, there would be no serious difficulties in their way. After the last snow had melted, the streams would go back to their lowest level. They would be easy to ford and would still contain enough water to meet the little group's needs. When they reached the Peel River, about a hundred miles from Fort McPherson, they would make a decision about how to cover the second half of the itinerary.

Why not admit it? They were all, with the possible exception of Summy Skim (who suffered from a painful lack of confidence), starting out full of hope. And is that not a surprisingly human feeling? Ben Raddle, Lorique, Neluto, even Bill Steel himself, who had never believed in Golden Mount before, now accepted its existence based on the clear assertions and the precise information given by Jacques Laurier. The scout, out of curiosity rather than greed, was the most eager of them all to find the famous volcano, and he would stop at nothing to reach it.

On leaving Dawson City, the wagon, with Neluto at the reins, carried the two cousins along at a brisk pace. It had to slow down, however, because the heavily laden carts could not keep up with it. Even so, it was possible to increase the length of the first days' marches without unduly tiring the animals and men. The vast, flat, open country presented no obstacles, and the southwest wind did not hinder their progress. To give the mules a break, the scout and his men would often walk part of the way, and then Raddle, Lorique, and the scout would talk about the subject that was uppermost in their minds. Summy Skim and Neluto scoured the countryside left and right, and since there was an abundance of ducks and partridges, they did not waste their powder. This meant that less of their canned goods were used when they stopped to eat at noon and in the evening. Then, even before nightfall (for it came late at that time of year and at that latitude), they set up camp for the night.

The caravan's northeasterly course took them away from the territory drained by the upper reaches of the Porcupine. The river made a wide bend toward the west and joined the Yukon near Fort Yukon.[3] There was no danger that Ben Raddle and his friends might meet Hunter's band, which had crossed the Porcupine much farther downstream. In any case, they were unaware that the Texans had undertaken an expedition toward the region near the Arctic Ocean under the guidance of the Indian Krasak. After the disaster at the Fortymile River, the rumor had spread that they were among the victims, but since the incident at

Circle City, their encounter with the police and their conviction, it became known that they had escaped unscathed from the cataclysm. What Raddle and Skim did not know was that their prison term was now up and that they were free again. Besides, they gave very little thought to the former owners of Claim 127.

On May 29, twenty-three days after leaving Dawson City, the caravan crossed the Arctic Circle, a little beyond the sixty-sixth parallel. They had covered the first two hundred miles of the journey without incident. They had not even met any of the parties of Indians that the Hudson's Bay Company agents still pursue across the region, driving them westward.

The weather was generally fine, and everyone was in good health. The robust crew were used to hard work and suffered no ill effects from a journey made under those conditions and at that time of year, even at such high latitudes. The mule teams easily found fodder on the grassy plains. When they camped for the night, it was always within easy reach of a clear stream at the edge of the forest of birches, poplars, and pines, which stretched to the northeast as far as the eye could see.

The landscape was now beginning to change. On the eastern horizon stood the crest of the Rocky Mountains. This is the part of North America where the mountain range rears its first peaks before continuing along almost the entire length of the New World.

One of the tributaries of the Porcupine had its source there, but the scout did not follow it, for it would have taken them too far to the west. But since the terrain was becoming more uneven because of the network of creeks and the hilly nature of the ground as they approached the mountains, he headed straight through the mountain passes, which were not too high in this part of northern Canada. This brought them to the Peel River, which runs past Fort McPherson and might have been useful to them.

Having reached the Arctic Circle, Bill Steel and his companions were still about sixty miles from the fort located almost at the point where the mountain range begins. Traveling became difficult, and there were several occasions when one of the wagon's axles or wheels would have been broken if Neluto had not been driving very carefully. There was no marked trail, and the Hudson's Bay Company traffic had not smoothed the way, but they had expected this, and Bill Steel knew what he was up against.

One day, as the caravan was making its way through a narrow pass, he remarked, "You know, this trail didn't seem so bad to me when I was over it about twenty years ago."

"But it can't have changed since then," said Summy Skim.

"Perhaps it's because last winter was so severe," said the engineer.

"That's what I think, Mr. Ben," said the scout. "The cold spells were so extreme that the frost went deep into the ground and broke it up."

"We have to be on the lookout for rock slides," advised Lorique. "Rocks could easily break loose from the sides of this gorge."

That actually did happen two or three times. Huge pieces of quartz and granite loosened by running water came rolling and bouncing down the slopes, smashing and crushing the trees in their path. One of the wagons and its team narrowly escaped being destroyed by those heavy boulders.

For two days the going was hard, and they were not able to maintain their average rate of progress. Ben Raddle and the foreman cursed the occasional delays, but Skim welcomed them with a philosophical equanimity.

"Golden Mount (if it exists)," he said, "will be there in two weeks just as it will be in one. Besides, I'm counting on having a well-deserved rest at Fort McPherson. After the distance we've covered, we'll be entitled to stretch out on a comfortable bed at an inn."

"If there are any inns at Fort McPherson," replied Raddle, who was not yet at the point of complaining about having camped in the open for the past three weeks.

"But are there any inns?" Lorique asked the scout.

"No," was the reply. "Fort McPherson is only a post fortified against the Indians, which the Hudson's Bay Company maintains for its agents. There are rooms, though."

"If there are rooms," observed Skim, "then there are beds. I wouldn't mind stretching out my legs for two or three good nights."

"First, let's get there," snapped Raddle, "instead of wasting our time with useless stops."

And so the caravan moved along as quickly as it could over the detours and obstacles of the mountain passes. But after it had crossed the end of the mountain range bordering the valley of the Peel River, it would move more rapidly.

Before they reached that point, however, the scout had to get himself out of an unfortunate encounter (although Summy Skim might have been inclined to describe it quite differently).

When they came out of the pass, the scout had called a halt near the bank of the Peel River under the overhanging branches of the tall pine trees grouped together on the left bank.

First of all, the question arose of whether to build a raft to carry them down the river to Fort McPherson. But Steel recognized that the stream was not navigable since it was still clogged by the last blocks of ice from the spring breakup. To build a raft big enough to carry the caravan's men and equipment would have taken some time, and to navigate it through the drifting ice would have been difficult. Instead, they would travel the remaining seventy-five miles along the Peel River, whose banks posed no serious obstacles.

"But by using those ice pans," said Steel to Raddle, "we can cross over to the right bank, and we'll be that much farther ahead, since Fort McPherson is on that side."[4]

That question having been settled, they pitched their tent and everyone got ready for an evening's rest, so eagerly awaited after the second leg of the day's journey.

But hardly had they settled in under the trees when Lorique, who had walked a short distance downstream, came running back. As soon as he was within earshot he shouted, "Watch out! Watch out!"

Summy Skim, like the experienced hunter he was, jumped up at once and grabbed his rifle, ready to fire.

"Indians?" he exclaimed.

"No," said the foreman. "Bears!"

"That's just as bad!" replied Steel.

In an instant, everyone was at the edge of the woods, while the mules snorted and the dog Stop barked furiously.[5] A trio of bears had come up the left bank and were now at the edge of the campsite. There they stopped and stood up on their hind legs. They were big animals, ferocious in appearance, belonging to the species of grizzlies that frequent the gorges of the Rocky Mountains.

Were the bears driven by hunger? Were they about to attack the caravan? Probably, because they were uttering frightful growls that terrified the mules.

Summy Skim and Neluto rushed forward. Two shots rang out and one of the bears, struck in the head and the chest, fell heavily to the ground and lay motionless.

That was the end of the attack. The other two bears immediately took to their heels. The few bullets sent in their direction did not touch them, for they bolted at top speed along the left bank of the river. But it was agreed that there would be a man on watch all night, for fear of another attack by the beasts.

It was a magnificent animal that they had shot. The meat, some of which is excellent, made a timely addition to the reserves of food. As for the splendid hide, Neluto undertook to remove it from the carcass.

"Since he doesn't need it for the winter," said Skim, "let's not let it go to waste. With a dressing gown like that, you could stand a temperature of sixty degrees below zero, which is not uncommon in this blessed Klondike!"

6

Fort McPherson

FORT MCPHERSON, at longitude 135 degrees west and latitude 67 degrees north, was the Hudson Bay Company's most northerly post in North America at that time. It commanded the whole area drained by the numerous branches into which the Mackenzie divides before emptying into the Arctic Ocean. It was there that fur hunters replenished their supplies and found protection against the Indian bands wandering across the northern plains of the Dominion.

This fort, built on the right bank of the Peel River, kept in touch as closely as possible with Fort Good Hope, 225 miles upstream on the Mackenzie.[1] Stocks of furs traveled from one to the other and were then transported under heavy guard to the company's central storehouse.

Fort McPherson was nothing more than a large store, above which were the factor's room, his men's quarters, and a room furnished with camp beds for about twenty people. Near the store were stables where the teams of horses and mules were kept. The nearby forests provided enough firewood to combat the severe cold of the winter. Fortunately, there had been no shortage of wood for many years, and there would be enough for many years to come. Stocks of food were maintained regularly by the company's suppliers at the beginning of the summer and were generously supplemented by hunting and fishing.

The factor in charge of Fort McPherson had about twenty men under his command, all Canadians or from British Columbia.[2] Discipline was strict and life was hard, given the severity of the climate to say nothing of the constant danger of attacks by wandering bands. For that reason the weapons rack was filled with rifles and revolvers, and the company was prompt to renew the supply of ammunition so that the fort was always well armed.

They could not be too careful. Indeed, the factor and his men had had an alert only a few days earlier.

It happened on the morning of June 4. The watchman had just reported that a body of men was coming down the right bank of the Peel River. It appeared to consist of about fifty Indians and foreigners, accompanied by several horse-drawn wagons.

As a necessary precaution, the gate of Fort McPherson was tightly closed as was usually done in such a situation. The only way to get into the enclosure would have been by climbing the walls.

One of the foreigners, who appeared to be the guide, came up to the gate and asked to have it opened.

The factor appeared at the top of the wall. He must have been suspicious of the new arrivals since he replied that no one would come through the gate.

He had given the right answer, for there was an immediate outburst of threats and insults. He recognized that the foreign members of the party were South Americans, always inclined to extreme violence. The Hudson's Bay Company had already had trouble with them, especially since the government in Moscow had sold Alaska to the United States, and there was a standing order to deny them entry into any of the forts in the northern region of the Dominion.

But those scoundrels did not confine themselves to words; they proceeded to take action. For one reason or another, either to obtain provisions or to capture Fort McPherson, which is a very important base commanding the Mackenzie delta, the South Americans and Indians tried to force the gate open. It held firm, however, and after a volley that wounded some of their number, they beat a hasty retreat but not without firing their rifles at the company agents who appeared at the top of the enclosure. Fortunately, none of them were hit.

After this fruitless attempt, the group decided to leave the area. But instead of going down the right bank of the Peel River, they headed northwest into the mountainous region.

The agents at Fort McPherson had certainly been well advised to be on their guard, and since there was some danger of a return attack, they kept watch day and night.

Five days later, on June 9, they had good reason to congratulate themselves on having maintained a close guard because another group was spotted coming down the right bank of the Peel, also heading toward the fort.

Great was the surprise of the scout's caravan—for that is who it was —to see a dozen company agents appear on the parapet with their rifles at the ready, ordering them to go away.

When it was explained to the head factor that this was a group of Canadians, he agreed to talk with them. By a fortunate coincidence, it turned out that he and Bill Steel were old acquaintances, having both served in the Canadian militia.

Fort McPherson's gate opened at once, and the caravan went into the inner courtyard, where they received a warm welcome.

The factor gave an explanation of his reaction at the approach of a group of strangers. He added that his caution, even mistrust, was justified by what had happened a few days earlier, when a party of South Americans and Indians had made hostile moves against the fort, attempting to force their way in, and he had been obliged to drive them back with rifle fire. What did they want, those prowlers, those bandits? Perhaps to steal food from the fort, for it was inconceivable that they intended to capture it. The Hudson's Bay Company would have wasted no time in driving them out.

"And what became of the gang?" asked the scout.

"After their planned attack failed," replied the factor, "they went on their way."

"In what direction?"

"Northwest."

"Well," said Ben Raddle, "since we're going north, we probably won't meet them."

"I hope you don't," said the factor, "because they looked to me like a pack of the dregs of humanity."

"But where are they going?" asked Summy Skim.

"They're probably looking for new gold deposits since they had prospector's equipment with them."

"Have you ever heard of any gold being found in this part of the Dominion?" asked Raddle.

"There is some, definitely," said the factor, "and I'm not surprised that they'd want to try digging for it."

But that was as much as the factor knew about it. He simply repeated what he had heard from Hudson's Bay Company hunters traveling through the Mackenzie delta and along the shores of the Arctic Ocean. He did not even mention Golden Mount, which could not have been more than 250 miles to the north of Fort McPherson.

Of course, Raddle did not want anyone to know Jacques Laurier's secret, but Skim was rather surprised. He still doubted that the Golden Volcano existed.

When he asked the factor whether there were any volcanoes to the north of them, the answer was that he had never heard of any.

The scout said only that the caravan was going in search of gold fields around the Mackenzie delta. They had left Dawson City six weeks ago and requested permission to rest for a few days at Fort McPherson. If the factor would be kind enough to offer them hospitality, they would be most grateful.

That was easily arranged. Since there was no one in the fort at the time except its small regular garrison and since the hunters would not arrive for another month, there was room available, and the caravan could settle in without causing any inconvenience. It was well supplied with food and would not have to depend on the fort's resources, which would be replenished at regular intervals by the Company's suppliers.

Ben Raddle thanked the factor heartily for his warm welcome, and in less than an hour men and equipment had moved in under excellent conditions.

There followed three days of complete rest for everyone except for Summy Skim and Neluto, who yielded to their hunters' instincts. They had good hunting in the surrounding area, whose abundant game provided the garrison with its main fare during the summer. There was no danger of exhausting the supply of partridges, ducks, and other representatives of the feathered family. There were even moose, only a few to be sure and difficult to approach. Skim spotted some but reluctantly had to give up the idea of following them for fear of being drawn too far away. Nevertheless, he was so well pleased when he returned on the second day that he said to his cousin, "You know, Ben, I'd much rather spend the summer at Fort McPherson than in Dawson City. At least we wouldn't be crowded in with that abominable swarm of prospectors."

"Which includes us, Summy."

"Which includes us, if you like. But here in the open country where you don't hear the rockers grinding or the pickaxes pounding, it's like a summer resort. I can believe I'm not so far from Green Valley—which we'll see again, by the way, before next winter."

And although he had already had to deal with a few disappointments, Summy Skim never doubted that he would be back in Montreal within four months.

The caravan's stay at Fort McPherson went by without incident, and when it came time to leave, everyone was well rested and ready to be on the trail again.

On the morning of June 12 the little company formed up under the scout's direction. They said good-bye to the factor and his comrades, offered their sincere and well-deserved thanks, and expressed the hope that they would see them again on the way back. The gate opened and closed again, and the caravan started down the right bank of the Peel River at a brisk pace.

Raddle and Skim were back in the cart driven by Neluto, and the other teams followed under the scout's direction. He was not familiar with the territory north of Fort McPherson of course, since he had never gone beyond that outpost. It was now the engineer's directions that were to be relied on. His map showed fairly accurately the location of Golden Mount as plotted by Jacques Laurier. The mountain should be situated at 68 degrees north and 136 degrees west. This being the case, the route from Fort McPherson veered slightly to the northwest, along the left bank of the Peel River, which would empty into the many mouths of the Mackenzie estuary 150 miles farther on.

At noon they halted near a stream at the edge of a forest of balsam firs. The animals were put out to pasture in a nearby meadow. A light, refreshing breeze was blowing from the northeast, under a cloudy sky.

The countryside was flat, and far to the east could be seen the first foothills of the Rocky Mountains. According to the map, the distance to Golden Mount should not be more than about two hundred miles. It would take a week at the most, barring any delays.

As they were chatting during the break, Bill Steel remarked, "Well, Mr. Summy Skim, no matter what happens, we're finally going to reach the end of our journey, and then we'll only have to think about getting back."

"My friend," was the reply, "a journey is not really over until you're back home, and I won't believe that this one is definitely finished until the door of our house on Jacques-Cartier Street closes behind us."

And who could have blamed him for speaking in such cautious terms?

It took four full days for the caravan to get to the confluence of the Peel and Mackenzie rivers, which they reached on the afternoon of June 16.

No problems interfered with their long days' marches made without undue exertion over the flat ground along the riverbank. The country was deserted, and they only met a few parties of Indians, members of the tribes who live by fishing in the Mackenzie delta. They did not encounter the gang reported by the factor of Fort McPherson, and it must be said that the scout, knowing only too well the type of scoundrels it included, made every effort to avoid coming into contact with it.

"Let's get to Golden Mount by ourselves," he kept saying, "let's come back by ourselves, and everything will work out for the best."

"But we'll defend ourselves, after all," said Lorique.

"It's better not to have to defend ourselves," declared Steel.

"And where we're going, it's better if no one follows us," added Ben Raddle.

As they traveled, Steel took every precaution. He always sent two men out ahead of the caravan, and on others its flanks, to act as scouts. Then, when they made a halt, the approaches to the campsite were always carefully watched, to guard against any surprise.

In short, there had been no unpleasant encounters so far. They did not pick up the slightest trace of the suspicious gang and assumed that it was now making its way through the mountainous part of the region east of the Mackenzie.

The estuary of this great river makes up a large hydrographic network that has perhaps no equal anywhere either in the New World or the Old. Its branches spread out like the ribs of a fan and are connected by a multitude of secondary branches, winding channels that become one enormous sheet of ice under the influence of the winter's deep cold. At this time of year, the last remains of the spring breakup had just melted into the waters of the Arctic Ocean, and there was not a block of ice to be seen in the Peel River.

To look at the complicated arrangement of the Mackenzie estuary, one might wonder if the West Channel was not formed by the Peel River itself, and joined to the main, or East Channel,[3] by the network lying between them.

That made little difference. What was important was that the caravan should be able to get back onto the left bank of the western branch, since the bearing of Golden Mount placed it close to that bank, almost at the edge of the icy Arctic Ocean.

This crossing was carried out with considerable difficulty during the halt on June 16. Fortunately, the water level was not high, and after careful searching the scout discovered a ford where the men and animals could cross, and the vehicles, too, once they were unloaded.

This operation took up the entire afternoon, and by evening Bill Steel and his friends were ensconced on the opposite bank. Huge clumps of trees provided shelter for them, and if a few shots rang out at that moment, they were not fired to defend the campsite against hostile bipeds, but against quadrupeds of the plantigrade family. Three or four bears, on meeting such a hostile reception, hurried away. This time they did not leave a second skin behind to complete the pair.

When dawn broke at 3:00 a.m. the next day, June 17, Bill Steel gave the signal to move out, and the teams made their way along the left bank.

The scout estimated that it would take three days to reach the coast near the Mackenzie delta. This would bring the caravan within sight of Golden Mount if the information given on the map was reasonably precise. Even assuming that the location given by Jacques Laurier was not absolutely exact, the mountain would certainly be visible since it would tower over the whole region.

They made their way along the western branch of the great river without meeting any obstacles. The weather was less favorable, however. Clouds were moving in swiftly from the north, and rain, sometimes very heavy, slowed their progress. Sometimes they had to seek shelter in the forests beside the river, and the overnight stops were always difficult. Still, all these irritations could be endured since they were now not far from their goal

It was fortunate, too, that the caravan did not have to cross the hydrographic network of the delta. The scout had good reason to wonder how he would have managed. Crossing all those streams would have presented serious problems if they were not fordable. Part of the equipment would have had to be left behind to be picked up later. There was even a possibility, if the thunderstorms brought heavy rain, that the entire surface of the delta might be flooded, making it impossible to cross either on foot or with the wagon teams and the cart.

No serious incident occurred, however, to delay even by twenty-four hours the arrival of the scout and his friends at the edge of the Arctic Ocean. On the afternoon of June 19, when they were not more than twelve or fifteen miles away, they made camp near the West Channel. The next day, they would undoubtedly come to a stop at the sandy coastline.

At five o'clock the sun was still fairly high above the horizon, but unfortunately fog patches were developing to the north.

Naturally, every eye turned in that direction, hoping to catch sight of the peak of Golden Mount. Even assuming that it was no more than five of six hundred feet high, it should have been visible at that distance, and certainly would be at night, if its crater was crowned with flames.[4]

Nothing appeared to those impatient eyes. The horizon seemed to have closed in a circle, as if the sea and the sky had joined all around it.

The level of tension experienced by Ben Raddle and the foreman, who shared all Raddle's hopes and illusions, can well be imagined. They could not stand still. If the scout and Summy Skim had not held them back, they would have started walking in the dark and not stopped until the dry land came to an end at the point where the Dominion is washed by the waters of the Arctic Ocean.

With telescopes to their eyes, they kept looking to the north, east, and west, studying the countryside, which would not be cloaked in darkness until late at night. They could see nothing through the light fog hanging in the air.

"Relax, Ben, relax," Skim kept repeating. "Be patient and wait until tomorrow. If Golden Mount is there, you'll find it in its place. There's no point in leaving camp just to locate it a few hours earlier."

This sound advice was seconded by Bill Steel, and Raddle and Lorique had to give in. There were still certain precautions to be taken against a possible encounter with Indians or—who could tell?—with the gang of scoundrels who had retreated from Fort McPherson.

And so the night passed. When dawn came, the fog had still not lifted, and Golden Mount would not have been visible even at a distance of five or six miles.

"Anyway," Skim logically pointed out, "if Golden Mount doesn't exist, we wouldn't see it even if the weather was clear."

Obviously, he still had some reservations with regard to Jacques Laurier's discovery, and perhaps Bill Steel was not far from sharing them.

As for Ben Raddle, his features were tense, his brow was gloomy, and anxiety was written on his face. He could not contain himself.

They broke camp at 4:00 a.m. It was broad daylight and the sun was already several degrees above the horizon. It could be felt behind the fog, which its rays had not yet dissipated.

The caravan set out again. By eleven o'clock it could not have been more than five miles from the shore, and Golden Mount was nowhere to be seen.

Summy Skim could only wonder whether his cousin was not going mad. He had endured so much weariness and run so many risks only to be disillusioned in the end!

But no. Before noon, the sky cleared to the north, the fog lifted, and Neluto could be heard shouting, "Look! Look! Smoke!"

At that instant the mountain appeared, the Golden Volcano, with its crater spewing sooty vapors.

7

Golden Mount

It took no more than two hours for the scout and his companions to cover the remaining distance to Golden Mount. They seemed to be attracted to this mountain as if it were an enormous magnet and they were made of iron.

"And in fact, that's what we are, aren't we?" said Summy Skim. "We must be made of iron to have endured everything we've been through so far." That was his way of completing the above-mentioned comparison suggested by the foreman.

It was not yet five o'clock when the caravan stopped at the foot of the volcano. Just as Jacques Laurier had indicated, there was the little stream named Rubber Creek flowing alongside the mountain's west face, on its way to the ocean. On its northern side, the base of Golden Mount was washed by the waters of the Arctic Ocean.

The region was completely uninhabited. Beyond the mountain and over toward the Mackenzie delta, there was not a native village to be seen, nor any of the Indians who frequent the coastal area. Off to sea there was not a single vessel, neither the sail of a whaling ship nor smoke from a steamer. And yet this was the time of year when whalers and seal hunters frequent the northern seas. No, no one had preceded Ben Raddle and his party to this remote region. Perhaps Jacques Laurier and Harry Brown were the only ones who had ever extended their exploration as far as the Mackenzie delta and discovered the existence of Golden Mount.

The scout made camp at the base of the east face, separated from Rubber Creek by a stand of birches and poplars and about a mile from the shore. There would be plenty of fresh water and wood to meet the caravan's requirements. Farther on, to the west and south, lay vast open country covered with greenery at this time of year and dotted with thickets. Skim thought there should be good hunting there. As they went along, he had noticed that there would be no shortage of furred and feathered game. The meat brought in by the hunters, together with the catch of fish, would ensure a steady supply of food for the encampment at Golden Mount without touching the reserves.

This gold deposit certainly belonged to the engineer, by right of first occupancy. No one had taken possession of it previously, and no one would have any right to interfere. No stakes marked out the limits of a claim, and no fees would line the coffers of the Canadian government.

Under Bill Steel's direction, the encampment was soon organized. Two tents were set up at the edge of the little wood. The cart and wagons occupied a spot in a clearing beside the stream. The mules were unhitched and turned out to graze freely in the nearby meadows. Needless to say, the usual precautionary measures were taken, and a watch would be kept day and night on the approaches to the encampment, although there seemed to be nothing to fear, unless perhaps bears, those habitual denizens of the Dominion's far northern regions.

No one doubted, moreover, that the mining of Golden Mount could be accomplished in short order. It would be simply a matter of scooping up the treasure in the crater and loading it into the wagons. There would be no need for a pick, no washing to be done. According to Jacques Laurier's information, the gold was in the form of dust and nuggets. All the work had been done long ago by the subterranean agents of Golden Mount.

But Ben Raddle would not be certain of that until he had climbed the mountain and studied the layout of the crater. According to Jacques Laurier, it was easy to go down into it. But something had occurred that might create certain difficulties, and that very evening, as it happened, the foreman Lorique had occasion to discuss it with the engineer.

"Mr. Ben," he said, "when the Frenchman told you about the existence of Golden Mount, didn't he mention an extinct volcano?"

"Extinct, yes, or at least there was no smoke or flame coming out of it when he visited it."

"And he had been able to climb right to the top of it, if I'm not mistaken?"

"Yes, he even went down into the crater," added Raddle.

"Laurier didn't think there was any imminent danger of an eruption?"

"No. There was no steam coming out of the crater. But that was six months ago, and eruptive forces may have come into play again since that time."

"They certainly have," replied the foreman. "There are wreaths of smoke rising at the top of the mountain, and I'm wondering how we'll be able to get down into the crater."

Of course, Ben Raddle had been thinking about this since their last overnight stop. They were no longer dealing with an extinct volcano, or even one just waking up from sleep. But if it proved impossible to get down into the crater, the engineer confided his thoughts to Lorique.

"Why couldn't an eruption save us all that work by emptying Golden Mount of all its nuggets? We'd just have to pick them up at the foot of the mountain, and that would be one less big job to do. Anyway, let's wait until tomorrow. When we've reached the top, we'll do whatever the situation requires."

The evening came to a pleasant end. The breeze had fallen well before sunset, and stars lit up the clear sky. The North Star cast its beams almost at the zenith, above the northern horizon.

The scout organized the watch on the encampment, and there was no disturbance during the night, except for the distant growling of bears, which did not venture as far as Golden Mount.

By five o'clock everyone was up.

Spurred on by his imagination, Summy Skim had gazed at the famous Golden Mount with considerable interest. Who knows? Perhaps he too was yielding to the temptation to scoop up handfuls of that enormous treasure.

238

"All right," he said to himself, "if Uncle Josias had made such a discovery, he'd probably have taken only a few weeks to collect millions and millions. Instead of dying in the Klondike, he would have come back home to associate with the billionaires of the New World. But fate decreed otherwise, and the opportunity now falls to his nephews, of whom one at least had never had such lofty ambitions, even in his dreams. Anyway, since we've come as far as the shores of the Arctic Ocean, let's try to go back with our pockets well lined—and when I say pockets, I mean our wagons and our cart loaded with gold to the breaking point. And yet, to tell the truth, no matter how much I study this mountain from every direction and how often I tell myself that there's enough precious metal in it to put Australia, California, and Africa to shame, it still doesn't look much like a strongbox to me."

In this case, however, in order to satisfy him Golden Mount would have had to resemble the vaults of the Bank of England or the Bank of America. It would have been a parallelepiped with perpendicular sides and an open door in the front wall, and since Ben Raddle didn't know the combination, how could he have opened it?

No, Golden Mount was simply a fire-spitting mountain, an irregular cone towering over that part of the coast. It was nine hundred or a thousand feet high, and as nearly as one could judge, its circumference at the base could not have been less than five miles. It was not exactly a cone, but a truncated cone, ending in a plateau at the top instead of coming to a point like a sugarloaf.

The first thing to reckon with was that the sides rose at an angle of at least seventy degrees. That would definitely make the ascent very difficult. But after all, it was certainly not impossible, since Jacques Laurier and his partner had been able to get up to the volcano's crater.

The north flank, facing the sea, was the steepest, nearly perpendicular. To attempt an ascent on that side was out of the question, and besides the base of the mountain there was in the water. There were no rocks coming out at its base, and it might have been called a cliff if it had been composed of chalk or some whitish material, instead of the blackish color that volcanic substances take on.

Ben Raddle and Lorique undertook to decide by which face they would try to get up to the summit of Golden Mount since Jacques Laurier had not indicated the route he had taken to reach the crater.

They were only a few hundred paces from the base since they had set up their camp precisely in the angle between Rubber Creek and the east face.

As for the slopes, they appeared to be covered with short grass, with a few woody clumps here and there that might give the climbers a foothold. Farther up, the grass gave way to a sort of dark humus, which might have been a layer of ashes and slag. There appeared to have been no recent eruption, which explained why Jacques Laurier thought Golden Mount had been extinct for a long time.

Raddle and Lorique returned to the encampment and reported the result of their explorations. The west face, where the slope was more gradual, would be the most suitable for making an ascent.

"Fine," replied the scout, "but let's build up our energy. Let's have breakfast right away."

"A wise move," added Skim. "It may take a good two or three hours to reach the crater, and if we spend that much time at the summit, we won't be back before afternoon."

Breakfast was soon ready. The game they had shot the previous day as the caravan went along was kept in reserve. Raddle, Skim, and their friends made do with ham and other canned meat, biscuits, and tea. In less than forty minutes, their hunger was satisfied.

On Bill Steel's advice, they decided to take some food along in case the climbers should need it. The flasks would be filled with gin and whiskey suitably diluted with water. They would also take a pick, spikes, and ropes, which they might have occasion to use on the steepest slopes.

The weather proved favorable for their undertaking. The day promised to be fine, and the sun, screened by clouds driven by a light north wind, would not be too hot.

Neluto would not take part in this first ascent. He would guard the encampment with the crew and was not to leave it for any reason whatsoever. There seemed to be nothing to fear, since the region was unin-habited, but it was important to maintain the practice of keeping a close watch.

About eight o'clock, then, Ben Raddle, Summy Skim, Lorique, and the scout set out. They skirted the base of the mountain on its southern side and reached the west face.

What struck them as rather strange was that along this side of the base they found no traces of volcanic material, not even under the vegetation. Of the last eruption (and when could that have been?) they found no sign nor anything resembling gold dust. Should they conclude from this that these materials had been flung out to sea and were now lying under the deep water off shore?

"It doesn't matter, anyway," was Raddle's response when the foreman drew attention to this. "It's likely—in fact, it's certain—that there's been no eruption since Jacques Laurier visited this volcano, barely six months ago.[1] He saw nuggets in the crater, and we'll see them too."

It was half past eight when he and his companions stopped at the base of the west face,[2] which extended all the way to the shore.

A careful examination revealed that this face presented a more gradual slope in the part that veered off to the north. It would be best to start out in that direction, even though they might have to change course later.

The scout took the lead and the others followed. At first the slope was not too steep—not more than forty degrees. The vegetation provided a fairly solid footing, and there was no need to use the spikes and ropes. Furthermore, Bill Steel, who had made many excursions in the Rocky Mountains, was a practical guide. His instinct was unerring, and he was so used to this kind of activity that his friends had difficulty keeping up with him.

"That's what comes of going over the Chilkoot Pass twenty times," said Summy Skim. "It gives you the legs of a chamois."

And truly, after the first third of the ascent, even a chamois might have found itself in trouble. It would have needed the wings of a vulture or an eagle.

241

The slope became so steep that it was necessary to use knees, feet, and hands, holding on to clumps of stunted shrubs. Soon the spikes and ropes were indispensable. The scout would go on ahead, drive in a spike through the vegetation, and tie a rope to it. Then he would uncoil the rope, and the others would pull themselves up toward him. They worked with the utmost care, since a fall to the base of the mountain would have been fatal.

By about nine o'clock, Raddle, Skim, and the foreman had joined Bill Steel at the halfway point. They all paused there to catch their breath and take a few mouthfuls from the flasks, then started out again, crawling up the slope.

They noticed that, although the summit of the volcano was plumed with smoke, indicating that subterranean forces were at work, there was no growling to be heard, and there was no perceptible tremor at the surface. The slope was probably thicker on that side, and the crater's chimney opened either on the northern or eastern part of the volcano.

They continued their ascent, which became more and more difficult and dangerous, but there was no question of their failing to reach the plateau at the top of the cone. It was unacceptable that the scout and his friends should not be able to do what the two Frenchmen had done a few months earlier.[3]

At one point, however, Summy Skim found himself in grave danger. He was hoisting himself up a very steep slope behind the scout when the spike holding the rope by which he was hauling himself gave way.

Ben Raddle uttered a terrified scream. He saw his cousin rolling downhill in danger of hurtling down to the foot of the mountain, where his friends would have found nothing to pick up but a corpse.

Fortunately, Lorique, who was at the end of the line, was able to grab hold of a strong clump of shrubs, and just as Skim came rolling near him, he seized him with his powerful arm and brought him to a stop. It was fortunate also that the shrubs withstood the shock, and there were no serious consequences.

"Ah! My poor friend!" exclaimed Raddle, sliding over toward him.

"Yes, Ben, I had a narrow escape."

"You're not hurt?"

"No. A few scratches, but they don't need the attention of good old Dr. Pilcox or the good Sisters Martha and Madeleine. Do you know what I said to myself as I was rolling downhill?"

"No, what?"

"That the volcano was spewing me out like an ordinary nugget."

"Another half-hour," said Bill Steel, "and we'll be up there."

"Let's get going, then," said Skim.

The distance separating the climbers from the summit of Golden Mount was no more than two hundred feet, but it was rough going. There was very little grass, and they had to exercise the utmost caution since there were no clumps of shrubs at that level, and the rocky surface offered no foothold. However, the spikes they drove into cracks did not give way, and by using ropes and by switchbacking, the scout and his friends continued to move upward, stopping to catch their breath. The smoke from the crater did not bother them, since it was drifting in the opposite direction.

It was exactly 10:13 by Ben Raddle's watch when the climbers stood together on the part of the truncated cone forming the mountain's plateau.

More or less exhausted, they all sat down on the quartz rocks surrounding the plateau, which must have been three or four hundred feet in circumference. Near its center was the crater, with sooty vapors and yellowish wisps of smoke issuing from it.

Before approaching this fire-belching chimney, which had no ash, debris, or lava coming out of it, Ben Raddle and his party stopped to catch their breath and survey the vast panorama stretching out before them. From that height, they could see twelve or fifteen miles in every direction, to the farthest limit of the horizon.

Looking southward, their eyes took in the verdant plains that the caravan had crossed on leaving the confluence of the Peel River to travel down its left bank. They could see as far as the distant hilly terrain behind which Fort McPherson commanded the surrounding region.

To the west, they saw the Arctic coast running northwestward in sandy beaches. It would be intersected by the northern end of the one hundred and forty-first meridian, the boundary between American Alaska and the British Dominion of Canada. Farther back, at a distance of about four miles, could be seen the expanse of a large forest.

To the east, at the foot of Golden Mount, lay the tangled hydrographic network of the Mackenzie estuary, whose many branches flowed into a large bay protected by an archipelago of small arid islands and dark shoals.

From there, the shoreline turned due north, ending in a promontory, a sort of enormous round hill, which shut off the horizon on that side. The region beyond the delta was covered with broad plains irrigated by a few small streams, but it was less flat. A few hillocks rising among the clumps of trees lent a certain relief to the ground. Farther still, the eye could make out the first foothills of the Rocky Mountains.

To the north of Golden Mount, beyond the vertical cliff whose base disappeared under water, the sea was bounded only by the surrounding sky.

The atmosphere, purified and cleansed by the breeze, its vapors dissipated by the sun's rays, was now perfectly clear. The sea sparkled in places as the sun rose toward the zenith. There was nothing to obstruct the view in that sector, which extended far into the distance. In fact, it could have extended ten times as far without meeting the shoreline of a continent, and would have encountered nothing but the ice floes of the Arctic Ocean.

During the summer, this huge ocean is always frequented by whalers, while seal and walrus hunters come to its shores and islands.

Ben Raddle and his friends saw no large islands. As far as their eyes could see, the bays, inlets, coves, and islets seemed to be deserted. There were neither aboriginals nor outsiders to be seen, even though the mouths of the Mackenzie are rich in marine mammals and several kinds of amphibians.

But farther out to sea, the picture was different. Through his telescope, the scout was able to make out several sails and plumes of smoke standing out against the northern horizon.

"Those are whaling ships," he said. "They've come through Bering Strait into the Arctic Ocean. Two months from now they'll head back to the strait. Some of them will put into St. Michael, at the mouth of the Yukon River, others into Petropavlovsk, on the Kamchatka peninsula. From there, they'll go and sell their catch in the Pacific ports."

"Do any of them put into Vancouver?" asked Summy Skim.

"Yes, some do," replied Bill Steel, "but that's a mistake, a big mistake, because it's very difficult to keep their crews. Most of the sailors desert to go to the Klondike."

That was only too true. Coming back after an arduous expedition to distant parts, the sailors caught the gold fever. To save them from this epidemic, the whaling captains tried as much as possible to avoid ports in British Columbia, preferring Asian ports.

After a much needed half-hour break, Raddle and the others stood up to explore Golden Mount's plateau.

The crater was not located exactly in the center, but in the eastern part. The opening of the chimney was seventy-five or eighty feet in circumference. Fumes and wisps of smoke were issuing from it with considerable force. However, by going up to it as close as possible, Raddle and Lorique saw that it was possible to go down inside it, as Jacques Laurier had told them. That was what the Frenchman had done at a time when there was no eruption in progress. He had even come to the conclusion that it was extinct. It was in this crater that he had noticed the presence of gold-bearing quartz, nuggets, and gold dust, which formed the soot, as it were, in the chimney. But what he had done, Ben Raddle had to forgo doing, because of the risk of being asphyxiated by volcanic gases.

The gold dust was to be found in the area around the crater, mixed in with the layer of volcanic ash. But after all, what they could collect there, as Lorique pointed out, what did it amount to in comparison with the prodigious heap of nuggets stored away inside Golden Mount?

To Lorique's remark, Raddle added, "We're going to have to dip into the crater itself. If this volcanic activity dies down, and if the vapors dissipate, we'll go down inside, just as Jacques Laurier did."

"And what if they don't dissipate?" asked Skim. "What if it's impossible to go down?"

"Then we'll wait, Summy."

"Wait for what, Ben?"

"Wait for an eruption to do what we couldn't do—throw out the material that's in the bowels of Golden Mount."

That would obviously be the only possible decision. For people who had camped at the Mackenzie delta, as many others did in Dawson City, who had faced the terrible winter season at this high latitude under just bearable conditions, yes, this decision was definitely indicated. But if the eruption was late in coming, if, after two months, the volcano had still not disgorged its treasure of nuggets, Raddle and Skim would be forced to leave their encampment and head back to Dawson City. Then, if they didn't start out for Montreal, they would have to spend another six or seven months in the capital of the Klondike.

This thought, which was shared by them all, led Summy Skim to ask, "And what if the eruption is delayed, Ben? What if it doesn't happen before winter sets in?"

Raddle turned his head away, and Skim did not press the point. He felt sure the force of circumstances would be stronger than Ben Raddle's will and tenacity.

After spending two hours on the plateau, the climbers started back down the sides of Golden Mount. The descent involved great danger of falling and required the utmost caution, but at least it only took half as long as the ascent.

An hour later the scout and his party, rather tired but safe and sound, were back at their encampment.

8

An Engineer's Bold Plan

ORGANIZING THE ENCAMPMENT in preparation for a stay of several weeks was best left up to the scout. When Ben Raddle had started out on this new expedition, he was convinced, relying on the precise information supplied by Jacques Laurier, that it would only be a matter of going to Golden Mount, scooping the nuggets out of the crater, loading them onto the wagons, and heading back to Dawson City. This simple task would have taken a week at the most, and the whole trip there and back would not last more than three months. If they left the capital of the Klondike on May 7, the caravan would be back there during the first few days of August. There would still be time before the severe cold set in for Bill Steel to take them to Skagway. They would then proceed to Vancouver and from there by train back to Montreal.

"What a train," said Summy Skim with a laugh. "What a train we'll need to transport us and our millions from Golden Mount! And what a lot of excess baggage we'll have!"

But while the millions were indeed at the designated place in the crater, now they could not be taken out.

The scout knew what he was doing and took steps to provide for his friends' subsistence and that of the animals until it became absolutely essential to leave the encampment. To try to spend the winter there would have been impossible. No matter what happened, then, whether the expedition was a success or not, they would have to leave by the middle of August at the latest. After that, travel through the region north of the Arctic Circle, assailed by strong winds and snowstorms, would become impossible.

"Besides," Summy Skim pointed out, "we have the example of those two poor Frenchmen who were overcome on the trail by the November cold, and died."[1]

Life would now be a time of waiting, which would tax their patience to the limit. Of course, they would have to keep an eye on the condition of the volcano and check on whether its activity was increasing in intensity. This would require several more trips to the summit, but neither Ben Raddle nor the foreman was daunted by the prospect of hard work, and they would keep a daily check on the development of the phenomenon.

As for Summy Skim, he could spend the long hours hunting across the plains to the south and west or on the marshes of the Mackenzie delta. There were ducks and other waterfowl there as well as furred and feathered game on the fields and in the woods. Perhaps he and Neluto would not find the days too long. They would be careful, though, not to go too far. There are certain tribes of Indians who visit the Arctic coast during the summer, and it is just as well to avoid contact with them.

As for the other members of the caravan, if they wanted to indulge in the joys of fishing, they would have every opportunity. The labyrinth of streams between the east and west branches of the river were teeming with fish. This alone would have guaranteed a supply of food until the streams began to ice over.

The next few days brought no change in the situation. Raddle observed no indication that the volcanic activity was becoming more intense, but on many occasions he was able to establish definitely that the volcano's chimney went up through the east side of the mountain. That was shown by the fact that the western slope was more gradual, and offered the best route to the top. From the encampment, set up almost at the foot of Golden Mount, in the very shadow of its east face, the dull noise of subterranean activity could be heard quite distinctly. That was the result of the crater's position on the plateau, which led the engineer to conclude that the east face of the mountain, rising abruptly to the chimney's walls, was probably not very thick. Lorique shared that opinion. But even assuming that a tunnel could be dug through to that wall, it would have been no more feasible to get into the chimney that way than through the orifice at the top, because the whole length of the tunnel would be filled with smoke and perhaps with flames. However, since the internal noises came through to the outside on that face, it would be easy to tell whether there were increasing signs of an imminent eruption without having to go all the way to the top.

Unfortunately, no flame or volcanic material issued from the mouth of Golden Mount during the first week. It was surrounded only by swirling, sooty vapors.

The first day of July arrived. It is not hard to imagine how impatient Raddle and his party had become. They were all irritated to some extent by the fact that there was nothing they could do to change the situation. Now that the camp was set up, the scout and his men had nothing to do from morning till night. Some of them spent their time fishing in Rubber Creek or in the main branch of the delta, while others set their nets near the shore, with the result that there was an abundance of both saltwater and freshwater fish. But that did not make the days seem any less interminable.

Several times, Skim invited Raddle to go hunting with him, but the engineer always declined. With the foreman and the scout, he either stayed in camp or wandered over to the foot of the mountain, talking, discussing, observing, but still unable to arrive at any definite conclusion. They climbed to the top twice more and found things still in the same state: there were wisps of smoke, sometimes more violent emissions of vapor, but nothing was being thrown out.

"Couldn't we do something to get that eruption started?" said the scout one day. "Or if not, couldn't we blow the mountain open with mines?"

Raddle looked at Bill Steel, shook his head, and said not a word.

It was Lorique who answered the question.

"Our entire supply of gunpowder wouldn't be enough for that," he said. "And besides, even if we could blast a hole, what would come out?"

"A flood of nuggets, perhaps," said Bill Steel.

"No, Scout," declared Lorique, "nothing but fumes. They'd come out there, instead of through the chimney, and we'd be no further ahead. What we know for sure is that Golden Mount was asleep for a long time, and now it's waking up. If we'd been here a few months earlier, we probably could have gone down into the crater. But luck was against us, and it will likely be a while before the eruption occurs. All things considered, the wisest thing to do is to arm ourselves with patience."

"In less than two months winter will be here," said Steel.

"I know that, Scout."

"And if the eruption hasn't happened, we'll have to leave all the same."

"I know that, too," repeated the foreman. "So we'll leave, we'll go back to Dawson City, and we'll come back here as soon as the fine weather returns."

"Do you think Mr. Skim will agree to spend another winter in the Klondike?"

"Summy can go back to Montreal if he likes," said the engineer, breaking into the conversation. "As for me, I'll stay in Dawson City, and all he'll have to do is meet me there next May if he wants to. Sooner or later, the volcano will erupt, and I want to be here."

Obviously, the engineer's plans had been carefully thought out and had now taken definite shape. But what would Summy Skim do?

The scout had the last word. "Yes," he said, "sooner or later, Golden Mount will throw out its nuggets and gold dust. But sooner would be better."

"Couldn't we do something to make it erupt?" asked Lorique for the second time.

And for the second time, Ben Raddle simply looked at him without answering.

During the next few days the weather took a turn for the worse. Heavy thunderstorms came up from the south, and the volcano seemed to be showing more activity under the influence of these atmospheric disturbances. A few flames appeared among the vapors, but they brought nothing out of the crater.

After the thunderstorms, which were of short duration, came torrential rains. There was a minor flood in the Mackenzie delta, and the area between the two main branches of the river was inundated.

Needless to say, Skim had to give up his daily hunting trips during that dismal time, and he found the days long. Moreover, the scout had decided that he ought to bring him up to date about Raddle's plans: to go back to Dawson City for the winter if necessary, leaving his cousin free to leave for Montreal with the option of coming back in the spring to resume the campaign.

Skim's first reaction was one of indignation, but he held himself in and said simply, "I knew it!"

And since Raddle did not confide in him, he also kept his thoughts to himself, waiting for the time when a definite explanation would be necessary.

On the afternoon of July 5, Ben Raddle invited Skim, the foreman, and the scout to join him in the tent. The engineer had reviewed in his mind the plan he had been pondering for some time. "Listen, my friends," he said when they had all taken their seats, "to what I have to tell you."

His face was serious. The wrinkles on his brow bore witness to the obsession that was gripping him. Summy Skim was deeply troubled because of his sincere friendship for his cousin. Had Ben Raddle decided to abandon this expedition, to give up the struggle against an uncooperative Nature? If so, Skim's joy would have been as great as Lorique's disappointment. Was Ben finally going to announce his decision to return to Montreal if the situation had not changed in six weeks, before bad weather set in?

"My friends," he continued, "we can have no doubt as to the existence of Golden Mount, or the value of its contents. Jacques Laurier made no mistake as we've seen with our own eyes. Unfortunately, the first signs of a new eruption have made it impossible for us to go down into Golden

Mount's crater. If we could have done that, our expedition would be finished by now, and we'd be on our way back to the Klondike."

"That eruption will happen, and maybe before winter sets in," said the foreman confidently. "We must hope so, anyway"

"If it does," affirmed Steel, "then everything will work out for the best."

"In six weeks at the latest," said Summy Skim.

A few moments of silence followed. Everyone had spoken his mind according to his own view of the matter. But the engineer obviously had a suggestion to make, and he seemed hesitant to express it in words to his friends.

He passed his hand over his forehead like a man who wonders whether he has really foreseen all the consequences of a plan he has been mulling over for a long time.

"My friends," he said, "a little while ago, our foreman Lorique put forward a suggestion to which I made no response. Possibly he made it out of frustration because we haven't been able to carry our task through to its conclusion. I've thought a lot about it since then, trying to find a way of carrying it out. I think I've found it. And when Lorique, seeing that the eruption isn't happening, exclaimed, 'Why not make it happen?' now it's my turn to say, 'Yes, why not?'"

The foreman jumped to his feet, impatient for Raddle to finish his explanation, because his comment really had been uttered out of frustration.

As for Summy Skim and the scout, they were looking at each other, apparently wondering whether the engineer was still in his right mind, or whether so many disappointments and worries had unhinged him.

But no, he showed all the lucidity of a man in complete control of himself. He was about to continue when the scout interrupted him.

"Create an eruption at Golden Mount? But how?"

"Listen carefully," Raddle went on. "Volcanoes, as you know, are all— and this can be definitely asserted—located at the edge of the sea or near it—Vesuvius, Etna, Hecla, Chimborazo—in the New World as well as in the Old. The natural conclusion to be drawn from this is that they must be in underground communication with the oceans. Water filters into them, quickly or slowly, depending on the composition of the soil. It reaches the interior fire, where it's heated and turns to steam. When this steam, trapped in the bowels of the earth, attains a high pressure, it creates an internal upheaval and tries to escape to the outside, dragging ashes, slag, and rocks out through the chimney, surrounded by swirling clouds of smoke and flame. That, without any doubt, is the cause of eruptions and probably of earthquakes, too. Well, if Nature can do it, why can't men do it also?"

All eyes were on the engineer at that moment. The explanation he had just given of volcanic phenomena was certainly an accurate one. It was equally certain that water from the Arctic Ocean must filter through to the interior of Golden Mount. And if the channels of communication had been blocked for a more or less lengthy period after the last eruption, they were now open, for the volcano was beginning to send out wreaths of steam, from the pressure of the vaporized water.

But was it possible to get through to those underground channels of communication, to send torrents of sea water into the central fireplace? Did the engineer have the audacity to attempt such a feat, to believe it could be done?

His companions refused to believe it, and Bill Steel questioned him about it.

"No, my friends," replied Raddle, "there's no question of undertaking such a task. It would be beyond my power. But we don't need to go down into the depths of the ocean—which might well be very considerable—to look for the line of communication between the volcano and the sea. Our plan of attack will be very simple."

Obviously, this aroused the curiosity of Lorique and the scout and it may be added that of Summy Skim as well, knowing as he did that Ben Raddle was too practical a man not to have based his remarks on a solid foundation.

"You noticed, just as I did," continued the engineer, "when we were at the top of Golden Mount, that the crater is located toward the east face of the mountain, where the chimney opens. Moreover, the noise of the subterranean activity is heard mainly on that side. Even now, the interior rumblings are clearly perceptible."

As if to confirm what the engineer said, those rumblings were coming forth with particular intensity.

"And so," Raddle went on, "we must assume that the chimney running from the bowels of the volcano to its crater runs through the part closest to our encampment. Now, if we could manage to dig an opening through that face and into the chimney, it would be easy for us to introduce huge quantities of water."

"Where would we get it?" exclaimed Lorique. "From the sea?"

"No," replied the engineer, "we won't have to look that far. Don't we have Rubber Creek, that little stream leading off from one of the branches of the Mackenzie? It's an inexhaustible supply, fed by the whole network of the delta, and we're going to send it pouring into the fireplace of Golden Mount."

"We're going to send it," the engineer had said as if the plan was already under way, as if a tunnel was already drilled through the massif, as if one last stroke of the pick would send the water of Rubber Creek gushing into it.

That was the plan Ben Raddle outlined. Audacious as it was, none of his friends, not even Summy Skim, thought of raising any objection to it. If it failed, the matter would be settled. If the man-made eruption did not occur, there would be nothing for it but to abandon any idea of mining Golden Mount. If it succeeded, and the volcano yielded up its riches, again the matter would be settled, and the heavily laden wagons would head back to the Klondike. It was true that sending water flooding into the volcanic fireplace might have violent and uncontrollable consequences. By assuming the role of Nature, were they not heading for disaster? Was there not a danger of having more than one eruption, an earthquake that would totally disrupt the region and annihilate the encampment and its inhabitants?

But no one wanted to consider those dangers, and work began on the morning of July 6.

The engineer took charge of the work. He considered, logically enough, that the first step was to attack the face of Golden Mount. If the pick encountered a rock that was too hard to break through, if a tunnel in to the chimney could not be opened, there would be no point in digging a trench to divert the stream, since the water would not reach the interior of the volcano.

The opening of the tunnel was set at about ten feet below the level of the stream so that the water would flow in. By a great stroke of luck, the material the tools encountered offered little resistance, at least for the first half of the tunnel. It consisted of loose earth, stony debris, pieces of hardened lava that had been buried in the mixture for many years, and bits of quartz that had probably been shattered during previous quakes.

The caravan's crew worked day and night, in shifts. There was not an hour to lose. Ben Raddle had no way of calculating the thickness of the face they were digging through, and the tunnel might possibly have to be longer than he had estimated. To be sure, the noises were fairly audible on that side and became louder and louder as the work progressed. But when would they know for certain that the tunnel had almost reached the wall of the chimney?

Summy Skim and Neluto had abandoned their hunting expeditions. Like the scout and Lorique, they did their share of the work, and the tunnel moved ahead five or six feet every day.

Unfortunately, after about ten days, they encountered quartz, which blunted their picks. They were not dealing now with fragments embedded in the earth but with a mass of extremely hard rock. They were afraid it might extend all the way to the wall of the crater, and how long would it take to penetrate that?

Ben Raddle did not hesitate. He decided to use explosives to break through the quartz. There was some gunpowder in the caravan's reserves, and even though Summy Skim would be deprived of it, they used it in the form of small explosive devices. True, this gunpowder was intended to be used for defense as well as for hunting, but the scout and his men did not seem to be in any danger, since the region was still deserted, and no party of natives or others had been seen near the encampment for nearly five weeks.

The use of explosives produced fairly good results. While progress was slowed down considerably, at least it had not stopped. There was no need now to shore up the walls to prevent cave-ins, and the tunnel cut through the hard substance without causing any rockfalls. Besides, the engineer was taking every precaution to avoid a catastrophe.

On July 27, after twenty-one days of work, the tunnel seemed to have been extended far enough. It was now sixty feet long and four feet in diameter, big enough to let in a great quantity of water. The growling and rumbling in the volcano's chimney were now so loud that the wall could not be more than three feet thick. It would require only a few blows with a pick, or a few explosive charges, to break through the wall, and the tunnel would be finished.

It was now certain the Ben Raddle's project was not going to be stopped by some insuperable obstacle. The open trench through which the water of Rubber Creek would be diverted could be easily cut through soil composed only of earth and sand. Even though it would be about three hundred feet long, Raddle estimated that it could be dug in about ten days.

"The hardest part is over," said Bill Steel.

"And the longest, too," added Lorique.

"Starting tomorrow," said Raddle, "we'll begin digging the trench six feet from the left bank of Rubber Creek."

"Well, then," said Skim, "since we have a day off, I propose to spend it . . ."

"Hunting, Mr. Summy?" asked the scout with a laugh.

"No, Bill," was the reply. "Climbing up Golden Mount one last time, to see what's going on up there."

"You're right, Summy," said Raddle. "The volcanic action definitely seems to be increasing, and it's a good idea to see with our own eyes."

This wise suggestion was adopted, and it was decided to devote the afternoon to the ascent of Golden Mount. As before, the climbers would be the two cousins, the scout, and the foreman.

All four of them walked around the base of the cone for a distance of about two miles, until they came to the long point of the slope, by which they had made a previous ascent. They had taken the precaution of bringing along a supply of spikes and ropes with which to haul themselves up the higher part of the face, which was extremely steep.

The scout took the lead, his friends followed, and this time, since they knew the way, they took only an hour and a half to reach the crater.

First of all, they went up to it as close as possible, but not as close as the first time. The fumes spewing out of the chimney were now thicker and blacker than before and rose twice as high. There were flames now, too, but no lava or slag was coming out.

"Obviously," said Summy Skim, "this Golden Mount is not very generous. It guards its nuggets jealously."

"If it doesn't want to give them up willingly," said Lorique, "we'll take them by force."

In any case, they could now see that the volcanic activity was becoming stronger. The internal rumblings sounded like those of a boiler under high pressure with its metal plates growling under the effect of the fire. An eruption was in the making, but it might be weeks, or even months, before the material contained in the bowels of the volcano would be flung up into the air.

After examining the condition of the crater, Ben Raddle decided not to interrupt the work they had begun with the object of speeding up the volcanic activity or even precipitating an explosion.

Before going back down, the climbers took a good look all around. Both land and sea appeared to be deserted. There was no campfire smoke rising above the plain and no sail was visible on the horizon. Under the circumstances, Raddle and his party had every reason to believe they were completely safe. Even the Indians had not made an appearance on the Mackenzie delta. The secret of Golden Mount was apparently not known in the Klondike.

They made their descent without difficulty. The weather had been as fine in the afternoon as in the morning. The temperature was higher than normal for those northern latitudes, and one might have thought it was midsummer in a more southerly region of the Dominion. But still, as Skim said to himself, even if the weather was as warm as in Green Valley, Green Valley was far away, and even if Golden Mount had been ten times, a hundred times, a thousand times higher, they would not have been able to see Montreal, more than two thousand miles off to the east,[2] not even with one of those telescopes that bring the moon within arm's reach.

But Summy Skim said nothing. The final phase of this expedition, whatever it might be, was approaching, and by mid-September the caravan would definitely be back in the Klondike.

By about five o'clock Raddle and his friends were back at the encampment, where work would be resumed the next day.

They enjoyed a very pleasant dinner since Neluto had succeeded in bagging some game during Skim's absence.

"But Ben," said Summy, as he was going into the tent to rest, "what if we extinguish the volcano with your flood?"

"Extinguish it!" was the reply. "There's not enough water in the Mackenzie River to extinguish it!"

"Besides," added Lorique, "if it was extinguished we could go down into the crater."

"And relieve it of its nuggets, obviously," said Skim. "Definitely, there is always an answer to everything."

9

The Moose Hunt

THE LEFT BANK OF RUBBER CREEK described a fairly sharp bend about a hundred yards from the opening of the subterranean tunnel leading to the volcano's chimney.[1] It was exactly at the angle formed by this elbow that the stream would be diverted. A trench would have to be dug along this three-hundred-foot distance to carry the water into the tunnel. The engineer laid out the route, and on the morning of July 28 everyone set to work.

It had been ascertained that the digging of this trench would present no great difficulties and require no great effort. The ground consisted of fairly friable earth to a depth of seven feet, below which there was rock. This would be deep enough, and the width would be about the same. The work could be done with pick and mattock, and there would be no need to exhaust their supply of gunpowder by resorting to explosives. It would be wise to keep a supply of ammunition, if not for their stay at the encampment, then at least for the return trip to Dawson City, for they might encounter Indians and outlaws along the way toward the end of the gold-mining season.

All the members of the caravan's crew applied themselves busily to the task, and there was not one of the brave Canadians who doubted that they would succeed. They knew Ben Raddle was trying to make Golden Mount erupt, and they also knew the eruption would spew out nuggets and golden lava. There would be enough for everyone, and no claim in the Klondike would ever have produced such results. Even the skeptical Summy Skim, it must be admitted, reached the point of saying, "Well, why not?"

Work on the trench went along quickly, and the weather was not too warm. The men worked in shifts, taking advantage of the long twilight period to work on into the night. They watched carefully to see whether the route of the trench crossed a lode anywhere, but there was no pay streak to be found.

"This stream is definitely not as valuable as Eldorado or Bonanza," remarked the foreman. "There are no nuggets moving along through it, but it'll get us the nuggets of Golden Mount, and that'll be something else."

Thirteen days went by, and by August 9 two-thirds of the trench was open. But as they got closer to the mountain the ground became stony and the earth was not as loose. Still, the tools did the job, and no explosives were used.

Ben Raddle estimated that it would take six or seven days to finish the operation. They would only have to make an opening five or six feet wide through the bank of Rubber Creek and break through the wall between the end of the tunnel and the chimney, and the water would flow of its own accord into the bowels of the volcano.

The unknown factor was how long it would take for the accumulation of steam to trigger an eruption. As the engineer had observed, however, the symptoms were growing more pronounced every day. The smoke above the cone was getting thicker and the flames were rising higher, lighting up the surrounding countryside over a wide area during the few hours of darkness. There was reason to hope, then, that the torrent of water, when it turned to steam in the central fireplace, would trigger an outpouring of volcanic matter.

That afternoon, on returning to camp, Neluto went to find Summy Skim.

"Oh, Mr. Skim," he said in a hurried and breathless voice.

"What is it, Neluto?"

"There are . . . there are . . . moose!"

"Moose!" exclaimed Skim.

"Yes, a herd of about half a dozen. I've just seen them."

"Are they far away?"

"At least two or three miles . . . over there."

The Indian pointed to the open country lying to the west of Golden Mount.

It was common knowledge that one of this fanatical hunter's keenest desires was to encounter some moose and bag a couple of them, but he had been unable to satisfy that desire since coming to the Klondike. In fact, not more than two or three moose had been sighted in the vicinity of Dawson City or in the Fortymile River area.[2] It is not hard to imagine how the news excited Summy Skim's hunting instincts, not to mention those of his fellow hunter.

"Come on," he said to the Indian.

Leaving the encampment, they walked for a few hundred yards along the base of Golden Mount. There they stopped, and Summy Skim could see with his own eyes the herd of moose calmly heading northwest across the vast plain.

He was sorely tempted to give chase immediately, but it was already late and he postponed his pursuit until the next day. All that mattered was that those ruminants had put in an appearance in the vicinity, and it would certainly be possible to find them again.

When he next saw Ben Raddle, Skim told him of his plan. Since there was no shortage of manpower for digging the trench, the engineer saw no difficulty in dispensing with Neluto's services for a day. The two hunters made plans to leave at five o'clock in the morning to pick up the trail of the moose.

"But promise me, Summy," said Raddle, "that you won't go too far."

"You should give that advice to the moose," said Skim with a laugh.

"No, Summy, the advice is for you. You can't afford to lose your way miles from camp, and we can't be forced to stop work to go and look for you. And then there's always the possibility of running into some kind of danger."

"No, Ben, the whole region is safe, precisely because it's deserted."

"All right, Summy, but promise me you'll be back in the afternoon."

"Let's say in the evening, Ben."

"Evening lasts half the night at this latitude," said the engineer. "No, Summy, if you aren't back by six o'clock, I'll start to worry."

"All right, Ben, all right," replied Skim. "Six o'clock, with a quarter-hour grace period."

"As long as your quarter of an hour doesn't last more than fifteen minutes."

All things considered, Ben Raddle might still have been afraid that once his cousin was in hot pursuit of a moose he would let himself be drawn farther away than he should. They could take comfort in the fact that no party of Indians or others had been seen at the Mackenzie estuary so far, but that could still happen any day. For that reason, once the expedition was finished, and successfully finished, the engineer would start back to the Klondike without losing any time.

The next day, before five o'clock, Skim and Neluto left camp, each armed with a long-range hunting rifle and carrying enough food for two meals, with their dog Stop frisking and barking around them.

The weather was fine, even a bit cool, although the sun had already begun to trace its long course above the horizon.

Every hunter will understand Summy Skim's very natural ambition to find the moose they had sighted the previous day and to bring down at least one of those magnificent ruminants. By and large, his hunting forays near Dawson City or around the Fortymile River had brought him only the usual small game, such as thrushes, grouse, and partridges. The big game had certainly withdrawn a hundred miles or more before the invading miners, and the Klondike did not have, in this respect, the resources to be found in the Cassiar forests or on the banks of the Pelly River. Summy Skim had of course encountered a number of bears, including the "silver tip," with its white throat, the brown bear, the black bear, the grizzly, and also the one commonly known as the "old miner." But he had never fired a shot at a mountain sheep, that wild quadruped whose favorite habitat is the Rocky Mountains. He had had more luck with the woodland caribou, a species of deer that differs in size from the ones he had already hunted in the Canadian forests. He had taken more than one shot at them, but since coming to the Klondike he had never once followed the trail of a moose.

The moose is an elk with magnificent antlers. It was once common in the area drained by the Yukon and its tributaries, but it has scattered since the discovery of gold claims in the Klondike.

As a result of that discovery, the moose, which was once rather sociable by nature, is tending to become more timid. It is difficult to approach and can be shot only under the most favorable conditions. That is unfortunate, because its carcass is valuable, its flesh is excellent (considered to be as good as beef), and sells on the Dawson City market for as much as a dollar a pound.

Summy Skim knew very well how easily a moose's suspicions are aroused. The animal's sense of hearing and smell are extremely keen. At the least sign of danger it runs away so rapidly, despite its weight of nine hundred or a thousand pounds, that pursuit is futile. The two hunters had to take the most careful precautions in order to come within range of the herd.

The animals had stopped at the edge of a forest about four miles from Golden Mount. There were clumps of trees standing here and there, and it would be necessary to scurry, or rather to crawl, from one to another in order not to be seen, heard, or even scented. Outside of the woods, to be sure, this maneuver would be useless, and the hunters would not be able to take a step without revealing their presence. The moose would then take to their heels, and it would be impossible to pick up their trail again.

After due deliberation, Skim and Neluto decided to head south, intending to get to the southern corner of the forest. From there, by moving from tree to tree, they might manage to come up to the herd without attracting attention. It would be important, though, to restrain their dog, which was showing signs of great impatience.

Three quarters of an hour later, after taking every imaginable precaution, Skim and the Indian stopped at the corner of the woods. The moose were still standing quietly at the edge of the forest, and by moving back up about a mile, the hunters would be close to their resting place.

"Let's follow along the edge, but just inside," said Skim, "and keep hold of Stop, Neluto. Don't let him run ahead and warn them."

"Of course, Mr. Skim," replied the Indian, "but you should keep a tight grip on me, too, because I need someone to hold me back."

Summy Skim could not help smiling at Neluto's remark. He understood and would have trouble enough holding himself back.

They began to make their move, which was not without its difficulties. The poplars, birches, and pines in the forest grew close together, and the thick undergrowth made walking difficult. They had to avoid stepping on the dead branches lying on the ground. The noise would have been clearly audible, especially since there was not another sound to be heard. The sun, which had grown hotter, shone down on the motionless branches. No bird calls greeted the ear, and no sound came from the depths of the forest. Summy had no idea whether the trees continued far across the region drained by the Porcupine and its tributaries such as the southern part of the Old Crow, and in any case, he had no intention of leaving the open country farther behind.

In short, it was nearly nine o'clock when the two hunters stopped at the edge of a little clearing less than three hundred feet from the spot occupied by the moose. The animals showed no sign of concern. Some were grazing or drinking from a stream that flowed out of the woods. Others were lying on the grass, probably asleep. But there was no doubt that the slightest sign of danger would put them to flight, in all probability toward the Porcupine basin to the south.

Summy Skim and Neluto were not inclined to rest, even though they needed to. Since the opportunity had arisen to take a lucky shot before their first meal, they would not let it slip away.

Here they were, then, rifles at the ready, picking their way through the undergrowth, crawling along the edge of the forest. Summy Skim admitted later that he had never experienced such a powerful emotion. It was not fear, certainly, since he was not dealing with fierce beasts. But the expectation of finally being able to satisfy one of a hunter's keenest desires was so great that his heartbeat quickened, his hand trembled, and he was afraid he would not be able to shoot straight. To tell the truth, if he missed such an opportunity to bring down the moose he so badly wanted, there would be nothing for him to do but die of shame.

Skim approached, followed by Neluto, making no more noise than a snake crawling through the grass. A few minutes of this silent creeping brought them within range, less than sixty paces from the spot where the ruminants were resting. Stop, held in by Neluto, was breathing heavily but not barking.

The moose seemed not to have caught wind of the hunters' approach. The ones that were lying down did not get up, and the others continued to graze.

But one of them, a magnificent beast with antlers like the branches of a young tree, lifted his head at that moment and turned toward the edge of the forest. His ears twitched and he stretched out his muzzle as if he wanted to sniff the air coming from the woods.

Had the animal scented danger? Was it about to run away and take the others with it?

Skim had a presentiment that this would happen. The blood rushed to his heart, but he controlled himself and said in a low voice, "Fire, Neluto, both of us at the same one, to make sure we don't miss."

At that instant they heard the sound of barking. Neluto had let go of Stop in order to raise his rifle, and the dog dashed into the midst of the herd.

Ah! It was over in a flash before Skim or the Indian even had time to take aim and fire. A flock of partridges would not have disappeared more quickly than the moose did.

Skim got to his feet, stunned.

"Damn dog!" he shouted.

"I should have held him by the throat," added the Indian.

"You should have strangled him!" Skim was absolutely furious, and if the dog had been there, he would not have got off lightly.

But Stop was already more than two hundred yards away by the time the hunters emerged from the forest. He had run off in pursuit of the moose, and it would be useless to call him back. Even if he had still been able to hear his master's voice, he would not have returned.

The herd was heading north, running faster than the dog, even though he was a very strong animal and a very fast runner. Would the moose go back into the forest, or would they turn east across the open country? That would have been the most favorable turn of events, for then they would have been approaching Golden Mount, whose smoke was swirling up four miles away. But it was possible also that they might veer off to the southeast toward the Peel River and seek refuge in the first gorges of the Rocky Mountains. In that case, the hunters would have to give up all hope of ever finding them again.

"Follow me," Skim shouted to the Indian. "Let's try not to lose sight of them."

They both began running along the edge of the forest in pursuit of the moose, which were now nearly half a mile away.

What were they hoping to do? And would they not have found it hard to answer that question themselves? But an irresistible urge, stronger than reason, impelled them along, the same urge that was driving their dog, Stop.

A quarter of an hour later, Skim was excited to see that the moose had finally stopped running. They could not keep on going north toward the coast, because there they would have been forced to turn back. But would they head southeast, in which case Skim and Neluto would have to abandon the hunt, or would they decide to lose themselves in the depths of the forest?

And after a few moments of hesitation, that is exactly what they did. The leader of the herd bounded into the forest and the others followed.

"This may be the luckiest break we could have," exclaimed Skim. "In the open we could never have come within range of them. In the forest they won't be able to run as fast, and we may be able to catch up with them this time."

Whether this line of reasoning made sense or not, it nevertheless took the hunters much farther west than they should have gone, into a forest of unknown size, from which they might have great difficulty getting out.

Stop had probably done the same as they had. He had dashed in among the trees and was already out of sight, although his barking could still be heard.

Here they were, then, making their way under the heavy branches, guided only by the dog's barking. The moose were definitely no longer in a position to run away quickly, since their lofty antlers would make it difficult for them to get through the thickets and shrubs. Under these circumstances, the dog would have the advantage over them since he could get through where they could not. He would catch up with them, and the hunters would only have to head in the direction of his barking.

That is what they did for two hours, but still they did not catch up with the herd. While they were not exactly walking aimlessly, they were carried along by an irrational urge. But—and this was more serious— they were traveling westward, and how would they ever find their way when it was time to go home?

Summy Skim noticed, however, as he went along, that the forest became less and less dense the farther in they went. There were still the same trees—birches, poplars, and pines—but they were farther apart, and the ground was less cluttered with roots and undergrowth.

But while they did not catch sight of the moose, Stop had not lost their trail. His barking continued, and he could not have been more than five hundred yards from his master.

Neluto and Skim kept pushing deeper and deeper into the woods. But shortly after noon the dog's barking was no longer audible.

They were now in a clearing where the sun's rays shone through. How far into the woods they had penetrated, Skim could not calculate, except on the basis of the time elapsed, but he estimated the distance to be two or three miles. They would have plenty of time to get back to camp after a rest, which they both badly needed. Exhausted and famished, they sat down under a tree and took the food out of their game bags. It can be positively stated that they ate with a ravenous appetite. Of course, they would have enjoyed the lunch much more if grilled moose meat had been on the menu.

And now, what was the wisest and most prudent course of action? Would it not be to head back to camp, even with the disappointment of coming home empty-handed? This time wisdom seemed to win out. But if it was unpleasant not to bring back a moose, it was even more so not to bring the dog home. And Stop had not reappeared.

"Where can he be?" said Skim.

"Chasing the moose," was the reply.

"I suspect you're right, Neluto. But then, where are the moose?"

"Perhaps they're not as far away as we might think, Mr. Skim."

This reply seemed to suggest that the Indian was not as determined as Summy Skim was to make the wise choice and abandon the hunt. He could not get over the disappointment of having hunted all morning without any luck.

There is no doubt that Skim felt a certain pleasure at hearing him speak in those terms. Still, he felt obliged to point out, "If the moose were not far away in the forest, we'd hear Stop barking."

At that very moment the noise of barking was heard less than half a mile away, to judge by the sound.

And the two hunters, without exchanging another word, got to their feet as if they had been activated by the same spring, picked up their game bags and rifles, and rushed off in the direction of the barking.

This time neither wisdom nor caution had any chance of being heard. Their advice was no longer heeded by those two foolhardy men, who might be lured farther and farther away.

In fact, the direction they took was neither north nor east. The herd of moose had turned toward the southwest. The forest probably extended in that direction for a dozen miles, as far as the first tributaries of the Porcupine. That would take Skim and Neluto even farther from Golden

Mount. After all, the sun was only beginning to decline toward the western horizon. If the hunters were not back at camp by six o'clock,[3] as they had promised, they would be there by seven or eight, when it would still be broad daylight. In any case, they surely did not pause to consider such matters. They heard Stop and were running toward him, never doubting that they were also running toward the moose they so badly wanted.

The animals were definitely not very far away, and the two hunters were now on their trail. Since the forest had become less dense, they found it easier going and made better time. Skim and Neluto pursued them as fast as their strength allowed. It did not even occur to them to call the dog, which probably would not have come back anyway, since he was as fanatical a hunter as his master. They paid no heed to the passage of time. They were still heading southwest, and there was nothing to indicate that they would soon come to the western edge of that vast forest. They ran as fast as they could, slowing to a walk only to catch their breath, but without stopping. They had no sensation of weariness. Skim forgot that he was now in an area close to the Klondike, not on the outskirts of Montreal. But while he had never had any trouble getting back to the farm at Green Valley, would it be the same now that he had to return to the encampment at Golden Mount?

Once or twice, he and Neluto thought success was within their grasp. A few antlers appeared above the bushes, not a hundred paces away from them. But the agile animals quickly disappeared, and there was no opportunity to take a shot at close range.

In short, several hours passed without either of the careless hunters even mentioning the time. By now the sound of Stop's barking was gradually growing fainter, indicating that the moose were increasing their lead. It would be impossible to catch up with them now. The sound of barking finally faded out altogether either because Stop was too far away or because such a long and arduous pursuit had left him hoarse and no longer able to utter a sound.

Skim and Neluto stopped, totally exhausted, and fell in a heap on the ground not sure whether they would be able to get up again.

It was now four o'clock by Skim's watch.

"That's the end of it!" he said, as soon as he could get a word out.

This time Neluto nodded in agreement, greatly disappointed.

"Where are we?" said Skim.

Yes, that was indeed the question, and it would not be an easy one to answer.

There was a fairly large clearing in that part of the forest, with a little stream running through it, probably on its way to join one of the tributaries of the Porcupine to the southwest. One whole side of it was bathed in sunlight, and farther on the branches seemed closer together, pressed against one another as they had been at the eastern edge of the forest.

"We have to get going," said Skim.

"Where to?" asked the Indian.

"Back to camp, of course!" replied Skim, shrugging his shoulders.

"And where's the camp?"

"That way, Neluto," answered his friend, turning his back to the sun, which was sinking toward the horizon.

"We can't start out again without eating something, Mr. Skim."

That was only too obvious. The two hunters could not have taken five hundred steps without fainting from hunger.

The game bags were opened and they dined as they had breakfasted in the morning, so heartily that there was no food left. Since game was not plentiful in the forest, it would have been difficult to replenish their supply of food unless they happened to find some edible roots that they could cook over a bed of coals.

But apparently that had already been done there. Neluto, who was following along the edge of the clearing, stopped at a little heap of ashes and called out to Skim.

"Look at this, Mr. Skim."

"Somebody has made a fire here, Neluto."

"There's no doubt about that."

"Does that mean there are Indians or other people in this forest?"

"Someone came, for sure," replied Neluto, "but that was a long time ago."

The white ashes had been stuck together, as it were, by the humidity, proving that the fire was not of recent date. That was not surprising and gave no reason to fear that there were people in the vicinity of Golden Mount.

But almost at once, another incident gave Summy Skim something more serious to worry about.

About a dozen yards from the old firepit, his glance fell on a shiny object lying in the grass. He walked over to it, bent down, and picked it up, uttering an involuntary cry of surprise.

It was a dagger, its blade set in a copper hilt.

"Look at that, Neluto," said Skim. He showed the dagger to his friend, who examined it carefully.

"The firepit may be old," he said, "but it isn't very long since this dagger was lost."

"Yes, yes," replied Skim, "the blade is very shiny. There isn't a trace of rust on it. It fell down into the grass not long ago."

There was no denying that fact.

Summy Skim turned the weapon over and over, studied it closely, and recognized that it was of Spanish manufacture. He even found the initial "M" engraved on the hilt and the word "Austin," the capital of Texas, on the blade.

"So," concluded Skim, "a few days ago, maybe a few hours ago, some foreigners camped in this clearing. I'm sure they didn't light this fire, but one of them lost this dagger."

"And they aren't Indians," observed Neluto, "because Indians don't have weapons like this."

"Who knows?" added Skim. "Perhaps they were going through this forest on the way to Golden Mount."

It was a reasonable hypothesis, and if the owner of the dagger was part of a large group, who could tell what grave danger might be threatening Ben Raddle and his companions? Perhaps, even at that very moment, the gang was prowling around in the vicinity of the Mackenzie estuary.

"Let's get going!" said Skim.

"Right now!" agreed Neluto.

"What about our dog?" asked Summy.

The Indian called in a loud voice, turning in every direction, but his call went unheard and Stop did not appear.

There was no question of moose hunting now. They had to get back to camp as soon as possible, so that the scout's caravan would be on their guard, and perhaps on the defensive. But the fastest way of getting there was to take the shortest route, and the shortest route was a straight line.

It was important to take their bearings as accurately as possible. Skim had no compass, but he did have a watch, and here is how he used it. It was a method he had used more than once when he went hunting in the Montreal region.

The sun, as we have seen, was shining into the clearing and, as it happened, the trunk of a very erect fir tree cast its shadow on the ground. Skim would use the line of this shadow to find his bearings. Standing directly over the line, he turned his back to the sun and took out his watch.

It was six o'clock. He would be able to find the north simply by putting the hour hand directly over the shadow. But since this watch was divided into twelve hours, he had to set the hour hand at three o'clock in order to get the same result. When the hand was parallel with the shadow, north was indicated exactly by twelve noon on the watch.[4]

As soon as he had determined his position, Skim held out his hand toward the east, the direction they had to take.

"Let's go," he said.

Just then the sound of a shot rang out, no more than three hundred yards from the clearing.

10

Mortal Dread

AFTER SUMMY SKIM and Neluto left to go moose hunting, Ben Raddle went to check on how the work was getting on. Barring delays or unforeseeable occurrences, the trench would be finished in two or three days. All they would have to do then would be to break open the left bank of Rubber Creek, strike the final blows of the pick against the walls of the crater's chimney, and a torrent of water would rush into the bowels of Golden Mount.

Would the eruption be long in coming? The engineer did not think so, nor did he have any doubts as to the ultimate result. The enormous masses of water, converted to steam by the central fire, would soon create a violent subterranean thrust that would expel the volcanic matter. It would no doubt consist largely of lava, slag, and other volcanic substances, but nuggets and gold-bearing quartz would be mixed with it and could surely be gathered up without the effort of extracting them. Obviously, it had to be assumed at the very least that the fumes from the eruption would fill the tunnel connecting the chimney with the trench. If necessary, then, they would move the encampment up Rubber Creek.

Furthermore, the action of the subterranean forces was tending to grow stronger. The internal bubbling was an indication of their violence. It was open to question whether it would be necessary to introduce water into the crater.

"We'll soon find out," was Ben Raddle's reply to the scout, who had made this suggestion. "We mustn't forget that our time is strictly limited. Here we are almost at the middle of August."

"And it would be unwise," added Bill Steel, "to spend more than another two weeks at the mouth of the Mackenzie. Let's say it will take three weeks to get back to the Klondike, especially if our wagons are heavily loaded."

"You can be sure of that, Scout."

"And in that case, Mr. Raddle, the season will be well advanced when our caravan reaches Dawson City. If we have an early winter, we could have real problems getting through the lake country on our way to Skagway, and you wouldn't find a steamer leaving for Vancouver."

"You're talking about gold, Scout old chap," replied the engineer jokingly, "and that's very appropriate when we're camped at the foot of Golden Mount. But don't worry. I'll be very surprised if our teams aren't on the way to the Klondike within a week."

Clearly, Raddle was speaking with conviction, and Summy Skim was not there to argue with him.

The day went by as usual, and by evening there were no more than thirty or forty feet of trench left to dig. The weather had been fine, with intermittent cloud and sun. The two hunters would have had nothing to complain about.

By about five o'clock in the afternoon, however, neither one of them had been seen in the open country to the west. True, Skim still had time to get home without breaking his promise. Several times, the scout walked out a few hundred paces to see whether he could spot him. There was no one. The two hunters' outlines were not silhouetted against the horizon.

An hour later, Raddle began to get impatient and made up his mind to speak severely to his cousin.

When seven o'clock came, and Summy and Neluto had not yet shown up, Raddle's impatience turned to worry. He was doubly worried when another hour went by and the missing men were still not back.

"They've let themselves wander away," he kept repeating. "With that devil Skim, when he has an animal in front of him and a gun in his hand, you can't tell what will happen. He just goes on and on and there's no stopping him."

"And when you're tracking a moose," declared Steel, "you never know where the animal will lead you."

"I shouldn't have let him go," added Raddle.

"It won't be dark until ten o'clock," added the scout, "and there's no danger of Mr. Skim getting lost. Golden Mount can be seen from a distance, and in the dark its flames would act as a guide."

The point was well taken. If the hunters had been seven or eight miles from the encampment, they would have noticed the glow from Golden Mount, and the theory that they were lost did not stand up. But what if there had been an accident? What if it was impossible for them to make their way back? And if they were not back by nightfall, what should be done?

Two hours passed, and it is easy to imagine the state Ben Raddle was in. He could not stand still. The scout and his friends made no secret of their concern. The sun was about to sink below the horizon and there would no light except that of the long twilight in the northern latitudes of the Arctic Ocean. What if Summy Skim and Neluto were not back by nightfall? What if they were not back by dawn?

A little after ten o'clock Ben Raddle and the scout, more worried than ever, left the encampment and walked along the base of the mountain just as the sun was disappearing behind the western haze. Their last look across the open country had shown it to be deserted. As they stood there, motionless, listening, their ears cocked in that direction, might they not have hoped that Skim, because he was so late getting home, would fire a shot to announce his arrival? Would he and Neluto not expect the engineer and the scout to come and meet them? Would they not have made a point of letting them know if only to spare them five or six minutes of anxiety?

But Raddle and Steel waited in vain for the sound of a gunshot. The plain was still as quiet as it was deserted.

"They've lost their way," said the scout.

"Lost their way?" The engineer shook his head. "Lost their way in this region, when Golden Mount is visible from ten miles away in every direction?"

"What do you think, then, Mr. Raddle? Moose hunting isn't dangerous, and unless Mr. Skim and Neluto got into a fight with some bears . . ."

"Bears, brigands, or scoundrels, either Indians or whites, Bill. Yes, I've got a feeling that they've come to some harm."

Just then—about half past ten—they heard the sound of barking.

"There's Stop!" shouted Raddle.

"They aren't far away," replied the scout.

The barking continued, but it was interspersed with whining, as if the dog had been injured and had had great difficulty getting home.

Raddle and his friend ran out to meet Stop. They had not taken more than two hundred steps when they encountered the poor animal.

The dog was alone, and his hind legs were red with blood coming from a wound on his hind quarters. It seemed that he no longer had the strength to walk and that he could not have made it to the encampment.

"He's wounded . . . wounded . . . and alone!" exclaimed Raddle, his heart pounding violently at the thought—almost the certainty—that Summy and Neluto had fallen victim to some disaster brought on either by men or by wild beasts.

"Perhaps," mused the scout, "Stop was wounded accidentally by his master or by Neluto. A stray bullet may have struck him."

"Then why wouldn't he have stayed with Skim if Skim could have treated him and taken him along?" asked Raddle.

"In any case," said Steel, "let's take the dog back to camp and dress his wound. If it isn't serious, perhaps he'll be able to come with us and put us on Mr. Skim's trail."

"Yes," added the engineer, "because I don't want to wait until morning. We'll take a good number of men with us, well armed, and as you said, Scout, if Stop can guide us . . ."

The scout picked the dog up in his arms and ten minutes later he and Raddle were back at the encampment.

The dog was taken into the tent, where his wound was examined. It did not appear to be serious, since it was only a flesh wound and did not affect any organs. It had been caused by a gunshot, and the scout, who was very competent in such matters, succeeded in extracting the bullet.

Ben Raddle took the bullet, held it up to the light, and examined it. He turned pale and his hand shook as he exclaimed, "This bullet is not of the same caliber as the ones Summy uses," he exclaimed. "It's bigger, and it didn't come from a hunting rifle."

Bill Steel examined the bullet and came to the same conclusion.

"They've had a brush with some scoundrels, some outlaws," exclaimed the engineer. "They had to defend themselves against an armed attack. Stop was hit during the attack and didn't stay with his master, because his master was taken away . . . or died along with Neluto. Ah! My poor Summy! My poor Summy!"

Raddle could not restrain his sobs. And what could Bill Steel say? The bullet had not been fired by either of the two hunters. The dog had come back alone. Did that not support the engineer's theory? Could there be any doubt that some misfortune had occurred? Either Summy Skim and his companion had died defending themselves, or they had been captured by their attackers since they had not been seen again.

At eleven o'clock, neither Skim nor Neluto was back at camp. The horizon had clouded over at sunset, and the twilight period would be dark.

It was decided that Ben Raddle, the scout, and their friends would go to look for the missing men. They got ready to leave at once. There was no need to take food, since the party would not go far from Golden Mount at least during the early stages of the search. But every member of the group would be armed in case they were attacked on the way or in case they had to use force to free the two prisoners.

Stop had been carefully bandaged. After the bullet had been extracted and the wound dressed, and he had been well fed and rested (for he was exhausted from hunger and thirst), he seemed eager to go looking for his master.

"We'll take him with us," said the scout. "We'll carry him if he's too tired, and perhaps he'll pick up Mr. Skim's trail."

If all their efforts during the night proved fruitless, if they had no success over a distance of three or four miles to the west,[1] the scout was in favor of returning to Golden Mount. They would break camp and the caravan would continue its search over the wide open country. They would scour the whole region between the Arctic Ocean and the Porcupine River. There would be no question of working at Golden Mount until Ben Raddle had found Summy Skim again, until he was sure what had happened to him—and who could say whether he would ever be sure?

After ensuring that the animals would not be able to leave the encampment, the scout and his party started out. They skirted the base of the mountain, which was making the earth tremble with its dull rumblings. Tongues of flame, clearly visible in the semidarkness, were shooting up through the smoke surrounding its summit, but no volcanic material was coming out.

Raddle and Steel were walking together with the dog at their side. The others followed, rifles at the ready. When they reached the point from which they had made their ascent of the volcano, they stopped.

What direction should they take now? Did they have any other option but to strike out at random? In any case, the most practical course of action was to rely on the dog's instinct. The intelligent animal understood what was expected of him and uttered muffled barks. If he happened on his master's trail, there would certainly be no mistaking it.

Stop hesitated for a few moments and then headed northwest. That was not the direction Skim and Neluto had taken when they left Golden Mount.

"Let's go wherever he goes," said the scout. All things considered, that was the best course of action.

For an hour the little group traveled across the open country in that direction until they came to the edge of the forest that the two hunters had entered two or three miles farther down.

What should be their next move? Should they plunge into the woods amid the pitch darkness of the trees? Or would it not be better, since they had found no trace, to go back to camp and resume their search in daylight?

Raddle, the scout, and Lorique discussed the situation. The engineer could not bring himself to go back, even though he realized how unwise it would be to start through the forest. Steel, with his greater self-control, was a better judge of the situation and insisted on returning at once. It seemed, though, that Stop was hesitating. He stood motionless at the edge of the forest, no longer uttering his dull barks, as if his instinct had failed him.

Suddenly he made a leap. He certainly did not feel his wound as he ran among the trees, barking loudly. He was obviously on the trail they had been vainly seeking until then.

"Let's follow him! Let's follow him!" shouted Raddle.

They were all about to rush into the forest, when the barking became more rapid.

"Wait," ordered Steel, motioning to the others to stop.

Almost at once, two men appeared, and in another instant Summy Skim was in the engineer's arms.

His first words were "Back to camp! Back to camp!"

"What happened?" asked Raddle.

"I'll tell you what happened when we get there," replied Skim, "but let's just worry about what may still happen. Back to camp, I tell you, back to camp."

Guided by the flames of Golden Mount, they all set out at a quick pace. An hour later they were at Rubber Creek. It was now past midnight.

Before joining Raddle, Lorique, and the scout in the tent, Skim stopped. He wanted to take a last look at the approaches to Golden Mount. The engineer and Steel followed his example. They knew they were in danger, but that was the only information they had been able to get out of Skim during the rapid passage from the forest to the mountain.

When they were alone, Skim gave a brief account of the events that had happened between six o'clock in the morning and five in the afternoon: reaching the edge of the forest, pursuing the moose, continuing the fruitless hunt until noon, stopping, resuming the hunt when they heard Stop barking, and finally stopping from sheer exhaustion at the edge of the clearing, where they found the ashes of a long-extinguished fire.

"It was obvious," he said, "that some men, either Indians or whites, had camped at that spot. There was nothing surprising about that. Besides, judging from the condition of the ashes, the firepit was already very old, and we had nothing to worry about."

"True enough," said the scout. "Sometimes the crews of whaling ships come ashore on the Arctic coast, not to mention the Indians who go there during the warm weather."

"But," continued Skim, "just as we were about to start back to Golden Mount, Neluto found this weapon lying in the grass."

Raddle and the scout examined the dagger and recognized, as Skim had done, that it was of Spanish manufacture. The thought occurred to them also that the dagger had been lost there very recently since there was not a trace of rust on the blade.

"This letter M engraved on the hilt," remarked Steel, "it didn't tell you anything, Mr. Skim."

"No, Bill, but all the same, I know what name it stands for."

"What name is that?" inquired Raddle.

"Malone, the Texan."

"Malone?"

"Yes, Ben."

"Hunter's crony?" suggested Steel.

"That's the one."

"They were there just a few days ago?" asked the engineer.

"And they're still there," replied Skim.

"Did you see them?" asked Lorique.

"Listen to the rest of my story, and then you'll know."

"Neluto and I were about to leave," he went on, "when we heard a gunshot not far away. We stopped, and our first concern was to make sure we wouldn't be seen.

"There could be no doubt that there were hunters in the forest. They were probably foreigners since Indians don't use firearms.[2] But whoever they were, it was best to be on our guard.

"I thought the shot had been fired at one of the moose that Neluto and I had been pursuing. But when you told me what had happened to my poor Stop, whom I thought I would never see again, I knew the shot had been fired at him."

"So," said Raddle, "when we saw him coming back without you, wounded by someone else's bullet, barely able to drag himself along, you can imagine what was going on in my head. I was already sick with worry because it was ten o'clock and you hadn't come back. What could I assume, except that you and Neluto had been attacked and that your dog had got that wound during the attack? Ah! Summy! Summy! How could I forget that I was the one who dragged you here?"

Raddle was overcome with emotion as he spoke and made no attempt to hide it. Skim understood very well what was going on in his cousin's heart, that he was thinking of the heavy responsibility he bore for becoming involved in such adventures.

"Ben, my dear Ben," he said, taking his cousin's hands in his, "what's done is done. Don't blame yourself. The situation may be getting worse, but it isn't desperate, and we'll get through it, I hope."

Skim shook hands warmly with the scout and went on with his story.

"As soon as we heard the shot, which came from the east, the direction we would have had to take to return to camp, I ordered Neluto to follow me, and we hurried away from the clearing, where we would have been seen.

"Besides, we heard voices, many voices, and we could tell that a group of men was coming from that direction.

"But while we didn't want to be seen, we did want to know who those men were. You can understand, Ben, how important that was to us. What were they doing here, an hour's walk from Golden Mount? Were they aware of the volcano's existence? Were they heading for it? Were we in danger of meeting them, perhaps on very unequal terms?

"It would soon be dark in the forest. To avoid falling into the hands of those scoundrels, I decided it would be wise to wait until later in the evening before starting out again. Once we reached the edge of the forest, we'd have the volcano's flames to guide us.

"In any case, there was no time to waste in thinking about it. The men were getting closer. They'd probably come and set up camp in the clearing, near the stream running through it. In a flash, we ran to a thick bush about a dozen paces to one side. Crouching among the tall grass and the undergrowth, we were in no danger of being discovered. Most important of all, we could see and hear.

"The group appeared almost immediately. There were about fifty men, some thirty of whom I was sure I recognized as Americans, and about twenty Indians.

"My hunch had been right. They were coming to make camp for the night at that spot and began by lighting fires to prepare their meal.

"I didn't know any of the men, and neither did Neluto. They were armed with rifles and revolvers, which they set down under the trees. They didn't talk much among themselves, and when they did, their voices were so low I couldn't hear them."

"But what about Hunter and Malone?" asked Raddle.

"They came along a quarter of an hour later," said Skim, "with an Indian and the foreman who had been in charge of operations at Claim 127.

"Ah! We recognized them all right, both of us. Yes, those villains had come to the neighborhood of Golden Mount, accompanied by a whole band of scoundrels, just like themselves, no doubt."

"But what are they doing here?" asked the scout. "Do they know about Golden Mount? Do they know there's a caravan of miners there already?"

"Those are exactly the questions I asked myself, Bill old boy," replied Skim, "and I finally got answers to everything."

Just then the scout motioned to Summy Skim to be quiet. He thought he had heard a noise outside. Stepping out of the tent, he looked all around the encampment.

The noise had been made by one of his friends crossing the trench. The first streaks of dawn, which comes so early at that latitude, were beginning to appear.

The vast open country was deserted. There was no group of men approaching the mountain, whose rumblings were the only noise breaking the silence of the night. The dog, stretched out in a corner of the tent, showed no sign of concern.

The scout came back in and reassured Raddle and his cousin.

Summy Skim went on with his story.

"The two Texans came and sat down at the very edge of the clearing, ten paces away from the bush where we were hiding. I could hear what they were saying. First of all, they mentioned coming across a dog, but said nothing about having fired at it. 'That was peculiar,' said Hunter. 'Yes, very peculiar—in the middle of this forest. There's no way it could have come here by itself, so far from Dawson City.' 'There are hunters around here,' said Malone. 'There's no doubt about it. But where are they? Has the dog caught up with them? They were running in that direction.' Malone pointed to the east as he said that.[3] 'Well,' exclaimed Hunter, 'who says they're hunters, the people who own that dog? No one ventures this far to hunt deer or wild beasts.' 'You're right, Hunter,' said Malone. 'There are miners here looking for new gold deposits. Hasn't it been reported that there are some in the Canadian north?' 'Yes,' replied Hunter, 'rich placers that those damned Canadians claim the sole rights to. But just let us get our hands on them, and they'll see how much is left for them.' 'Not enough to fill one pan,' replied Malone, laughing between his dreadful oaths."

"Did they say anything about Golden Mount?" asked Ben Raddle.

"Yes," replied Skim, "because Hunter went on to say, 'Besides, that Golden Mount, which the Indians often talk about and which our guide Krasak knows about, can't be far from here on the Arctic coast, and even if we have to cover the whole shoreline from Point Barrow to Hudson Bay, we'll find it sooner or later.'"

The engineer looked thoughtful. His worst fears had been realized.

The Frenchman, Jacques Laurier, had not been the only one to know about the existence of Golden Mount. This Indian, Krasak, must have given the secret to the Texans, and they had not taken long to determine its location, without having to travel along the whole shoreline of the Arctic Ocean. They would spot the volcano as soon as they stepped out of the forest where they were camping. They would see the smoke and flames swirling over its crater. In an hour they would have reached the base of Golden Mount, and when they came close to the encampment occupied by the former neighbors of Claim 127 on the Fortymile River, what would happen then?

Turning to Skim, he asked, "You noticed that Hunter had a lot of men with him?"

"About fifty armed men," was the reply, "and in my opinion he didn't recruit them from among the few honest men to be found in the Klondike."

"That's very likely; in fact, it's certain," declared the scout, "and what it all means is that our situation is serious."

With this comment from Bill Steel, the conversation came to an end. Precautions were taken to guard the encampment during the night, and there were no further incidents before morning.

11

On the Defensive

As the scout had said, the situation was serious.

Was there any reason to hope that the gang of Texans would not discover Golden Mount, at least not immediately? Hunter would spot it as soon as he emerged from the forest at its eastern edge. Then, too, he had as a guide that Krasak, whose name Summy Skim had heard mentioned. They would not have to travel along the whole Arctic coast, since they must have come from that direction after they passed the source of the Porcupine River. If they had taken the scout's route from Dawson City to the mouth of the Mackenzie, they would have been seen a long way off, as much as twenty-four hours ago, and they would have gone straight toward Golden Mount. That meant they had come from the west, from Fort Yukon, on the right bank of the great river.

There were about fifty men in the gang, while Ben Raddle and his party numbered only about twenty. Their courage would not be able to make up for this numerical inferiority, even though they were determined to defend themselves to the death.

There was nothing to do, then, but to wait for events to take their course, and they would not have long to wait. In forty-eight hours at the most, perhaps even that very day, Hunter would be on his way to Golden Mount. As for abandoning the encampment on the Mackenzie, starting back to the Klondike, retreating before the Texans, that was out of the question. The scout would not have suggested it to his friends, and their reaction would have been to refuse. Did they not consider themselves, as the first occupants, to be the legitimate owners of this volcanic deposit? They would not let it be snatched away from them without a fight. Even Summy Skim himself, the wise Summy Skim, would not have agreed to let Hunter force him to retreat. He had not forgotten the man's uncouth actions when they had met, first when disembarking from the steamboat at Vancouver and then on the border between Claims 129 and 127 on the Fortymile River. There was a quarrel to be settled, and since the occasion had arisen, he would settle it in person.

What would happen when the Texans reached the foot of the mountain? Here is what Bill Steel was thinking, and here is what he said to Ben Raddle the following day when the two men resumed their earlier conversation.

"In a few hours, I suppose, we'll see the gang heading for Golden Mount. When they get there, will Hunter stop and set up camp, or will he follow around the base of the mountain and camp on the side next to the Mackenzie, as we did?"

"I think, Bill," replied the engineer, "that the Texans will first want to climb Golden Mount. That would be their wisest move. They'll want to reconnoiter, as we did, to see whether there's any gold-bearing quartz or nuggets at the summit."

"No doubt," replied the scout. "But after they've looked at the crater and realized that it's impossible to get through the smoke and flames, they'll come back down. That's when the question arises of whether they'll want to wait until the volcano erupts or wait until the eruption is over. In either case, they'll have to set up camp."

"Unless they go back the way they came," exclaimed Skim, joining in the conversation. "That would be their wisest decision."

"But they won't," declared Raddle. "You can be sure of that."

"I am sure of it, Ben. However, it won't occur to those villains to speed up the eruption of Golden Mount, as we're trying to do."

"All right, Summy. Then they'll wait."

"And while they're waiting," added the scout, "they'll camp in the neighborhood. Besides, let's not forget that the sight of a dog in the forest has aroused their suspicions. They'll want to see whether some group of miners has reached the mouth of the Mackenzie ahead of them, and they'll carry out their search as far as the estuary."

"We'll have to assume that they will," replied Skim. "They'll soon discover our camp. They'll try to drive us away, and then I'll be face to face with Hunter! Well, if it takes a good duel, either in the French or the American fashion—I'll give him his choice—to settle the quarrel and rid us of this gang, after we've got rid of its leader . . ."

That was obviously not going to happen. The Texans would be able to take advantage of their numerical superiority to destroy the scout's caravan or at least drive it away and retain sole control of Golden Mount.

They had to be ready, then, to repulse an attack. All steps were taken in preparation for an imminent raid.

First of all, Bill Steel brought the wagons into the corner between Rubber Creek and the mountain. The animals were brought back from the pastures, which were unprotected, and led across the trench to the shelter of some trees about 150 paces away, where there was enough grass to feed them for several days. The teams had to be saved at all costs in order to get back to the Klondike before the first frost of winter set in. In addition, the tents were taken down and kept ready to be put up again at night beyond the trench. The trench, of course, would serve as a line of defense. The attackers would have great difficulty crossing it in the face of rifle fire when it was filled to the brim with water from the stream.

If necessary, to prevent the encampment from being invaded, Ben Raddle would give the order for the last blows of the pick to be struck against the bank of Rubber Creek. For the time being, however, he would wait since he had nothing to gain by precipitating an eruption as long as Hunter was at the foot of Golden Mount.

Weapons were made ready for the defense of the caravan. Of the twenty men in the party, about a dozen had guns, revolvers, and cutlasses, in addition to Raddle, Skim, Lorique, Steel, and Neluto's rifles.

It goes without saying that from then on the hunters would do no more hunting, although the fishermen continued to fish in the creek and the inlets along the shore in order to save the caravan's reserves of food.

Work on the trench, of course, was not interrupted. It would keep moving toward the mountain. It was important to be able to fill it from end to end between the creek and the entrance to the tunnel that had been cut into the mountainside. But the engineer would not use explosives now, since the noise might be heard. The charges would not be set until the moment came to blow open the wall between the tunnel and the volcano's chimney.

The volcanic activity showed no sign of intensifying. The noises from inside were not becoming any louder. The flames and smoke were not rising higher or spreading out. Weeks, even months, might go by before Golden Mount would be in full eruption.

All that day the scout and his friends remained on the alert. The men stayed in the remotest part of the encampment. In order to see them, one would have had to go as far as the left bank of Rubber Creek or to the West Channel of the Mackenzie delta.

Several times, however, Raddle, Skim, Steel, and Lorique went out to look farther out over the open country. Since they saw nothing suspicious approaching, they went on to the western end of the base.[1] From there, they could see as far as the first row of trees in the forest that closed off the horizon nearly four miles away.

The countryside was deserted. There was no body of men to be seen there, and no one in the direction of the coast along which the gang might have come if they were following the shoreline.

"It's certain," said the scout, "that the Texans haven't left the forest yet."

"That's right," added Skim. "They've headed west."

"I can't believe that," replied the engineer. "Their guide knows where Golden Mount is, and they must have seen it from the edge of the woods. They're probably still camped in that clearing where you saw them, Summy."

"Then they can't be in a very big hurry, Ben."

288

"If they suspect some miners are here ahead of them, they may want to reconnoiter the situation before making a move. Perhaps they won't push on to Golden Mount until tomorrow night."

"Probably not," said Raddle, "because it's impossible that they haven't seen it."

"So," said Steel, "we'll be on the lookout for any surprise."

Raddle, Skim, the scout, and Lorique took one last look to make sure the countryside was deserted and then went back to camp. By evening, Steel had taken all the necessary precautions for the night.

The night was uneventful, and Summy Skim slept right through until morning as usual. Raddle, on the other hand, enjoyed only a few hours of sleep. His mind was troubled by worry and irritation. Irritation, because at the very moment when he was about to achieve his goal, luck was turning against him. Worry, because he had no doubt that Golden Mount would be hotly contested. Would he be able to hold out against Hunter's gang? He felt a heavy weight of personal responsibility.

Was it not solely on his initiative that this trek to the mouth of the Mackenzie had been organized? Had he not been the leading spirit of this expedition, which was in danger of ending so badly? Had he not, so to speak, forced Summy Skim to spend a second year in these remote regions of the Dominion? It was understandable that he had wanted to come to the Klondike after the death of Uncle Josias to take possession of his inheritance, and it was only natural that Summy Skim should have come with him. It was also understandable, in a way, that on arriving at the Fortymile River he should have yielded to the temptation to work Claim 129 and take all the profit from it without listening to the objections raised by his prudent cousin. But after the earthquake and the flood, after the destruction of the claims on that whole part of the Klondike adjacent to the American border, what would have been his wisest move? To abandon forever the life of a prospector last winter, to leave Dawson City as soon as winter was over and his leg was fully recovered, and to head home to Montreal, instead of going back up to the Arctic Ocean.

It was regrettable, then, that Raddle had come into contact with the Frenchman Jacques Laurier, who had revealed to him the existence of Golden Mount. It was equally regrettable that he had decided to use that information, which was no longer his secret alone, and that a gang of scoundrels was about to take it from him by force.

That was what Ben Raddle said to himself during his long hours of insomnia, expecting the sentinels to sound the alarm. He had gone out two or three times to check on the approaches to the encampment.

Undoubtedly, the caravan was threatened by a most serious danger. If Hunter attacked, they would have no chance of putting up a successful resistance, since the attackers outnumbered them two to one. Would it not be the better part of valor to retreat before they were driven out? That very night (since the Texans had not yet appeared) it would have been easy to break camp and head the teams back toward Dawson City. The caravan would have been out of sight before daybreak. But to abandon the profits of the expedition after so much effort, after enduring so much fatigue, on the very eve of success. No! Ben Raddle could never have allowed himself to give the order to leave, and in all probability his companions could not have allowed themselves to obey it.

At five o'clock in the morning Raddle and the scout walked out past the trench two hundred yards or so but did not go as far as the eastern face of Golden Mount. They returned without having seen anything new.

The fine weather promised to continue and the barometer was above normal. It was rather warm, but a cool wind off the sea had a moderating effect and sent the smoke from the crater drifting southward. The engineer and Bill Steel noticed that it was not as thick and black as it had been the previous day.

"Is the volcanic action dying down?" asked Raddle.

"Well" said the scout, "if the crater died out, then our work would be simpler."

"And Hunter's work, too," replied the engineer. "All the same, let's not stop working now. Let's finish the trench."

"It'll be finished today, Mr. Raddle."

"Yes, Bill. All we'll have to do then will be to break through the bank of the stream and the wall at the end of the tunnel. We'll do that when the time comes. But that will depend on the circumstances."

The men set to work, and in only a few hours the last blow of the pick had been struck and the last shovelful of earth removed. Now, along the three hundred feet of trench and the sixty feet of tunnel, the water from the creek could go rushing into the chimney of Golden Mount.

After lunch they were allowed a short rest but without neglecting to keep watch on the approaches to the encampment.

In the afternoon Neluto set out toward the open country, accompanied by Stop, who had almost fully recovered from his wound. If even one of Hunter's men, let alone the whole gang, had ventured as far as the base of the mountain, the intelligent animal would certainly have picked up his trail.

About three o'clock, as Raddle and Skim were inspecting the bank of the stream near the spot where the opening was to be made, they were suddenly put on their guard.

There was a sound of rapid barking coming from the direction in which the Indian and Stop had gone out to reconnoiter.

"What can that be?" exclaimed the scout.

"Our dog has probably flushed out some animal," said Raddle.

"No," replied Skim. "He wouldn't bark like that."

"Come on," said the engineer.

They hadn't taken a hundred steps when they saw Neluto hurrying back.

A few minutes later, the Indian shouted in a loud voice, "Look out! Look out!"

As soon as he had joined the other three, he added, "They're coming!"

"All of them?" asked Steel.

"All of them," was the reply.

"How far away are they?" inquired the engineer.

"Seven or eight hundred yards from the volcano, Mr. Ben."

"And they didn't see you?" asked Skim.

"I don't think so," replied Neluto, "but I got a good look at them. They're coming in force, with their horses and wagons."

"And where are they heading?" asked the scout.

"Toward the creek."

"Did they hear the dog barking?" asked Summy.

"No, they couldn't have. They were still too far away."

"Back to camp," ordered Raddle, "and let's get ready to defend ourselves."

A few minutes later they all reached the trench, crossed over it along the bank of the creek, and took shelter under the trees.

Would Hunter, Malone, and their gang stop when they reached the corner of Golden Mount? Would they make camp there or go on to the Mackenzie estuary?

The latter hypothesis was certainly the more likely. Since they also needed to camp for a few days, they would look for a site where there would be plenty of fresh water. There was no creek flowing through the open country to the west of Golden Mount, and Hunter must have known that the great river emptied into the ocean a short distance away. It was to be expected, then, that he would head toward the estuary. At that point, how could the work on the trench fail to attract his attention? What hope was there that he would not discover the encampment under the trees?

Ben Raddle and his friends were in danger of an imminent attack, and they made ready to repel it.

But the afternoon went by and the attack did not materialize. Neither the Texans nor any of their men made an appearance in the vicinity of Rubber Creek.

Did that mean that Hunter had chosen to call a halt at the foot of Golden Mount, on this side? But that would not be a suitable site for a lengthy stay.

"It's possible, though," the scout pointed out, "that Hunter may have wanted to climb the volcano before making camp at its base."

"That's possible, yes," replied Skim. "After all, he does have to reconnoiter the crater, make sure there are nuggets in it, and at the same time see what's happening with the eruption."

It was a good point, and Raddle nodded in agreement.

Be that as it may, the day ended without a visit from the Texans. Would they not come until the next day, then, and make camp near the Mackenzie after they had climbed Golden Mount? It seemed likely that they would.

But in order to be ready for any eventuality, the scout and his friends decided to stay up all night, prepared to defend themselves. They took turns crossing the trench along the bank of the creek to the foot of the mountain, where they took up a position that afforded a good view of its base.

Until half past eleven it was still light enough to see any men who might have been heading toward the creek, and by two o'clock the first light of dawn appeared.

No incident occurred during that short night, and when the sun rose, the situation was just as it had been the day before.

Would Hunter and Malone appear at the top of the volcano during the day? That was what they needed to know. And would it be possible to see them without being seen?

To withdraw to the south was out of the question. The countryside in that direction did not have a single clump of trees that they could hide behind. If they moved back to the spot where Rubber Creek branched out from the main stream, it would also be impossible to find any shelter where Hunter and Malone could not see them from the plateau at the top of Golden Mount.

There was only one place from which they could see the Texans walking around the crater without being seen themselves. That was a clump of old birches standing two hundred yards from the encampment on the left bank of the creek, downstream from the place where its water was to be diverted. It would be possible to move between the encampment and the trees by crawling behind a hedge of bushes.

Raddle and Steel went out early to make sure that anyone approaching the ridge of the plateau would be clearly visible. This ridge, as they had noticed when they climbed the mountain for the first time, consisted of blocks of quartz and hardened lava, which offered a secure foothold. Below that, the mountainside dropped vertically like the wall of a tower, both on that side and on the side facing the sea.

"This is a good place," said the scout. "We won't be seen either coming or going. If Hunter climbs up to the plateau, he'll certainly want to have a look at the Mackenzie delta from the direction of this ridge."

"So," remarked Raddle, "we'll keep a man on duty here all the time."

"I might add, Mr. Ben, that our camp can't be seen from the top now. It's sheltered by the trees. We'll make sure all the fires are out and there's no smoke. If we do that, I'm pretty sure Hunter's gang won't be able to find it."

"That would be most desirable," replied the engineer. "It would also be desirable for the Texans, once they realize they can't go down into the crater, to abandon their plans and go back the way they came."

"And may the devil be their guide!" exclaimed the scout. "If you like, Mr. Ben," he added, "since I'm already here, I'll stay and you can go back to camp."

"No, Bill, I'd rather you left me here to keep watch. Go and make sure everything necessary has been done and see to it that none of our animals can wander away."

"All right," replied the scout, "and I'll ask Mr. Skim to come and relieve you in two hours."

"Right. In two hours," said Raddle. He stretched out under a birch tree from which he could keep an eye on the ridge of the volcano's plateau.

Bill Steel went back alone to join his friends in the little thicket. The tents had been taken down in the morning, and there was nothing to reveal the presence of a caravan in the corner between Rubber Creek and the face of Golden Mount.

A little before nine o'clock, at the scout's suggestion, Summy Skim slipped between the rocks, his rifle slung over his shoulder as if he were going hunting, and went to join the engineer. Stretching out beside him, he began the conversation, quite naturally, by asking, "Anything new, Ben?"

"Nothing, Summy."

"None of those brutes from Texas have come to perch up there on the rocks?"

"Not a soul."

"It would give me great pleasure to take down one or two of them," continued Summy, indicating his rifle loaded with two cartridges.

"At this distance, Summy?" wondered the engineer.

"That's true. You're right. It's a little too high and a little too far."

"Besides, Summy, it's more important to be cautious than to be skillful. One man less in the gang wouldn't make it any less dangerous for us. If we aren't discovered, I'm still hoping Hunter and his crew will get out of our way after they realize there's nothing they can do."

That was still Ben Raddle's wish, but there were so many solid reasons why it might not come true!

After they chatted for a few minutes, Raddle got up to go back to camp. It was now nine o'clock.

"Keep good watch, Summy," he said. "If you see the Texans on the plateau, come and warn us right away. And be careful not to show yourself."

"Right you are, Ben."

"The scout will come and take your place so you can come and have lunch."

"Bill Steel or Neluto," replied Skim. "He's a good man and we can have every confidence in him. He's got the eyes of an eagle—or the eyes of an Indian, which amounts to the same thing."

Raddle was about to start back between the rocks on his way to the encampment when Skim suddenly seized him by the arm.

"Wait a minute," he said.

"What is it?"

"Look up there!"

295

The engineer raised his eyes to the plateau at the top of Golden Mount. A man appeared beside the ridge, followed by a second.

"It's them! It's them!" repeated Skim, stretching out his arm.

"Yes, it's Hunter and Malone," said Raddle, scurrying quickly behind a clump of trees.

It was indeed the two Texans, and no doubt a few of their gang were on the plateau with them. They had very likely examined the condition of the crater and then walked around it, intending to take a good look at the region to the east, especially the immense hydrographic network that makes up the Mackenzie delta. It would certainly occur to them to move their encampment there if they decided to wait for the eruption, at least until the first cold spells forced them to leave.

"Ah!" murmured Summy Skim. "Those two villains! And just think that I'd have two bullets with their names on them if only they were in range. To be sure, there's an affair of honor to settle between Hunter and me. Yes, honor! And if it hadn't been for the flood on the Fortymile River, it would have been settled in my favor, I hope."

But that was definitely not what Summy Skim should have been thinking about at that moment, and Ben Raddle was certainly not thinking about everything that had happened on Claims 127 and 129 the year before. His only concern was with the two men who had come to challenge his claim to Golden Mount. In fact, his hatred for Hunter and Malone was as deep as Skim's, although for a different reason.

For about half an hour they could see the two Texans going back and forth on the ridge of the plateau. Clearly, they were studying the region intently, sometimes leaning over to see the base of the volcano on the side next the estuary.

If they had discovered the encampment at the foot of the mountain and if they had realized that another caravan had reached the Mackenzie delta ahead of them, that would have been revealed simply by their attitude. There was no doubt, however, that Hunter and Malone were staring fixedly at the creek flowing past its base, and there was no doubt that they saw it as an ideal location to set up camp for a few weeks.

Just then they were joined by two other men. Raddle and Skim recognized one of them as the foreman from Claim 127. The other, an Indian, was unknown to them.

"He's probably the guide who led them here," said the engineer.

"He's definitely the one I saw in the clearing," exclaimed Skim.

Watching them on the ridge of the plateau, the idea occurred to him that if they happened to lose their balance and fall eight or nine hundred feet, that would certainly simplify the situation, perhaps even settle it once and for all. With its leaders dead, the gang might very well abandon the expedition.

It was not the Texans who were precipitated from the top of the volcano but a rather large block of quartz, which broke off from the ridge. They hurriedly moved back in order not to be dragged along with it.

As it fell, the piece of rock struck a projection on the mountainside and broke into several pieces, which fell amongst the trees sheltering the encampment.

Skim could not suppress a cry, but Raddle put his hand over his mouth.

"Be quiet, Summy, be quiet!"

"I just hope none of our friends have been crushed."

They could only hope so. But as it happened, the falling rock startled one of the horses, which broke its tether, dashed out of the thicket, ran to the trench, cleared it in a single bound, and headed for the open country.

Shouts were heard, faintly because of the distance, and they came from the top of Golden Mount.

It was Hunter and Malone who had shouted, calling their friends.

Five or six of them came running up to the ridge, and it was not hard to guess from their gestures that Hunter now knew there was a caravan at the mouth of the Mackenzie. That horse could only have escaped from an encampment, and that encampment was right there, at their feet.

"Come on," said Raddle to Skim.

Leaving the thicket and crawling between the rocks, they made for the woods, where the scout, Neluto, Lorique, and their friends were anxiously waiting for them.

12

Attack and Defense

BILL STEEL AND THE OTHERS still did not know whether their encampment had been discovered or not. From its location at the foot of Golden Mount, they could not see the ridge on the plateau. They were not even aware that Hunter and some of his gang had climbed to the top or that they had seen the horse that escaped. But since it could have been seen running across the open country, Neluto had set out after it and soon brought it back.

Everyone was briefed on the situation, and they were sure they would soon have to fight off an attack.

"We'll defend ourselves," declared the scout, "and we won't yield any ground to those American villains."

His words were greeted by a unanimous hurrah.

Would the attack come that same day? It seemed likely. It was to Hunter's advantage to bring matters to a head. True, he would not be so reckless as to act without knowing what forces he would be facing. He would obviously try to find that out before joining battle. He might even try to get what he wanted by negotiating if he had numerical superiority on his side. In any case, he and Malone still did not know they were dealing with their former neighbors, the owners of Claim 129 on the Fortymile River, with whom they had already had very violent altercations. And the situation would not become any easier when Hunter found himself in the presence of his enemy, Summy Skim.

And so the scout busied himself making final preparations for defense on the assumption, based on Skim and Neluto's report of what they had seen in the forest, that Hunter's gang was twice the size of their crew.

After the question had been discussed, the engineer made a suggestion to Steel.

"Right now, our camp is inaccessible," he said, "because it's protected on one side by the face of Golden Mount and on the other by Rubber Creek, which Hunter and his men can't cross without exposing themselves to our rifle fire."

"That's true, Mr. Raddle," replied the scout, "but in front our only defense is the trench running from the creek to the mountain, and a trench seven or eight feet wide and seven or eight feet deep isn't likely to stop the attackers."

"No, it isn't," said the engineer, "as long as the trench is dry, but if it's filled to the top with water, it'll be harder to cross."

"I agree, Mr. Raddle. Would you be thinking of flooding it, then, by cutting through the bank of the creek?"

"I'm thinking of that, Bill," replied Raddle. "The water would completely fill the trench."

"But later on," the scout pointed out, "if we want to blow up the wall between the tunnel and the chimney, how can we do it if the tunnel is full of water?"

"It won't be, because it is still closed off by a narrow dam that we'll leave in place until the time comes to break it open with a few strokes of the pick."

"Fine, Mr. Raddle," said the scout. "That's what we have to do, and we have to do it right away. We've got a few hours before the gang has time to come back down and show up at our camp. Let's get to work!"

Bill Steel called his men together and told them what had been decided. Tools in hand, they went to the bank of the creek and attacked it at the point where the trench began.

It only took half an hour to make an opening, which the water enlarged as it rushed through. But it was held back by the dam at the opening of the tunnel, and when the water level between the trench and the creek was equalized, the flow of water subsided.

Every approach was now cut off in front of the triangle where the encampment was hidden by masses of trees.

While this work was going on, Skim and Lorique, with Neluto's help, busied themselves putting the rifles and revolvers in working order and the cutlasses, too, in case it came to hand-to-hand fighting. There was still a sufficient supply of powder and bullets, as well as ready-made cartridges.

"We've got as many shots for those villains as they deserve," said Skim, "and we won't go easy on them."

"In my opinion," said Lorique, "if they meet with heavy gunfire, they'll go back the way they came."

"That's possible, Lorique, and since we're protected behind the trees, and they'll have no protection on the other side of the trench, that will offset the handicap of being one against two. If ever there was a time to aim straight and not waste a shot, this is it. Don't forget that, Neluto!"

"You can count on me, Mr. Skim," replied the Indian.

The preparations for defense were soon finished. There was nothing to do now but wait and keep a lookout on the surrounding area. Men were stationed in front of the trench, from which they could observe the whole southern base of Golden Mount.

Everyone in the caravan understood the position they were in. There was no other way out, now that the dam, just wide enough to allow the teams to pass over, had been kept in place at the entrance to the tunnel. If they had to retreat, to give up the place to the Texans, they could only get out through this narrow passage and reach the open country by going up the left bank of Rubber Creek. But everyone was confident that Hunter would definitely not succeed in crossing the trench. The passage in question was easily barricaded, leaving only an opening that would be closed when the attack began.

While a few men stood on guard, the others, waiting their turn to replace them, ate their lunch under the trees with Raddle, Skim, and the scout. The fishing had been excellent during the past few days, and the canned goods were still practically untouched. They had started a fire, but that presented no problem, now that the encampment had been discovered. Smoke rose freely through the branches.

The meal was not disturbed in any way, and when the watchmen who had been relieved came back, they had no report to make of the gang's approach.

"Perhaps," suggested Skim, "the villains would rather attack us at night."

"But night lasts barely two hours," replied Raddle, "and they haven't a hope of taking us by surprise."

"Why not, Ben?" said Skim. "Mightn't they think we don't know they're on Golden Mount? They don't know we saw them when they were standing on the edge of the plateau."

"That's possible," agreed the scout, "but they saw the horse that ran away. First a dog in the forest, then a horse running across the countryside. That's more than enough to prove there's a caravan camped here. So, either this afternoon or tonight, we can expect to see them."

About one o'clock Bill Steel crossed the dam and joined the men watching the surroundings.

While he was away, Raddle and Lorique went back to the clump of trees from which they had seen Hunter and Malone on the ridge of the plateau. The smoke from the volcano was visible from there, rising some fifty feet above the crater and swirling furiously. Sometimes a few flames leaped to the same height. The intensity of the internal fire was becoming more violent. Was there any reason to believe that the eruption would take place soon, perhaps within the next few days?

Such a turn of events would be very unfortunate and very damaging to the engineer's plans. The volcano would throw out the gold-bearing substances, nuggets, and gold dust along with its lava and slag, and the Texans could simply gather them up. The eruption would work to Hunter's advantage, and how could Ben Raddle challenge his claim? The game would be irrevocably lost. At the encampment, the caravan had some chance of success. In the open country, it would be impossible to fight with any advantage.

The engineer was very worried when he came back, but he clearly understood that he would have to let events take their course.

As soon as he arrived, Summy Skim drew his attention to the scout, who was running back as fast as he could. The two cousins went out to the dam to meet him.

"They're coming!" cried Steel.

"Are they still far away?" asked the engineer.

"About a mile," replied the scout.

"Have we got time to reconnoiter?" asked Lorique.

"Yes," was the reply.

All four of them immediately crossed the trench and quickly reached the spot where a few men were standing on guard.

It was easy, without being seen, to survey the part of the countryside leading up to the base of Golden Mount.

A closely packed group of men was advancing along that base. The entire gang must have been there. Light glinted on the barrels of their rifles. But they had neither horses nor wagons. All their equipment had been left at the place where the Texans had been camping for the past two days.

Hunter, Malone, and the foreman were walking in front. They advanced cautiously, stopping occasionally and even going a few hundred paces out of their way to look at the top of Golden Mount.

"They'll be here in less than an hour," said Lorique.

"They obviously know about our camp," said Skim.

"And they're coming to attack it," added the scout.

"If I wait here until Hunter is within range," exclaimed Skim, "I could take a shot at him, and at a hundred paces I guarantee I'd bring him down like a duck."

"No," order Raddle, "let's go back."

All things considered, it was the wisest move, as the Texan's death would not have prevented the others from attacking.

Raddle, Skim, the scout, and Lorique returned to the trench, followed by their men. They crossed the dam in single file and the opening in the barricade was blocked with stones already collected for that purpose. There was now no passageway from one bank of the trench to the other.

They all then moved back about sixty paces, behind the first trees, where they would be protected if there were an exchange of gunfire, as seemed highly likely. With their weapons loaded, they waited.

The scout's advice was to let the gang approach as far as the trench and not make a move until they tried to cross it.

Half an hour later, Hunter, Malone, and their men rounded the corner of the mountain. Some crept along its base with short steps. Others went as far as the creek and followed down its left bank, weapons at the ready, revolvers thrust into the red belts around their waists.

Most of these men were miners whom Raddle, Skim, Lorique, and Neluto had seen working at Claim 127 on the Fortymile River. There were about thirty of them, plus about twenty Indians whom Hunter had hired at Circle City and Fort Yukon for this expedition to the Arctic Ocean.

When they reached the bank, Hunter and Malone stopped, and the whole gang gathered together.

The two Texans and the foreman now engaged in a conversation that must have been very animated to judge by the violence of their gestures. There can have been no doubt in their minds that there was an encampment set up behind those trees, and they were motioning in that direction with their hands. But what seemed to cause them genuine disappointment was the trench, an obstacle they would find very difficult to cross if gunfire broke out sixty paces away.

They had immediately recognized, moreover, when they saw the freshly moved earth and the footprints still visible on the ground, that this trench had been dug only recently. But why it had been dug, they could not have imagined. As for the entrance to the tunnel, it was completely screened by a jumble of branches. In any case, would they ever

303

have dreamed that the tunnel was designed to carry water from the creek into the bowels of Golden Mount?

But Hunter and Malone walked back and forth along the bank, wondering, no doubt, how they could cross the trench. It was absolutely necessary for them to move up as far as the thicket, either to make contact with its occupants or to make sure they had abandoned the place the day before, which they thought after all was a possibility.

They were joined at that point by the foreman, who showed them the barricaded dam, the only passage by which they could cross the trench dry-shod.

They all headed in that direction. When they saw there was no opening in the barricade, they must have said to themselves that the thicket was definitely occupied and that by breaking down the barricade they would reach the encampment.

Ben Raddle and his friends, hiding behind the trees, followed the gang's every move. They could tell that Hunter was about to open a path by moving the stones piled on the dam. The time had come to stop him.

"I don't know," whispered Summy, "what's to stop me from giving him a bullet in the head. I've got him right in my sights."

"No, don't shoot, Summy," said Raddle, lowering his rifle. "If their leader was killed, they wouldn't stop. Perhaps it's better to negotiate before we start firing. What do you think, Scout?"

"I think we can always try," replied Steel. "It can't make matters any worse. If we don't come to an agreement, then we'll see."

"In any case," remarked Lorique, "let's not show ourselves. We can't give Hunter a chance to count us."

"That's true," replied the engineer. "I'll go myself."

"And I'll go with you," added Summy Skim, who would never have consented to let his cousin go without him to meet the Texans.

At the very moment when a few of Hunter's men were moving up to break through the barricade, Raddle and Skim appeared at the edge of the thicket.

As soon as Hunter saw them, he motioned to his men to move back, and the whole gang took up defensive positions about ten paces from the trench.

Hunter and Malone approached alone, holding their guns.

Raddle and Skim each had a rifle, which they held with the stock to the ground.

The two Texans followed their example, and the first to speak, with an element of surprise in his voice, was Hunter.

"Ah!" he exclaimed. "It's you, the gentlemen from 129."

"Yes," replied Skim, "here we are."

"I didn't expect to find you at the mouth of the Mackenzie," continued the Texan.

"Any more than we expected to see you follow us," replied Skim.

"As a matter of fact, there's an old quarrel to settle between us."

"And it can be settled here just as well as at the claims on the Fortymile River."

Hunter's surprise was giving way to anger as he found himself standing face to face with Summy Skim. He raised his gun, and Skim did the same.

There was a stir among Hunter's men, but he motioned to them to be still. He wanted to know before starting a fight how many men Raddle had, but he tried in vain to see into the interior of the thicket. None of the men from the caravan showed themselves between the trees.

Deciding the time had come to intervene, Ben Raddle walked up to the bank of the trench. He and Hunter were about twelve paces apart. Malone had stayed farther back.

"What do you want?" asked Raddle in a loud voice.

"We want to know what you're doing here at Golden Mount."

"And what right have you to ask that?"

"It's not a question of right, it's a question of facts, and the fact is that you are here, over three hundred miles from Dawson City."[1]

"We came here because we wanted to," retorted Skim, who was beginning to lose his self-control.

"And what if we don't want to see you here?" continued Hunter, his voice revealing an anger that he could barely suppress.

"Whether you like it or not, we're here," replied Skim. "We didn't ask your permission to come, and we won't ask your permission to stay, either."

"I repeat," went on the Texan, "what was your purpose in coming to Golden Mount?"

"The same as yours," replied Raddle

"You intend to mine this gold deposit?"

"Which is Canadian, not American," replied the engineer, "because it's located on Canadian territory."

Obviously, the question of nationality would not stop the Texans. Motioning toward the volcano, Hunter replied, "Golden Mount doesn't belong either to the Canadians or to the Americans. It belongs to everyone."

"So be it," replied Raddle, "but at least it belongs to those who occupy it first."

"Occupying it first is not the point," declared Hunter, who was gradually losing his calm.

"What is the point, then?" asked the engineer.

"The point is to be in a position to defend it," retorted Hunter, with a threatening gesture.

"Against whom?"

"Against those who claim the sole right to mine it."

"And who might they be?"

"Us," exclaimed Hunter.

"Just try, then," was Raddle's reply.

Malone gave a signal, and several shots were fired. Neither Raddle nor Skim was hit, and they both darted back toward the thicket. Skim turned, hastily raised his rifle and fired a shot at Hunter.

The Texan jumped to one side to avoid the bullet, which struck one of his men in the chest, mortally wounding him.

Firing broke out on both sides, but the scout's men, protected by the trees, suffered much lighter losses than Hunter's, some of whom were killed, while the caravan's crew had only a few wounded.

Hunter now saw clearly that he was in danger of letting his gang be decimated if he did not manage to cross the trench, push back the scout's caravan, and drive it away, with the numerical superiority that he believed he enjoyed—as in fact he did.

Malone and two or three others rushed to the dam to force their way through the barricade. Crouching down behind the rocks and piles of stones, they tried to make an opening that they could get through.

The defenders now turned their full attention to that spot. If a passage were opened, if the gang got to the edge of the woods and invaded the encampment, resistance would eventually become impossible, and the greater number would have the upper hand.

Hunter, on the other hand, realized that he could not leave his men exposed to heavy fire and ordered them to lie down on the ground. The earth thrown up beside the trench formed a sort of breastwork, which protected them as long as they were lying down. From there, by opening little loopholes, they would be in a position to direct their fire at the thicket, although there was no one there at whom they could aim directly. The two or three of the scout's men who were wounded had been struck by stray bullets.

At this point Malone and two of his men, crawling along the ground, managed to reach the dam. Protected by the rocks in the barricade, they began gradually removing the stones, which fell into the trench.

A number of shots were fired from the thicket without touching them. Then Bill Steel, who wanted at all costs to prevent them from crossing the dam, decided to engage them in a hand-to-hand fight.

It would have been dangerous to expose himself over that open space of some sixty yards between the thicket and the trench. But Hunter and his men would run the same risk after they passed the barricade and rushed toward the encampment.

Raddle advised the scout to wait a bit before leaving the thicket. There was a possibility that Malone and the others, who were busily tearing down the barricade, might be put out of action, and that still others might suffer the same fate. It would not be surprising if Hunter gave up the fight at that point for fear of needlessly sacrificing his men down to the last one. But a steady fire had to be kept up against the dam, and the shots coming from the breastwork along the trench had to be answered.

This situation continued for about ten minutes. None of the men working at the barricade had been wounded, but after the opening had been enlarged, the bullets began to strike home.

One of the Indians was knocked down. After he was carried away, another took his place beside Malone.

Just then, Neluto got off a lucky shot. He had taken aim at Malone and hit him full in the chest.

The Texan fell, and a terrible cry rose from the whole gang.

"Well done," said Summy Skim to Neluto, who was standing near him. "That was a great shot. But leave Hunter to me. We've got some business to settle, and I'll take care of it."

But after Malone had been lifted up and carried back to safety, Hunter seemed to give up the idea of continuing the attack. There was absolutely no chance of success under those conditions, and every one of the attackers would be killed eventually. Not wanting to expose his men any further, he raised his voice above the noise of the shots being fired on both sides and gave the signal for retreat.

Carrying their wounded under the hail of bullets that marked their flight, his gang went back up the left bank of Rubber Creek, turned out onto the open country, and disappeared behind Golden Mount.

13

The Eruption

So ended hunter's first attack on the encampment. It cost him a number of casualties, including Malone, while two or three of the scout's men had been only slightly scratched by stray bullets.

Would this attempt be repeated, perhaps under more favorable conditions? Given Hunter's hateful and vindictive nature, driven by a fierce desire to keep control of Golden Mount, would he not try to seize the encampment if he found out the numbers were in his favor by nearly two to one?

"In any case," declared the scout, "the villains have retreated, and they won't be back today."

"No," replied Summy Skim, "but maybe tonight."

"Well then," said Ben Raddle, "we'll keep watch. Even during the two or three hours of darkness, Hunter would have just as much trouble crossing the trench as he had today. I'm almost sure he won't dare, because he knows very well we'll be on our guard."

"But it's important to rebuild the barricade on the dam," Lorique pointed out.

"That's what we're going to do," replied Bill Steel, calling a few of his men to help him with the work.

"But first," said Skim, "let's see whether the gang is going back to their camp over there."

"Let's see," agreed the scout.

Raddle, Skim, Lorique, Steel, and Neluto, rifles in hand, crossed the dam and walked as far as the southeast corner of the mountain. From there they could see along the base to the Texans' camp, taking in that whole part of the open country.

It was only six o'clock and still broad daylight.

When they reached the corner, Raddle saw that they would not have to go any farther.

Hunter and his cronies were no more than five or six rifle shots away. They were walking slowly despite their fear of being pursued. Even the scout had wondered whether it might be a good idea to go chasing after them in full force. On the other hand, it was better if the Texans did not know there were only about twenty men in the caravan. Besides, regardless of what Skim thought, it was possible that they might have abandoned the idea of making a new attack on the encampment.

The gang was walking slowly because they were carrying their wounded, most of whom, apparently, could not walk, and Malone was likely one of those.

For nearly an hour, the scout and his men stood watching the retreat. They saw Hunter swing around the far side of Golden Mount's base, and since he did not head across country in the direction of the forest, he must have gone back to his camp.

By eight o'clock the scout had finished rebuilding the barricade on the dam.

Two men took up their positions there, and everyone else went back to the thicket for the evening meal.

The conversation centered on the day's events. After the attack, Hunter's retreat could not be considered as the end of the matter. It would not be final unless the gang left Golden Mount. If the Texans persisted in staying on in the neighborhood, what other incidents might be expected? If the eruption occurred naturally, would there be an armed fight over the nuggets thrown out by the volcano?

On the other hand, as long as the Texans were there, should Raddle carry out his plan to induce an eruption by channeling water from the creek into the crater?

Then again, in a few weeks the cold season would begin, with its storms, blizzards, and snow. It was absolutely essential for the caravan to be back in Dawson City before then. Would the engineer decide to spend a second winter in the Klondike and put off work at Golden Mount until the following summer? And why might Hunter not come back too? Would it be necessary to recruit a troop of Canadians and Indians more numerous than his in order to drive him away?

Could Ben Raddle persuade his cousin to postpone returning to Montreal for another year?

That was something Summy Skim had probably never counted on and could not have foreseen. Whether the expedition succeeded or not, he certainly was expecting that he and Raddle would leave the Klondike within two months.

The evening was uneventful, but all measures of security were taken before anyone thought of enjoying a little rest. The scout, Lorique, and Neluto had volunteered to take turns guarding the dam, and their vigilance could be depended on.

The tents were set up—their being visible no longer created a problem—and everyone slept more or less peacefully, depending on their temperament. But the one who was kept awake longest by insomnia was Ben Raddle because of the plans and worries with which he was obsessed.

Very early the next morning, the scout and Raddle crossed the trench and went to look out over the open country. It was deserted. There was no squad of men marching toward the forest. Hunter had not decided to leave for good, and after all, no one expected him to.

"It's too bad we can't climb Golden Mount by the face nearest the camp," said Steel. "By walking over to the other side of the plateau, we'd have seen them."

"It's impossible, Bill, unfortunately," replied Raddle.

"There's no danger, I guess," continued the scout, "in going out a few hundred yards away from the mountain."

"None at all, Bill. There's no one in sight, and even if we were seen, we'd have time to get back to the trench and close the barricade."

"Come on, then, Mr. Ben, and we'll see the smoke from the volcano. Maybe it's thicker. Maybe the crater is starting to throw out some lava."

They went out about five hundred yards and stopped.

There was no change in the crater. Smoke was rapidly swirling out of it, mixed with flames which the south wind blew toward the sea.

"It's not going to erupt today," remarked the scout.

"No," replied the engineer, "and right now I'm hoping the eruption won't happen until after Hunter has left—if he does leave."

Just then, Steel noticed smoke rising from the base of the farthest foothill of Golden Mount.

"Yes," he said, "they're still there, making themselves at home! And since we're not trying to drive them away, they'll say to themselves—correctly—that there aren't very many of us."

It was sound reasoning, but not reassuring to Ben Raddle.

After surveying the open country one more time, they went back to the trench and into the encampment.

It was now August 15, and Raddle felt pangs of anguish as he watched the days go by with no result. By the end of the month, as the scout pointed out, it would already be almost too late to start back to the Klondike, which the caravan would not reach before September 15. By that date, the miners who spend the winter in Vancouver have already left Dawson City, and the last river boats are steaming down the Yukon, which would soon be blocked by the freeze-up. No matter what happened, their departure could not be postponed more than two weeks. In fact, if winter came only a little early, Bill Steel would have great difficulty crossing the lake region and going down through the Chilkoot Pass to Skagway.

Summy Skim often discussed this point with him, and that was exactly what they were talking about after lunch while Ben Raddle was strolling along beside the trench.

After examining the spot where the creek had been diverted, Raddle went and stood on the dam. Picking up the branches that concealed the opening, he entered the tunnel and moved along to the wall separating it from the chimney.

He wanted to satisfy himself that everything was in order. He checked the position of the six holes drilled into the wall, where the explosive charges would be set, enough to break through it when they were detonated. Then, when the dam was demolished with a few blows of the pick, the stream would go rushing into the bowels of the mountain.

As a matter of fact, if the Texans had not been there, who knows whether Raddle might not have induced the eruption that very day? Why would he have waited any longer since time was of the essence and the eruption seemed unlikely to occur naturally?

Yes, the engineer would only have to light the fuses, which would set off the charges in a few minutes, and then break open the dam. After half a day, or two hours, or perhaps only an hour, the pressure of the steam accumulated within it would activate the volcano.

In front of the wall, Raddle was deep in thought, cursing his inability to carry out the last step then and there and bring his daring scheme to its conclusion. Since the Texans would have been the first and no doubt the only ones to benefit from it, he had to wait, and keep waiting. What if the gang did not go away? What if Hunter stayed until the place was no longer habitable? What if he delayed his departure as long as possible? What if his plan was to spend the winter in Circle City or Dawson City instead of going to Vancouver and to mount an expedition again as soon the weather permitted? Where would Ben Raddle be then? He would be thousands of miles away in his own country, having seen all his efforts fail lamentably, both at the Fortymile River and at Golden Mount.

Such were the thoughts that occupied the mind of the engineer, who was more concerned with the present than with the past or the future. Yes! Had he been free to act, he would not have hesitated. That very day, he would have "played his last trump" (if one may use that very French expression). And if his plan had succeeded, if the volcano had yielded up the riches accumulated deep within it, it would only have taken twenty-four hours to load the wagons with the precious nuggets, and the caravan would have been on its way to the Klondike.

As he was thinking about this, Ben Raddle could hear noises coming from the volcano's central chimney. The rumblings seemed to be louder. He even thought he could hear something like stones and large rocks moving around as they were lifted by the steam and fell back again. Were these noises the signs of an imminent eruption?

Just then, there was the sound of shouting outdoors. Raddle thought someone was calling him. Then the scout's voice came through the opening of the tunnel.

"Mr. Raddle, Mr. Raddle!"

"What is it?" asked the engineer.

"Come here, come here!"

Raddle must have thought the gang had launched a new attack against the encampment. He crawled back through the tunnel and onto the dam.

There he found Summy Skim, who had come to join Steel.

"Are the Texans back?" he asked, turning to his cousin.

"Yes, the villains!" replied Skim. "But not in front or from behind— from up there!"

He motioned with his hand toward the plateau on Golden Mount.

"Look, Mr. Ben," added the scout.

Having failed on the previous day to force their way across the trench, Hunter and his men had given up the idea of a direct attack in favor of another, which might result, at the very least, in forcing the caravan to abandon its encampment.

They had climbed the volcano again, walked around the crater, and reached the crest of the plateau, out of reach of the belching clouds of smoke. Using picks and levers, they had attacked the ridge, which was composed of irregular blocks of rock, lava, and boulders piled up by the hundreds. Pushed to the edge, those pieces were beginning to fall like an avalanche, breaking and overturning trees, and making huge holes in the ground. A few stones even rolled as far as the trench, causing the water to splash over its banks.

"You see," shouted Summy Skim, "you see. They couldn't drive us out and now they're trying to crush us."

Raddle did not answer. He and his friends had to crowd against the face of the mountain to avoid being pelted by the hail of falling rocks. The thicket was no longer safe, and hundreds of blocks of stone were falling on the encampment.

The men had to abandon it and seek refuge on the left bank of the creek, beyond the reach of the avalanche. But two of the wagons had been smashed. Three men, who had been hit by falling rocks earlier and quite seriously injured, had to be moved to the rear.

As for the equipment, there was nothing left but wreckage. The tents had been knocked down and torn, the utensils destroyed. It was a disaster. At the same time, two of the mules were lying on the ground and the others, driven mad by fear, had leaped across the trench and were scattering over the open country.

From above came the sound of fierce shouts and horrible yells from the gang, as they rejoiced in this abominable devastation. And the rocks continued to fall, sometimes hitting one another as they fell and scattering fragments over the area between the creek and Golden Mount.

"They're going to throw the whole mountain down on top of us!" cried Skim

"What can we do?" said Lorique.

"I don't know what we can do now," replied Skim, "but I certainly know what we should have done. We should have put a bullet in Hunter's chest before parlaying with him."

There is no doubt that if they had disposed of the Texan the day before, the situation would not have been as dangerous as it was now, for the idea of crushing the encampment must have come from him.

"Soon we'll have no equipment left," said the scout, "if we don't save at least what we still have. Let's drag our wagons to the bank of the creek, where they'll be out of range."

"And then what?" asked Lorique.

"Then?" replied Steel. "Then we'll take our rifles and we'll go to the camp of those bandits while they're still up there. We'll wait for them there and fire at them at close range as they're coming back down. Their wagons will replace the ones we've lost."

It was a daring plan, but it might succeed. Hunter and his men would certainly be in a very bad way, exposed to the fire of some twenty rifles as they rappelled down the slope of Golden Mount. Since they were still busy prying rocks loose from the ridge, they would not leave the place until they had no stones left.

This would give the scout and his men time to move along to the other end of the base without being seen. If they found a few men from the gang there, they could easily overpower them and then wait for Hunter and the others and kill them as they made their way down the mountain like chamois.

"That's it!" exclaimed Skim. "Let's call our men. Most of them have their weapons, and we've got ours. Let's cross over the dam. We'll be there in half an hour and it'll take those rogues at least two hours to get down."

Although Ben Raddle had not been asked directly, it was up to him to respond, to say whether he approved the plan. It was really the only one that could be carried out, the only one that offered any hope of success.

But Raddle held his peace, as if he had heard nothing of what had just been said. What could he have been thinking about?

The engineer had indeed heard his friends, and just as they were signaling their men to join them, he spoke up.

"No," he said. "No."

"What do you want to do, then, Ben?" asked Skim.

"I want to answer Hunter's gang the way it deserves."

"And how is that?"

"By setting off the eruption. Perhaps it will destroy the lot of them."

That is certainly what it would do if it happened suddenly and caught them by surprise at the edge of the crater.

Raddle moved toward the opening of the tunnel.

"What are you going to do, Mr. Ben?" asked the scout.

"Blow up the wall and send the creek pouring into the volcano's chimney."

The explosive charges were ready. There was nothing left to do but light the fuses.

Just as the engineer was about to enter the tunnel, Lorique, who wanted to take his place, spoke up.

"Let me go," he said.

"No," replied Raddle, and he disappeared through the opening screened by branches. He crawled along until he came to the wall at the end, lit the fuses of the charges that had been set in the holes, and hurried back.

A few minutes later the charges exploded with a dull sound. The mountain seemed to shudder on its base.

There was no doubt that the explosion had broken through the wall. Almost immediately a boiling sound was heard in the tunnel, through which the lava was probably beginning to flow, and thick clouds of black smoke burst out through the opening.

"Let's get to work!" shouted Raddle.

Now they had to break open the dam, to connect the creek with the chimney.

Everyone set to work, smashing the dam with their picks and tossing shovelfuls of earth onto the banks. It took no more than a quarter of an hour to finish the job, for the water finished it when it was only half done.

The slope of the trench and the tunnel sent a torrent of water fed by the inexhaustible Rubber Creek under the flank of Golden Mount. Would this torrent overcome the force of the smoke and lava coming through the tunnel? That was the one remaining question, and it would soon be answered.

The engineer and his friends waited anxiously, keeping out of range of the boulders that were still falling from the plateau above.

Half an hour went by, then an hour. The water was still flowing in full force and disappearing through the entrance to the tunnel. Pushing back the smoke, it rushed tumultuously into the side of the mountain.

All of a sudden, there was a terrible explosion. Flames and smoke burst from the volcano and rose five or six hundred feet into the air, accompanied by hundreds of stones, bits of hardened lava, slag, and

ashes, all swirling about with a tremendous noise. At the top, a wide section of the plateau had obviously collapsed. Perhaps, under the pressure
of the volcanic matter, the plateau had been ripped apart along its entire
width. Perhaps the crater had been enlarged to make way for the igneous
mass spewed forth by the action of the central fire.

But then the whole eruption tilted toward the north. The accumulation of rocks, lava, and ashes was thrown in that direction and fell into
the sea!

Yes, Golden Mount emptied its entire contents into the Arctic Ocean.

Summy Skim uttered an involuntary cry.

"Ah!" he said, "our nuggets!"

And if Raddle, Lorique, and Bill Steel himself did not cry out with him,
that was because they were stunned into silence. They were not thinking
of the Texans at that moment, but of all the wealth of the richest gold deposit in North America vanishing into the depths of the icy sea.

When all was said and done, Ben Raddle had been right. By introduc-
ing water into the volcano's chimney, he had caused it to erupt in one
hour. The earth shook as if it were threatening to open up. The air was
shaken by roaring flames and hissing steam. A thick cloud hung over the
plateau at the top of the cone to a height of several hundred feet. A few
of the blocks that were hurled to that height burst like bombs, releasing
a shower of gold dust.

"Our nuggets are exploding!" Skim kept repeating.

In despair, they all watched the terrifying spectacle. The engineer had
been able to hasten the eruption, but he could not control its direction,
and his expedition was ending in disaster.

True, the caravan had nothing to fear now from the Texans. Right
from the outset, Hunter and his cronies must have been caught off guard
by the suddenness of the phenomenon and had no time to get out of the
way. Perhaps the plateau had collapsed under their feet. Perhaps they
had been swallowed up in the crater. Perhaps they had been flung into
space, burned and mutilated, and were now lying in the depths of the
Arctic Ocean.

"Come on," cried the scout. "Come on!"

Since they had taken the precaution of staying on the other side of the trench, it was easy for them to reach the open country and follow along the base of Golden Mount. Running as fast as they could, they headed for the Texans' encampment. It took them no more than twenty minutes to get there.

There they stopped. About a dozen of Hunter's men who had stayed at the encampment were already running toward the forest. Their horses, terrified by the noise of the eruption, were scattering over the countryside.

When the scout and his friends came to a halt, the encampment was deserted. But five or six members of the gang, who had managed to escape from the plateau, were sliding down the slopes of Golden Mount at the risk of breaking arms and legs.

Among them was Hunter, gravely wounded no doubt, barely dragging himself along about a hundred yards from the bottom of the slope. He was catching hold of clumps of shrubs, falling, getting up again, well behind the others who took to their heels when they got to the bottom.

At that moment a gunshot rang out. It was Neluto, who had fired before anyone could stop him.

Hunter, hit in the chest, leaped into the air, rolled from rock to rock, and landed in a heap at the foot of Golden Mount.

14

From Dawson City to Montreal

So this was the unexpected way the expedition was to end! What a finale it was, not the one Ben Raddle and his friends had some reason to expect, which would have made them the possessors of the volcano's incalculable treasures. The Texans' actions had certainly thwarted Raddle's plans. To protect the personnel of the caravan, the engineer had been forced to bring matters to a head by setting off the eruption. But after all, even if he had done it at a time of his own choosing, the gold in the crater would still have been lost to him, since the volcano's contents were hurled out toward the Arctic Ocean.

"All the trouble started," said the scout, "because the volcano was already active when we got to the Mackenzie estuary."

"That's right," replied Summy Skim. "Jacques Laurier thought it was extinct, but it was only asleep, and it woke up a few weeks too soon."

That was true. Bad luck had robbed Ben Raddle of all the profit from his expedition. No matter what anyone might say to him, he would never be consoled for that loss.

"Poor old Ben," said Skim. "You need a little philosophy and a little wisdom. There's nothing for us to do now but go back to the land we love so much. We've been away from it for eighteen months."

Instead of answering, Raddle started back to the encampment. However, since Hunter's camp was abandoned, and the survivors of the gang had disappeared, Bill Steel thought it would be appropriate to take two of their wagons to replace the ones that had been crushed by the rocks. His men also succeeded in bringing back two or three of the horses that had run away across the open country. They were hitched to the wagons and everyone returned to Rubber Creek.

The departure date was set for the following day. As the scout kept repeating, they could not afford to wait if Raddle and Skim wanted to reach Dawson City in time to be on their way to Vancouver before snow squalls made the route impassable and before the first frosts blocked navigation on the rivers and lakes.

The encampment was put back in order, after a fashion, for the last night.

As for the diversion of the creek, it kept on flowing. For all anyone knows, all the water in the huge estuary might continue to pour into it for weeks and months.

"Who knows?" said the scout to Summy Skim. "Perhaps the flood will finally extinguish the volcano."

"That's quite possible, Bill, but let's not say anything about it to Ben. He might want to wait. And besides, there'd be nothing more to get out of the crater. The claim on Golden Mount is as worthless now as Claim 129 on the Fortymile River. One was flooded out and the other was emptied into the sea."

Their last night was a quiet one. It was not even necessary to keep watch on the surrounding area. But during the few hours of darkness, what a beautiful sight the eruption was in all its power! Flames were rising as high as the clouds, showers of fireworks were set off with extraordinary force, and wreaths of golden ashes swelled out above Golden Mount.

At five o'clock the next morning, the scout's caravan made its final preparations. Before the signal for departure was given, Raddle and Lorique explored around the base of the volcano for half a mile. Had the eruption thrown out any blocks of gold-bearing quartz or any nuggets? That was what they wanted to know as they were leaving, probably forever, those northern regions of the Dominion.

No, there was nothing. The eruption had not changed direction, and its entire contents—stones, slag, lava, ashes—were still being thrown northward and falling into the sea, sometimes nearly a mile from shore. Out in the open country there was nothing. The violence of the phenomenon was extremely intense, and it would have been impossible to climb up to the crater. If Ben Raddle had any thought of making one last ascent of Golden Mount, he had to abandon it. And what would have been the use, anyway?

The caravan got into formation, headed by the engineer and Summy Skim in the carriage, with Neluto driving. The wagons and their teams followed under the scout's direction, carrying only the camping equipment. Since this was not a heavy load, the Canadians and Indians who made up the personnel were able to ride also,[1] making for rapid progress. As they had done on the way up, they would only stop for two hours at noon and eight hours at night.

There was food enough for two weeks since hunting and fishing had enabled them to save their canned goods during their several weeks at Golden Mount. And as they went along, the hunters would find plenty of partridges, ducks, and larger game. If Summy Skim could finally bag one of those famous moose, might one venture to say that he would not regret the long journey and the long absence?

The weather was uncertain, and summer was almost over. There was reason to hope, however, that they would reach the capital of the Klondike before the September equinox. The temperature was dropping since the sun's daily trajectory across the sky was becoming lower every day. They would have to endure cold nights during their stops, often without shelter, as they crossed this treeless country drained by the Mackenzie and its tributaries.

When the caravan stopped for the men to have lunch and turn the animals out to pasture, Golden Mount was still visible on the horizon. Ben Raddle turned around, unable to take his eyes away from the priceless eddies swirling above its summit.

"Come on, Ben," said Skim. "Everything is going up in smoke, like so much else in this world, so let's concentrate on one thing, that we're still more than seven thousand miles away from our home on Jacques Cartier Street in Montreal."[2]

And so the caravan moved on as quickly as possible along the left bank of the Peel River toward Fort McPherson, the Hudson's Bay Company outpost on the river's right bank. Inclement weather was already bringing showers and snow squalls, which made traveling very arduous. And so, when the caravan reached the fort on the afternoon of August 22, they had to stop over for twenty-four hours.

The scout's men did not conceal their regret at the disappointment they had suffered. They, too, had been counting on the riches of the Golden Volcano, riches they would have shared, and now they were going home empty-handed.

They started out again on the morning of August 24. The weather had taken a turn for the worse, with gusts of snow that Bill Steel found very worrying.

After leaving Fort McPherson, the caravan turned away from the course of the Peel River, which veered off to the southeast, through the region bounded by the enormous chain of the Rocky Mountains. They now headed southwest, taking the shortest route from Fort McPherson to Dawson City. They crossed the Arctic Circle at about the same point as they had on the way up, leaving the source of the Porcupine River on their right.

Their journey was now very exhausting, heading into a strong wind from the south. The teams moved ahead with difficulty. Skim and Neluto, furthermore, were having no luck hunting, for the game was already moving back to more southerly regions. They had to make do with ducks, and those would soon be gone, too.

Fortunately, everyone was generally in good health. The sturdy Indians and Canadians, accustomed to such exertions, remained tough and able-bodied.

Finally, on September 3, they came within sight of the hills rising to the east of the Klondike's capital, and that afternoon the caravan stopped in front of the Northern Hotel on Front Street.

Not surprisingly, news of the scout's arrival with his caravan spread immediately throughout the whole town. What had taken the engineer to the shores of the Arctic Ocean would soon be common knowledge.

The first person to come hurrying to the hotel was Dr. Pilcox, still eager to help, still cheerful, showering the two cousins with his friendliest greetings.

"Are you well?" was his first question.

"Very well," replied Summy Skim.

"Not too tired?"

"No . . . not too tired, doctor."

"And you're satisfied?"

"Yes," replied Skim. "We're glad to be back."

Dr. Pilcox was now brought up to date. He heard about all the trials and tribulations of the fruitless expedition and the various incidents that had occurred—the meeting with the gang of Texans, the attacks on the encampment, how and under what conditions the engineer had set off the eruption, Raddle and his friends' escape from the criminals, and the futility of all their efforts since the nuggets of Golden Mount were now lying in the depths of the Arctic Ocean.

"You see," exclaimed the doctor, "you see, that volcano couldn't even vomit in the right direction. There was really no point in administering an emetic!"

By "emetic," the doctor meant the diversion of Rubber Creek, which had sent torrents of water into the stomach of Golden Mount.

The only consolation he could offer Raddle was to repeat what Skim had already told him, with a slight variation.

"Be philosophical about it. Philosophy is the most hygienic thing in the world. If people were really philosophical . . ."

But what would be the consequences of that medical "if," Dr. Pilcox never said.

That same day, the two cousins went with him to the hospital. Sisters Martha and Madeleine were delighted to see their former traveling companions again. When Summy Skim met the two nuns, he found them just as he had left them, completely devoted to their mission.

"With helpers like them," the doctor told him, "our work carries on all by itself, and we'd be in a position to deal with the 315 kinds of illness that afflict the human race."

During the evening he spent with his compatriots, the question of their departure came up.

"Well," declared the doctor, "you have no time to lose, unless it suits your fancy to undertake another winter in this adorable Klondike."

"Adorable, if you will," replied Summy Skim, "but I prefer to save my adoration for Montreal."

"As you wish, Mr. Skim, but what a town this young Dawson City is, and what prosperity the future has in store for it!"

In the course of the conversation, Ben Raddle made reference to Claim 129 on the Fortymile River.

"Well, Mr. Ben," said the doctor, "it's still submerged under the water of the new stream, and may God grant that the stream may never dry up."

"Why so?" asked Skim.

"Because it now bears my name," replied the doctor, "Pilcox Creek, and I take a certain pride in being included in the geographical nomenclature of this beautiful land of the Klondike."

No, there was no danger of such a misfortune occurring, and both claims, 129 and 127, were submerged forever under the waters of Pilcox Creek.

Since Raddle and Skim had made up their minds to leave, it was important for them to be on their way without delay. Winter promised to come early just as summer had that year, and the miners who were going to live in Skagway or Vancouver until the following spring had left Dawson City two weeks earlier.

On the whole, it had been a good season. Fortunes had been made on both mountain claims and river claims in the territory drained by the tributaries of the Yukon, especially the tributaries of Bonanza and Eldorado creeks. The predictions of the surveyor Ogilvie continued to come true, and the mines of the Klondike would produce as many billions as the deposits of Africa, America, and Oceania had produced in millions.

The day after their arrival, Raddle and Skim had a discussion with the scout about their departure. They were counting on having the services of that trusty and intelligent Canadian to take them to Skagway. Steel gave the matter serious consideration.

"Gentlemen," he said, "I'd have been glad to continue acting as your guide, but I can't close my eyes to the fact that it's now too late to undertake a journey across the plains of the Pelly. In two weeks, the rivers and lakes will be frozen, navigation will be impossible, and we'd be forced to come back to Dawson City."

Perhaps this prospect would not have frightened Ben Raddle, but he did not express such an opinion, which would have made Summy Skim jump like a chamois.

"Besides," continued Steel, "the weather is getting colder all the time, and even if we were able to cross the lakes, we'd certainly find the Chilkoot Pass closed, and you wouldn't be able to get to Skagway.

"What can we do, then?" asked Skim, too impatient to sit still.

"What you have to do," replied the scout, "is go to St. Michael at the mouth of the Yukon. You'll find steamboats there that make the trip to Vancouver."

"But how can we go down the Yukon?" inquired Raddle.

"The last boat will leave Dawson City in two days, and it'll certainly reach St. Michael before ice jams put a stop to navigation all along the river."

That was wise advice, coming from such a practical man as the scout, and it had to be followed without hesitation.

"But what about you?" asked Skim.

"What I'll do," said Steel, "is spend the winter in Dawson City as I've often done before and wait until it's possible to go back to Bennett Lake."

When this plan was reported to Dr. Pilcox, he gave it his approval, especially since he also believed that some very cold weather was imminent, and his experience could be relied on. Besides, he was not a man to be terrified by temperatures of fifty or sixty below zero. Even a hundred below would not frighten him.

It was decided that they would leave within twenty-four hours. Their preparations would be neither long nor difficult.

Raddle suggested to Lorique that he go with them.

"Thanks, Mr. Ben," replied the foreman, "but I'd rather stay in Dawson City. Next season I'll find a spot on a claim somewhere, and there'll be plenty of work for me. And then, you're still the owner of 129, and no matter what anyone may say, Pilcox Creek may give you back your property some day."

"And on that day, Lorique," replied Raddle in a voice that his cousin could not hear, "a telegram . . ."

"Yes, a telegram addressed to Engineer Ben Raddle, Jacques Cartier Street, Montreal, Canada," replied Lorique.

The engineer and the foreman were definitely of one mind.

But while Lorique did not accept Raddle's offer, Neluto's reaction was different when Summy Skim, who appreciated the honest Indian's loyalty, said, "Neluto, are you planning to stay in this country, with the wind and the snow fighting over it eight months of the year?"

"Where else would I go, Mr. Skim?"

"Why don't you come to Montreal with me?"

"If that's all right with you, Mr. Skim."

"I'll put you up in Green Valley, and when spring comes we'll go hunting together. Since the moose will soon be leaving this abominable Klondike, which is only fit for people like Hunter and Malone, we'll bag a few of them sooner or later."

"Mr. Skim, I'm ready to leave," said Neluto, his eyes shining with pleasure.

There was nothing left to do but settle up with the scout for the expenses of the expedition to Golden Mount, and it was a generous settlement. This made a substantial hole in the cousins' finances. What a disappointment it was for the engineer to think that all those expenses should have been paid, first, with the profits from 129, or then with the profits from the Golden Volcano.

On the morning of September 7,[3] the moment came for the final fare-wells. Sisters Martha and Madeleine and Dr. Pilcox accompanied Raddle and Skim to the Yukon boat on which they had reserved two passages for themselves and one for Neluto. Lorique was waiting for them there.

The nuns had tears in their eyes and Summy Skim felt a pang of an-guish at the thought of those two saintly women whom he would prob-ably never see again.

The doctor could not hide his emotion when he shook hands with his compatriots, and Raddle's last words, whispered in Lorique's ear, were, "Don't forget. A telegram."

The boat cast off and soon disappeared around a bend in the river.

The distance from Dawson City to St. Michael via the Yukon River is about 1500 miles. The Yukon boat, two hundred feet long and sixty in the beam and propelled by a powerful stern wheel, moved rapidly down-stream among the ice floes that were beginning to form. Fifteen miles from Dawson City it passed between the Pic du Vieux to port and the Pointe de la Vieille to starboard. After a few hours' stop at Fort Cudahy, it crossed the frontier ninety miles from the capital of the Klondike and arrived at Circle City, the village of some fifty huts from which Hunter had started out for Golden Mount. Then its journey took them through a picturesque region among hundreds of islands covered with spruce, birch, and poplar, where the sound of its steam whistle made the river banks ring. It stopped for half a day at Fort Yukon, the former capital of the Klondike,[4] three hundred miles downstream from Dawson City, in a region that was probably very rich in gold deposits.

From there, where the Porcupine flows into the great river at its most northerly point, the Yukon curves toward the southwest and empties into Norton Bay.

Raddle and Skim were constantly fascinated by the incidents of this river voyage, with stops at Fort Hamlin, an ordinary supply depot, and Rampart City, at the mouth of Munook Creek, which had a population at that time of about a thousand miners. No exploration had been carried out beyond that point. What avaricious longings were inspired in the hundreds of passengers on board the Yukon boat, most of whom were going home empty-handed after a fruitless summer's work!

The weather was changeable, with rain and even some snow. There was a chill in the air, and farther downstream there were more ice floes than had been expected. Ice jams were beginning to form, considerably slowing the progress of the boat, which incidentally stopped every night. As a result, the journey took twice as long as usual, twelve days instead of six or seven. There were stops at the Tanana Mountains, at Novikakat, Nulato (opposite Volassatuk), Kaltag, Fort Get There, and Anvik, where a mission had been established that attracts many Indians. These are all simple tribal encampments, rather than villages. At Starivilipak the boat reached the most southerly point of the river, which then turns to the northwest and empties into the Bering Sea at Kullik.

From there, the journey of eighty miles to St. Michael took only half a day, since the boat's progress was no longer hampered by ice.

Mr. Arnis Semiré says that at that port, where the Yukon navigation companies are located, it is always raining, with annual precipitation of more than six feet. Naturally, then, when Ben Raddle, Summy Skim, and Neluto disembarked on September 29, after a fourteen-day journey, they were greeted by a downpour.

Fortunately, they were able to book passage for the next day aboard the *Kadiak*,[5] bound for Vancouver. They were still 2,875 miles away from that city, from which the railway would take them directly to Montreal. But the *Kadiak* encountered violent storms, especially off the long Alaskan peninsula, and had to take shelter for forty-eight hours in the lee of the Pribilof Islands.

All in all, the return journey was not as long, and especially not as tiring, as it would have been across the lake region to the Chilkoot Pass. The scout had given Raddle and Skim wise advice when he urged them to go down the Yukon.

In short, it was October 17 when the *Kadiak* sailed into the port of Vancouver.

Four days later, Ben Raddle and Summy Skim, followed by Neluto, walked into their house on Jacques Cartier Street in Montreal after an absence of eighteen months.

What keen regrets and unfulfilled desires filled the engineer's soul! His personality was affected, and he seemed ready at any moment to burst out in recriminations against his bad luck.

Then Summy Skim would say cheerfully, "Yes, poor Ben! He's always ready to erupt. After all, when you've had a volcano in your life, part of it always stays with you."

Notes

Notes by the editor of the French edition, Olivier Dumas, are indicated by "Ed." Notes by the translator, Edward Baxter, are indicated by "Trans."

Preface to the French Edition

1. "Obviously," Jules Verne conceded to the elder Hetzel in 1883, "I will always stay with *geographical and scientific* themes as closely as possible, since that is the object of the entire work, but . . . my intention for the novels that are still left for me to do is to spice them up as much as possible by using every means provided by my imagination in the rather restricted milieu in which I am condemned to operate." (*Bulletin de la Société Jules Verne* 70, [2nd quarter 1984]: 59.)—Ed.

2. Jules Hetzel was the son of Verne's publisher Pierre-Jules Hetzel and took over the publishing business after his father's death.—Trans.

3. *En Magellanie*, ([Paris]: Société Jules Verne, 1987) out of print; *La Chasse au météore*, original version, Société Jules Verne, 1986, out of print; reprinted Grama. coll. "Le Passé du futur", 1994, (distributed by Vilo).—Ed.

4. Bibliothèque nationale, fo 345, October 24, 1899.—Ed.

5. Part 1, chapter 14.—Ed.

6. *Seconde Patrie*, [Paris: Hetzel, 1900], chapter 11.—Ed.

7. *En Magellanie*, chapter 15; *Seconde Patrie*, chapter 32.—Ed.

8. Part 2, chapter 1.—Ed.

9. "The cursed thirst for gold" (Virgil, quoted by Verne, part 1, Chapter 5).—Ed.

10. *Le Volcan d'or*, Michel Verne's version, [Paris: Hetzel, 1900], part 2, chapter 6.—Ed.

11. Part 2, end of chapter 6.—Ed.

12. Another ridiculous example: a block of gold thrown out by the volcano—in the opposite direction!—lands precisely on the head of the "villain," neatly eliminating him and making it possible to recoup the expenses of the expedition.—Ed.

13. *Sans dessus dessous*, [Paris: Hetzel, 1889], chapter 13.—Ed.

14. *Cinq semaines en ballon*, [Paris: Hetzel, 1863], chapter 22.—Ed.

1.1. An Uncle's Legacy

1. Michel Verne changed nearly all the chapter titles. Here he replaced it with "An Uncle in America," which is ridiculous, since everyone lives in America.—Ed.

2. Verne calls this stream "Forty Miles Creek, but every reference I have consulted uses the name "Fortymile River."—Trans.

3. Since the Klondike was never recognized as a political entity, it did not have a capital as such. Dawson City was the capital of the Yukon at the time.—Trans.

4. Verne used the spelling "Hunter."—Trans.

5. Verne uses the term "emigrants," which, from his point of view, they were. But once in the Klondike, they were "immigrants" and have been so described throughout.—Trans.

6. Montreal had not been the capital of Canada since 1849, when the parliament buildings were burned by an angry crowd. Toronto and Quebec City served alternate three-year terms as the capital of the province of Canada until 1858, when Queen Victoria was asked to choose a capital and picked Ottawa. In 1867 Ottawa became the federal capital of the new Dominion of Canada.—Trans.

7. The official title "Dominion of Canada" was adopted at the time of Confederation in 1867.—Trans.

8. J.V. wrote Ben Braddle.—Ed.

9. According to the Random House dictionary, Jonathan is an archaic term for an American, especially a New Englander.—Trans.

1.2. The Two Cousins

1. Cariboo is the name of a district in British Columbia.—Trans.

2. This distance, left blank in the original, has been supplied by reference to a map.—Trans.

3. Verne later corrects this to read one hundred and forty-first.—Trans.

4. There actually was a company in the Klondike known as the North American Trading and Transportation Company. It was founded by a man named Healy. Verne refers to it in this chapter as the Anglo-American Trading and Transportation Company.—Trans.

1.3. From Montreal to Vancouver

1. Although the Peace River rises in British Columbia, it flows eastward into Alberta and from there northward through the Northwest Territories.—Trans.

2. J.V. adds another variant here, writing "Ben Craddle."—Ed.

3. Referred to here as "Ben Naddle."—Ed.

4. The reference to "Ottawa, the country's capital," conflicts with the statement in chapter 1 that Montreal was the capital. (See part 1, chapter 1, note 6)—Trans.

5. Verne referred to this town as "Carlton Junction." (Toronto would certainly not be visible from there.)—Trans.

6. Verne used the spelling "Ebrehorn" for Elkhorn. Since the buffalo had largely disappeared from the Canadian west by about 1880, it is unlikely that our travelers would have seen thousands of them.—Trans.

1.4. Vancouver

1. New Westminster is not on Vancouver Island but on the mainland of British Columbia very close to Vancouver.—Trans.

2. Vancouver harbor actually opens onto Georgia Strait (not Georges), which runs north and south between Vancouver Island and the mainland of British Columbia. Juan de Fuca Strait runs east and west between Vancouver Island and the State of Washington and connects with Georgia Strait south of Vancouver.—Trans.

3. I have found no evidence that Vancouver Island was ever named "Quadra," but Quadra Island, which lies between Vancouver Island and the mainland of British Columbia, takes its name from the Spanish naval officer Bodega y Quadra, who commanded a Spanish naval base on Vancouver Island in 1792. Verne appears to have combined the two islands into one.—Trans.

4. St. Michael is actually about one hundred miles from the mouth of the Yukon.—Trans.

5. Verne wrote "*Foot-Ball*."—Trans.

6. Verne used the spelling "Chilcoot."—Trans.

7. Although the metric system had been legal in Canada since 1871, it was not generally used. It was not until the 1970s that Canada adopted the metric system, first for temperature and later for weights and measures.—Trans.

8. Verne wrote "Westminster Hotel," forgetting that they were staying in the Vancouver Hotel.—Trans.

9. As the *Football* moved from Queen Charlotte Strait into Johnston Strait, it would have been much too far from Vancouver for any signal to be heard.—Trans.

1.5. On Board the *Football*

1. We were told in the last chapter that the *Football* did not carry cargo.—Trans.

2. Christiania is the present-day Oslo.—Trans.

3. Virgil, "The cursed thirst for gold."—Ed.

4. The distances in this paragraph are omitted in the original and have been supplied by reference to a map.—Trans.

5. Here and in the next paragraph, Verne wrote "Princess Charlotte Island."—Trans.

6. Since Alaska became the forty-ninth state in 1959, Verne's count is not quite accurate here.—Trans.

7. The Canada-Alaska boundary was settled in 1903 (after Verne had written *Le Volcan d'or*), not by a treaty but by an international tribunal. Skagway and Wrangell, which Verne refers to as being located in Canada, were included in the part awarded to the United States. (The Canadian members of the tribunal, resenting the fact that the British member had voted with the United States, refused to sign the agreement.)—Trans.

1.6. Skagway

1. In previous chapters Verne has referred to "Canadian Pacific" steamships, which would be more accurate. It is interesting that Verne specifically refers to "railways canadiens" and "railroads des États-Unis." Could he have been aware of this minor difference between Canadian and American usage?—Trans.

2. The word *easy* was omitted from the original.—Ed.

3. Skagway is located in the area that was in dispute between Canada and the United States at that time.—Trans.

4. For much of the book, Verne uses the spelling "Stell."—Trans.

5. Earlier in this chapter, we were told that Bill Steel was in Skagway "at that very time."—Trans.

1.7. The Chilkoot Pass

1. Verne used the spelling "Lindeman."—Trans.

2. The word *shelters* was omitted from the original.—Trans.

3. These elevations are missing from the original and have been supplied by reference to *The Canadian Encyclopedia*. Verne erroneously wrote that the Chilkoot Pass is the lower of the two.—Trans.

4. This sentence is incomplete in the original and has been reconstructed in accordance with a note from the Editor: "J.V. . . . intended to describe the hope of fortune and the reality of disappointment."—Trans.

5. Verne gave this date as May 6, which is inconsistent with the date mentioned previously.—Trans.

1.8. Lake Lindemann

1. The spelling of "Bennett," "Lindemann," "Laberge," "Takhini," and "Lewes," which Verne spelled "Benett," "Lindeman," "Labarge," "Takheena," and "Lewis," respectively, has been corrected.—Trans.

1.9. From Bennett Lake to Dawson City

1. Verne wrote "northeast," but in fact the river turns to the northwest. —Trans.

2. The word *opportunity* was left out in the original.—Ed.

3. Verne spelled this "Hootalinga."—Trans.

1.10. The Klondike

1. The Monroe Doctrine did not call for the annexation of the entire Western Hemisphere to the United States, as Verne seems to suggest, but declared it to be off limits to European colonizing powers.—Trans.

2. Vitus Bering, a Dane in the Russian navy, discovered Alaska in 1741.—Trans.

3. Verne wrote "northeast," but in fact the Yukon River flows southwest from Fort Yukon.—Trans.

4. This was the Rev. Robert MacDonald, an Anglican missionary.—Trans.

5. Yukon became a separate territory in 1898.—Trans.

6. The word *fifty* was left blank by Verne and has been supplied by reference to a map.—Trans.

7. Some of the streams mentioned here flow into the Klondike River, some into the Yukon. The spelling has been corrected in some cases. As Verne states two paragraphs farther on, Bonanza Creek flows into the Klondike River, not the Yukon.—Trans.

8. This was Joseph Ladue (not Leduc, as Verne spelled it).—Trans.

9. William Ogilvie, a surveyor and commissioner of the Yukon from 1898 to 1901.—Trans.

1.11. Dawson City

1. British Columbia was already a part of Canada at that time, having entered Confederation in 1871.—Trans.

2. Judge McGuire (not MacGuire) was the Hon. Thomas Horace McGuire. Mr. Wade was probably Frederick Coate Wade, acting land commissioner and advisor to the Yukon Council.—Trans.

3. Father William Judge, a Jesuit missionary.—Trans.

4. Probably Capt. Cortlandt Starnes of the North West Mounted Police.—Trans.

5. This number was left blank by Verne and has been supplied by reference to a map.—Trans.

6. Verne left a blank for the price of whiskey.—Trans.

7. The fort at the confluence of the Fortymile and Yukon rivers is Fort Cudahy and not, as Verne wrote, Fort Reliance. According to the late Pierre Berton, a Canadian author and expert on the Yukon, the Fortymile River was so named not because of its length, but because it flows into the Yukon forty miles downstream from Fort Reliance.—Trans.

8. The dispute between Canada and the United States had to do with the boundary between the Alaskan "panhandle" and British Columbia. There was no disagreement about the 141st degree of longitude.—Trans.

9. Since the company had its headquarters in Chicago, this should not have been a problem.

1.12. From Dawson City to the Alaskan Boundary

1. In fact, they would be following the course of the Yukon River.

2. The Morse was probably Moose Creek.—Trans.

3. Verne wrote "left bank," obviously an oversight, since we were not told that they crossed the Fortymile River and since we learned in part 1, chapter 1 that Claim 129 was on the right bank.—Trans.

1.13. Claim 129

1. Earlier in this chapter, the shafts are said to be fifteen or twenty feet deep.—Trans.

2. From here on, J.V. calls the foreman "Lorrique."—Ed.

1.14. Working the Claim

1. Verne wrote "between sunrise and sunset."—Trans.

2. Verne wrote "left bank," but we have already seen that Claim 129 was on the right bank.—Trans.

3. Alaska was sold to the United States by Russia in 1867.

4. The original offer (part 1, chapter 2) was five thousand dollars, not forty thousand.—Trans.

1.15. The Night of August 5–6

1. Verne wrote "Earvay" and "Gripple," which appear to be misspellings. —Trans.

2. Again, we have 127 and 129 (odd numbers) incorrectly placed on the left bank.—Trans.

3. Summy may have shot black bears in Green Valley, but there are no grizzlies in eastern Canada.—Trans.

2.1. A Winter in the Klondike

1. Verne wrote "north," which would have been the left bank.—Trans.

2. Earlier in this chapter, the water was said to be five or six feet deep.—Trans.

3. Since the Fortymile River flows into the Yukon from the left, the travelers must have crossed the Yukon at some point. This is not mentioned.—Trans.

4. "*Klondyke Nugget*" is the correct spelling.—Trans.

5. It may be noted that the district produced ten million in 1898 and sixteen million in 1899.—Ed.

6. The editor of the 1989 French edition inserted the word *froid* (cold) to fill a blank left in the original manuscript.—Trans.

7. By mid-November the bears would have been hibernating in their dens.—Trans.

8. The name "François" has been crossed out and replaced by "Jacques." —Ed.

2.2. The Dying Man's Tale

1. The original manuscript reads "François" [see part 2, chapter 1, note 8]. Why did Michel Verne change the name "Laurier" to "Ledun"?—Ed.

2. Three French naval vessels named *Borda* served successively as the French Naval Academy from 1840 to 1913.—Trans.

3. Verne seems to be jumping to an unwarranted conclusion here.—Trans.

2.3. The Aftermath of a Secret

1. Verne probably did not intend to include the southern United States and Mexico in this comment.—Trans.

2. And yet it was so cold that Skim nearly froze to death when he stepped outside.—Trans.

3. At zero degrees centigrade, the snow banks would not melt in a "few hours."—Trans.

2.4. Circle City

1. Verne wrote "sixty-third."—Trans.

2. Since the earthquake and flood occurred on the night of August 5–6 (see part 1, chapter 14), there would be only one month of summer left.—Trans.

3. J.V. now calls the Indian "Karrak." Michel Verne chose "Karak."—Ed.

4. Verne left this distance blank. It has been supplied by reference to a map. This applies also to the next reference to Fort Yukon.—Trans.

2.5. A Journey of Discovery

1. The distances given in this chapter have been corrected by reference to a map. In almost every case the distance given by Verne was incorrect.—Trans.

2. Verne gives the number of people in the group as sixteen.—Trans.

3. Verne wrote "toward the north."—Trans.

4. To cross the Peel River on drifting ice pans, with all the caravan's wagons, animals, and equipment, would have been a very hazardous undertaking.—Trans.

5. The author forgot to mention the purchase of the hunting dog that makes its appearance here.—Ed.

2.6. Fort McPherson

1. Verne omitted this distance. It has been supplied by reference to a map.—Trans.

2. British Columbia became part of Canada in 1871.—Trans.

3. Verne, by an obvious slip of the pen, wrote "West Channel."—Trans.

4. They were expecting to find an extinct volcano.—Trans.

2.7. Golden Mount

1. Verne wrote "eight," which conflicts with his earlier reference to six months.
—Trans.

2. Verne wrote "east face," obviously a slip of the pen.—Trans.

3. J.V. forgets that Harry Brown is an English-speaking Canadian.—Ed.

2.8. An Engineer's Bold Plan

1. See part 2, chapter 7, note 3.—Trans.

2. Verne wrote "five hundred leagues" (1,250 miles).—Trans.

2.9. The Moose Hunt

1. J.V. now uses the name "Buller" when referring to Rubber Creek.—Ed.

2. In part 1, chapter 14, we were told that "moose and caribou were frequently seen in the woods."—Trans.

3. Verne wrote "five o'clock" here.—Trans.

4. A watch can be used as a compass by pointing the hour hand at the sun and counting back, counterclockwise, halfway to the number twelve on the dial. In the morning this point will indicate due north. After twelve noon, it will indicate due south.—Trans.

2.10. Mortal Dread

1. Verne wrote "east," but Skim and Neluto had headed west on their hunting trip.—Trans.

2. Indians had been using firearms for many years by this time.—Trans.

3. Verne wrote "west," but they would have been going east, toward their encampment.—Trans.

2.11. On the Defensive

1. Verne wrote "eastern," but the forest lay to the west.—Trans.

2.12. Attack and Defense

1. The distance was omitted from the original.—Ed.

2.14. From Dawson City to Montreal

1. The personnel listed in part 2, chapter 5 did not include any Indians.
—Trans.

2. The distance was omitted from the original.—Ed.

3. The date in the original is September 17, obviously a slip, since they got to Dawson City on September 3, spoke to Steel the next day, and were told that the last river boat would leave in two days.—Trans.

4. Since Fort Yukon is located in Alaska, it could not have been the capital of the Klondike.—Trans.

5. Verne probably meant to write "Kodiak."—Trans.

IN THE BISON FRONTIERS OF IMAGINATION SERIES

Gullivar of Mars
By Edwin L. Arnold
Introduced by Richard A. Lupoff
Afterword by Gary Hoppenstand

A Journey in Other Worlds:
A Romance of the Future
By John Jacob Astor
Introduced by S. M. Stirling

Queen of Atlantis
By Pierre Benoit
Afterword by Hugo Frey

The Wonder
By J. D. Beresford
Introduced by Jack L. Chalker

Voices of Vision: Creators of Science
Fiction and Fantasy Speak
By Jayme Lynn Blaschke

At the Earth's Core
By Edgar Rice Burroughs
Introduced by Gregory A. Benford
Afterword by Phillip R. Burger

Back to the Stone Age
By Edgar Rice Burroughs
Introduced by Gary Dunham

Beyond Thirty
By Edgar Rice Burroughs
Introduced by David Brin
Essays by Phillip R. Burger and Richard
A. Lupoff

The Eternal Savage: Nu of the Niocene
By Edgar Rice Burroughs
Introduced by Tom Deitz

Land of Terror
By Edgar Rice Burroughs
Introduced by Anne Harris

The Land That Time Forgot
By Edgar Rice Burroughs
Introduced by Mike Resnick

Lost on Venus
By Edgar Rice Burroughs
Introduced by Kevin J. Anderson

The Moon Maid: Complete and Restored
By Edgar Rice Burroughs
Introduced by Terry Bisson

Pellucidar
By Edgar Rice Burroughs
Introduced by Jack McDevitt
Afterword by Phillip R. Burger

Pirates of Venus
By Edgar Rice Burroughs
Introduced by F. Paul Wilson
Afterword by Phillip R. Burger

Savage Pellucidar
By Edgar Rice Burroughs
Introduced by Harry Turtledove

Tanar of Pellucidar
By Edgar Rice Burroughs
Introduced by Paul Cook

Tarzan at the Earth's Core
By Edgar Rice Burroughs
Introduced by Sean McMullen

Under the Moons of Mars
By Edgar Rice Burroughs
Introduced by James P. Hogan

The Absolute at Large
By Karel Čapek
Introduced by Stephen Baxter

The Girl in the Golden Atom
By Ray Cummings
Introduced by Jack Williamson

*The Poison Belt: Being an Account of
Another Amazing Adventure of
Professor Challenger*
By Sir Arthur Conan Doyle
Introduced by Katya Reimann

Tarzan Alive
By Philip José Farmer
New Foreword by Win Scott Eckert
Introduced by Mike Resnick

The Circus of Dr. Lao
By Charles G. Finney
Introduced by John Marco

Omega: The Last Days of the World
By Camille Flammarion
Introduced by Robert Silverberg

Ralph 124C 41+
By Hugo Gernsback
Introduced by Jack Williamson

*The Journey of Niels Klim to the
World Underground*
By Ludvig Holberg
Introduced and edited by
James I. McNelis Jr.
Preface by Peter Fitting

The Lost Continent: The Story of Atlantis
By C. J. Cutcliffe Hyne
Introduced by Harry Turtledove
Afterword by Gary Hoppenstand

*The Great Romance: A Rediscovered
Utopian Adventure*
By The Inhabitant
Edited by Dominic Alessio

Mizora: A World of Women
By Mary E. Bradley Lane
Introduced by Joan Saberhagen

A Voyage to Arcturus
By David Lindsay
Introduced by John Clute

Before Adam
By Jack London
Introduced by Dennis L. McKiernan

Fantastic Tales
By Jack London
Edited by Dale L. Walker

*Master of Adventure: The Worlds of
Edgar Rice Burroughs*
By Richard A. Lupoff
With an introduction to the Bison Books
Edition by the author
Foreword by Michael Moorcock
Preface by Henry Hardy Heins
With an essay by Phillip R. Burger

The Moon Pool
By A. Merritt
Introduced by Robert Silverberg

The Purple Cloud
By M. P. Shiel
Introduced by John Clute

Lost Worlds
By Clark Ashton Smith
Introduced by Jeff VanderMeer

Out of Space and Time
By Clark Ashton Smith
Introduced by Jeff VanderMeer

The Skylark of Space
By E. E. "Doc" Smith
Introduced by Vernor Vinge

Skylark Three
By E. E. "Doc" Smith
Introduced by Jack Williamson

*The Nightmare and Other Tales of
Dark Fantasy*
By Francis Stevens
Edited and introduced by
Gary Hoppenstand

Tales of Wonder
By Mark Twain
Edited, introduced, and with notes by
David Ketterer

The Chase of the Golden Meteor
By Jules Verne
Introduced by Gregory A. Benford

*The Golden Volcano: The First English
Translation of Verne's Original Manuscript*
By Jules Verne
Translated and edited by Edward Baxter

*Lighthouse at the End of the World:
The First English Translation of
Verne's Original Manuscript*
By Jules Verne
Translated and edited by
William Butcher

*The Meteor Hunt: The First English
Translation of Verne's Original Manuscript*
By Jules Verne
Translated and edited by
Frederick Paul Walter and
Walter James Miller

The Croquet Player
By H. G. Wells
Afterword by John Huntington

In the Days of the Comet
By H. G. Wells
Introduced by Ben Bova

The Last War: A World Set Free
By H. G. Wells
Introduced by Greg Bear

The Sleeper Awakes
By H. G. Wells
Introduced by J. Gregory Keyes
Afterword by Gareth Davies-Morris

The War in the Air
By H. G. Wells
Introduced by Dave Duncan

The Disappearance
By Philip Wylie
Introduced by Robert Silverberg

Gladiator
By Philip Wylie
Introduced by Janny Wurts

When Worlds Collide
By Philip Wylie and Edwin Balmer
Introduced by John Varley

UNIVERSITY OF NEBRASKA PRESS

Also of Interest by Jules Verne:

The Chase of the Golden Meteor

The Chase of the Golden Meteor is vintage Verne, artfully blending hard science and scientific speculation with a farcical comedy of manners. This unabridged edition will be sure to delight Verne's legion of fans and attract new ones.

ISBN: 978-0-8032-9619-0 (paper)

Lighthouse at the End of the World
The First English Translation of Verne's Original Manuscript

At the extreme tip of South America, Staten Island has piercing Antarctic winds, lonely coasts assaulted by breakers, and sailors lost as their vessels smash on the dark rocks. Now that civilization dares to rule here, a lighthouse penetrates the last and wildest place of all. But Vasquez, the guardian of the sacred light, has not reckoned with the vicious, desperate Kongre gang, who murder his two friends and force him out into the wilderness. Alone, without resources, can he foil their cruel plans?

ISBN: 978-0-8032-6007-8 (paper)

The Meteor Hunt
The First English Translation of Verne's Original Manuscript

This is the story of a meteor of pure gold careening toward the earth and generating competitive greed among amateur astronomers and chaos among nations obsessed with the trajectory of the great golden object. Set primarily in the United States and offering a humorous critique of the American way of life, *The Meteor Hunt* is finally given due critical treatment in the translators' foreword, detailed annotations, and afterword, which clearly establish the historical, political, scientific, and literary context and importance of this long-obscured, genre-blending masterpiece in its true form.

ISBN: 978-0-8032-9634-3 (paper)

Order online at www.nebraskapress.unl.edu or call 1-800-755-1105. Mention the code "BOFOX" to receive a 20% discount.